G000125122

# The Purest Form of Chaos

*Eliza S Robinson*

**Purple Pluto Press**

First published in the UK 2019 by Purple Pluto Press

This edition published in 2020.

© Eliza S Robinson

ISBN 978-1-5272-5447-3

Cover art by: Sanni Lindroos

*To the friends I would follow
blindly into battle*

# The Purest Form of Chaos

## Chapter One
*February 2149*
*Tartarus Settlement*
*Western Russia*

Phoenix Kashnikova did not dare to scream. The kidnapper's arms gripped her body like a vice, and thrust a dark hood over her head. She dragged her feet against rough, wooden floorboards in an effort to slow him down. The kidnapper grabbed her hands, and enclosed her wrists in a strong grip. Loose nails caught on her soles, drawing blood that dripped in lazy droplets onto the floor like a trail of scarlet breadcrumbs.

"Ow," she whimpered. His grip shifted from her wrists. The man took her waist in his hands, and flung her over his shoulder. Now she screamed.

"Shh, girl." He spoke to her in English, but his accent was Russian. Muscovite, like her mother's. It had been years since she had heard a Russian accent. "Shh, Phoenix."

*He knows my name,* she thought. *He's from Western Russia, and he knows my name.* Her mind raced.

*Mum!* she thought. *It must be!*

Her heart quickened, beating to the irregular rhythm of panic and hope. Had her mother stepped up after all these years? The thought was uncomfortable. Any aid from her mother came tangled in a web of ulterior motives. Phoenix refused to think of it. For now, she must enjoy the thrill of her kidnap, the sweet journey out of hell, and into purgatory.

Phoenix woke to the unsteady rock and sway of a horse-drawn carriage. Her head was still covered with the hood. Heat radiated from a spot some inches away – the heat of a fellow body. As her ears grew accustomed to the clickety-clack of hooves on cobbled streets, she detected other sounds. These came from within the carriage: heavy breathing, from the same direction as the heat. And cursing, lots of cursing.

"Gotcha!" said her companion. The exclamation was closely

7

followed by the sound of tearing fabric. Phoenix lay still. Perhaps if he thought she was asleep, he wouldn't be tempted to harm her. For the second time that night, she felt another person's hands on her body. These were not the hands of her kidnapper. Where *his* had been silky smooth, these were calloused, with short fingernails and gentle pressure. She understood why he was touching her.

With a final tug, Phoenix's companion tore the hood from her head, and the blackness of her vision was eased by the light of the full moon, which streamed through the glass windows of the carriage. Her fellow kidnappee was only a boy: sixteen, perhaps, with black hair, wide eyes, and white skin. His eyebrows were dense and bushy. The boy's face was marred by an inherent sourness, and the fullness of his lower lip made him exude an air of petulance.

"Look at the world!" He was captivated by the sight before him. She recognised his accent: English, like her own. He must also be from the Settlement. "There's a whole world out there, a whole city."

"It must be Moscow," Phoenix said. She pushed her back up against the wall of the carriage, and covered her mouth with her hand. Even in this light, she didn't want him to see.

She felt the hope being sucked out of her. If this boy was here too, her mother could not be their saviour. Phoenix drew her eyes away from the luminescence of the midnight city, where lights glowed in windows, on street corners, reflecting against glass and falling into shadow. She peeled her eyes for an indicator of who had taken her, or where she was going. Large television screens were mounted upon tall poles in every street. A montage played out upon them, a silent news bulletin. Images flashed back and forth of a tall man in a heavy crown, with hair as yellow as butter.

"Did you see him?" she asked. Her voice was muffled through her hand. "When he took you?"

"No," the boy said. "I felt him though, his hands were smooth."

"He must be rich," said Phoenix. "This is velvet." She fingered the fabric of her hood. The last time she had worn velvet was when she was ten years old. It had been her father's turn to host the annual meeting of Settlement presidents. Back when she was still a sight fit to be seen in public.

8

"Why would he want us?" he asked.

"That's what I'm trying to figure out."

"Maybe he wants to sell us as sex slaves," the boy said.

Phoenix shuddered. She had only just escaped one series of tortures, this kidnap was the closest she had come to liberation. She shifted her hand, and fed long strands of hair into her mouth, which she anxiously chewed.

"Promise you'll kill me," she said. "If it comes to it, promise you'll kill me."

"I'll try." She didn't believe him. "How do you want me to do it?"

Phoenix considered. She had contemplated the nature of her own death on many occasions, but choice of method had never been a factor.

"If we had a gun," she said, "I'd want you to shoot me. It's brief, humane. A single bullet through the heart, and I'd be gone. Don't shoot me in the head, my brain is far too precious."

The boy laughed. "What if there's no gun?"

"I suppose you'll have to strangle me."

"Why are you covering your mouth?" he asked. "I can hardly hear you."

"It's disgusting. My teeth... They're broken and rotten. I'm repulsive."

"Hi Repulsive," he said. "I'm Sol."

Phoenix laughed, in spite of herself. She let her hand drop to her lap, but turned her face away from Sol, towards the window. She was transfixed by the view of the city, even at this dark hour. The Settlement walls had separated this world from her for sixteen years, and a little case of kidnapping wasn't going to kill her curiosity.

"I know who you are," he said casually. "You used to be in my classes when you were younger. I haven't seen you in years."

Phoenix nodded slowly. "We'll speak no more of it," she decided. "We have more immediate things to worry about. Do you want me to kill you, if he tries to sell or abuse us?"

Sol hesitated. He shook with cold.

"No," he said. "I don't want to die. I'll never give them that pleasure."

"Fair enough."

The carriage came to a halt.

Their captor stood at over six feet tall, and held an electric lantern in his pale hands. It cast sufficient light to capture the details of his face and physique. His hair was blond, and his eyes were an unsettling shade of blue. Like ice. His face was a mask of calmness.

Sol elbowed Phoenix's shoulder, and tilted his head ever-so-slightly to the view from his window. Her gaze shifted from the open door on her side of the carriage, to the vast city square opposite. A grand palace loomed in the near distance, casting a shadow across the pavement. It was a bizarre architectural specimen, a pastiche of brutalist starkness, and lavish, golden domes. This building couldn't make up its mind what it wanted to be.

"You removed your hoods," observed their kidnapper. "Put them back on before you step outside."

Phoenix shivered. She was still dressed in her white nightie, and the February air bore the chill of the formidable Russian winter, weather that had stopped both Napoleon and the Nazis in their tracks so many hundred years ago. The kidnapper inspected the bare skin of Phoenix's shaking legs, and looked up, over the carriage roof, and back to her again.

"Take this." He unbuttoned his black fleece jacket.

"Thank you," Phoenix said through her hand. She slipped her arms into the heavy sleeves, enveloped in the residual body heat. It smelt of cigarettes.

"Put your hoods back on," he repeated.

Sol complied immediately. Phoenix eyed her kidnapper.

"Why?" she asked, raising her voice loud enough to pass the shield of her hand.

"It is my responsibility as your new guardian to protect you. All you have to do is wear a blindfold for a short amount of time. Once we're inside, you're free. I can give you everything you could ever want. You're safe now, Phoenix."

"What's the catch?" She didn't trust him. For all his sparkle, she saw only the ice at his core. Every instinct told her to run.

"The catch," he said, "is that you stay within the confines of your new home. No running away."

10

"I'm not your Eve," said Phoenix. "You can offer me paradise as much as you please, but I'm not playing your game. I've eaten enough apples in my life to know they're all poison. You may have kidnapped me, but I am not your property. I'm happy to give this arrangement a chance – I'm more than happy to. But if ever the time comes when I wish to leave, I'll be gone. Do we understand each other?" In the rush of passion, her hand slipped from her mouth. Icy eyes watched with horror as crumbling, rotten fragments of teeth stared back like an apocalyptic wasteland. Phoenix slammed her palm back over her mouth, biting down against her own skin to stem the flow of tears that threatened, and prevent the gasping roar from leaving her throat.

"I'll take you to a dentist first thing in the morning," he said. "You look like you could use a visit to the doctor as well."

"Who are you?" Phoenix asked. The accidental revelation made her brave, and when her hand fell this time, it was no accident.

"I'm the Tsar," her kidnapper said with a smile. His teeth glowed pearly white in the light of his torch. She trusted him even less. The single atom of vanity that remained in her yearned for the day when she could bear to look in a mirror again, when her own face was not an attack on her spirit.

✝

*January 2150*
*Moscow*
*Western Russia*

"Sol said you wanted me," Phoenix announced as she entered the Tsar's library. She addressed him in Russian. His English was good, but she spoke Russian like it was her native tongue.

Her bare feet padded across the dense, red carpet to join him by the floor-to-ceiling windows that overlooked the cityscape beyond.

"How does it feel to be seventeen?" the Tsar asked. He wore a fitted blue suit, and his blond hair was slicked back against his scalp, separated into neat lines by the teeth of a comb.

"The same as sixteen," Phoenix said. She watched the winter sunshine bounce off the snow on Moscow's rooftops. "I'm still living on borrowed time. My life is rented, I own nothing."

"Does that bother you?" the Tsar asked. His face showed no sign of interest or emotion.

"Not yet," said Phoenix. "I've done nothing, I owe you nothing. I've been here eleven months and I'm still myself. I'm content, for now."

"I'm glad I've kept you satisfied." The Tsar smiled. Phoenix still didn't trust him. No man would kidnap two teenagers without a reason, and until she discovered his motives she would remain wary of him. "How are the teeth doing?" he asked. "It's been a while since I last checked in with you." The Tsar rarely spent time with his young charges. Apart from the initial act of kidnapping, he took a hands-off approach to his role as benefactor.

"They're excellent!" Phoenix beamed, showing off a collection of perfect neat white teeth.

"And your health? Are you eating properly now?"

"Can't you tell? I'm not half as skinny as I used to be. You employ excellent chefs." She walked closer to the window, ill at ease in the Tsar's presence.

"How about your happiness?" he asked. "Have you read all the books I gave you?"

"Several times."

"I noticed some books out of place in here last week. I wondered if, perhaps, that was your doing?" His voice was neutral. She stood with her back to him, and couldn't gauge his mood from his facial expression.

"I'm sorry," Phoenix said. "I returned all the books I borrowed, I promise I did. I needed to read more, and–"

"I'll find more books for you," the Tsar said. "I don't want you to be bored."

"I'm not bored, I want to expand my mind. I can't do that if I read the same books over and over."

"Of course." The Tsar joined her by the window. "How is Sol? Is he a good companion for you?"

"Sometimes," Phoenix said. "Other times he's so moody I can't stand it. I'm not a people person at the best of times, if I'm going to be confined with someone they need at least some redeeming features."

"What you need is another girl, someone you can connect with."

"Ooh, are you going to kidnap someone else for me?"

The Tsar met her with an ice-cold stare. "I don't like the term *kidnap*," he said. "I'm much fonder of the word *liberate*. Would you agree that that is a more accurate depiction of the circumstances?"

## Chapter Two
*March 2150*
*Olympus Vineyard*
*Greece*

Persephone sat curled up in the corner of her bed. She painted her toenails with one hand, and pushed chunks of thick, white bread into her mouth with the other. She hummed a tune that came out garbled through her bread-clogged throat.

"Persephone!" bellowed a voice from the floor below. "Persephone, where are you?" It was Demeter, the manager of the vineyard and the bane of Persephone's existence.

She attempted to swallow her mouthful of bread, and choked on it.

"Persephone!"

"I'm–" she coughed. "I'm coming!" She dipped more bread into a bowl of olive oil, and popped it into her mouth, before rushing out of the dormitory. Persephone hurried down the path towards the vineyard's main building, and descended the steps to the cellar. The heat of the sun was absent down here, though a shaft of its light penetrated the darkness of the staircase. The slabs of grey stone were cold, and Persephone couldn't help but shiver as her bare feet came into contact with them. She hopped on alternate legs to limit her interaction with the icy chill.

The cellar was divided into small stone production booths. Shelves ran along the side walls, and a desk filled the centre wall. Identical, stark, efficient. Persephone sat at the last vacant desk. She took blank labels down from a shelf, and began to draw. Her movements were simultaneously precise and careless, her slender fingers danced with an art only routine can bring. She drew in thick, black ink around stencils of grapes, and coloured the image on the wine label with burgundy watercolour. Many of her days were spent like this. While the other vineyard workers spent the summer in the fields, picking grapes, Persephone was kept indoors all year round. Demeter said her skin burned too easily for her to spend hours in the sun.

Persephone grew weary as she coloured in the fruits. The routine bored her. This monotony could have been comforting, if

14

her life contained more than this. If the vineyard were a home to return to after grand adventures, she could stomach the dull life she lived. But it was all Persephone had ever known, and she ached for change like the air she needed to breathe.

✝

It was midday by the time Demeter came to check on the workers. The hard clack of her shoes on the floor alerted Persephone to her presence. Demeter was quite young, a few years past thirty, but she walked and moved within a cold cage of strictness. Every movement held the assertion of authority.

"Can I go outside?" Persephone asked when the clacking came to a halt behind her. She turned to meet Demeter's cold stare. Respect for authority had been instilled into Persephone since before she could walk, but in recent years a new logic had budded in her mind: if she must respect authority, it followed that authority must respect her.

"Why?" Demeter asked sharply. Her brown eyes shifted in expression, she was anxious.

"Because I want to." Persephone's curiosity was piqued by the unfamiliar look in the woman's eyes. "Are you alright?"

"I'm perfectly well. Thank you for asking." Her voice came out thick and stilted.

"You're afraid." It unnerved Persephone to see her like this. "Do you want to talk?"

"No. Not to you, child." The frown lines twitched below her lips. "This isn't your battle."

"Battle?" The word sparked an ache within her, a yearning for the conflict her simple life had failed to provide. It burned like indigestion, an acid in her throat with the power to stop her thoughts in their tracks and veer her mind completely off course.

"Trouble's coming." Demeter wrung her hands together. She tapped her right foot against the floor. *Clack. Clack. Clack.* "Do you know how long I've worked here, Persephone?"

"No," she said. "Certainly as long as I have; I can't remember a time without you."

"I was seventeen," said Demeter. Her stern face was almost

15

kind. "The same age as you are now. I arrived just a month before you did." Her voice caught in her throat. "I've known you your whole life. I've seen you grow from a fat little baby into a woman... a woman who's old enough... Never mind." Her fleeting vulnerability stiffened in an instant, and she reverted to her default sternness.

"Old enough to what?" Persephone asked.

"Old enough to make decisions," Demeter said carefully. Her black eyebrows drew together in concern. "Decisions like whether you can go outside during your break. You have an hour, don't waste it."

"Thank you!"

Persephone ran up the stairs and out the door, her hair flying in the wind behind her. Demeter's words were weighted in her mind. Decisions meant change, change meant progress. Persephone hurtled down the pebble paths until she neared the edge of the vineyard. The white gauze of her dress snagged on the branches of bushes; they scratched her calves from the side of the path. Her breath came out in weak gasps, and the muscles in her legs burned. She came to a stop on a rocky ledge at the very edge of the vineyard. From here, Persephone could see the neighbouring orange grove through the barbed-wire border fence, and beyond to the mountains that separated this valley from the sea.

Twigs crunched in the near vicinity.

"Morning," said a voice behind her. Persephone turned to see the man who addressed her. His expression gave no indication of whether he wished her morning to be good or ill.

"It's afternoon," Persephone said, taking him in. He was tall, and conventionally attractive, with light blond hair. His eyes were a peculiar shade of icy blue, like they had been cut from a glacier. He reminded her of the sun in winter – warmth too weak to melt the frigid ice.

"My mistake," he said with a charming smile. Persephone wasn't quite impressed. She found the prospect of a real-life stranger exciting, but there was something about this man that unsettled her.

"What are you doing here?" She twisted her long red hair into a rope, and tied it in a knot atop her head. The midday sun was hot

16

upon her temples.

"I haven't decided yet. Maybe I'll buy some wine. Maybe I'm here to make friends." He smiled again. This time it sent chills down her spine, like someone had walked over her grave with feet as light as a feather.

"Why would you travel this far to make friends? Or buy wine, for that matter?"

"Who says I travelled?" There was a look of perplexity on his face that Persephone couldn't understand. The stranger was indeed strange.

"The lack of tan is a big clue," she said. "If you'd been here more than a couple of hours, you'd be a nice shade of brown."

"You aren't." His gaze feasted on her. Discomfort rippled through her, manifesting in a burning blush that spread from her cheeks to her neck and ears. "Everything about you is light and pale."

"I don't tan," she said. "I burn, it's the curse of the ginger. And you're avoiding my question." She looked up into his eyes, trying to find any sign of warmth, humanity, emotion. All she could think of was ice.

"No, I'm not from here."

Persephone noticed his accent for the first time: foreign, no place she could name.

"Me neither, I guess." She gestured to her red hair.

"Evidently." His face twisted into something that was meant to be a smile. "I'm Haden, by the way."

"Persephone."

"That's a mouthful."

"I didn't choose it."

"Evidently."

She glared at him. His gaze bore an unpleasant aftertaste.

"Have you lived here long?" Haden asked.

"Since I was a baby," Persephone said. "I don't know where I came from, just that it was part of the Vineyard Scheme. I guess I was just the second-born child of some unfortunate family."

"Don't you ever wish to leave? See the world?"

"Every day."

"Would you like some pomegranate?" Haden asked. He

17

produced a crimson fruit from the pocket of his black trousers, and sliced it in half with a pocketknife.

Persephone hesitated.

"It's just fruit," he said. "It doesn't bite."

"Alright." She forced a small smile. "Thank you."

She bit into the pomegranate. Bitter-sweet juice burst on the tip of her tongue as her teeth crunched the seeds. It tasted like temptation.

Persephone smiled again. "It's lovely, thank you."

"I grow them myself," Haden told her. "I have a laboratory where we grow special fruit." He smiled again, and Persephone wondered how she could have had any misgivings about him.

"I have to go now," she said.

"I'll walk with you," he decided.

"If you can keep up!" She started off at a fast pace, leaving him running to catch up. His long legs were far shorter than her competitive streak.

Persephone decided to enjoy Haden.

"Persephone! For goodness sake, where are you, girl?" Demeter's voice squealed like a strangled cat as it ricocheted off the stone steps down to the cellar. Persephone groaned, and made her way up to the door of the vineyard's headquarters. This mansion was built from dark-grey stones that bore a cold contrast to the sticky spring weather. Only two weeks prior, it had been snowing. The climate became more unpredictable with each passing season.

"What is it?" Persephone asked as Demeter dragged her by the arm up two flights of stairs. The staircase was steep and spiralled, with a banister carved from dark mahogany. Demeter's grip tightened as they ascended the stairs. By the time they reached the dimly lit room on the top floor, Persephone was sure her bones would snap.

"Lord Zeus wishes to see you," Demeter finally explained.

Lord Zeus was a tall, formidable man, with dark hair and a thick beard. He was a figure of legend, in many ways, and rarely interacted with the residents. Persephone had only ever seen him from a distance.

"Why?" Persephone asked.

"It's beyond me," Demeter said. She gave the girl a hard push into the room.

"Lord Zeus?" Persephone asked. "You wished to see me?"

"Yes." His voice was as chilly as the room. He was younger than she had expected, no older than 40. He had the hint of a foreign accent, perhaps the same as Haden's. The shape of his face also reminded her of the man she had met earlier.

"Why?" Persephone asked. "Have I done something wrong?"

"This young man," Haden stepped out from behind Lord Zeus's throne-like seat, "has made me an offer. He will shortly return to his home country, and he wishes to take you with him."

Persephone was shocked. A chance to escape? She had wished for this her whole life! She was too euphoric at the chance of freedom to wonder what Haden could want with her. She wasted not a moment on thoughts of the danger of strangers.

"Absolutely not!" intervened Demeter. "There's no way I'm letting you leave." Her dark eyes pleaded with Persephone.

"Why? You don't care about me, no one does. I'm nothing if I stay here, I'm no one. I need more than this place."

"What are you talking about? Of course I care for you. You were always like a daughter to me."

Persephone snorted. She had spent many hours, many days, imagining her mother, picturing the family that had been forced to relinquish her. She didn't know what a real mother was like, but she was certain the woman would be nothing like Demeter.

"A daughter? You hate me! You're forever telling me I'm too naive, too careless, that I'm a waste of space without even half a brain." Persephone paused, and made the decision of a lifetime in the shortest of instants. "I'm going!"

"It's settled," Haden said with a smile to himself. Was there a hint of disingenuousness in his wolfish smile? Persephone didn't seek to notice.

"Persephone," Demeter pleaded, "you don't know what you're getting yourself into! You think you're running away from your demons, girl, but you're running straight towards them."

"That may be the case," Persephone said, "but I can't live my life knowing I passed over a chance to leave this place. I don't belong here, you know I don't. If you truly care for me, then I'm sorry for you. And if you don't... my leaving won't be a loss. I have to take this chance, no matter the risk." Persephone felt empowered for the first time in her life. Something shifted deep inside her as she finally found her voice.

They left the next day. Haden didn't speak as they headed to the train station. He walked ahead of Persephone. She picked her way carefully across the rocky paths, enchanted by the landscape that opened out in front of her. The terrain was near identical to that of the vineyard, but it was outside its gates, beyond the confines she had lived inside for her whole life. The hot sun bore down on Persephone's shoulders, and the dust beneath her feet billowed up into her eyes.

"We'll reach Moscow in two days," Haden said.

"Moscow?" Persephone asked.

"My city." He stopped still, to give her time to catch up. "We'll take an underground shuttle through the Dead Zones, and travel by train once we've crossed the Western Russian border."

"What are the Dead Zones?" Persephone asked. She knew nothing of Haden's world.

"Bulgaria, Romania, Ukraine, Belarus." She stared at him blankly, the words were foreign to her. "They're the lands between Greece and Western Russia," Haden explained. "They were decimated in the Third World War. Much of the planet was."

"How big is the world?" Persephone asked. "Come to think of it, there's no way you can answer that. I have no scale to understand it by."

"We live in a wide world," Haden said. "Alas, much of it has been destroyed. Between war and climate change, we lost most of the planet in one way or another. There are still clusters of countries huddled together, but most are separated by Dead Zones and have little to do with each other. We still had refugees fleeing to Western Russia even a couple of decades ago."

"That's tragic," Persephone said. "And beautiful, in a way. Our species lived on in spite of all that. It's incredible."

"I see you are an optimist." Haden laughed to himself. "You

20

find beauty in the strangest of things."

"When your world is as small as mine was, there isn't much of a choice. You have to find something to live for."

They took the train to Athens. This was Persephone's first train journey, and she found it both exciting and illness-inducing. The train was old and rickety; it wobbled along the tracks and gave her motion sickness. Haden read a newspaper for most of the journey, and Persephone contented herself with watching Greece fly past the window.

"Our shuttle will leave shortly," Haden said when they arrived in Athens central train station. "Come this way."

He led her up from the platform. They descended a flight of stairs that seemed to go on forever. The tang of cold metal permeated the air. This world was more built-up than Persephone was used to. The Vineyard had been like a village. Athens was her first experience of a metropolis. She was daunted and thrilled by the promise of the world she had yet to discover, of towns and cities, and people. So many people.

The shuttle pulled up to the platform just as they arrived. It was a sleek, silver train carriage, with a crest bearing a double-headed eagle embossed on its side. The interior was decorated in rich purple. Persephone sat down on a plush seat. Haden sat opposite. They stowed their luggage on the shelves just in time before the shuttle shot off. It travelled faster than the train, and the speed made Persephone feel queasy.

She wanted to interrogate Haden about the world he was taking her to, but she had too many questions to ask, none specific enough to verbalise. He took out his newspaper, and went back to ignoring her.

Haden was different when they arrived in the Western Russian station. As they climbed out of the shuttle, he stood up straighter. In Greece, he was calm and relaxed. Now his shoulders were stiff, and he held his head high. His face was expressionless. Persephone watched him with interest.

"Wait here," Haden said when they ascended above ground. He

directed Persephone to a wooden bench in the corner of the train-station waiting room. "I will be back shortly."

Haden crossed the room, and spoke to a flustered man at the ticket desk. They stood too far away for Persephone to eavesdrop. The man Haden spoke to wore a navy-blue uniform, and had thin, dark hair. He was, perhaps, in his forties. Even from this distance, she could see the power dynamics at play. The ticket seller was excited and a little afraid. Haden was cool and collected. Persephone wondered if the two men knew each other. She couldn't imagine how else Haden could cause a grown man to flounder like this.

"That shouldn't have taken so long," Haden said when he returned. "I've dealt with my fair share of incompetent staff, but this one set a new low."

"What did he do?" Persephone asked.

"Never you mind. Come, our private carriage will be ready soon."

"Private carriage? Are the trains here different to in Greece?"

Haden chuckled to himself.

"The trains are similar if not slightly better," he said. "But circumstances are different here. We will travel privately from now on. It wouldn't be wise to share a train with the commoners."

Persephone felt uncomfortable with the way he spoke, but she kept quiet. She didn't know enough about this man or this country to feel confident in her opinions.

A woman clad in the navy-blue train-staff uniform approached them. She opened her mouth to speak, but Haden shushed her. She led them forward in silence.

Persephone had imagined their private carriage to be part of a larger train, but this carriage was a vehicle in its own right. It bore the same crest as the shuttle, and its interior was decorated in the same shade of purple. The journey lasted five hours. It was night-time when they finally reached Moscow. They departed from the train station through a quiet back exit, and Haden led Persephone to a horse-drawn carriage, in which they travelled across the city. She couldn't make out much in the dark, only the contrast of lights with the shadows cast by vast buildings. They passed through the gatehouse of a grand palace, situated in an even grander square. Through the carriage window, Persephone could see a large courtyard, lit by flaming torches that hung in chains from the oppressive stone walls that seemed to be closing in on her. Haden opened the carriage door to let her out. In the centre of the courtyard was a fountain in the shape of a woman, with wide eyes and long hair. Water spewed from metal hands into the pond below, where coins glinted in the light from the torches.

"Put this on," Haden demanded of Persephone. He handed her a black-velvet blindfold.

"Why?" she asked. He had grown more secretive the closer they were to Moscow, but this final step seemed ludicrous.

"Because I want you to."

Persephone raised an eyebrow at the absurdity of his request, but obeyed nonetheless. He was her saviour, after all. Haden took her hand and led her through the darkness of his own creating. Persephone held his hand, feeling the smooth surface of his palm. It was the hand of a man who had never worked a day of manual labour in his life.

"These are your rooms," Haden said after a long time. He removed the blindfold, and freed her from the darkness. "Try and stick to these, make sure you don't go through the large oak door. You'll know the one if you see it." With that, he left her on her own.

Persephone looked around the room. Everything was a shade of lilac or cream. Little light came in through the large window that overlooked a courtyard. A double bed jutted out from the centre of the wall on her left-hand side. The bedspread was fashioned from fine material in a dull shade of lavender. The only view from the window was of the walls across the courtyard.

Persephone glanced around the room again. This time she noticed more: a door on her left she thought must lead to a bathroom, an empty bookshelf on the wall opposite the bed – nothing that caught her interest. It was late and she was tired from travelling. Persephone crawled into bed. She would explore her new home in the morning.

✝

Persephone woke with excitement on her first morning in Moscow. Sunlight shone through her bedroom windows, and her heart pulsed with the thrill of adventure.

Breakfast was set out on her bedside table. Persephone ate the fruit salad with her fingers. Sticky juice dripped down her chin, and across her hands. After she had eaten, and cleaned herself up, she meandered through the quiet corridors, ready to satiate her curiosity. Each room was identical to the last: pristine, empty, and uninhabited.

When Persephone reached a large, gold-studded oak door, it seemed only natural to ignore Haden's warning and venture beyond the majestic barrier. For a few moments she stood in hesitation. He had told her not to go past the door for a reason. Her mind ran away with itself, creating bizarre fantasies of what could be behind the door. Guillotines and gallows—all sorts of horrors—filled her imagination, and she told herself it was for her own sanity that she take a small look.

The door creaked open at the touch of Persephone's hands.

# Chapter Three

A cavernous room appeared before Persephone. Long tables with decadent gold-footed legs ran alongside the vast walls. A throne of red velvet and gold stood near the door she had entered through. There were no guillotines, she noted thankfully. Another door was set in the wall at the far side of the room. Persephone crossed the room, and opened the door. It revealed a corridor, with dozens of smaller doors leading off it. She chose one at random, the third door on the left. It opened to a large chapel, ornately decorated in bright colours. Persephone had only been there a moment, when she was startled by the sound of two men's voices arguing.

"In here! Quick!" a girl called from behind her. Before Persephone could move, two pairs of arms hauled her through another door. She turned to her rescuers: a boy and a girl, both around her own age.

"Hello?" Persephone said.

"Who are you?" the girl asked. She inspected the ginger intruder.

"My name is Persephone."

"Purr-seff-ann-ee." She lingered on each syllable. "It's a pretty name."

"Thank you." She sensed the girl was making fun of her.

"I'm Phoenix," the girl announced, "and this is," she gestured in the vague direction of the boy, "Sol."

"Phoenix, like the bird?" Persephone asked.

"That's born out of its own ashes? Yeah. The room caught on fire just as I popped out of my mother, so I was literally born in ashes." She laughed. "What brings you to Icy Boy's palace?"

Persephone assumed 'Icy Boy' was a reference to Haden's eyes. "I came here because he wanted me to."

"You came of your own accord? Oh lord!" Phoenix sighed dramatically.

"Didn't you?"

Phoenix didn't answer, she changed the subject instead. "Where are you from?"

"Greece, I lived on a vineyard there. I was brought there as a baby. I don't know where I was before that."

"You never met your family? Spent your life confined to the

vineyard?"

"You know about the Vineyard Scheme?" Persephone asked, surprised.

"She reads a lot," said Sol.

"From the Tsar's personal library," Phoenix said with a wink. "He's rather lax about security."

"What's a Tsar?" Persephone asked.

"Old Icy," Phoenix said with distaste. "Tsar Haden Olympovski of Western Russia. I know you've met him. I heard you talking in the courtyard last night. I have a sixth sense for hearing people speak English, it's so rare here. A Tsar is a king or emperor in this part of the world." She looked Persephone up and down again. "So, are we friends?"

"We can be."

"Fabulous! What can I call you? Is there anything your name shortens to? It's rather long."

"I'm not sure."

"How about…" She thought for a moment. "Perse— Sphennie… Sphenya?"

"I guess so."

"Wonderful!" said Phoenix. "Do you want to come see the great city of Moscow?"

"I'm not allowed to leave," Persephone told her.

"Neither are we. He doesn't have eyes in here. And even out there… For all the cameras, he never seems to look at them. I'll grab you a change of clothes, and meet you back here in ten minutes?" She walked off before Persephone could protest.

"Welcome to my world." Sol followed the disappearing figure of Phoenix with a dark look.

"You don't like her?"

"She's an acquired taste." He didn't elaborate.

"Have you known her long?"

"Sort of." He hesitated a moment. "We came from the same Settlement. We didn't meet properly until we were brought here, last year."

"Settlement?" Persephone asked.

"I'll let her answer that one. I'm sure she has a story to spin."

They lapsed into silence until Phoenix returned.

26

✝

The clothes Phoenix brought Persephone were simple but stylish: a forest-green button-down blouse, and loose black trousers, with fabric that floated about her ankles as she walked.

"Are you decent?" Phoenix asked. She had given Persephone privacy to change.

"Yep."

"We're going to jump out the window." She climbed up onto the windowsill. "It's a bit of a drop, but you'll be fine."

Persephone looked at her in horror. She suspected Phoenix's idea of "a bit of a drop" would be a hundred-metre dive.

"It's about three metres," Sol said.

"I can't jump that far!"

"Sure you can." Phoenix swayed precariously on the window ledge, teasing them with her catlike balance. Her self-assurance shone through. She knew she wouldn't fall. "Are you coming or not?"

"I guess." Persephone glumly watched the light-brown legs teetering on the windowsill.

"Wonderful!" Phoenix was birdlike as she jumped. Her body flew through the air to the ground below with a grace that seemed at odds with her demeanour. She landed with a large thump on the pavement, and jumped up, unfazed.

"Come on!" she called.

Persephone glanced to Sol for reassurance, but he had stalked off in silence. She stood alone on the sill, contemplating the crushing stony death that awaited her.

"Are you coming, Sphenya?" Phoenix spun around in circles, like a tornado, in the courtyard below.

"Yes." She took a deep breath—sure it would be her last—and jumped. A cold blast of wind hit her abdomen. Persephone had never felt so alive.

Phoenix stopped spinning, and grabbed her by the hand. Her skin was cool and soft, but not clammy. It was evident she took good care of herself.

"Sol disappeared," Persephone said.

"What a surprise." Phoenix led her through the courtyard to a narrow gate hidden in the wall.

"How often do you do that?" Beyond the gate was a crowded square. People swarmed as far as the eye could see. "Jumping out of buildings?"

"Not a lot," Phoenix said. A smile crept onto her face. "Normally I just sneak out the back entrance. But Sol doesn't know that. Plus," she turned to Persephone and looked her dead in the eye, "I wanted to see what you're made of."

"Did I pass your test?"

"Absolutely." She dragged Persephone through the crowd. "Sol didn't. It's been over a year, and he's never left the palace. God knows what he gets up to all day!"

"Why don't you tell him there's another way out?"

"And have him follow me around all the time like a depressed cockroach? No thank you! Wait here, Sphenya, I'll be back in two minutes." Her dark hair flapped around her face as she ran towards the marketplace.

Cities were a new experience for Persephone. She stared, awestruck, around the magnificent square. Grand architecture ruled the skyline, in bright pinks and greens, oranges and blues; street vendors sold every kind of food imaginable. The Tsar's palace—the crowning jewel—stood before them all, unbeatable in magnitude and glory. Persephone delighted in the sights she had waited a lifetime to see.

"Here," said Phoenix when she returned. She handed Persephone a cardboard container, separated into four compartments. Three contained food, and the fourth a glass bottle, filled with dark brown liquid.

"Thanks." She assessed her new friend in the bright daylight. Phoenix was taller than Persephone. Her dark-brown hair was cut just below her chin, straight except for a slight wave on the left-hand side. A slight smirk was permanently embedded in her face. Strong, dark eyebrows drew attention to high cheekbones that rose like mountains below her stormy blue-green eyes. The eyebrows were plucked to perfection, and her light-brown skin gleamed with moisturiser that had not yet dried. She wore little makeup, but it was clear she took great care in curating her appearance. Faint freckles exploded across her nose, and her neat, pouting lips concealed straight, pearly teeth. Her accent had hints of Sol's, but only when she talked fast. When Phoenix was in control, she spoke with the same accent as the Tsar.

"Where are you from?" Persephone asked. She sank her teeth into a pastry. Sugary almond paste oozed luxuriously onto her tongue, and flaky crumbs fell through her fingers like snowflakes onto the cobbles below.

"Settlement." Phoenix shrugged her distaste.

Met with a blank stare, she explained. "Last century the planet went to shit. War, climate change, all the fun stuff. Many countries were destroyed. They're now Dead Zones, unsafe to live in or travel through. Refugees came from the United Kingdom and America. Western and Eastern Russia took in British refugees, but refused the Americans. Greece got the Americans, but they bred too quickly, hence the Vineyard Scheme. In the Russian countries, refugees weren't allowed to integrate into society. They were kept in Settlements, basically prisons, and have been made to live there ever since. Sol is from a British Settlement. As you may have figured, you come from an American one."

"What about you?" Persephone asked. "Your accent isn't like Sol's."

"I'm Russian," Phoenix said. "Born right here in Moscow. I was raised in a British Settlement, but we'll speak no more of that."

"This place is truly beautiful," Persephone said in an effort to change the subject.

"It has its charms. The palace was built 75 years ago, for Tsar Khaos Olympovski, Icy Boy's great granddaddy. The Kremlin, that stood there before it, was destroyed in a fire. Rumour has it Tsar Khaos started the fire himself – he certainly lived up to his name. Do you want to stand here gawking at buildings all day, or shall I show you around?"

Persephone's gaze drifted up towards the sky, but she was met with more than a view of clear blue, or white-grey clouds. Up above the square loomed vast structures. They looked like a mirror, but didn't reflect her own image. Instead, she saw Haden in various scenes and locations. The images played on loop, and Persephone couldn't decide if what she saw was the result of technology or magic.

"Either's fine with me," she said in answer to Phoenix. It was near impossible to remain calm. The whole world stood before her, and she wanted to simultaneously jump in the air with joy, and lie down on the ground beneath her to soak up the energy of the Earth, the energy of freedom.

"Finish eating, then we'll go." Phoenix smiled brightly, beaming up at the sky. Her face was like reflected sunshine.

"What's this?" Persephone asked. She eyed the green pickled vegetables as if they would attack her. She missed Greek food.

"Gherkins!" said Phoenix. She plucked one from her own container and munched on it enthusiastically.

Persephone nibbled tentatively at the tiny cucumbers. Her face contorted with disgust.

"It tastes... unusual." Why must the food of freedom taste so foul?

"Exactly! You'll get used to it."

"Never!"

Phoenix laughed. It was a beautiful laugh, like bells tinkling out across the busy square.

"What do you usually eat?" she asked. "Tomatoes and olives?"

"And grapes," Persephone said. "Lots of grapes."

Phoenix pulled a face. "I hate fruit."

"You can't hate all fruit, there's such a variety!" A cloud passed over the distant sun, sending the square into sombre grey gloom. The onion dome turrets of Saint Basil's Cathedral cast circular shadows that fell across Phoenix's face. Persephone still stood in the sunlight.

"I do. I can't eat it without being sick."

"What's this?" Persephone held up the bottle of brown liquid.

"Kvass. It's a soft drink. Made from black rye bread."

"A drink made from bread?" Persephone laughed at the thought of it.

"Welcome to Western Russia." Phoenix tapped her foot impatiently. "Try not to take all day to eat."

Persephone bit into the second pastry – this a savoury one, filled with sautéed potatoes and green cabbage, spiced with caraway seeds. She slipped the bottle of kvass into the pocket of her trousers, not quite ready to drink bread juice. She took a final look around the square. Her eyes wandered languidly across each building, memorising the glow of the sun and the shadow of the clouds. "Okay," she said. "I'm ready."

Persephone spent the rest of the day exploring Moscow, with Phoenix playing the role of tour guide. Phoenix skipped through life with an endearing passion for living, but her new friend soon discovered a number of topics were off limits if this pleasant mood were to be preserved. In spite of the initial hiccups of navigating Phoenix's tempestuous waters, Persephone was happy to spend the day like this. Phoenix was unlike anyone she had ever met, and she offered Persephone something she had never had, something she didn't know she had even desired: *a friend.*

The next five months vanished into a thousand moments, as the flowers of friendship began to bloom. Persephone spent most days with Phoenix, exploring the city. Phoenix was noticeably absent three days a week, and refused to offer an explanation of why. Persephone spent these days with Sol. He wasn't a talkative boy, but he challenged her to board games, and the two soon fell into a comfortable companionship. In the evenings, Phoenix and Sol joined Persephone in her room. Together they would eat, and sometimes share bottles of wine Phoenix scavenged from the kitchen.

One day in late summer, Persephone and Sol sat on either side of the fireplace, resting their backs against the wall to soak up the heat. It was late August, but a bitter chill had crept into the air. Phoenix lay sprawled out on the floor. Her feet traced a path up the wall, soft within her ankle-socks.

This was life now. An intimate life, where the world belonged only to Persephone and her two companions. It had been months since she had seen the Tsar. The enigma of why he had brought her here was a frequent topic of conversation. Persephone tried not to think about it, but it gnawed away at Phoenix, and she couldn't go a day without raising the subject.

"I have a theory," she said. "Don't think it's silly, and it's only a theory, but…"

"Yes?" Persephone and Sol asked in unison.

"Icy Brains wants to marry you, Sphenya." She let her words hang in the air for a moment, allowing the weight of them to sink in. "I have good reason to think it's true." Phoenix watched her friends' reactions, and was not disappointed.

"Why would he want to marry her?" asked Sol. He rarely took interest in Phoenix's musings about the Tsar, but this time she caught his attention. "Sphenya's barely an adult, and he's what? 28?"

"I think his father's putting pressure on him to marry," Phoenix said simply. She flipped slowly through a book, pulling faces at the page, both amused and horrified at its contents. Her eyebrows were a performance in and of themselves, dancing with the vivacity of her reactions.

"Phoenix?" Persephone asked sternly. She sat up out of her slouching position, shifting away from the fire. She was warm all over.

"What?" came the all-too-innocent response. Phoenix continued her perusal of the book. She lay on her back now, with her bare legs leaning flat against the wall. Persephone saw each expression upside down, and it did little to calm her nerves.

"Why would his father pressure him to marry?" she demanded.

"The Tsar rules about a quarter of what was once the Russian Federation," Phoenix said. She didn't look up from the book. "That is Western Russia. His dad rules the rest—Eastern Russia—which is mostly Siberia."

Persephone looked blankly. The name meant nothing to her.

"Siberia," Phoenix repeated. "Big, snowy place. Lots of natural resources, huge mining industry. It's where Eastern Russia's wealth comes from. Whoever has control of Siberia has a monopoly on industry, so even if Tsar Kronus wasn't the Ice Cube's father, he'd still have a lot of influence over him. When you throw in family obligation, Old Freezer Face is basically his daddy's puppet."

"I don't see why he needs a wife," Persephone objected. Even if the two situations were connected, she didn't see why that wife had to be her.

"He's never been popular," Phoenix said. "Whether his laws

are liberal or strict, the public hates him. He changes laws on a whim, messes up the system everyone's used to. He's lost his citizens' trust, and he's too far gone to earn it back. So what to do? There's nothing disillusioned people love more than a royal wedding. Investing the Crown's wealth in a wedding no one wants? Splendid! Then there's the matter of heirs…"

"Why me though?" The idea of marrying Haden seemed unnatural to her. "I'm hardly bride material – I'm eighteen years old!"

"You're totally bride material!" Phoenix said. "You're foreign, which provides mystique. And you're young, in the prime of your fertility. Not to mention you're a ginger. They say redheads make men desirous." Phoenix grinned mischievously, watching her friend cringe.

"There must be another explanation," Persephone said. "He wouldn't go all the way to Greece just to find a bride. Why'd he want me anyway?"

Phoenix rolled over, and sat up to face Persephone. Phoenix's hair was tousled, and her shirt was scrunched.

"Honestly?" she said. "Because, to men like him, the only thing better than a vagina is a foreign vagina."

"I don't even know how to respond to that." A deep blush crept across her face.

"Listen, Sphenya," said Sol, who finally deemed it time to come to her rescue. Phoenix smirked smugly at the traumatised Persephone. "You need to be careful. You don't know what you're getting yourself into with that man."

"You think I'm going to marry him?" she asked. "Give me some credit!"

"Yes," Phoenix mused, "you wouldn't marry just anyone. You're quite stubborn – it's your only defining personality trait."

"Gee, thanks," Persephone said. She could sense Phoenix's desire to keep prodding, to continue provoking her until she elicited a strong reaction. "I don't want anyone—you, or Haden—to reduce the meaning of my life to a single body part. Can we just forget you ever had this stupid theory?"

"Sure." Phoenix returned to her earlier pastime of flipping through the book.

"What are you reading?" Sol asked. "You keep pulling faces."

"It's a picture book," she said dismissively. Phoenix didn't try to hide her dislike of him.

"Like for small children? Aren't you a bit old for that?"

"No, it's a *picture* book." She raised an eyebrow suggestively. Sol looked confused.

"It's porn," Persephone said. "It says so on the cover."

"You'd like it, Solly Boy," Phoenix said. "Or maybe you wouldn't." She shot Sol a look that sent him back to silence. His eyes, when they dared to meet hers again, burned with rage.

"I don't find the pictures themselves amusing," she continued to Persephone. "They don't do much for me, I find this stuff somewhere between fascinating and repulsive. It's the fact this book belongs to the Tsar, and the thought of him doing any of this, that I find hilarious. Wouldn't you agree?" She held the book open, revealing a graphic, black-and-white image of two men and a woman engaging in a sexual act.

Persephone blushed scarlet and turned away for a moment. Her eyes soon crept back to the page. All she could think of was Haden, in a way she had never thought of him before. Sol glared at Phoenix. He was redder than Persephone.

"Sorry." Phoenix looked pleased with herself. "I didn't realise you were both so squeamish."

"Sphenya…" Sol stared from the book, to Persephone, and back again. "Since when could you speak Russian?"

"What do you mean?" she asked.

"I thought you only spoke English."

"I do only speak English."

"Holy shit." Phoenix dropped the book, which fell open to an unfortunate page, and gazed at Persephone with excitement. "Sphenn, look at the front of this book! It's written in Russian, in the Cyrillic alphabet. This isn't English. How can you read it?"

"I don't know," Persephone said. "I just can."

"Can you understand spoken Russian?" Phoenix asked. "Can you understand people talking when we're outside?"

"Yes. I never thought about it before."

"To be clear," Phoenix asked, "you've never learnt to speak or read Russian? Ever? You just have the knowledge innately, like

34

the language has been programmed into your brain?"

"I've never learnt Russian," Persephone confirmed.

"This is amazing." Phoenix couldn't stop staring.

"Why do you two live here?" Persephone asked in an effort to change the subject. For all their conversations about the Tsar's intentions for her, Phoenix had never let slip the purpose of his other two charges,

"Haven't you guessed?" Phoenix lay back down and pointed her toes in the air, staring up at the ceiling. "We're prisoners."

"Why?" Persephone asked.

"Um, let's see? Your future husband is a megalomaniac, and kidnapping makes him feel powerful. Plus, it sent a message to the Settlements, let them know who's really in charge. Those damn Settlement Presidents act like they're the heads of their own little states, but the Tsar rules over us all."

"Why don't you escape? You know how."

"Oh, that is the question!" Phoenix said dramatically. "He knows where we lived. He'd only bring us back and lock us up somewhere we couldn't escape from. No, this is better. We've got our own rooms, clean clothes, lots of food, not to mention the library." She was silent for a moment, watching the ceiling with a pensive expression. "No one cared when we were kidnapped. Why should we go back to them? This is better." Again, Phoenix and Sol exchanged a non-verbal argument. Persephone could no longer tell who wished to silence whom.

# Chapter Four

Persephone woke slowly that morning. She clung to the warmth of her duvet, hiding from the world for just a little longer. Adventures were things for afternoons, she believed, and mornings should be devoted solely to sleep. As she rolled over, Persephone heard a crunch of paper beneath her. She groggily opened her eyes, and found a note on her pillow that simply read:

> Meet me by the oak door at noon
> *– Haden*

Phoenix's theory of a marriage plot flooded into her head. The weight of it hit her forcefully, a hard pressure in her chest. Persephone shuddered. She had come here for freedom. Marriage would steal that freedom from her. It would strip her bare. She sat up in bed, and took her breakfast from the bedside table. An assortment of fruits were arranged neatly: slices of cantaloupe shaped like crescent moons, spiralled rows of raspberries, a small bunch of grapes. Persephone tore off a handful of red grapes, and shoved them into her mouth as she hurriedly dressed – it was already eleven thirty. She wore fitted, black trousers, and a lilac blouse she had borrowed from Phoenix. She brushed her long hair up into a ponytail on the top of her head. This hairstyle made her feel powerful, like she was a business woman, not a teenage girl.

"I just need my war paint," Persephone said to herself. She reached for a tube of mascara, and walked over to the mirror. Damp, black eyelashes soon stood out magnificently beneath ginger eyebrows. She applied a subtle, nude shade of lipstick to her lips, slipped her feet into a pair of black platform heels, and was ready to go. Marriage was not the plan, but she was prepared to negotiate.

Persephone just had time to alert Phoenix and Sol to this new development before she went to meet the Tsar. There was a skip in her step as she hurried down the dark corridor to her friends' bedrooms. Persephone was adamant nothing would happen between her and Haden, but she looked forward to his attempts. If she was being honest with herself, she was excited by the attention, by the notion that she, and only she, could fix Haden's problems. Would that not make her more powerful than the Tsar?

"Good morning!" she exclaimed, as she danced into Phoenix's room.

"I think I must be dreaming," came the sarcastic response. Phoenix lay on her bed, reading a novel. She wore a pair of dark-green dungarees and a white t-shirt. "You're awake, before midday, and you're telling me it's a good morning? Okay, what's happened? When did you have a personality transplant?"

"I had a note from Haden," Persephone explained. "He wants me to meet him at noon."

"That's why you're happy?" Phoenix hit her head against her pillow in exasperation. "You are one of a kind, Sphenya, honestly!"

"It's a good thing!" Persephone tried to bring her around. "It means something's going to change. It means I might find out what he wants with me."

"Good luck." She laughed. "You don't have to be a genius to figure out what he wants with you, Sphenn. He wants you to make royal little babies for him." Phoenix folded down the page of her book, and watched Persephone pityingly. "If he asks you to marry him, say no, for goodness' sake! I don't want you becoming the Ice Tsarina!" She got up from the bed, and squeezed her friend's hand.

"I'll walk with you," she said. "You're so giddy, you'll fall over if I'm not there to stop you. Where are we going?"

"The big oak door," Persephone told her.

"How do you feel?" Phoenix asked. Her tone was uncharacteristically serious, concerned. This had been happening often lately. Persephone wondered whether it was purely part of the girl's growing up, or if there was something going on that she hadn't been privy to.

"I feel powerful," Persephone answered. Her heart raced as her shoes clacked purposefully across the floor.

"You have no power, Sphenya," Phoenix said bluntly. "Why can't you see that? You're as much a prisoner as Sol and I are."

"I consented to coming here," Persephone argued. "I'm in control. I was in control then, and I'm in control now. If he asks me to marry him, I can say no. And I will say no. I have that power. More than that, I will see him with his power reduced. I can ask for what I wish, I can bargain with him!"

"You're kidding yourself," Phoenix said. "Unless there's a drastic reversal of circumstances in the next few minutes, the Tsar will be, as he always has been, more powerful than you. 'No' is just a word, Sphenn. You can say it a thousand times, but it only has meaning if people listen to it. Consent isn't about what you wish, it's about how far the other person respects your wishes. I don't think the Tsar does respect them."

"Why are you so jaded?" Persephone asked. "Haden is a good man. He gave me a new life, he rescued me!"

"I'll see you later, okay?" Phoenix changed the subject. She hugged Persephone impulsively, and hurried off before Haden arrived.

"Persephone," Haden greeted her. He emerged through the oak door only moments after Phoenix's departure. His blond hair was slicked back, highlighting the chiselled landscape of his high cheekbones, and the strength of his jawline. His icy blue eyes shimmered under the yellow light from a lantern on the wall. He walked with an easy confidence, and his lean muscles and good posture exuded sex appeal. Persephone saw through it, saw that— for all his beautiful facades—this man was not comfortable in his own body.

*I could be comfortable with his body*, she thought to herself, eyeing him up. Just because she didn't want to marry him, it didn't mean she couldn't admire the scenery.

"Hello," Persephone said with a warm smile. All she could think about was Phoenix's theory. And Haden's body. Fear and excitement danced within her chest. She had greeted him in Russian. He didn't seem surprised by this.

"I thought you might like to see my fruit laboratory," he said in his native language. He flashed her a charming smile.

"Yes, that would be nice." Persephone breathed a sigh of relief, the marriage proposal seemed to be off the table for now.

He led her through a door that she had never noticed before, due to its concealment behind a red, velvet curtain to the right of the oak door, and immediately down several flights of steps, lit by golden lamps. The floors were carpeted, and Persephone's heels did not clack. She wondered if the staircase was soundproofed, if anyone would hear her scream – or make any other kind of noise. Every inch of her body was on high alert. They came to a stop at the next door – a heavy, ornate beast of a door, carved from mahogany, and varnished in a deep red. Haden stopped Persephone, his hand resting authoritatively on her shoulder. He handed her the black-velvet blindfold, which she remembered from her arrival here.

"What's this for?" Persephone asked, offended. "Don't you trust me?"

"The location of the laboratory is top secret," Haden explained. His face was open, charming, but the pressure of his hand made her uneasy.

"I don't want you having your wicked way with me, Haden," Persephone teased. "After all, we are alone down here."

"You can trust me," he promised.

"But you can't trust me?" She wanted to provoke him, to break through the charming cool of his demeanour, to make him snap. She wanted him to throw her up against the wall, to release the passion she knew must lurk just below his icy surface.

"Silence, woman."

He was joking, she knew he was joking. But the see-saw of desire and discomfort tipped again as he spoke. Persephone had no interest in men who used her womanhood as a source of jest. She pouted her painted lips, and snatched the blindfold from his hands, tying it herself to allow a sliver of vision to remain below its blackness.

Haden led her further down until she was sure they were well below the palace. Persephone concentrated her eyes on that tiny splinter of light at the base of the blindfold. Anything important enough to be kept from her was worth memorising, if she were to have power over this enigma of a man. The path was simple: staircase after staircase, a corridor, left, then right, until they finally reached their destination.

"Here." Haden removed the blindfold. His smooth hands

lingered on her silky red hair for a few moments longer than necessary, claiming her as his own. Persephone's palms began to sweat, and her heart thudded in her chest. She was afraid of him, perhaps for the first time. She had been attracted to him before, but his touch now made her uncomfortable. She shuddered with anticipation, a nervous panic. The feeling subsided as she viewed the room in which they stood. Persephone's body buzzed with excitement. She could almost taste the power contained here.

"It's amazing!" she whispered, intoxicated by the scent of myriad fruits. Pungent raspberries fought against apples and pomegranates to dominate the air, their aromas bursting with ripeness.

Haden and Persephone stood in a room built from fruits, but this was no orchard, no garden or grove. This was a laboratory, a scientist's take on nature. Each scent, each sight, each taste that rode on the air, was heightened to the very brink.

The walls were fashioned from fruit. Blackcurrants and blueberries flourished – a dizzying mass of indigo blue that seemed to be constantly shifting. There were times when Persephone thought she caught a glimpse of greens and reds beneath the purple and blue. She wondered how many layers there were to this cave of creation. The floors were a mass of large, green coconuts, packed closely like a cobbled street. The remainder of the room was stuffed with row upon row of fruits, growing in glass incubators that rested upon sturdy green vines, rising up from the coconut floor, tended by robot workers. Persephone found herself drawn to the robots. They were mere machines, humanoid in shape, with white, metallic exteriors. They were methodical, mechanical, nothing much to see. But they took her right back to that Greek vineyard, to the robotic life she had once lived, where each day followed the monotonous routine of painting and production.

"It is rather extraordinary," Haden agreed, pleased by her reaction. "Come with me." He took Persephone by the hand, leading her across the vast room and through another door. She lagged behind him as they walked, twisting her neck to watch the laboratory receding from view, the robot workers continuing as normal.

It occurred to Persephone that the life she lived in Haden's palace was no more a part of the real world than her life at the vineyard had been.

They continued walking through labyrinthine corridors, lit by old-fashioned lamps that cast shadows across their path. Persephone couldn't help remembering stories she had read as a child, of princesses from the past residing in ancient castles. She imagined herself in a floor-length pink, corseted dress, ginger hair flowing down her back. The image was laughable to her; she knew she was nobody's princess.

Haden led her into a dimly lit room, much smaller than the laboratory. The room had a romantic air, and candles burned on a table set for two.

"I thought you might be hungry," Haden said. He pulled out a red velvet-backed chair for her, before taking a seat himself.

"Thank you." Persephone smiled. Her ponytail swished about her shoulders as she tipped her head to gaze up at the ceiling. The hair on the back of her neck prickled as she sensed Haden watching her, observing her, enjoying her. A slow smile spread across his lips as he saw her expression. He didn't say a word.

They ate in silence, which gave her time to observe the Tsar. This was the man who had uprooted her life, and changed it for the better, yet Persephone knew nothing about him. She knew he was the Tsar, but what of his other side? Who was he when he was just Haden?

The meal was a trial for Persephone, who was yet to develop a taste for Russian food. She made it through the first course—borscht, served with black rye bread—with little discomfort. She took great joy to see the next course was composed of Greek food: a platter of pita bread, falafel, black and green olives tossed in rosemary and olive oil, and hummus. Persephone crowed with delight at the sight of it. Haden smirked to himself, still not deigning to speak.

By the time they had finished dessert—cherry chocolate cake with almond ice cream—the candles had burned low, casting garish shadows across the walls of the room. Haden poured them each a glass of red wine, and pulled a chess set off a shelf. "Do you play, Persephone?"

Her hair glowed orange in the candlelight; her youthful face

41

flushed from the strong wine. Though she had spent her life on a vineyard, Persephone had never grown used to drinking alcohol, and it barely took a glass to make her tipsy.

She nodded in response to his question. Sol had taught her during her first week in Moscow. The first time they had played together was a rainy Monday. Phoenix was nowhere to be found, and Sol was desperate to avoid making small talk. They played game after game, on the floor by the fire in Persephone's room, until the sky outside had grown dark, and Phoenix's footsteps pattered softly in the hallway. Persephone had little interest in remembering facts or reading books, but she had an interest in strategy, in winning each game she dared to play. These were the skills she would need in her life as an independent woman: the ability to plan ahead, to know which moves to make to ensure the outcome suited her.

"Shall we play together?" Haden asked. His eyes teased her. The wine had loosened his inhibitions as much as it had hers. Persephone could see he wanted her. She could no longer tell if she wanted him. All she knew was she wanted to play a game, chess or otherwise.

"Sure," she said. Her smile gave him all the answers he needed.

"Would you like to be black or white?" asked the Tsar. His eyes never left her face. The ice devoured her; unmelted by her fire.

"Black," Persephone said. "I prefer other people to make the first move, that way I know where I stand." Her pulse quickened. "In chess, of course." She looked up from the board. Her blue eyes met his.

"Black you are then." He set out the chessmen. "A good piece, this," he held up the white king, "though people tend to underestimate him, because his moves are restricted. He is still the most powerful piece on the board."

"Powerful?" Persephone scoffed. "He's the weakest! He can be completely trapped, and he's always the one who ends the game. He can't keep himself out of trouble!"

"Well, well," Haden laughed. "You have a little spirit after all." Persephone's eyes lingered on the neck of his white button-down shirt, noticing the blond hairs at the top of his pale, muscular chest.

"I prefer the pawns," she said. "People overlook them because they're dispensable and boring, but I think they're extraordinary.

42

In a game of predictability, only they can beat the odds. They can rise above themselves, become important. Kings are an open book, whereas the pawns are almost like a phoenix: born out of nothing, and reborn powerful."

"Yes," Haden said, "it would be most terrible to overlook the biggest threat in the game."

✝

Persephone was somewhat less giddy when she returned to her quarters. The wine clouded her senses, and she swayed a little as she walked. She sat down on the carpeted floor, and pulled off her heels, letting her sore feet relax in the cool air. A laugh escaped her lips as she thought over the events of the afternoon. Laughter soon turned to uncontrollable giggles. Persephone rocked back and forth where she sat.

"Oh my god," called out an all-too familiar voice. "What have I missed?" Phoenix plonked herself down on the ground beside her friend. "What happened? What did you do? Please tell me you didn't!"

Tears of laughter streamed from Persephone's eyes.

"As if!" she said. "Come on, I have standards!" She laughed harder, burying her face in her knees.

"So?" asked Phoenix. "Are you going to tell me about your date with Mr Deep Freeze?"

"It was strange," Persephone said, glancing out the window. She was on edge, unable to concentrate properly on anything, even once the laughter ceased. Something was wrong. She couldn't function. Her bloodstream called out for some missing chemical.

Phoenix's eyes lit up. "Strange?" she asked. For her, that word hinted at excitement; for Persephone, it forewarned danger.

"It was enjoyable," she said, turning away to hide her expression. She wanted to arouse Phoenix's intrigue, to wind her up a little. It was time for the tables to turn. "I had fun with him," she continued. "Lots of fun..."

"You're not going to tell me what happened, are you?" Phoenix asked sulkily.

"Nothing happened," Persephone giggled. "He only touched

43

me to take off my blindfold."

"He blindfolded you?" Phoenix asked. "What a kinky little creep."

"He took me to his top-secret fruit laboratory," Persephone continued; her voice dripped with innuendo. "He showed me where he grows all his coconuts. He had really big coconuts."

Phoenix burst out laughing. "I didn't come here for you to tell me about the Tsar's coconuts, Sphenya," she said with mock severity. "I have no patience for your vulgarity."

"At least he didn't show me his bananas."

"Sphenya! Are you the same girl who blushed at some harmless pornography?"

"That book was not harmless," Persephone protested. "Don't remind me of it! I'd only just managed to remove that image from my mind!"

"Come on, Sphenn. I want details of your date – but please, no talk of his coconuts."

"It wasn't a date," Persephone said, as she wriggled into a more comfortable position. She sat cross-legged now, a half-smile on her face as she prepared to recount the tale to Phoenix. "Story time," she announced, still tipsy. "He took me to his fruit laboratory, which was all kinds of wacky. The walls and floors were made of fruit, and—"

"Where is this elusive venue?" Phoenix asked, stretching her legs out on the floor.

"You know the velvet curtains by the big oak door? There's another door behind there, and a few flights of stairs – it's down that way."

"I've never found it," Phoenix said. "I've been down there a few times, never found anything interesting. I guess I didn't go deep enough. What happened next?"

"We had lunch together."

"So it *was* a date?"

"No," Persephone said. "Not a date. We barely spoke during the whole meal. But there was Greek food, and I could have cried with happiness! I never realised just how much I missed falafel. And hummus! I was in heaven." Persephone beamed up at the ceiling. "After we ate, we played chess. That was when it got

44

weird. He made these comments about the king piece being the most powerful."

"The queen's the most powerful," Phoenix said automatically. "Girl power will always beat the patriarchy."

"The king's a weakling, and I said so, but Haden tried to convince me the king was the biggest threat in the game. I don't think he was talking about a chess piece."

"The king hides behind the queen."

"As I said: weakling."

"Did he mention marriage?" Phoenix asked. She pulled her hair towards her mouth, trying to chew on strands too short to reach.

"No," Persephone answered. The topic hadn't arisen.

"Maybe I was wrong." Phoenix bit her lip, evidently worried.

Persephone knew she didn't like to be wrong. She wracked her brains. "I think you were right about one thing."

"Of course I was!" Phoenix quickly regained her bravado.

"He feels completely powerless. That's why he uses the little power he does have to control everyone. Perhaps his father *is* using him as a puppet. And perhaps he *is* an unpopular tsar."

"Excuse me! I was right about two things, not one!" Phoenix said. She hugged her knees to her and rocked from side to side.

Persephone watched with amusement. Her affection for Phoenix grew each day, in spite of their bickering. She knew their friendship was special, and she wouldn't trade it for anything in this new wide world.

"Where's Sol?" she asked after a moment.

"He went to bed. He wasn't feeling well, apparently." Persephone sensed that the weight Phoenix gave to the last word was carefully placed.

"Oh." She knew something else was going on with Sol, something Phoenix was aware of, but reluctant to share. There were times when Persephone felt left out, in spite of their closeness. Phoenix and Sol, for all their sniping, had an impenetrable world that she wasn't allowed in. It was easy to feel like an outsider when those two could communicate without even a word.

"Want to go out?" Phoenix asked. She appeared preoccupied now, her mind exploring thoughts far distant to the topics of either Sol or the Tsar.

"Sure," Persephone agreed. "I might go and see Sol first." She felt an unexpected bout of misery creeping up on her. She wondered whether it was a further effect of the wine, or if it related more to Phoenix's secrecy surrounding Sol.

"I wouldn't go if I were you. He wants to be alone. He's sulking, he won't want anyone disturbing his self-pity," Phoenix said. There was a cutting edge to her tone, it contained the same knife she used to speak of the Tsar.

"What's up with him?"

"He has personal stuff going on." She spoke flippantly, as though Sol's 'personal stuff' didn't rank highly in her estimation. "It's a difficult situation – there's no way it could ever turn out in his favour."

"That's sad," Persephone said. "Sol should know he can talk to us – about anything."

"It'll come to light soon anyway," Phoenix predicted. "You can't keep things hidden in the closet forever." She sighed wearily as she hopped up from the floor. "Let's go."

"Ready to fly?" Persephone asked as they walked over to the windowsill. The courtyard below was a dull shade of grey in the afternoon light. Heavy clouds loomed low in the sky, closing in. Persephone was the first to take to the window. The air blew icily beneath her blouse, teasing her skin to tautness. She shivered, thinking of the Tsar. Reality claimed her with the scratch of gravel against bare feet.

"I forgot my shoes!" she called up to Phoenix.

"You think those will do you any good?" she laughed. "You're better off without them, Sphenn!"

"Can you grab me another pair before you come down?" she begged. "I'm not going barefoot!"

"What did your last slave die of?" Phoenix grumbled, before letting out an elongated, grudging "Fine!"

Persephone waited in the courtyard. Her bare feet paced, and she twisted yellow flowers around her fingers absent-mindedly. She glanced up at the palace wall, waiting for Phoenix. The glimmer of blond hair, peeking out from behind a red-and-gold curtain, caught her eye. Persephone ducked hurriedly behind a large green bush,

46

praying the Tsar hadn't seen her.

✠

"Jumping drunk," Phoenix said when she returned. "That's a first for you." She tossed a pair of shoes out the window. Persephone caught one, and scrambled in the bushes to find the other. Twigs scratched at her arms, and she giggled, still lulled into a dreamlike state by the strong wine. Everything felt softer, like she was contained in a cosy bubble that held no danger of being popped.

"It's good to be brave sometimes," she said absently.

"It would've been more sensible to take the back exit," Phoenix said when she landed on the ground.

"When have you ever cared about sensible?"

"Unlike you, I don't have a death wish." She slipped through the narrow gate, and out of the palace confines.

"Where do you want to go?" Persephone asked, following at her heels. "Are you finally going to tell me where you disappear to all the time?"

"It's private," Phoenix said. Red Square was busier than usual. She elbowed her way through the crowd with little regard for the people in her way, walking with brisk steps away from the palace, away from Persephone. The harsh clatter of feet on cobbles grated against Persephone's ears, even in her drunken state she couldn't shake the feeling that something wasn't quite right.

"Phoenix!" she called. "Where are you going? Wait for me!" She struggled forwards, through the undulating sea of people. Just as she was about to be swallowed by the crowd, Phoenix stopped still. Her head was tilted upwards, to the screens. Persephone followed the line of her gaze. The news clip was captioned "Annual Meeting of Settlement Presidents." Men in suits congregated around a large table. A tall man, with a dark beard and heavyset brown eyes, stood at the head of the table, giving a speech. His words weren't audible from the video. Before Persephone could take in any more, Phoenix had grabbed her arm, and dragged her away from the screens.

"Are you okay?"

47

Phoenix didn't answer.

"Where are we going?"

"I have some business to attend to," she said when they were finally through the thick of the crowd. "Since you're so desperate to know all the rest of my secrets, you may as well come with me."

‡

The walk from the train station could have been pleasant, if it wasn't for Phoenix's sombre mood and stony expression. Blue-green eyes burned, eyebrows arched in an expression of stoic martyrdom that looked almost genuine. Dark hair was whipped back by the wind, and her nose pointed in the air with determined resolution.

Tired of viewing her friend's display, Persephone entertained herself with watching the landscape. Whilst Moscow was now familiar, the Western Russian countryside was as alien to her as the moon. The grass here was greener than in Greece, and the air smelled different – fresh, sweeter, and colder; always colder. Trees were scattered across meadows and farmland, but as they drew further from the train line, the fields gradually emptied out, until they were barren save for dry grass.

"Why are there no farms here?" Persephone asked. Phoenix didn't respond, but the answer soon became evident.

A building loomed in the distance: gargantuan, twenty storeys tall, with a width three times its height, fashioned from ugly grey bricks. They couldn't be more than ten miles out of Moscow, but the energy of oppression that emanated from this place heralded a different world.

"Is this the Settlement?" Persephone asked. Phoenix hadn't told her where they were going, but she had soon figured it out. The very sight of the building threatened to steal her soul, to cast a dark shadow over her heart. The windows were mere slits, and barbed wire covered the walls. Although no security guards were visible, she was sure some must lurk nearby.

"Yes," Phoenix confirmed. A deep tremble shook her voice. "Lovely, isn't it?" She gave a mocking smile. Her eyes expressed a level of fear that made Persephone want to cry. Phoenix wasn't

48

putting this on; her terror was not exaggerated for attention.

"It reminds me of a prison," Persephone said. She desperately longed to hug her friend, but Phoenix stood purposefully out of reach. She shook, fragile as a paper doll. Persephone gazed in horror at the forbidding walls that reached up to the clouds. At the vineyard there had been sunlight, fresh air, freedom in the basic sense. She had been deluded to ever think the two Settlements were comparable.

"Oh Sphenya, it *is* a prison!" Phoenix's voice shook with anger and fear. "I hated it here." She hid her face, turning to the horizon. "Hate is too small a word to convey the horror of this place." She deeply inhaled, exhaled, inhaled, exhaled, her ragged breaths audible above the roaring wind. "We were all treated like dirt. We had no freedom, and nothing can erase the memories. It haunts me; I can't escape the nightmare of what happened here."

"Why did you come back?" Persephone couldn't understand it. If she were Phoenix, she would run as far away from here as she could, and never stop running until the memories ceased. To run was to fight, that was the only logic that made sense to her. Even so, Persephone was not naïve enough to believe Phoenix returned here bearing an olive branch. Perhaps coming here was a greater act of war than attempting to leave it behind.

"It's too late for me." Phoenix's voice no longer shook. She arched her shoulders back, stood tall, like the warrior she told herself she was. "But it's not too late for everyone else. Don't judge me Sphenya, you haven't lived here! You don't know what he— what it was like!" She pulled a packet of matches from her pocket, and held them up. "I'm here to make a difference. Some crimes are too great to go unpunished. I must get revenge, not just for myself, but for every victim."

Persephone's eyes widened with horror. Her gaze swivelled from the matches, to the wall, and back, until it sank in. "People could die!" Her words were quiet, but firm. She knew right from wrong, but what of here, where the lines were so deeply blurred? This place was an institution of oppression, and every instinct told her its only hope for redemption was to burn to the ground. Persephone knew that just by bringing her here, Phoenix had finally torn down the fortress she enclosed herself within, that it was a sign of her deepest trust. That didn't make a wrong right.

"I knew you wouldn't understand!" Phoenix's words stung. Her tongue seemed specially trained for venom, any sentence could become a fatal blow. Persephone watched her, torn between opposed senses of justice. Phoenix's tired voice filled with bitterness and remorse as she spoke again. "You're my friend, Persephone, and I'm trying to share the darker side of myself, let you see who I really am. For some dumb reason I thought you would stand by me in spite of that. I guess I was wrong. But don't you see? These people would rather die than live here! Doesn't that show you what kind of a place this is? You don't know what it's like to live without hope! For every day to be the same as the last, and the same as the next! You think living in a vineyard was bad? You think your life was so terrible because you were confined to a couple-of-miles' worth of grape fields? Whatever your life was like before you came here, it was nothing compared to this."

"What about you? How can you smile and laugh and act like an idiot half the time? How can you be happy when you've lived like that?"

Phoenix looked at Persephone pityingly. There was a beauty in her naivety, in the dimpled smiles and ginger curls that radiated sunshine. Her eyes and hair were an unnatural hue. Too bright to be from nature. Phoenix didn't see beauty there today, she saw a battlefield. From here on out, Persephone would become either her ally or her adversary. Phoenix breathed deeply, and forced herself to look Persephone in the eye, to choose friendship, in spite of the agony confiding would bring. "It's all an act, Sphenya," she finally said. "Can't you see that? It's fake, I'm a fake. I smile and laugh, because that's who I am, but believe me, I'm torn into a thousand tiny pieces. I fell apart long ago, and I've never found anyone to put me back together again. I never will." She wove her fingers together, clutching her own flesh and blood and bone, the only thing she could rely on. "There is no glue strong enough to piece me back together. So I shall stay broken forever. Broken and hollow and empty, and completely alone!"

"You're not alone," Persephone said. Phoenix's pain resonated with an ache deep inside her. Perhaps it was merely an acknowledgement of the intrinsic loneliness, *otherness* of a fellow Settlement child. Perhaps it was something more, a bond between the two girls themselves, rather than their circumstances. "I'll help you."

"You'll help me?" A glimmer of hope entered her voice. "You'll really help me?"

"Of course I will." Persephone took Phoenix's hand and held it tight, feeling the chill of her skin. Something passed between them then, an invisible pact of unity, a promise that any obstacles that blocked their way would be faced together. Persephone could see how much damage Phoenix had suffered. She felt guilty for never noticing it before. She silently vowed to be more vigilant, to truly see her friend, to support her no matter what. The first step was to light this fire.

"What do you want me to do?" Persephone asked.

"The bricks contain an accelerant," Phoenix explained. She tilted her head in the direction of the Settlement, whilst keeping her eyes as far away from it as possible: she couldn't bear to look.

"What does that mean?" Persephone asked.

"It's highly flammable," Phoenix explained. "When this place was built, they wanted a way to dispose of it quickly, if they had to. Y'know? Brutally murder a few thousand people if they caused too much trouble? Welcome to Western Russia, where murder is easier than integration!" She sighed dramatically. "I don't know if this will work – once the guards realise what's happening they'll put the fire out. But I have to try, Sphenn. I'll light a fire at the base of the wall, and once it catches we'll run as far away from here as humanly possible. Got it?"

"Got it."

The two girls scouted through the open fields, fetching armfuls of wood and twigs, which they built up into a mountainous pile. The air was thick with the odour of wood, grass, and fungi. Wind billowed through the girls' hair, whipping it across their faces.

"Before we do this," Persephone said, as Phoenix struck the first match, "I have to ask: are you sure this is right? I'll stand by you, whatever you decide, but I have to know you're sure. There's no going back from this."

"Of course it isn't the right thing." Desperation permeated

Phoenix's voice. "But the right thing and the best thing aren't always the same."

She dropped several lit matches into the heart of the heap of wood. The girls stood and waited while sparks crackled, soaring like fireflies into the darkening sky. Persephone couldn't shake the feeling she was taking part in something terribly wrong.

"Okay, on the count of three: run like your life depends on it," Phoenix yelled above the ever-increasing roar of the flames. "One, two, *three!*"

Persephone began to run, but Phoenix tripped on a branch, and fell, sprawled out on the ground.

"Phoenix!" She screamed as she ran back to her friend. "Get up!" Smoke rose, filling her nostrils.

"I can't," Phoenix wailed as the ravenous flames leapt towards her.

"Come on!" Persephone yelled. She hauled Phoenix up, off the ground, dragging her by the arm. They both coughed furiously, and clamped their hands over their mouths and noses, trying not to breathe in the acrid smoke that clawed its way into their lungs.

"I can't walk," Phoenix said, tears of pain and frustration brewing in her eyes. Persephone kept a firm hold on her arm, pulling her as best she could until they were both safely out of burning range. They stood and watched as the fire caught onto the building, and the exterior wall burst into a violent array of fierce, yellow flames. Fire alarms wailed at a tremendous volume, and a swarm of guards in black uniforms emerged through the doors. There was no sign of any Settlement citizens.

"We've got to get out of here!" Persephone shouted over Phoenix's coughing. Fire alarms rang out, shrill in the girls' ears. "If these bricks have this accelerant in, which I think they just proved they do, that fire's gonna spread quickly. We'll be cooked within minutes!"

"Yum." Phoenix gave a faint smile. "Look, Sphenn, I've twisted my ankle. I can't walk, let alone run. Leave me here."

"I'm not going without you!"

"I keep forgetting how stubborn you are."

"Just lean on me, do your best," she begged.

"Okay." Phoenix leant an arm around Persephone's neck, and

tried to walk fast, but her ankle ached, and she limped heavily.

"I'm going to try and carry you now. It'll be quicker."

Phoenix nodded, and let her friend lift her. Persephone glanced behind her when they had travelled a suitable distance away from the Settlements. The guards had quelled the fire completely, the girls' efforts had been in vain. She didn't have the heart to tell Phoenix.

# Chapter Five

Persephone and Phoenix made it back to the train station unscathed, but as they stepped onto the platform in Moscow, they began to feel discontent brewing in the air, in the hostile glances of the locals, in the angry sound of feet on pavement. When they reached Red Square, they were shocked to see people engaging in open protest: smashing windows, throwing flaming torches at the palace, yelling and chanting in anger at the Tsar and his regime. The screens suspended high above the square were shattered. Wires hung precariously from their broken frames.

"Shit," Phoenix said under her breath.

"What's going on?" Persephone asked a man who stood nearby. He was middle-aged, and a little taller than her, with deep wrinkles submerged in his tanned forehead. His brown eyes burned with fury.

"We're teaching the Tsar a lesson!" he shouted back. "Showing him he's powerless over us, declaring our freedom!"

"Shit! Shit! Shit! *Shit!*" Phoenix whispered. "They're not grand on timing, are they?"

"How are we gonna get back?" Persephone began to panic. She had kept her cool up until this point, taken deeps breaths and told herself everything would be okay. Moscow was still unfamiliar to her, and she had no idea which backstreets would take them home, let alone how they would get back into the palace unnoticed.

"It doesn't look like we can, or at least, it doesn't look like I can. You should go on alone."

"And leave you to be trampled to death? No way!"

"Go get Sol then. Maybe you'll be able to get me back, between you." Phoenix glanced worriedly across the square, assessing the level of disruption caused by the protests. She wondered just how much of the city would be inaccessible. "He wasn't really ill, he's just sulking."

"I'll be back as soon as I can," Persephone promised. She wiped sweat from her soot-covered brow, and pulled her long hair out of its ponytail, letting it ripple across her back in the wind. She was worn out, worried about the riots. Her legs ached, and she was sure traces of alcohol remained in her system. Persephone had lived more today than she had in the past eighteen years. "Try to stay away from the violence," she added.

Persephone embraced her friend. She clung to her so tightly that Phoenix squealed out in protest.

"You're squishing me!" she complained at regular intervals. Persephone didn't relent. Her affection for Phoenix had magnified in the past few hours. The adrenaline rush of witnessing these riots only increased Persephone's desire to do all she could to protect her friend from the cruelty of this world. When she finally released Phoenix from her grasp, Persephone summoned all the bravery she possessed, and ducked through the wild crowd to the concealed palace entrance.

Phoenix limped away from the crowd. The pain in her ankle was excruciating. Watching these riots, she was three years old again. There had been riots in the settlements. She was too young to remember the politics of it. All she knew was that the people had rebelled, and many of them were killed. Then too, she was only an onlooker. Phoenix had been a small child, and didn't remember much, but this frantic array of people brought it all back, almost as vividly as the equally awful events of that next year of her childhood.

"Ow!" she protested, as someone knocked into her. The combination of the collision and her twisted ankle sent her falling to the ground. She lay there, head spinning, unsure if she could get up, when someone lifted her. At first she thought it was Sol, but he spoke in Russian.

"Are you hurt?" the man asked, as his strong arms carried her through a nearby door.

"You've no idea," she replied, "unless you've ever tried to run on a twisted ankle." The strangest idea came to her then: this man looked almost like the Tsar. His face was completely different, both in structure and skin tone, but his hair was that particular yellow shade of blond, and his eyes were familiar icy blue.

"Now that is one of the few things I haven't done," he said. "It sounds painful. You were limping before you fell. How did you twist it?"

"I tripped," she said.

"You should probably stay by the window, so you can see your friend when she returns. She is coming back for you, isn't she?"

Phoenix shook her head slightly. "I don't know if she'll get back. By choice, she would. She's incredibly loyal, it turns out: loyal and stubborn. But she'd have to go through the worst of the trouble – twice. I don't know."

"How come your face is covered in soot?" the man asked.

"None of your business," Phoenix said. She didn't take well to prying strangers.

"I'll go and find your friend," the man said. He didn't seem offended. "What's your name?" The apartment was bare, empty of any furniture. She wondered if he lived here at all.

"Phoenix."

"Appropriate." He nodded at her soot-covered face. "Okay, Phoenix, I'll find Persephone for you, and you wait here."

She nodded obediently, and sat cradling her ankle, mewling like a wounded kitten, as he returned to the melee outside. It was only after he left that it occurred to Phoenix she had never told him Persephone's name. The minutes passed and turned into hours.

The sun had almost set by the time the man returned with Persephone and Sol.

"Sorry we took so long," Persephone said hurriedly, running to her friend. "It was hard to get back here, we had to take a detour."

"It's fine," Phoenix said. "I'm grateful you came back at all."

"I should come with you," said the man. "If I carry you home, it will be easier for your friends."

Persephone glanced at Sol. Phoenix could see the questioning look in her eyes. They all knew it would be plain stupid to tell him they lived in the Tsar's palace, but even between them, they wouldn't be able to carry Phoenix for long. In order to get back home safely, they couldn't take the direct route across the square.

"We need to go back through the city and around," said Persephone, "and when we get to a certain point, we must go on alone."

"Fine by me." He scooped up Phoenix, and they started on their way to the palace.

"Have you lived in Moscow long?" he asked Persephone.

"Since March. They've been here longer." She gestured at her friends. "You?"

"I'm from anywhere I want to be." He smiled mysteriously.

"I envy you greatly. It seems wherever I go, I get stuck."

They didn't speak for a while. Eventually, Persephone said "We go alone from here."

"If that's what you wish." He transferred Phoenix to Sol, and turned back down the narrow street.

"Come on," Persephone said hurriedly. They had nearly reached the palace by now, and she was worried someone might have noticed their absence. Her mind wandered back to earlier in the afternoon, when she had noticed the Tsar lurking behind the window. If he had indeed seen her—and, most likely, Phoenix—leaving the palace, surely he would have checked their rooms to see if they had returned.

"Ow." Phoenix winced as Sol quickened his pace.

"Who was that man?" Persephone asked.

"I don't know. I fell over and he picked me up. I don't need to be told I shouldn't go off with strangers—I'm not stupid—but I didn't fancy getting trodden on by half the city."

"Okay."

They went the rest of the way in silence, but soon encountered a problem. The back entrance to the palace was barricaded shut; they had no way to get in.

"Hang on," Phoenix said, clapping a hand across her forehead to make the others aware of her eureka moment. "The library is in the dome of the roof. He never bothered to fix the broken skylight. If we could somehow get up there, we could go through that window."

"You'd have to climb."

"Yes, but I can crawl once we're up on the roof, plus, no one's going to see us up there."

"How do you propose we reach said roof?" Sol asked. He was particularly irritable today.

"The tree," Phoenix said. "We can hardly turn up at the front

57

door – the Tsar would practically murder us if he knew we'd been out."

Persephone's heart thumped in her chest. The more she considered it, the more certain she was that Haden had seen her that afternoon.

"What if we're seen?" she asked. "What if the rioters see us?" The uppermost branches of the tree rose above the palace garden wall; the three climbers would be visible to the rioters below.

"If anything," Phoenix answered, "they'll think we're some of them, breaking into the palace. It's not them we need to worry about, it's Old Icy Boy."

After arguing for several minutes, Sol and Persephone agreed Phoenix's idea was the best one they had. They carried her to the tree.

"What was that?" Persephone yelped. A colossal crashing sound ricocheted across the nearby square, bouncing off the palace walls with violent vibrations.

"It's a gunshot," said Sol.

"Sphenn," Phoenix said, "climb up onto the tree. We need to see what's going on."

Persephone obliged immediately. She hooked her foot onto the lowest branch, and hoisted herself into the tree. The bark was rough beneath her fingers; she bled.

"Well?" Phoenix demanded. Persephone climbed quickly, not daring to look beneath her. Now was not the time for caution.

As Persephone reached a height parallel with the top of the palace garden wall, her eyes caught sight of a view that instilled fear in her exhausted mind. Red Square loomed below her, and it was indeed red. A hoard of blue spilled from the palace doors: the Royal Guard, brandishing black rifles that gleamed in the light of the setting sun. Blood soaked the square, soaked the rioters.

*No,* Persephone thought, *not rioters, people.*

She shuddered. Further shots rang out.

"Who's killing who?" Phoenix called. "Have the people of Western Russia finally grown a backbone after a century, or…" she tailed off.

"Or," Persephone answered. She had never witnessed this level

58

of violence. "Or."

"He's got the military involved, hasn't he?" Sol asked. He squeezed Phoenix's hand. Together, they gazed up at Persephone as she watched over the palace garden wall.

"It's a bloodbath," she said, her voice accompanied by another round of gunshots. "He's got the army there, and they're killing. They're killing blindly! They're just shooting into the crowd." Her voice caught in her throat. Where before, Persephone had been fearful of the rioters, she now watched them with pity. She ached for them, these people who were forced to die because they dared request a better standard of living. The more she watched, the more Persephone succumbed to the feeling of solidarity with the downtrodden citizens of Moscow.

"Come on, Sphenn," Phoenix sighed, "there's nothing we can do. That wall right there is the least of the barriers between us and them."

Persephone dwelled on those words as she waited for Sol and Phoenix to join her amongst the branches. It had never occurred to her before just how privileged she and her two fellow prisoners were. They lived in luxury, lived lives of leisure for which they didn't have to work a single day. Perhaps the time they had each served in the Settlements outweighed the injustice of this stroke of luck – made better, somehow, the disparity between their living conditions and those of the general public. Perhaps.

"You can't let yourself think about it," Sol said in a low voice, as he joined her on her branch. Phoenix was still some metres below; each movement was painstaking.

"I can't stop," Persephone said. She leant her head against Sol's shoulder. All she wanted to do right now was sleep.

"Because you're asking yourself: how can we live like this, when they're forced to live like that?"

"No," she said. "Not quite. I'm asking myself: how can Haden be so kind to us, allow us to live here free of charge, providing him with nothing in return, yet he can shoot his own people without blinking an eye? How can one man be both so kind and so callous?"

"He's a different breed," Sol said, after some thought. "He doesn't know what the real world is like. He was taught this is his right, his duty. He was taught to protect himself above all else. We

59

all have that self-preservation instinct, but for the Tsar… It's not himself he has to protect, it's his position."

"Are you saying it's not his fault?" Persephone considered. The thought was infinitely more palatable, and infinitely more horrific.

"I agree," said Phoenix, between groans of pain, as she joined them on the branch. "Don't look so surprised, Sphenya!" she added. "Okay, okay, disclaimer: I do not support the Tsar, nor do I support his use of military intervention in this situation. But he's doing his job, just like they're doing theirs. All parties involved are responding to the situation in the most natural way for their social group. Including us. It's all rigged, Sphenn, we all do what we're told to do."

"Told by whom?" Persephone asked.

"Told by our good old-fashioned fight-or-flight instinct," Phoenix said. "Come on, we should get inside. I don't fancy being hit by any stray bullets."

They climbed the rest of the way in silence, before finally hoisting themselves out of the tree and onto the roof. Persephone and Sol walked from that point; Phoenix crawled.

"Is this the library?" Sol asked as they came to the dome of the roof. It was a vast, golden structure, interspersed with skylights.

"What do you think?" Phoenix asked, pain in her voice. She pushed the window further open, and peeked glumly into the room below.

They each jumped. Phoenix stifled a scream as she landed on the floor. Pain seared through her twisted ankle, making her see stars. They were poised, ready to leave the library, when they heard the sound of voices, growing increasingly louder. There was nowhere to hide.

☦

Panic beat through their hearts like a drum: rhythmic, primal, the music of their basest fears.

"Under here!" Phoenix whispered, gesturing at a bookshelf. Persephone and Sol stared blankly, their confusion heightened by terror. "Now!" she insisted. "It's a narrow space, but there's just enough room. Hurry up!'

Persephone quickly crawled out of sight, squishing herself into the tight space between bookshelf and floor. Sol carried Phoenix over to the bookshelf, and followed Persephone under. Phoenix disappeared in the nick of time, just before two sets of footsteps entered the room. She held her breath, squeezing her limbs as close together as possible. She knew one false move could be fatal. They listened to the heated argument ensuing above them.

"Why is it my fault?" shouted the Tsar. "You told me what to do and I did it! You have forgotten who the Tsar of this country is!"

"You have forgotten who made you the Tsar," came the stern reply. This man's voice was low and threatening. It made Phoenix think of another man's voice, in another vast building isolated from the outside world.

"It was Uncle Hyperion, not you. And he's been dead a long time."

"It may have been his death, but it was my decision, Haden. Remember that."

"Thank you, it was what I always wanted!" No one could mistake the sarcasm in the younger man's voice. "I never wanted to rule! Don't you see my life has been stolen from me? I could have been a scientist, Father!"

"And what then?" asked the Tsar of Eastern Russia, his voice deeply condescending as he addressed his son. "You know what you're capable of, but so do I. Keeping you away from your science is the best thing I could have done for you! I thought you were losing your mind when you told me what you had created. It shouldn't have even been possible! You were a young child. Damn you and your prodigious talent! I should have known you'd be just like your mother. You need to learn control, Haden. I mean control over yourself, not other people. There is only one man of whom you can be master, and he is yourself."

"I didn't do it to cause harm!" Haden's voice was filled with agony. "I was lonely. Don't you see this is your fault, not mine? I was a child! My mother was dead not even three years, and you were never around! I needed somebody, and I had nobody!"

"Rhea's death was no excuse for your absurdity."

"My mother was everything to me," Haden said bitterly. "She loved me, and I know you never did. I was trying to replace her. I should have known no one could fill my mother's place."

"So you sent it away, irresponsible as ever."

"She is a fully functioning person, father, not an 'it'."

"Your experiments are of no consequence to me, as long as you keep them to yourself. That is not the issue at hand."

"What is this 'issue' you speak of?" Haden asked.

"You! You are the issue. You should be grateful for this country. Your brothers would have killed for this!"

"If only I were one of my brothers. But I'm not one of them. I'm not a lot of things, father, and we both know it!"

"You must pretend to be the things you're not! This silly phase you're going through, I want to hear nothing of it."

"It's not a phase." Haden's voice ripped through the air, far louder than it had been before. He roared with the might a grown man, but, to Phoenix, he sounded like a child. Or a wounded animal. "There's nothing wrong with me. You don't have to limit yourself to one thing. You were the one who taught me that. I'm not going to do anything to embarrass you. Don't you worry about the damage I could cause to your pristine reputation."

"You always had to have everything. But you can't play for both teams, Haden. If you were anyone else, this wouldn't matter so much, but you are the Tsar and you must act like one. You have barely earned your people's respect as it is. You fix this now—and let me hear no more of it—or I will."

"Tell me what I have to do?" the young Tsar pleaded. "Marry a pretty girl? Have a few babies? Just tell me what I'm meant to do!"

"Find a suitable bride by the end of the month, or you will lose everything."

"Father, I am working on it!"

Phoenix, Persephone, and Sol listened to the echo of receding footsteps. When the coast was clear, they clambered up from under the bookshelves, covered in dust.

"That was close," Persephone sighed.

"Ow," Phoenix moaned.

Sol remained silent.

"We should get cleaned up," Persephone said. They stood beside the door to her room. All three of them were in foul moods. "You come with me, Phoenix. I'll run you a bath, and get you something for your ankle." She ached for her own company, yet she dreaded spending any time with the thoughts that rattled around in her frazzled brain. At least Phoenix's presence would distract her from her haunted mind. When Persephone dared close her eyes, all she saw was blood. All she heard was Haden's voice.

Phoenix nodded, and Sol stalked off without so much as a 'goodnight', leaving the girls on their own.

"What's wrong with him?" Persephone asked, turning the bath's taps until they expelled a flood of steaming water. Sol had been quieter than usual, lately, and it was obvious something was going on with him.

"He's an eighteen-year-old boy," Phoenix said, brushing her ash-strewn hair with Persephone's hairbrush, "what's not wrong with him?"

"He just seems… I don't know. He's upset about something."

"Yeah, well, you've never been in love," Phoenix said, the words gushing from her mouth with considerable speed. It was clear to Persephone that Phoenix couldn't wait to get this off her chest. "Not that I have for that matter, but I read a lot. I can tell the signs a mile off."

Persephone stood still for a moment, wondering what the other girl meant. Then it hit her.

"He's in love? With whom?"

Phoenix didn't reply. She paid close attention to the act of brushing her hair, and watched herself in the mirror. She raised her eyebrows ever so slightly, and pouted her lips a little, tipping her head to find the kindest lighting.

"With me?" Persephone asked, trying to read Phoenix's face for any sign of an answer. That face, however, refused to comply. All it did was pout and observe its own sombre self.

"No. Not with you," she answered finally.

"With you?" She didn't think it likely.

"No. Not with me."

"Who is it then?" Persephone asked. If it wasn't Phoenix or herself, who was left?

Phoenix stopped brushing her hair, and turned away from the

mirror. She looked Persephone in the eyes. Something passed over her face, an unreadable expression that was perhaps edged with a tinge of guilt. And then she said it, the last thing Persephone would have expected. "He's in love with the Tsar."

# Chapter Six

The words slowly sank in. Persephone's jaw dropped, her mouth formed into a gaping circle. Her left eyebrow raised itself spontaneously as she stared at Phoenix. Persephone sank down onto her bed, whilst the revelation lodged, ill-fittingly, in her brain. "He's in love with Haden?" she asked, to confirm her mind wasn't playing tricks on itself.

"Yeah," Phoenix said. "I didn't think the Tsar was that loveable either. He's kinda gross if you ask me. It would be like pining after the inside of a freezer."

"I didn't mean Haden was gross," Persephone said, her stomach churning. "He's not, not at all. I just—"

"Was under the closed-minded impression that all boys liked girls? What did they teach you at that vineyard?"

"No, not at all." Persephone said, shaking her head at Phoenix's lack of faith in her. "It's just... Sol... and the Tsar. I didn't know you two had even spent much time with Haden."

"I haven't," Phoenix said. "I've only met him a couple of times. I know he saved me and all that, but he's so cold – and that's not me making fun of his creepy eyes, I'm saying his personality's cold. I don't know how much time Sol has spent with him. I asked him about it, but it's like talking to a brick wall."

"Sol hardly knows him, why would he love him? What makes you think he does?" Persephone asked. Discomfort settled in the pit of her stomach.

"Think about it: when I mentioned Frost Face wanted to marry you, Sol was adamant it couldn't happen. Earlier, when you spent the day with the Tsar, he pretended to be ill. And then, upon hearing that his love has to take a bride by the end of the month, he went all sour. I know his Russian isn't good, but he would've understood enough of that conversation to know he has no chance."

"Okay, say it is true, why wouldn't he tell us? We're his friends."

"Because he likes to put the 'Sol' into 'Solitude'? Or he's embarrassed. You'd be, wouldn't you, if you had a crush on someone? I know I'd be."

"I guess so, but I'd still have to tell someone. I couldn't just keep it to myself."

"Would you tell me?" Phoenix asked. Persephone could sense a deep uncertainty hidden behind the question, an uncertainty as to where their friendship stood, after the tumultuous events of that day. As though Phoenix, with her tendency towards secrecy, needed assurance of Persephone's continued openness.

"Of course!" She moved to hug Phoenix, who stood in the doorway of the bathroom. "Now, you get clean."

Persephone returned to her bed. She sat up against her pillows, knees hugged to her chest, with her eyes fixed on the window. All she could see was the courtyard; her heart longed for cityscapes, or open fields. Or grapevines. She explored her mind, skimming through memories of the two men in question, and tried to figure out how she felt. All she was aware of was a strong stab of jealousy stirring inside her, but she didn't know whether it was for Haden, or for Sol. Persephone felt different things for each of them. When she was with Haden there was an uneasy attraction, a spark that wouldn't go out, but wasn't yet ready to burst into flame. Sol was steady, reliable.

Phoenix emerged from the bathroom, wrapped in a soft, white robe. Her dark hair was dripping wet.

"Are you gonna have a bath?" she asked, shaking her hair like a wet puppy. She wrapped it into a towel turban atop her head.

"Yeah," Persephone said, "I need a minute first."

"Are you okay?" Phoenix asked. Her lips were pressed together in worry, and her blue-green eyes were thoughtful.

"I'm fine."

"Fine never means fine. Tell me what's wrong: is it Sol or the Tsar?" She immediately sussed out the root of the problem.

"I think it's both,' Persephone sighed.

"Both? Ouch! That'll be messy." Phoenix sat down beside her friend, carefully positioning her bathrobe to cover her naked legs. "You're saying you're upset because Sol likes the Tsar, and you like Sol, but you also like the Tsar?"

"Yeah," Persephone said. "I don't like Sol in the sense you're thinking," she added hastily. "I don't know if I even like Haden in that way. But they're both… They're my people."

Phoenix snorted. "Your people? They're not possessions, Sphenn."

"Sol's my friend," Persephone said. "We're comfortable together, I don't have to pretend around him. Haden makes me feel uncomfortable – in bad ways and good. There are times when I could swear I hate him, and times when I want to push him up against the nearest wall and have my way with him."

"If you have to do that with him," Phoenix said, "do it in a bed, for everyone's sake."

"I'm not doing anything with him," Persephone assured her. "I just said it to illustrate my point. Sol is my friend, I wouldn't want more from him. Haden awakens the fire within me, and I never know whether I want to burn alongside him, or let my flames devour him completely. The idea of him and Sol, it doesn't sit right with me, because they're so far apart in my mind. Sol is safety, and Haden is danger. I hate him right now, after what I saw in the square. I wouldn't be with him if he begged me."

"Men like him don't know how to beg," said Phoenix. "If he wanted you, he would take you. Ice is water, Sphenn. Water extinguishes fire. You'll only burn as long as he lets you."

Persephone remained silent.

"The worst isn't over yet," Phoenix continued. "It's barely begun. The Tsar has to find a wife by the end of the month, and odds are that wife is gonna be you, which will hurt Sol. If you say no to the Tsar, he loses his throne, and you'll lose your home. What if you don't want to be the Tsarina? There are so many bad things about this situation, and no matter how it turns out, at least one person is going to get hurt. It's a disaster no matter what happens!" Phoenix became increasingly worked up as she spoke. She gestured with her hands, and her face was a mural of frustrated excitement, the muscles of her jaw dancing with exuberance.

"I hadn't thought about all that." Persephone knew Phoenix had a point, but she couldn't help feeling her friend was being a little melodramatic. Surely Haden wouldn't kick her out for refusing his proposal? Her mind drifted back to the violence in Red Square. How well did she really know this man?

"Whatever you're going through, it's going to be ten times worse for Sol. Western Russia has a long history of homophobia, so even if the Tsar felt the same—which, frankly, I don't think is likely, despite all that in the library earlier—nothing could happen between them. The Cold Creeper is hardly going to sacrifice his reputation to get it on with an eighteen-year-old boy. Sol loses, no matter what happens between you and the Tsar."

"I know it's awful for him," Persephone said, "but I can't help that Haden doesn't feel the same way, or that we live in a country full of bigoted homophobes, or whatever else is getting in the way of Sol and the Tsar living happily ever after. How is it my fault?"

Phoenix bit her lip, deeply troubled.

"What?" Persephone asked.

"Sometimes I think there's more going on than just us three." Phoenix chose her words carefully. "It's like there's a greater force at play, like you and Sol are puppets and someone's pulling all your strings. It's so subtle, whatever it is, that's it's barely noticeable. It's only when you look at the bigger picture that you see something doesn't quite fit."

"What do you mean?"

"I don't know. It's nothing. Go and have a bath."

Persephone could tell Phoenix knew a lot more than she was letting on, but she didn't press her. It could wait until tomorrow.

She twisted the taps, and watched morosely as steaming water gushed into the bath, fogging up the mirror above the washbasin. The bathroom was grander than the bedroom, though simple in design. The uniformity of the white-tiled walls was broken by a single line of midnight-blue tiles, decorated with orange hieroglyphics, which ran parallel to the rim of the bathtub. The taps were made of gold.

Persephone peeled off her clothes, which were now slick with sweat and stained with ash. She tossed them in the laundry basket, and climbed into the tub. The water burned her skin, but she didn't care. If only water could burn away memories. She shuddered at the thoughts of blood and fire and voices heard in libraries.

Phoenix bit back a yelp of pain as her sore ankle twisted beneath her again. She fell with a thump on the floor outside Persephone's door, the last place she wanted to be. She prayed her friend was still asleep, but Phoenix soon found she was all out of luck.

"Are you okay?" Persephone stood above her in the doorway.

"Never better." She tried to hoist herself off the ground, but fell back to the floor in a heap.

"Where are you going?" Persephone narrowed her eyes at Phoenix, who wore a hooded black jacket, dressed to be inconspicuous.

"It's private."

"You're not going anywhere alone in that state. Plus, wherever it is can't be as bad as what we did yesterday."

"Why are you awake?" Phoenix glanced at her watch, she didn't have time for this. "It's 7:30, you're never up this early."

"Stop dodging the question."

"Ugh!" She finally pulled herself up off the floor. "Get dressed."

"You're taking me with you?" A glimmer of excitement flashed across Persephone's pale face. For a moment she was like her old self, before the sombre look of yesterday returned. Her eyes were smudged with makeup she had forgotten to wash off, and her hair was a tangled orange mess. Even in this state, she looked like a porcelain doll animated with human life force.

"Do I have a choice?" Phoenix asked. "Hurry up! If you make me late I'll abandon you in the metro." She followed Persephone into her bedroom, and sat uneasily on the crumpled bed as she waited for her friend to dress.


Red Square was eerily silent that morning. The bodies had been cleared away, and blood no longer spattered the cobbles. The screens still dangled precariously from their poles, and no market stalls had been erected. Phoenix hobbled on her twice-twisted ankle, clutching at Persephone for support. They walked in silence to the metro station.

"He saw me leave yesterday," Persephone finally said, when they sat side-by-side on the busy train. "We need to be more careful, no more jumping out the window."

"He's not stupid," Phoenix said. "He has cameras in every corner of this city, he knows we leave."

"Why doesn't he stop us?" Persephone scratched at the green polish on her thumbnail.

"There's no reason to. Don't be fooled, Sphenn, he's still in control. We're only as free as he allows us to be."

"Doesn't that bother you?"

"I know how to pick my battles. Come, this is our stop." Persephone helped Phoenix up from her seat, and let her friend lead her through the metro station. The street outside was a uniform row of tall buildings with soft-pink walls. The lower storeys contained shops—clothes stores, grocers, pharmacies—and the upper levels were residential areas.

"Are you going to tell me where we're going?" Persephone asked. Phoenix walked with more purpose now, although she winced with pain every time her sore ankle touched the pavement. She turned a corner, into a run-down alleyway. The plaster of the walls was riddled with cracks, and graffiti covered every available surface. Phoenix stopped outside a faded yellow door, and took a key from her pocket. She twisted it in the lock, and the door swung open. Before them stood a narrow staircase. Phoenix gestured for Persephone to enter, and locked the door behind them.

"Are you taking me here to murder me?"

Phoenix didn't dignify the question with an answer. She shoved past her friend, and climbed up the stairs. There was no lighting in the stairway. Persephone followed Phoenix through the dark, until they reached a corridor at the landing. Light glowed at the far end of the corridor: natural light, streaming through windows, and electric lights glaring down from the ceiling. Persephone followed Phoenix through a doorway, and was surprised to find herself standing in a bookshop.

"You're late," said a good-natured voice, from somewhere behind a haphazard stack of old books. "Don't worry, I won't tell the boss." The voice belonged to a young man. He had light-brown hair that was long overdue for a trim, and he lounged in a chair, reading a book on astrology.

"I twisted my ankle." Phoenix dragged herself towards him, leaning heavily on a bookshelf for support. "My commute took longer than normal. It won't happen again." She turned to Persephone. "Sit down somewhere and don't get in the way."

The man hadn't noticed her until now. "Is this a friend of yours?" he asked Phoenix in a low voice.

"Something like that," she said. "Don't worry, she won't get in the way."

"You're not meant to show people the back exit." He folded down the page of his book, and regarded Persephone with a look of curiosity and apprehension.

"We can trust her," Phoenix said simply. She sat down in a chair behind a desk at the far side of the room.

"I still don't understand what's going on." Persephone went to join Phoenix, who gave her a warning look, and pointed to a pile of cushions on the windowsill. "This is a bookshop, right?" She took a seat. "What's with the secrecy?"

"Sphenya," Phoenix said, and gestured at the man, "this is Drew. Drew, meet my room-mate, Sphenya." She paused a moment, and finally said. "It's a radical bookshop. I work here."

"Radical?"

"We sell all kinds of books," said Drew. "Some of them are political, books that wouldn't make it past the Tsar's censorship."

"We're also a prime meeting place for literati types," Phoenix said. "It's not just underpaid workers who don't support the Tsar's rule. Whilst the working class and students take to the streets in good old-fashioned protest, the middle classes prefer to explore their revolutionary sides behind closed doors."

Before Persephone could decide what to make of this information, a bell dinged on the far side of the shop, and a customer entered through the front door. Whilst Phoenix spoke to the customer, Drew came and sat beside Persephone on the window seat.

"I'm sorry if I came across as rude," he said. "Security is important here. But Phoenix doesn't trust anyone, so if she says you're trustworthy, I believe her."

"I'm so confused," Persephone said quietly, watching the customer out of the corner of her eye. "It's a bookshop. People must come in and out of here all the time. Why am I a threat?"

"Everyone's on edge after what happened yesterday," Drew said. "It's one thing to buy a banned book, but selling them is far more dangerous."

☦

"I'm surprised," Persephone said. She stared down into the depths of the River Moskva. Evening sunshine glittered across the surface of the water. Phoenix stood beside her on the riverbank, eating a pastry. She was quiet and contemplative, not like her usual self. "You're working against the Tsar."

"Shh!" Phoenix hissed. "Announce it to the whole city, why don't you?"

"I'm sorry, I'm sorry!" Persephone said.

"You need to learn to keep your mouth shut, anyone could be listening." She broke off a crumb of pastry and dropped it to a pigeon at her feet. "You can't just accuse someone of working against the Tsar, not in public." The pigeon cawed at her feet, begging for more crumbs. She stomped her foot to scare it away, and continued. "I'm not working against him, I'm just working."

"He wouldn't see it that way."

"If you still have a soft spot for him after what you saw yesterday, I swear to god—"

"That wasn't what I meant," Persephone said carefully. "Why don't you just say you have a foot in both camps? I'm not judging you for it, it's a smart move, I just don't see why you're pretending it's not what you're doing."

"I don't get involved in politics," said Phoenix. She ate the last mouthful of her pastry, and scrunched its paper wrapper into a ball.

"Phoenix, you work in a radical bookshop. Even I know that's a political move. Especially given your living arrangements."

"You're so naïve sometimes," Phoenix said. "It's a bookshop. We sell pieces of paper bound up together. I love books as much as the next person, but they're never going to," she glanced around to make sure no one was listening, "overthrow the Tsar. You can call me political the day I take to the streets in active protest. Right now all I'm doing is making a living."

The next time Persephone accompanied Phoenix to work was two days later; an evening this time. The bookshop cafe had been closed due to short staffing the previous time, but now it was filled with the hustle and bustle of event preparation. Phoenix was dressed in a black-and-white waitressing uniform, and her brown hair was held back by a lilac headband. She wore dark purple lipstick, and her eyes glittered with an emotion Persephone almost read as pleasure.

"You need to stay out of the way," Phoenix said. They stood in the shadow of a bookshelf. The lights in the bookshop were dimmed, as the gathering was set to take place in the cafe. "I'll explain to my boss who you are and why you're here."

"How are you going to wait on people with your ankle like that?" Persephone asked.

"With great difficulty, but I don't have a choice."

"I could do it," Persephone suggested.

"No!"

"Why not? It can't be that hard."

"First of all," Phoenix said, "waitressing is a lot harder than you'd think. Secondly, you need to stay out of sight."

"Why?"

"If a certain someone takes you as his bride, your face will be everywhere."

"You're being paranoid. Plus, I have no intention of marrying Haden."

"Phoenix, there you are." A woman approached them. Her hair fell in glossy black curls over her shoulders, and her lips were painted a pretty pink. She didn't smile, but her green eyes were warm.

"Hi, Elizaveta," Phoenix said. "Did you get my note? I twisted my ankle, and I had to get my friend Sphenya to help me with my commute. She'll stay out of the way, don't worry."

"I hope you're okay," said Elizaveta. "If you're not up to working I'm sure we can manage."

"I could fill in for her," Persephone offered. Phoenix shot her a warning look.

"I should be fine if you let me stay behind the bar. Sphenya is more used to filling wine bottles than pouring from them." She glared at Persephone again, and smiled sweetly at her boss.

"If you're sure," Elizaveta said. "I'll be in and out throughout the evening, I still have some work to finish up for the newsletter, but I'll be in my office if you need me."

Elizaveta walked away with a graceful ease. She disappeared through a door behind the counter in the bookshop.

73

"I have to get to work," Phoenix said, and hobbled towards the bar.

Persephone reacquainted herself with the window seat. She watched as light drops of rain began to spatter against the glass, blurring the lights from the street below. At least last time she had had Phoenix and Drew to talk to. Now she was alone, with nothing but books for company. Persephone crept between the shelves, reading the titles of different sections: 'Feminism', 'Politics', 'History'. She chose a book from the Feminism corner, and took it back to the windowsill with her. The light here was too dim, and she could scarcely make out the words. Words like 'solidarity', 'discourse', and 'patriarchy' loomed at her from the shadows of the page. They were like whispers in her memory, their meanings familiar, but too far away to make out. Persephone returned the book to the shelf, and thought bitterly that what she really needed to read was a dictionary. Dissatisfied with the literature around her, she edged towards the border of the cafe. Making sure to stay hidden behind a bookshelf, Persephone watched the the clusters of people that milled about the cafe.

"I didn't see it," said a tall man with a protruding stomach, and a twirled moustache the colour of dark chocolate. He wore a red bow tie, and his neck was slick with sweat. "I did hear the gunshots. And the screaming."

"I heard the Tsar of Eastern Russia was visiting," said another man. He was small, with hair like straw, and wore an ugly tweed jacket. "If the Tsar called in his father over a little protest, I can't see him lasting the rest of the year."

The first man looked into the dark of the bookshop. His gaze rested directly on Persephone. She ducked behind a bookshelf, far from prying eyes and intriguing conversations.

Persephone rolled over in bed. It was early, she knew that even without checking the time.

"Good morning," said the Tsar. Persephone screamed.

"Sorry, I'm sorry," he said hastily. Haden stood awkwardly over her. He was well put together for this time of morning, dressed in a

74

turquoise suit, with his hair neatly combed.

"What are you doing here?" She sat up in bed, her eyelids still heavy with sleep. Persephone's brain couldn't compute why the Tsar was in her bedroom.

"I'm having a ball on the 31st. You are invited." Haden shifted his weight from foot to foot, and watched her face closely. He was more uncomfortable than she was. "By that, I mean you must come. I will send someone to pick you up at 8:30pm." He turned to leave.

"Haden!" Persephone called after him. "Why do I have to be there?"

"Because I say so." The door closed behind him with a loud *thunk!*

The 31st was the final day before the ultimatum came into place. The Tsar's last chance at keeping his throne. In that moment, Persephone knew Phoenix was right. This had to be the reason for the ball: a way to test her performance in public. It was certain: the Tsar wanted her to be his bride.

# Chapter Seven

Persephone wanted to scream. She knew she was trapped, once again. She was intrigued by Haden, but not enough to marry him. Not after what she had seen in Red Square. A memory crept back to her of the day she had met him: she had felt uneasy, there was something about him she couldn't bring herself to trust. The feeling subsided, and she had started to like him. She couldn't remember why.

"Breakfast, Miss," declared a servant after knocking on the door. She came and placed a tray on the bedside table.

"Thank you." Persephone did her best to smile as the servant curtsied and left.

She glanced at the colourful array on her plate. The Tsar's fruit was served as it was grown: neat and sterile, a work of art rather than a meal. It sang to her, sweet juices calling out to the liminal spaces in her mind, where thought failed to reach and reflexes didn't dare to lurk.

The fruit tasted good. The chunks of melon were sweet and fresh, and lulled her mind into relaxation. The imminent prospect of her marriage didn't seem so intimidating now, and she blamed her earlier worries on an empty stomach.

When Persephone returned to her room that evening, she found clothes laid out on her bed: an elegant dress with an accompanying mask. Beside these lay a note, printed on gold-edged paper, written in a neat hand. It read:

> *My dearest Persephone,*
> *This is your costume for the masked ball on the 31st.*
> *I want you dressed and ready by eight thirty that evening.*
> *A servant will come to collect you, and escort you to the ballroom.*
> *– Tsar Haden of Western Russia*

This was the first time Haden had informed Persephone he was the Tsar. She wondered if his choice to reveal his identity was linked to a future proposal. Or had it to do with his seeing her leaving the palace earlier in the month? This was a power game, she knew that much. He was making certain she knew who was in charge.

Persephone skimmed her fingers across the black-satin skirt of the dress, feeling the lumps and bumps of the gold embroidery that patterned its surface. Beside it lay the mask, the same black satin and gold thread as the dress. It was shaped to conceal the top half of her face.

A wave of nerves crashed through her as she thought of the ball. Throughout her time in Moscow, Persephone's social interactions remained within a limited group of people: Phoenix, Sol, and the Tsar. The prospect of a ball filled with strangers was both terrifying and exhilarating. This would be a chance to interact with so many new people! She was excited, in spite of herself, but the underlying threat of a marriage proposal kept that excitement in check. Persephone knew the ball would be the beginning of the end; her peaceful days would now be few.

Persephone sat in front of her bedroom mirror, whilst Phoenix twisted and knotted her hair into a complicated style. The pressure on her head was claustrophobic, like her brain was trapped within a cage of woven hair. It was 6pm, August 31$^{st}$.

"What're you gonna say if he proposes?"

"I don't know," Persephone said. "I'll decide when, or if, I have to."

Phoenix applied makeup to her friend's face, skilfully finger-painting a wall of foundation across Persephone's skin. After the foundation came the lip liner, followed by lipstick in a vibrant red.

"I don't have a choice, do I? If I say no, he isn't going to let me stay here, is he?" Persephone asked.

"Do you want an honest answer?"

"Yes."

"He might send you back to the Vineyard," Phoenix said, "or lock you up somewhere, or knock you out and get married while you're still unconscious. He could kill you, or—"

"Enough! I get the picture."

"Good," said Phoenix. "You need to think before you make such an important decision."

Persephone pouted at her. "I do think! And," she pointed to her costume, "I look stupid!"

"No, you don't. Come on, we have two hours, and your hair isn't half done!"

Persephone let her friend work on her hair and makeup for the next hour-and-a-half. Phoenix constructed a façade through which Persephone barely recognised herself.

"I'll be back in a sec," Phoenix said when the makeover was complete. She took a moment to smile indulgently at her handiwork, before darting out of the room. Her bare feet slapped against the floor with careless agility.

When Phoenix returned, she held a camera.

"What's that for?" Persephone asked, aghast.

"If you get engaged tonight, and disappear from my world and into his, I need evidence you existed."

"You must know I wouldn't leave you like that," Persephone said. "Even if I were to marry him, which is the last thing I want to do right now, I wouldn't leave without saying goodbye. I couldn't do that."

"Just let me take the damn picture," Phoenix said. She held up the camera. "Smile."

Persephone obeyed, though smiling was her last instinct. Her mind was heavy, clouded with both fear and intrigue at the prospect of what awaited her. A printed photograph flew out from the camera. Persephone's face smiled up from the floor, the concern in her eyes hidden by the mask.

"Let's get one together." Phoenix jumped onto the bed beside Persephone.

"How're we going to do that?"

"We'll just turn the camera around and hope for the best," Phoenix said. "I don't know why it never occurred to me to get pictures with you." Tears hid in the corners of her eyes, waiting patiently to spill over once she was alone.

78

"Phoenix." Persephone grabbed hold of her shoulders, forcing her to make eye contact. "Listen to me, I will not leave you. I am never going to abandon you, I promise. No matter what happens with Haden, I will make sure you're not alone. I've got your back, you don't need to worry."

Phoenix nodded, and blinked repeatedly to clear the tears from her eyes.

"I just love you so much." She wrapped Persephone into a tight hug. "There are times when I absolutely can't stand you, but I do love you. You're the best friend I've ever had."

"I love you too." Persephone's words were muffled by Phoenix's shoulder. Her mouth filled with fabric when she spoke.

"Don't ruin your lipstick!" Phoenix squealed. "I put effort into that."

"Too late, sorry." Persephone laughed. "I think I ruined your shirt, too."

"It'll wash out. Come on, let me finish the artwork."

"Let's take the picture first, it'll be more real."

"Okay," Phoenix agreed. "That way I can remember you as the beautiful mess you are." She slung her arm around Persephone's shoulder, and held up the camera. The girls laughed as Phoenix repeatedly clicked the button, and tens of photographs landed on the floor.

"I think that's enough," she decided, hopping down to inspect them. "Take your pick," she added. "But I want this one." Phoenix held up the photograph: her head was tipped to one side, eyes squeezed shut with laughter, white teeth bared, hair flying in every direction. Persephone beamed widely, her smile the only part of her face not hidden by the mask.

"Then I'm taking this one." Persephone brandished the photograph of her choice.

"That one's dreadful!" Phoenix said. In the picture, her lips were pursed into a pout, her eyes were widened, and her hair was in tangles. Persephone's head was leant back in laughter, and only her chin and smudged lipstick were visible.

"It's lovely," she said. "It's the most accurate one – you're a poser and I'm a mess."

"I'm taking all these." Phoenix scooped her favourite

79

photographs into a pile beside her crossed legs.

"That only leaves me with five," Persephone said. "How many have you got there, twenty?"

"Something like that," said Phoenix. "Tell you what, if you don't marry Old Icy, we'll make a whole photo album, and document our friendship for years to come!"

"Sounds like a plan." Persephone smiled, but her heart was heavy. Tonight would change everything, she could feel it in the air.

"Here it is, Miss," announced the servant who escorted Persephone to the ballroom door. He was a tall man, with thick, dark whiskers, and an elegant posture. He seemed somewhat pompous for a man of his rank, but Persephone respected him for the pride he took in himself. Self-confidence was a hard skill to learn, and she admired those to whom it came naturally.

Persephone's heart thumped as she stepped inside the ballroom, she felt its beat pulsating throughout her body, down to the tips of her toes. The room was filled with sumptuously dressed, masked people. Some danced, talked, drank, whilst others stood by tables filled with exotic foods. Even in their current attire, Persephone could see these people were of a breed she had never before encountered. They were the uppermost elite of Western Russian society. Persephone edged her way around the room, and attempted to avoid the large groups of people. She would try to mingle later, but right now she was starving, and food was her priority. Her journey towards the nearest buffet was cut short when she caught sight of a table laid out with bottles of wine: wine from her home vineyard. With an unwelcome dash of homesickness, she wondered if she had painted the labels herself. Persephone had shed few tears for the life she once lived, but now she found herself on the verge of it. The homesickness that had dissipated so quickly once she arrived in Moscow returned with a vengeance. She wanted to cry for how far she had come, and how far back she would fall. If she married the Tsar, Persephone would lose the freedom she had gained. She allowed herself to consider what this life had to offer her, where she wanted to be in a decade's time. She could still be incarcerated with Phoenix and Sol. Or she could be the Tsarina, the most powerful woman in Western Russia. Persephone wasn't made to spend her life hidden away, trapped in the back rooms of a royal palace, distanced from grandeur. As long as there were ladders before her, she would ache to climb them. She would reach the top, whether through work or marriage.

Persephone brushed her fingertips gently against the surface of the wine label. The familiar feel of the paper beneath her fingers brought back bittersweet memories of life before the Tsar.

"Are you a collector?" asked a young man, as he poured himself a glass of red wine. "They say Olympus wine is the finest in all of Greece." He had a warmth about him that shone out, radiant in comparison to the aloofness exuded by rest of the party.

"No." Persephone didn't know what to make of him. "I prefer to indulge in things that don't give me headaches and nausea after over-consumption."

He laughed. "You must be smarter than the eighty percent of this room that are already dead drunk."

"If I'm smarter than them, they must be really dumb."

"Can I tell you a secret?" he leaned in, and she felt the warmth of his lips against her ear. "They are really dumb."

Persephone laughed, and allowed herself to observe him more closely. He was almost as tall as the Tsar, with light-brown curly hair, and tanned skin. A dark-blue mask embroidered with thick emerald threads obscured his face so the only visible feature was his mouth. His full lips curved into an easy smile.

"What's your name?" Persephone asked.

"I thought the point of the masks was anonymity?" he teased. She could hardly see his eyes through the slits of the mask.

"Sorry," she said. "I thought the whole point of social occasions was to make new acquaintances?"

"Oh, you are a terrible flirt." He grinned. "Certainly a terribly pretty flirt. First names?"

"There goes your anonymity." Persephone couldn't help smiling as she looked up at him. There was something deeply likeable about this man. He seemed out of place in this environment. With his dark tan and friendly manner, he belonged to a different world.

"Andrei," he said. "One of my mother's many terrible choices."

"Persephone," she said. "All I hear is that it's too long."

"I think it's a pretty name," he told her. "Forgive me for being forward, but I think you're a pretty girl."

"You've said that twice now. Don't you have any other lines?" She enjoyed compliments, but it was more than his words that brought the silly smile to her face. She felt giddy, giddier than she had ever felt for the Tsar.

"Oh, my dearest Persephone, the words I utter are no lines," he said with all the drama of an actor on a stage, "they come from the deepest corners of my heart!"

"Deep corners?" She laughed, resting a hand on the table to steady herself as her shoe caught on the skirt of her dress.

"Why, yes," he grinned. "I am an artist, Persephone. Don't mock the poetry of my mind."

"You're strange."

"You're honest."

"And pretty, so I'm told." Her blue eyes sparkled as she looked up at him, attractive even through the mask. Persephone smiled flirtatiously. She felt herself wanting him, wanting him not for security or status, or even good looks, but for the raw energy he exuded, the life force, the substance, the charm-that-ran-deeper-than-charm.

"Most of your face is hidden," he said, "but you have pretty hair, and a pretty smile. A smile is the greatest indicator of a person's beauty." He nodded philosophically.

"Are you a professional charmer?" Persephone asked, unused to so many compliments in such a short space of time. Phoenix threw them around as liberally as she did insults, and even Sol found time for kind comments about Persephone. But in her mind, she was still a child in the vineyard, a constant annoyance to the staff, who criticised her for her curiosity, her daydreaming, and used the word 'pretty' like a curse.

"No," Andrei said, "I am merely the Tsesarevna's brother." His voice rumbled with laughter at his own words. Persephone sensed an irony in his comment, a bitter joke that she could neither locate nor understand.

"Is that even a thing?" It certainly didn't sound like one.

"Yes, it is indeed a thing."

"Is it a royal thing?"

"It could be a royal thing."

"Sorry," Persephone said, "I'm Greek, or American-Greek, or something. I don't know much about Russian titles."

"Settlement?" he asked in English. "Me too. High five!" He held his hand up for Persephone to hit. She slapped it hard. "Ow!" Andrei exclaimed. "I'm from an Eastern Russian Settlement. The best one, in fact. They haven't hacked up any kids there recently."

"Is that what happens in the Settlements?" Persephone asked, horrified. Phoenix's desire to burn her home to the ground made more sense.

"Ignore me," Andrei said. "I haven't been in polite society for a while, I forgot which topics are taboo."

Persephone nodded.

"I'm sorry if I upset you," he continued. "It's a rumour that goes around from time to time. There's never been any evidence."

"The more I learn about Western Russia, the less I like it here." She spoke more to herself than to Andrei.

"I agree."

"Does it get easier?" she asked. "Being part of this society?"

Andrei didn't have time to answer.

"Persephone." She spun around at the voice of the Tsar.

"Hi," she managed to squeak. He loomed over her. The features she had, at times, found enticing had lost all appeal since their last meeting. His face was hardened, his jaw tight, his eyes brittle and icy.

"Will you dance with me?" Haden asked. It wasn't a question, but an order. Persephone nodded, and let him lead her out to the dance floor. His mask was black, embroidered with red silk, and encrusted with rubies. She couldn't help noticing how well their attires matched.

"You don't care much for etiquette, do you?" He took her hand in his, and placed his other on her hip. They danced in synchronicity, like robots programmed to move in unison: timed to perfection, unnatural.

"I grew up on a vineyard, remember?" Persephone said. "I was hardly taught to bow and curtsey." He made her skin crawl now.

The feel of his body so close to hers, and the twirling motion of the dance, made her want to vomit. Sweat trickled down her back like an icy ghost.

"Yet you dance so beautifully." the Tsar said. There was no kindness in his polite tone. Tonight he seemed to be a machine, rather than a man.

"They taught us," Persephone said, "I don't know why." The dance lessons had been pleasant. They were one of the rare times she had been allowed to socialise with the other girls. She remembered the feel of their hands on her shoulders as they twirled around the room. The memory was imprinted on her mind; she had been so starved for touch back then.

"One of the rules of the Vineyard Scheme is that they teach an accomplishment," the Tsar explained. Their eyes met for a brief moment. He was the first to turn away.

"What's the point of it all?" Persephone asked. Her face grew red from anger and over-heating, and she stepped out of time with Haden, causing him to trip on her foot. The room spun before her, and she closed her eyes for a moment to ground herself. Persephone's mind drifted back to the turbulence in Red Square, the day she and Phoenix set the Settlements alight. "What's the point of the Settlements, and the Vineyard Scheme? Why didn't they just let the refugees mix with everyone else? Was it purely xenophobia, or they had nowhere to put them, or what? It's ridiculous! These people came to Western and Eastern Russia, and Greece, because their own countries were about to be destroyed, don't you think they deserved better than this?"

"As admirable as I find your conscience to be, Persephone," the Tsar said, "I don't think such a discussion is appropriate at a dance. If you wish to discuss history and politics with me on some other occasion, I would be happy to oblige."

"Whatever you wish," Persephone said curtly. She wanted to slap him. "Nice ball," she added. With the exception of Andrei, she felt a growing dislike for the people in this room. Without speaking a word to them, she saw their vapidity, the triviality of their existence.

"I know," Haden said with a smile that didn't quite seem genuine.

"Wow! Talk about full of yourself!" she burst out before common sense could prevail.

"You have to be, when you're the Tsar."

"Yeah," she said, "about that: why did you take so long to tell me?"

"I thought our little friend might have mentioned it to you."

Persephone didn't reply. She knew now he must have seen her through the window that day, to know of the friendship between her and Phoenix. Another thought occurred to her. The girls' bedrooms were separated only by a corridor and a staircase, surely the Tsar had known their paths would converge. Had he planned for them to meet all along?

Phoenix and Sol's roles as Haden's prisoners seemed nonsensical. Her own could be explained away by his supposed intentions of marriage, but Persephone couldn't imagine what her friends had to offer to the Tsar. A precocious girl and an embittered boy? They were about as much use to a Tsar as democracy.

"Phoenix did," Persephone said.

"Yes," Haden mused, "she doesn't seem able to keep things to herself."

"No." Persephone felt guilty for saying it. There were plenty of occasions when Phoenix had been perfectly capable of keeping secrets, though these were always her own.

"I know you've been out of the palace. Don't do it again," the Tsar ordered. "There have been a number of security threats recently. If my intelligence serves correct, I believe you witnessed the worst one with your own eyes. If I find you've been out again, I will have you moved to the dungeons. Do you understand?" Their eyes met, and Persephone was struck by the power he held over her. She was his now.

"I understand." She understood all too well: one false move, and her life would collapse around her. "Perhaps Phoenix would be less inclined to go walkabout if she was given something to eat other than fruit," Persephone said before she could stop herself. If they weren't allowed to leave, she had to do something to make life easier for her friend. "Phoenix doesn't eat fruit. It makes her ill."

"Interesting," Haden said. "She's not an anomaly after all."

They moved in silence for the rest of the dance. When the music finally came to a stop, the Tsar gave Persephone a slight bow, and left her to her own devices.

"Are you okay?" asked Andrei. She hadn't noticed he was there.

"I'm fine," Persephone said. She thought of the conversation she had overheard in the library. Haden's father had implied he was dangerous. It had hardly registered at the time, when her mind was consumed with shock at the bloodshed in Red Square, and Phoenix setting the Settlements alight. Now, with a clear head, Persephone found herself scared.

"You're shaking," Andrei said. "Did he upset you?"

"He threatened to lock me in the dungeons, but other than that, I'm wonderful." Persephone glowered. She wanted to knock the tables upside down, smash the wine bottles against the varnished floorboards until the glass shattered into razor-sharp crystals. Her blood boiled. Her body burned with the need for annihilation; she ached for war.

"He did? Why?" He seemed unfazed by her terrible mood.

"Does it matter?"

"Yes, but if you don't want to talk about it, I won't pressure you. Would you like to dance with me?"

Persephone considered for a moment, still fuming from her encounter with Haden. She looked Andrei over, from top to bottom, and decided to accept his offer. Perhaps it would help distract her.

"I would love to dance with you."


"How did you meet the Tsar?" Andrei asked as they danced.

"It highlights my naïve nature," Persephone told him. "Do you mind if I don't say?"

"Yes, I mind terribly, but it's not up to me." He added in a low whisper "In my opinion, that man is a creep. You'd do well to stay away from him – and his dungeons. Whereas me, I'm everything that meets the eye. Charming, honest, single..."

Persephone laughed. She found Andrei endearing, despite him making his interest in her so obvious. It took a rare breed of man to pull off his lines with success. If the same words came from anyone else's mouth, they would have made her deeply uncomfortable.

Persephone realised, as Andrei spun her around the floor, that the reason his flirting stayed firmly on the right side of harmless, was because he didn't ask for anything from her, didn't expect validation and false smiles. He met her as an equal.

They found themselves together for dance after dance, comrades against the superficiality of their fellows. The conversation that bubbled initially—sweet and silly, of great comfort and little substance—soon fizzled into an easy silence. Persephone had no desire for their interaction to mean anything; it was fun, and that was all she wanted.

"The night's nearly over," Andrei said. His face was close to hers, his arms circled loosely around her back. There was no formality to their dancing now: they rocked, and swayed, and laughed more than necessary. "All good fairytales end at midnight."

"Are we a fairytale?" she asked. He took her hand and twirled her around.

"Why, of course we're a fairytale!"

Persephone slid her hands up to Andrei's shoulders. The slits of his mask were too narrow for her to see his eyes.

"If this was a fairytale," Persephone told him, "I'd be dancing with the Tsar. Those damsels in distress like to marry their way to the top, remember?"

Before Andrei could respond, Persephone felt the vice-like grip of a hand resting possessively on her arm. Her captor dragged her through a concealed door, into a dark room.

"What the hell?" demanded a furious Persephone, as the heavy door slammed shut behind her. The walls and door were so thick she knew no one would hear her scream. A match struck, and a stout, red candle flared into flame. By the dim light it exuded, she identified the person who had dragged her here: the Tsar.

"We need to talk," he said.

"Here I was thinking you pulled me into a dark room just to scare me." The space seemed drained of oxygen. Persephone forced herself to breathe deeply, yet each gasp for air felt too weak to suffice. The Tsar loomed over her. The candle cast red shadows across his icy eyes. Persephone shuddered as she tried to see through the gloom. Surely there must be an escape route! The light from the candle barely reached beyond the pair of them, but Persephone deduced that the darkness beyond only extended a couple of metres. This must be some kind of closet.

"I want you to be my wife," he said. To Persephone, the words sounded rehearsed. She knew it wasn't a question.

"Why?" she asked immediately. If she were to entertain such a ridiculous proposition for even a moment, she must find out his reason.

"I need to marry. I need to marry you." His voice was emotionless, cold as the shivers that ran down her spine.

She sighed at the absurdity of the situation. Persephone wondered what her own part was in this. She rested her hands on her hips, and stared him straight in the icy eyes, through the windows of his black mask. "I don't plan on marriage in the immediate future. I'm not even nineteen years old."

"You have to marry me!" Haden burst out, in an uncharacteristic display of emotion. Persephone was unused to his passion, she had only heard it that day in the library. "My future depends on it!" He gripped her shoulders forcefully; his fingers burned into her skin. She was sure they would leave bruises.

"I don't want to marry you, and I'm not going to!" Persephone shook his hands off her. Her eyes did not leave his the whole time. He angered her; she wanted to slap that condescending expression right off his face. But now was not a time for reckless rage: oh no, now was the time to bargain. She held the power here.

"You don't understand!" He took her wrists now, circling her skin beneath his smooth thumbs. Persephone felt her stomach gurgle. She had been so busy dancing with Andrei that she had forgotten to eat. The fruit she had consumed that afternoon seemed a lifetime ago. She felt weak, and the Tsar's touch made her palms sweat with discomfort. "This country, it's all I have. Everything of my own was stolen from me a long time ago. I lost the life I wanted, I can't lose the life I have earned. If I lose this country…" His voice cracked. Tears glistened in his frozen eyes. "I'll have lost everything. You're the only chance I have!"

She stared up into the glaciers of his eyes, and for the first time saw vulnerability there. Persephone pitied him. But she knew she must draw a line on this pity: he was trapped, and he was scared, but what of those he oppressed? It was one thing to pity Haden the Person, but another to pity Haden the Tsar. He had made choices she could never condone, and she refused to tie herself to him based on one instance of vulnerability.

"Persephone," the Tsar pleaded. "I will be good to you. I've looked after you, haven't I? I will try to be a good man, a good husband."

"It's not about me," she said. "It's not about how you treat one woman, it's about how you treat every woman, and every man, and every person. You don't gain humanity by picking favourites. I can't be your wife unless I know you'll better yourself for the world, not just for me."

"You are a very demanding lady," the Tsar said. He was relieved. He had misread her protestations. He thought she was his. Persephone knew better.

"I'm a woman who knows what she wants," she said. "Never forget that, Haden." She paused, ready to strike a bargain with this man who scared and disgusted her. "If I agree to marry you, it will be on one condition."

"What condition?"

"I get a say in what happens in this country." Persephone eyed him confidently. She had seen him at his weakest, seen the lengths that weakness had driven him to. Ambition got the better of her. Marriage seemed a small price to pay for power.

"There is no way in hell I would agree to that!" His voice ripped through her, tearing the silk of her skin, shattering the china doll before him. The Tsar looked upon a little girl and expected her to crumble. But Persephone was a woman, this man couldn't break her.

"I saw those riots," she said. 'I went through them. I saw how much your people hate you." She thought of Phoenix as she spoke, imagined her friend standing beside her, cheering her on. "I saw the Royal Guard shooting innocent people. You are despised, Haden. You need me. If things don't change soon, you won't have a country to lose!"

"What would you change?" the Tsar asked.

89

"I'd give more power to the people," Persephone said. "You're meant to be a Tsar, not a dictator."

"Please don't tell me I proposed to a Communist!" Haden laughed. He wasn't taking her at all seriously.

Persephone didn't know what the word 'Communist' meant, but she could gather enough of its meaning from the way he mocked her. "There shouldn't be such disparity between the poor and the elite," she said finally. "That is why your country is eating itself alive and your reign is a disaster." Persephone's body was on fire. She craved this discussion, craved the opportunities it could bring. She wanted to climb to the top of the ladder, and she wanted to change the world. How wonderful to combine those two ambitions! All the irony of her own thoughts was lost on her.

The Tsar considered for a few moments. He looked Persephone up and down, weighed up the passion of her ideals versus her lack of real power. A slow smile spread across his face: this girl was no threat. Oh no, she was the answer to his prayers.

"I think, Persephone," Haden said, his smile broadening into a wide grin, "we have a deal." He kissed her cheek, just below her mask. She forced herself not to cringe away from him. "Now, we must announce our engagement."

The masks still covered their faces as the Tsar took Persephone's hand in his, and led her through the ballroom to a raised platform. Her heart pounded with panic. The room spun before her, and vomit rose in her throat. Breaths squeezed through her constricted lungs, and tears burned behind her eyes. He had tricked her, surely! This couldn't be happening, this couldn't be real.

*No,* she thought. *I tricked myself.*

They stood in silence for a moment, before Haden announced through a microphone: "Ladies and gentlemen, let me present to you the future Tsarina, my fiancée: Persephone."

Haden nodded towards her mask. She fumbled with the knotted ribbon, her numb fingers forcing it to unravel. The Tsar proceeded to remove his own mask. When the black and gold were gone, and pale skin and blond eyebrows were restored to view, Persephone saw this was not the only mask he had cast aside. She saw him now: saw the smug stretch of his pink lips, pulled taut to reveal straight, smiling teeth. She saw the arrogance in his high cheekbones, and the gloating glint in his icy eyes. Persephone knew with dreadful certainty that Haden's previous vulnerability had been nothing more than a cruel, manipulative act. He had fooled her.

The sound of applause was deafening in Persephone's ears as reality set in. She would be the Tsarina. From this moment on, she would never make a decision for herself. She would be unable to utter a single word without being the subject of gossip. Persephone clasped her hands in front of her, and stared out into the crowd. She watched as Andrei wiped a pretend tear from his eye. Persephone recoiled in horror when she realised only one man would touch her for the rest of her life. She stepped sideways, attempting to further the distance between herself and the Tsar.

The rest of the night passed by in a blur, her head spinning like a tornado. The Tsar was determined to introduce his new fiancée to what seemed like an infinite succession of 'dearest friends'. After an hour of small talk and queasiness, Persephone finally whispered to him "Please let me go now. I need to sleep. I can barely stand up."

The Tsar raised an eyebrow. He didn't believe her.

"I think I'm going to vomit," she said. "I think I'm going to vomit all over the next person you introduce me to. If you don't let me go, I'll make that a promise."

"I will escort you back to your room," he decided. "Just give me five minutes."

"No," Persephone said firmly. "Let me go alone. Give me that freedom."

"Fine," the Tsar dismissed her.

Persephone stalked back to her bedroom, fuming. She didn't know who she hated more: the Tsar, or herself. The journey seemed endless, wobbling in her high-heeled shoes. She wanted to crawl into bed and cry.

Phoenix and Sol sat in wait. She heard them talking when she reached her corridor. Although she couldn't make out the words, she knew they were discussing her and the Tsar.

"So?" Phoenix demanded, at the creak of the door. She and Sol sat crossed-legged on Persephone's bed, leaning against the headboard. They looked tired – more than tired, she realised, upon seeing a half-full bottle of red wine resting on her bedside table. She made a beeline for it, and took a long swig, straight from the bottle.

Phoenix snorted, raising her dark eyebrows with judgemental flair. "Was it that bad?" she asked.

"I'm his fiancée," Persephone said, after another gulp of wine. "He knows about us leaving the palace, and threatened to put us in the dungeons if we do so again. Is that all you want to know?" She flopped down, face first, onto the bed. Phoenix's toe prodded her sympathetically. "Can you leave me alone now? I'm tired." Persephone buried her face into the duvet, and scrunched the fabric between her fists.

Phoenix was about to protest at this dismissal, but Sol gave her a stern look. They left without a word.

Persephone stripped off her ball gown, and dumped it on the floor without a second glance. She would be glad if she never laid eyes on that dress again. She pulled a nightgown over her head before crawling under the covers of her bed and bursting into tears. Persephone sobbed into her pillow. She had given away her future, and there was nothing she could do to get it back.


Phoenix crept back later in the night, a small figure in her lilac nightgown, arms wrapped around a wicker basket. She sat down gently on the side of Persephone's bed, and flicked on the lamp switch.

"Wakey wakey," she said.

"Wakey wakey, big mistakey," came the morose response. "Let me sleep. I want to die."

"I come bearing chocolate," Phoenix announced, wriggling under the covers. "I know food can't solve your problems, but chocolate triggers lots of happy hormones. I figured it might cheer you up."

Persephone wrapped her arms around her friend, burying her

face in Phoenix's abdomen.

"So where's this chocolate?" she asked.

Phoenix hoisted the basket up onto the bed. "There weren't any shops open this late," she said, "so I had to go on an expedition to the kitchens, and they only had posh chocolate. There's white chocolate with lavender, dark chocolate with almonds, and an overly fancy one filled with some kind of alcoholic goo."

"Why can't I just marry you?" Persephone asked. "At least you know how to look after me!"

"Two reasons," Phoenix said. "One: I'm not into girls, so I doubt our marriage would be fulfilling. Two: same-sex marriage is illegal in Western Russia."

"There should be friend marriages," Persephone said. "We could swear off relationships forever, and live happily ever after together, with chocolate and cats and wine."

"If only." Phoenix stroked Persephone's hair, her fingers running nimbly across the ginger waves. "Are you scared?" she asked. "Of marrying him?"

"I'm terrified," Persephone said. She stretched out her legs, and snuggled her head into the soft pillow of Phoenix's thigh. "I have to marry him, and I didn't think about what marriage actually meant. Oh my god, I have to have sex with him! I don't want to do that. He's ten years older than me. He's ancient!" Persephone sobbed into Phoenix's leg, soaking the fabric of her nightgown with salty tears.

"I wish I could say he can't make you." She squeezed Persephone's hand. "But he will. There are no laws to protect you. He is the only law."

"I'm so stupid," Persephone said. "I've always been stupid, but now I'm doubly stupid!" Her face crumpled once again, and a fresh bout of tears escaped her.

"Maybe this engagement isn't as scary as you think it is," Phoenix reasoned. "It's not what you bargained for, and you're tired and overwhelmed. Perhaps you'll feel better in the morning."

Persephone sat up, her face streaked with mascara, and tore into the packaging of the lavender chocolate. It melted luxuriantly on her tongue, but her mouth felt heavy and awkward from crying, and even chocolate became unpleasant.

"What would you have done?" she asked. "You wouldn't have agreed to marry him would you? You'd have kicked him in the crotch, and jumped out the nearest window."

"Fantasy Phoenix might have," she agreed, brushing her dark hair back with her fingers and tying it into a half-ponytail. "But Real Phoenix, the oh-so-wonderful person sitting beside you... She has no idea what she would've done. Free choice is an illusion. He only let you think you had a choice so you can blame yourself for the rest of your life. He has you trapped. For all we know, if I was in your position, I'd have agreed to marry him too. That's the only option he'd allow."

"I can't imagine you married to the Tsar," Persephone said.

"I don't want to imagine it. Ugh! I think *I'm* going to cry now!"

"Did I bring this on myself?" Persephone asked. "Did I create this? I said all that stupid crap about wanting to throw him up against a wall and have my wicked way with him."

"If everyone who fancied the Tsar ended up with him, he'd have screwed Sol a hundred times by now," Phoenix pointed out. "And we all know that's never going to happen. Stop trying to claim responsibility, Sphenn. This isn't your fault. The Tsar's playing mind games with you. He's a prick, and we hate him – don't we, Sphenn? But we won't give in to his crap. I refuse to let you blame yourself for this. You can blame him, and you can blame the patriarchy, but I won't let you blame yourself."

"But I said yes. I agreed to marry him. I'm at fault!"

"It was hardly an isolated incident," Phoenix said. "He must have had this planned from the moment he brought you here, perhaps even from when he chose to visit Greece. You're not free, you are his pawn. It's that simple."

Persephone broke off another chunk of chocolate. She stared at it mournfully before placing it in her mouth.

"What do I live for now?" she asked, her mouth clogged with the paste of chewed chocolate.

"You live for life," Phoenix said. She sat up straighter, cleared her throat, and put on her best Motivational Speech voice. "You live because you are an amazing woman who is going to conquer this world, and will not be subdued by that ice-cold creep. You are brave, and you are brilliant, and you will make the best of your situation. You can't get around the fact you're marrying that bastard, but you can use it. You are going to have access to things that—"

"We both know he won't give me access to anything."

"You'll have access to your children," Phoenix said. "You'll raise them. You'll give birth to the future Tsar or Tsarina of this country, and you will mold them into the shape you see fit. Raise a feminist revolutionary, and watch the Tsar's world come crashing down around him. It's a long game, sure, but it's the only one you can afford to play."

# Chapter Eight

Persephone's wedding date to the Tsar of Western Russia was set: May 3rd. Each mention of the occasion triggered chronic nausea. She soon found herself on the verge of panic attacks.

Persephone was woken early the morning after the ball, by a young, blonde woman named Tatiana, whose oval face was marred by a subtle sourness, well-hidden behind a façade of friendliness and efficiency. Five hours had passed since Tatiana's arrival, and it was now midday. Persephone had passed the time by devouring plate after plate of fruit.

"You still haven't explained why Haden wants you to chaperone me," she complained through a mouthful of pomegranate seeds. She wore a pair of scruffy denim dungarees over a white t-shirt. Her orange hair was tied above her head in a messy topknot, and an adolescent pout was planted firmly on her face. She spat the pomegranate seeds back into her bowl.

"Come on," Tatiana said. "I'm bored."

"Haden told me I can't leave the palace," Persephone said.

"He doesn't want you going out unsupervised. You're safe with me." Tatiana winked, and pulled Persephone up from the bed by her hand. Tatiana's wrists were laden with silver bracelets, and her nails were painted pistachio green.

"Where are we going?"

"Somewhere I can teach you how to be a Tsarina."

Persephone's face loomed larger than life, broadcast on the screens in Red Square. The news headlines declared that the Tsar was engaged to be married to a Greek girl from Olympus Vineyard. The footage showed Haden announcing their engagement at the ball the previous night. The scene changed, and Persephone saw herself, painting wine labels in Greece, talking to her supervisors, running across the vineyard on the day she met Haden. She had never seen the cameras.

"First on the agenda," Tatiana said, "is to teach you to dress right. You look like a child in that outfit; no one's going to take you seriously." She didn't pay much attention to the screens, this was normal to her.

"I look like a child because I am one," Persephone said. "I'm not even nineteen and I'm expected to marry a man who's a decade older than me." She shuddered at the images on the screens. Her life was broadcast in videos she had never seen being filmed, and Persephone couldn't help wonder how long Haden had been planning this marriage for.

"I was married at fifteen. Do you see me complaining?" Tatiana shrugged her shoulders and continued at a fast pace across the square.

"That's child abuse."

"We don't have child abuse in the Russian countries."

"Only in the Settlements?" Persephone couldn't help herself.

"The Settlements treat their children with an impeccable standard of care. My father was the president of Eastern Russia's largest Settlement, and I know first-hand that its citizens were well looked after." The wind blew through Tatiana's hair, causing it to billow around her shoulders and fly across her face. Whilst her speech stayed composed, her hair and dress rebelled against her, shattering the illusion.

"I heard people chop up children in the Settlements." Persephone wanted to provoke her. But more than that, she craved answers about this world she had entered into. The façade had begun to crumble since the riots in Red Square, and where there had once been excitement, she now felt a growing sense of dread.

"I'm going to kill Andrei!" Tatiana burst out. "I heard you two talking last night, but I didn't think you were naive enough to take him seriously."

Persephone looked at Tatiana, sizing her up. "Wait, you're Andrei's sister?" Her hair was lighter than her brother's, but she was tall like him, and had the same mouth, although her full lips tended to frown whereas her brother's were forever smiling, in Persephone's memory.

"Unfortunately."

"What did he mean by it? About the children in the Settlements?" She couldn't let it go.

97

"Andrei has a fanciful imagination," Tatiana said. "He's travelled enough to think he understands the world, and he takes rumours a little too seriously."

"How do you know the rumours aren't based on fact?"

"A couple of years ago, there was major flooding around Tartarus Settlement. Some dismembered child's bones washed up just outside the property lines, and they were found by a farmer. It was thoroughly investigated, and no evidence was found."

"I've heard Tartarus is an awful place."

"I've never been there," Tatiana said. "But I've met Jakob, and as Settlement presidents go, he's the better sort. He's a little too intellectual, and impossible to hold a decent conversation with. But he's never made a pass at me, so he's not half as creepy as the rest of them."

"Whatever you say." They walked in silence for a little while, before Persephone couldn't resist asking "What about the Tsar? Has he ever hit on you?"

"Haden's never been one for the ladies. Good luck there." She laughed. "I'm not one to gossip, but I've been part of this family for a decade, and I've never seen him with a woman. He's either a mad celibate genius, too devoted to his science to care about sex, or he has a taste for the boys. The jury's still out on which. All I'm saying is: his father thinks it's the latter, and that's where you come in."

"Why me?" Persephone asked. "Why go all the way to Greece, pick some random girl from a vineyard, and drag her back to Moscow? Why couldn't he marry someone Russian?"

"I don't know why he went to Greece, but I can see why he picked you."

"What do you mean?"

"Have you ever looked in a mirror?"

"Several times a day, for 18 years."

"You don't quite look human. Your hair and eyes are too bright, your skin too pale and smooth. You're not of this world. You match his aesthetic. That whole family looks a little odd. With Haden it's the eyes, with the others it's just their unnatural perfection of features. They don't like to marry ordinary. I only ended up amongst their numbers because Poseidon's intended bride died.

It's even creepier if you go back a generation. Both Tsar Kronus's brides were called Rhea. Both are dead. I'm surprised he hasn't found a third one."

"Is this normal for royalty?" Persephone asked. "Because it all sounds weird to me."

"They're a special breed," Tatiana said. "You'll get used to it eventually. Don't expect normal from that family, they're all insane."

✝

When Persephone returned to the palace, she found Phoenix lurking in the corridor outside her bedroom. Her eyebrows were scrunched together and her lips were plumped out in a pout.

She didn't make an attempt at conversation, but followed Persephone silently into the bedroom.

"How was it with Icy Boy's sister-in-law?" she asked finally, flopping down onto the bed.

"It was nice. She took me shopping, and then we went to this fancy restaurant. It was unlike anything I've ever experienced!"

"Sounds fun."

"We're going out again this evening. She's taking me to a cocktail bar."

"It must be nice to leave the palace." Phoenix's voice was bitter. She stared out the window as she spoke. "I hate being cooped up in here. It can't've taken a year for him to figure out we leave. He's only bothered about it now you're here. And now you get to swan around the city with your sparkly new chaperone, whilst I'm locked up in this prison!"

"Wait," Persephone asked, "are you jealous of Tatiana?"

"Me? Jealous?" Phoenix laughed. "Oh please!"

"You are!" Persephone sat down on the bed and took Phoenix's hand. "You have nothing to worry about. Yes, I'm enjoying the Tatiana experience, but that doesn't mean I view her as a friend. She's this shiny thing to play with, that's all. She spends money on me and she's nice to look at, but it doesn't mean I like her as a person."

99

Phoenix burst out laughing. "Are you saying Tatiana's your sugar mummy?"

"I'm saying she's not a threat to you."

✝

The cocktail bar was not what Persephone had expected. Unlike their escapades earlier in the day, this place was not glamorous. Tatiana led her down an alleyway in a far corner of Moscow.

"You've changed your style," Persephone said as they entered the bar. The room was dimly lit. Yellow candles hung in jars on the midnight-blue walls. Greasy-haired old men slumped on benches, with bedraggled dogs lounging against their legs.

"I want to get drunk," Tatiana said, "and no sensible woman gets drunk where the cameras can see her. We don't want our night to be broadcast all over the country, so here we are."

"You make a fair point."

"Bartender!" Tatiana called, as she sashayed over to the bar. "Hit me up with two of your finest green-apple Martinis." She hopped onto a barstool, and beckoned for Persephone to join her. "This place may look like a dump," she said, "but they make damn good drinks. It's a hidden gem."

"Well, well, well, look who it is," said a second bartender, sidling out of the back room. He was a tall man, with dark hair and tanned skin. His grey eyes didn't leave the figure of Tatiana.

"Delinov," she said, "fancy seeing you here."

The first bartender passed them their drinks. Persephone gulped down her Martini and observed Tatiana and Delinov. There was no mistaking the flirtation between them.

"How's Blayk?" Tatiana asked. The tone of her voice changed; it became more tender. She glanced quickly at Persephone, and mouthed something to Delinov.

"He's doing well," he said. "Do you plan to visit while you're in Moscow?"

Tatiana shook her head slightly. "No. I'm busy looking after this one." She nodded in the direction of Persephone. "I can't get away long enough. It's for the best, I'll just confuse him."

100

"He misses you."

"He barely knows me."

"He knows you in his heart."

"Sentimentality doesn't work on me Delinov. It's been five years, you should know that by now."

"If you insist." He left Tatiana and walked to the other end of the bar.

"What was that about?" Persephone asked.

"Nothing," Tatiana assured her. "Don't mention it to Haden." She took a sip of her drink. "Damn these are good."

"They are indeed," Persephone said, placing her empty glass back down on the bar. "It tastes like juice!"

"You've finished that already?" Tatiana asked. "Slow down. I don't want you getting drunk while I'm still sober." She watched Delinov from across the room. He stole glances at her as soon as she looked away. She downed her drink, and held up two fingers to the bartender. He proceeded to make two more cocktails.


"My husband doesn't want me," Tatiana said after her fourth Martini. Her face was flushed with drunkenness, and her long, pale legs gleamed in the light from the candles. She looked younger now. Her skin was soft and her lipstick had worn off from touching so many glasses. Persephone watched her sadly. She wanted to comfort her, to reach out and touch her, show her that she was wanted. "We've been married a decade," Tatiana continued. "Ten whole years – hasn't touched me once." She shook her head from side to side, and blinked her eyes in confusion. "I swear to God, that family... Those brothers... Good luck to anyone who marries them! One is most likely gay, my one's celibate, and the other is fucking his sister. I guarantee you this is the last of the Olympovski line." She cackled to herself. "Good riddance! That family is a plague on this country."

Persephone didn't know what to make of that comment. Her mind was clouded with alcohol. Her thoughts were unclear and her instincts were taking control. Her eyes skimmed over Tatiana's body, over the silky legs, the breasts pushed up by the black lace bra that peeked out from under her silver dress. She forced herself to think.

"It's not a reflection on you," she said finally. The words were slow to leave her mouth. "People can't control whether or not they feel attraction. There's nothing wrong with him, and there's also nothing wrong with you."

"Other men want me," Tatiana said. "Delinov wanted me. But my own husband? No. I'm shackled to a man who won't meet my needs. It's such a waste. Look at me!" There were tears in her eyes now. "These are supposed to be the best years of my life. I'll never be this beautiful again, and it's all going to waste."

"You are not a waste," Persephone said. Before she knew what she was doing, she reached out and stroked Tatiana's cheek. The skin was softer than she expected. Her fingers danced across the smooth surface. Persephone cupped Tatiana's face in her hands, and leaned in towards her. She felt the electric pull of tension between them. She could barely breathe. Tatiana's lips called to her like a siren's song and she knew she would not be complete until their mouths became one. Persephone didn't know what to do. She had never been kissed before, and there was no instruction manual on how to do it right, but she was too drunk to care, and she followed the calls of her body. Tatiana's lips were soft and plump, and her mouth tasted like green apples and gin. Persephone's hands skimmed over Tatiana's shoulders, lingered on the bare skin just above her breasts. The kiss lasted a few seconds but it felt like an eternity. The sharp sting of a slap across her face broke the illusion and eternity was shattered.

"You fucking idiot!" Tatiana said in a low voice. She spoke in slow English, like the language was almost lost to her. "What were you thinking?"

"I'm sorry," Persephone said, embarrassed. "You were sad, and I— I wanted to show you how beautiful you are."

"Haden found himself the perfect bride," Tatiana said with a harsh laugh. "What you do behind closed doors is your own business. I'm not going to judge, but let's make two things clear. One: you will never kiss me again. I want no part of this. And two: if you have half a brain, keep this private. This is Western Russia, Persephone. If you want to survive here, you can't go around kissing girls in public. Do you understand?"

Persephone nodded ashamedly. "I'm sorry," she said. There were tears in her eyes.

"It's a good thing there are no cameras here." Tatiana glanced around in spite of herself, paranoid. "If you're going to make it as a Tsarina, you must kill your impulsive side. You're going to put yourself in danger if you don't watch out." She seemed considerably more sober now.

"I'm sorry," Persephone said again. She wanted to sink beneath the floorboards and hide.

"Shut up. Come on, let's get you home. We'll speak no more of this. Don't do it again, don't tell anyone, and don't let your guard down so quickly. You're an idiot, girl. You won't last five minutes in that marriage, I can assure you."

Persephone was not the only one returning home at that hour. She heard the patter of footsteps on the stairs below, and looked down just in time to see a hooded figure ducking out of sight.

"Phoenix!" she called. Silence. "Phoenix, I know it's you." She descended the stairs, and knocked loudly on Phoenix's bedroom door.

"What?" She had changed quickly, and was now dressed cosily in her nightgown. The hooded coat stuck out from under the bed, and her full face of make-up gave her away.

"Where did you go? You know we're not allowed out!"

"I have a job, Persephone," Phoenix said. Her tone was defensive. "I have responsibilities, I can't just up and disappear the moment it suits me. Not that other people have a problem doing that." It seemed Persephone's presence wasn't the only thing bothering her.

"What happened?"

"Drew quit," she said. "I have 2.5 friends in the world. One of them is marrying the fucking Tsar, and the other has quit his job to go start a commune or some shit."

Persephone slumped against the wall. Her mind was still on Tatiana.

"Wait, are you drunk?" Phoenix asked.

103

"Something like that."

"I envy you."

"I need to go out," Persephone said.

"Where?"

"I don't know. The river, maybe. Or even your bookstore, if it's still open."

"They have an event tonight," Phoenix said. "They'll be open till all the drunk poets muster up the life force to fall down the stairs."

"Let's go."

"Wait." Phoenix went to her wardrobe, and pulled out another black hooded jacket. "Your face is everywhere. If you leave the palace, you need to be inconspicuous."

"How many of those things do you own?" Persephone asked.

"A few. Drew would say it's because I have a Scorpio ascendant and want everyone to think I'm mysterious. Never tell him your time of birth, he'll read you like a book."

"I don't know my time of birth," Persephone said. "Stolen from my family, remember?"

Phoenix didn't respond. She changed out of her nightgown and into day clothes, and slipped into her coat. She switched off the light behind them, and the girls carefully made their way out of the palace.


They entered the bookstore through the customer entrance. This staircase was wide and welcoming, not steep like the staff stairway. Persephone struggled to walk properly, the cold night air had tired her out, and the gin that churned in her stomach made her sleepy and wobbly on her feet.

"Phoenix, why are you back here?" Elizaveta greeted her. "Hello again – Sphenya?"

"She's here with me," Persephone said. "I'm looking for a book."

"That's news to me," Phoenix said.

"Any book in particular?" Elizaveta asked. "I'm sure Phoenix can help you find it, I swear she knows her way around these shelves better than I do!" The shallow lines around her green eyes crinkled a little, the closest she came to a smile.

"I'll know it when I see it," Persephone said.

"Sphenya." Elizaveta watched her closely, with a look of compassion. "There are no books on how to survive loveless marriages. My advice is to read about feminism, feminist theory, that is. I've often found comfort in the voices of women who came before me, it helped to know I didn't suffer alone. Build yourself a support network of women you can rely on. You don't have to fight alone."

"Thank you," Persephone said. She felt the gin wreaking havoc in her bloodstream. It was an effort to stand up, let alone hold a conversation.

After Elizaveta walked away, Persephone asked "Did you tell her my real name?"

"Nope." Phoenix plonked herself down on the windowsill. "I told you, people will recognise you now."

"How did she know I don't love him?"

"Because you look petrified in those videos. It doesn't take a genius to see you're repulsed by him."

Persephone headed towards the Feminism section.

"Honestly," Phoenix said, "I love Elizaveta, I kind of wish she was my mum, but feminist support networks aren't going to mean shit when Icy Boy's locked you away in his ivory tower. You'd do better to read a history book or ten – at least that will give you an idea of how to destroy him."

Tatiana faded in and out of Persephone's life over the next few months. The threat of her presence was like a bitter chill in the air, enough to set Persephone on edge, rattle her teeth and paralyse her bones, but not enough to freeze her completely. In Tatiana's presence, Persephone stayed quiet and reserved, a placid rag-doll that played every role asked of her, but could never retain animation without the hands of her puppeteer. When she left, Persephone could breathe again. She was reluctant to leave the palace, after Haden's warning, but she sneaked out at night, wrapped herself in one of Phoenix's jackets, and squished herself into the crowded metro trains. She darted through darkened streets, and finally came to the refuge of the bookshop, where soft yellow light glowed from electric lamps, and the bookshelves stood sturdy around her. On nights when the shop was closed, she and Phoenix would sit together and read by the fireplace, using their coats as blankets. Persephone worked her way through vast volumes that recounted the Russian countries' history. Phoenix read books Persephone couldn't understand, and muttered to herself in a strange, melodic language that sounded like it was spoken by elves.

"Sphenya?" Phoenix asked one night in February. It was almost 3am. The fire was down to its last embers, and Persephone had almost fallen asleep where she sat.

"What?" she asked groggily.

"It's never occurred to me before, but can you understand me?"

"When you're whispering in gobbledegook, or in general?"

"I'll take that as a no." Phoenix closed the book, and turned to face Persephone. "I wondered if maybe you could understand every language the way you can understand Russian. Somehow it's stranger that it's only happened with one language."

"Why are you learning it?" Persephone asked. She pulled her coat around her shoulders, and shivered. "What's the point of learning another language, unless you're planning to leave Western Russia?"

Phoenix didn't meet her gaze. "Never you worry about that," she said. "As long as you're here, I'm not going anywhere. Come on," she stood up, "we should get home."

"We could just run away," Persephone said. "We could leave in the dead of night, he wouldn't know until it's too late."

"The Tsar has cameras everywhere, Sphenn, you know that."

"Only in Western Russia. Even I know there's more to the world than this."

Phoenix slotted her language book back into the shelf. The section was titled 'Estonia.' Persephone didn't know what the word meant.

"Persephone." Phoenix reached out a hand, and helped her up from the floor. "You can't go to war without a battle plan. Running away might seem like the most appealing option right now, but there's stuff going on that you and I don't fully grasp. If we try to cut our ties now, I fear they'll only strangle us."

"That's easy for you to say, you're not engaged to him."

"I lived my first sixteen years in the Settlements, I understand more than anyone what it's like to be trapped. Please trust me, Sphenn. We need more information before you go and do something drastic."

✞

In the days leading up to her wedding, Persephone was overcome with nausea. The only food she could stomach was fruit. The more she ate, the worse she felt, but by this point, eating was a compulsion. She lay in bed as hot sweats tore through her body, stripping her of her strength.

Phoenix sat in the chair in the far corner of the room, watching with apprehension as Persephone stuffed her mouth with blackberries. It was May 2nd, Persephone's 19th birthday, and the day before her wedding.

"I should have helped you escape," Phoenix said finally. She chewed on a lock of hair, and stared morosely at a point on the wall above Persephone's head. "I thought I had an answer, but I couldn't find it in time – it's still out of reach. I feel like I've failed you."

"I want to marry him," Persephone said. "This is what I want, this is what I have always wanted." It was the first full sentence she had spoken in days. Her eyes were clouded with sickness, and it was an effort to force the words out of her mouth.

Phoenix stood up, and went to the window. Her mind was buzzing with abstract images that refused to combine into a coherent thought.

"I guess you succumbed to Stockholm Syndrome after all," she said to buy herself time.

"I want to be his bride," Persephone continued. "He can give me everything I ever dreamed of. He's the richest man in this country. He's powerful, he's attractive. He's everything I could hope for in a husband." She crammed more blackberries into her mouth.

"Bullshit," Phoenix said.

Persephone forced a fistful of fruit into her face. "I... deserve...

107

this." She choked on the berries, and vomited all over her bedspread.

Phoenix stared from Persephone, to the fruit in her hand, to the mess of purple vomit, and ran from the room.

*May 3<sup>rd</sup>,*
*2151*

Persephone's hands shook like a rickety cage, constraining her bouquet, as she entered the palace chapel. The vast crowd on either side of the aisle made her wish she could sink into the ground. Being buried alive would be preferable to this. Yet having so many eyes upon her worked as a form of twisted motivation.

*Once I've made it to the altar*, she told herself firmly, *the worst of it will be over. I won't have to look at them; I'll only have to look at Haden. He won't be such a bad husband. He will be good to me.* A smaller, more malignant voice added *because I own him.*

Persephone raised her eyes to the morning light that streamed through the stained-glass windows. The vast expanses of coloured glass portrayed the crucifixion of Christ, barely visible through the thick lace of her veil. She tilted her face further toward the ceiling, and focused on the image of the Virgin Mary, trying to find solace in a religion that was completely foreign to her. She looked up at the bizarre paradigm of the Virgin Mother, and thought further into her near future, past the wedding, and to the wedding night. In spite of an initial rush of embarrassment, Persephone revelled in the idea that, for the first time in her life, she would have someone with whom she could be intimate. Persephone's childhood had been devoid of tenderness and care, she had never felt wanted. In spite of her apprehension, she yearned for her wedding night, and the lifetime that would follow. She would finally have someone to love her, someone whom she, too, could grow to love.

At war with Persephone's vivid fantasy of marital bliss was the hard truth that her union with Haden meant the sacrifice of all her freedoms. The blushing bride transformed into a condemned prisoner mounting the steps to the gallows, and the dream was crushed. Haden, blissfully unaware of Persephone's torment, stood by the altar, dressed from head to toe in a fitted, white suit, that highlighted his lean, muscular shape.

108

In spite of her desperate search for warmth, all Persephone could see in Haden's image was ice: sharp, hard, and cold. It was a contrast to the suppressed fire that haunted her heart. The last embers in the ash-filled wasteland within her chest kindled into brilliant flames as she saw two faces peeking out from behind one of the purple velvet curtains in the far corner of the chapel. Both Phoenix and Sol looked deeply sombre, the inner demons of each playing across their faces. Phoenix gave Persephone a forced smile and a thumbs-up, mouthing the words *"good luck"*; Sol's desolate eyes were fixed solely upon Haden. If Persephone hadn't known the emotion upon his face was love, she would have read it as hatred or disgust.

By the altar stood Haden, and, alongside him, the highest Patriarch of the Orthodox Church: the two heads of Western Russia's most powerful institutions.

The first stage of the ceremony was the Betrothal, where Persephone and Haden were blessed by the Patriarch, and given white candles to hold for the duration of the ceremony. Persephone started to lose focus as the Patriarch began reciting prayers; she hardly noticed as the rings were placed on the third finger of her and Haden's right hands, in the Russian tradition. This act was followed by a second succession of prayers and blessings, leaving Persephone weary by the time the ceremony progressed to its second stage: the Crowning.

The Patriarch guided bride and groom to step onto a small sheet of rose-coloured cloth, symbolising their entry into the Sacred Mystery of Holy Matrimony, and the new life that awaited them. Persephone was shaken out of her daze by the Patriarch's next words.

"Do you, Persephone, willingly testify that you are marrying this man through your choice alone, and that you are not promised to another man?"

Persephone endeavoured to answer, but her mouth had dried up, preventing any vocal response.

"Persephone?" Haden implored in an urgent undertone.

She nodded weakly. "I do."

"Do you, Haden," the Patriarch asked, "willingly testify that you are marrying this woman through your choice alone, and that you are not promised to another woman?"

"I do," Haden said immediately.

A third prayer-filled interlude occurred, giving Persephone time to regain control over herself. The Patriarch then called upon Poseidon, Haden's elder brother, and Tatiana, to place crowns upon the couple's heads. The crowns were woven from myrtle, orange leaves, and branches, and threaded with ribbons of red and gold, to symbolise the royal union of marriage. More prayers followed, before the couple were invited to drink red wine from the Common Cup, after which the Patriarch proceeded to wrap his epitrachelion around Persephone and Haden's linked right hands. This stage of the ceremony culminated in the wedded couple being led thrice around an altar, on which a crucifix and Gospel Book rested, to symbolise the pilgrimage they were to embark on, the journey of life they would share together.

The next phase of the ceremony began with Kronus, Haden's father and the Tsar of Eastern Russia, offering both bride and groom a crystal glass to shatter upon the floor, each ragged shard a symbol of the years they would share together, and the happiness and devotion that should occur between them.

Persephone's hand shook as she dropped her glass, causing it to land on the soft red carpet, rather than the altar at which it had been directed. Her glass remained whole. Haden's, which had reached its intended destination, broke into twenty-one pieces. Persephone heard a snort of laughter from behind Phoenix's curtain. Of course she would be the first person to take pleasure in the flaws of a religious tradition. Phoenix had never been silent in her atheistic views, and Persephone was certain she would have to endure a rant about religion the next time she saw her friend. This direction of thought led Persephone to realise she may never see Phoenix again. The thought of losing her friends hit like a thousand rocks crashing into her chest. She watched the spot where she knew Phoenix and Sol were hiding. She longed to be beside them.

The rest of the wedding day was filled with further traditions and events, leaving Persephone exhausted by its end. She hardly ate all day, unable to face the increased weariness that food would bring to her. As day turned to night, all Persephone could think was *I've made a mistake.*

Once the guests finally deserted the palace's grandest dining hall, Persephone was left alone with her husband for the first time since their wedding ceremony. Haden glanced up at an elegant clock that hung from the wall.

"It's getting late," he said.

"Yeah." Persephone's breath caught in her throat. Nervous energy built up inside her as she thought of the next step in committing herself to Haden.

"Come on." He led her out of the dining hall, up a narrow, carpeted staircase.

"Why are there so many red carpets in this palace?" Persephone asked, breathing heavily from the exertion of climbing the steep stairs. "It feels sinister, like we're treading on soft, fluffy blood."

"Fluffy blood?" Haden raised an eyebrow at her. The corners of his lips twitched in the briefest of smiles. His attention soon drifted from her again, his eyes flickering away from her anxious face.

"I don't particularly have a way with words," Persephone said.

"On the contrary, I think you do." He allowed himself to resume eye contact. "Fluffy blood, it's an interesting concept." His eyes were impassive, as always. Persephone found her gaze drifting to his body for cues. The Tsar held an erect posture, with proud shoulders and a puffed out chest. His hands, however, hung limply by his sides, searching impotently for some form of occupation. He caught Persephone staring at him, and folded his arms across his chest. She watched him breathe, watched the slight flare of his nostrils, and the place where his pale skin met the tight collar of his shirt. Her eyes fell to his crotch with unnecessary frequency. Her body tensed up at the thought of him, her stomach tied itself in knots.

"Are you happy?" she asked. "Are you happy, now you've married me and you get to keep your country?" A deep coldness permeated the windowless corridor, hiding this passageway from the warmth of May. Persephone felt the dense chill penetrate the neck of her wedding gown. Hair rose up on the back of her neck. Her body was supercharged, electric in anticipation of the consummation of marriage. Even the cold set her on fire.

"I am very happy," he said. "I am the happiest man in Western

Russia."

"That's not hard," Persephone said under her breath. All she could think of was the violence in Red Square, and the hardship it was bred from.

"What was that?" The ice in his eyes caught her then; a sharp slash of coldness that said he understood her perfectly.

"I said it must be hard," she quickly covered herself. "Marrying someone who's practically a stranger, having no control over your own fate." Her words were cutting enough that Haden finally stopped his ascension of the stairs.

"Is it? You tell me," he asked, catching her arms in his hands and pinning her against the wall. The air was thick and heavy in the confined closeness of the staircase. The ice of his eyes met the fire of hers in a fierce tug-of-war, and Persephone didn't know whether to fear him or yearn for him. She felt weak from hunger. All she had been able to eat in her nervous state was a small amount of fruit. Haden loomed over her, the epitome of strength, inciting in Persephone feelings of deep passion. It wasn't passion for him. Seeing the contours of his muscles straining against his white suit, feeling the grip with which he constrained her, all she could feel was an expanding sense of envy. He was a form of power, and she one of apparent weakness. She envied him for his power—his strength—and envy soon turned to anger. He could overpower her in an instant, if he chose to, and very soon, she knew the time would come for him to take her in any way he wished. Persephone shuddered involuntarily as she envisioned a darker end to the evening than the naïve fantasies she had allowed herself to indulge in.

"Haden," Persephone said as the pressure of his fingers on her arms began to ache. "Please let go of me. I am your wife and you should not hurt me."

Haden released her abruptly, without a word. They continued up the stairs in silence.

"This is your new room," he informed her, opening a vast, gold-plated door to a grand bedroom decorated in a variety of shades of gold and white. In spite of the obvious grandeur, it was evident this room was not inhabited. Persephone eyed Haden confusedly.

"This is your room," he explained. "Goodnight." He turned to

112

leave.

Persephone watched Haden's retreating figure, letting it slowly sink in that she was as alone as she had always been.

"Haden!" Persephone called impulsively, running after him. The white silk of her wedding dress tangled between her legs, trapping itself beneath her feet and inhibiting her movement. "Haden!"

"Persephone?" He turned to her, stopped, waited. His eyes followed her expectantly.

Bravery budded softly in her lonely heart as she considered the weight of a wedding night spent alone. Persephone knew what she had to do. Her hands caught Haden's stiff shoulders, and shoved him hard against the wall, pinning down this man who towered over her. His body was unyielding, rigid at the shock of her touch. Persephone stood on her tiptoes, and kissed her new husband firmly on the mouth. There was no heat, none of the passion of her fantasies: only a desperate girl, attempting to seduce a stone-cold man. The Tsar pushed her away from him, disgusted. His strength almost knocked her to the floor. Persephone reached out an arm to steady herself against the wall behind her. She turned away to hide her crumpling face, surprised by his abrupt dismissal. She bitterly bid him goodnight, and returned to her room. Persephone was sure she did not imagine the scrape of the key in the lock. Trapped. Again.

She threw herself on the bed and burst into frustrated tears. She had pledged her life away to a man who wouldn't even share a bed with her, a man who didn't trust her enough to leave her door unlocked. Persephone screamed at the top of her voice, finally giving up the obedience and deference she had forced herself to show to her husband. She didn't care if her screams were heard. In that moment, she cared about nothing but herself.

Persephone engaged herself in fantasies of driving a knife through her husband's heart, of watching his blood soak across his chest. She imagined him crying out with pain. In the throes of anguish, destruction was her only solace. Persephone screamed until her throat was raw and she had become a sweating, sobbing mess. She stripped off her wedding gown and threw it to the floor. She crawled into bed in her undergarments, and stared up at the ceiling, wishing for even a temporary respite. Hope of sleep was non-existent.

It was three o'clock in the morning when she realised the thing she wanted most in the world was to hear one of Phoenix's crazy theories. She sobbed harder at the thought of being permanently separated from her friends. By five o'clock Persephone had decided she would confront the Tsar, ask him why he married her if he had no intention of being a husband to her. She yearned to understand what his true motives for marrying her had been, and why it was so hard for him to love her. By six o'clock, she finally fell asleep.

Slumber was short-lived. Three loud raps on the window startled Persephone into consciousness.

## Chapter Nine

The dim light of dawn entered through the window, closely followed by a human figure, camouflaged against the night in a dark-green shirt and black trousers. She jumped through the window, blurry in the early morning light. Her brown hair was tousled from the climb, and a look of disgust crossed her face as she inspected the room.

"Good morning, Sphenya." Phoenix perched on the windowsill.

"What the hell was that for?" Persephone asked. "You scared me half to death! Death would actually be preferable right now." She pulled her duvet up over her shivering shoulders.

"I'm sorry, Sphenn," Phoenix said. "I thought you might need a friend."

"My lack of companions is the least of my worries." Persephone was angry at her friend, and she could think of no logical reason why.

"I'm sorry," Phoenix said.

"Next time you have some stupid theory about me, do everyone a favour, and keep it to yourself!"

"Don't shoot the messenger." Phoenix leant against the wall by the windowsill. "All I did was warn you. I've got another theory about your husband, but I'll let you figure that one out for yourself. When you spend your life doing his bidding, having no opinions of your own, and eating his toxic fruit, don't blame me for your losses. All I wanted was to be your friend." Phoenix leapt from the window onto a balcony several metres below. She fell with a loud thump. A quiet sob escaped from her. It drifted up through the window like a ghost of her presence.

In no way did it cross Persephone's mind that Phoenix was in the right. She found herself repulsed by the way the girl acted, and began to wonder how they had become friends in the first place. Persephone's mind was in turmoil, it pulled her in a thousand directions. The more she questioned, the less she knew.

*Who am I?* she wondered. In the space of a year, Persephone's whole identity had transformed. The naïve girl from the vineyard had been reincarnated into a woman: a woman with passion, with drive, a woman who yearned for a purpose, and found she had none. Persephone had been forced to grow up the moment she said yes to marrying Haden. She had grown up the moment she relinquished her girlish fantasies and realised marriage was not an escape, but a final, permanent prison. Being a girl meant making choices, hoping for a better world. Being a woman meant understanding that each choice comes with consequences that cannot easily be undone.

A few hours after Phoenix's departure, a key turned in the lock, heralding the arrival of another visitor: Sol.

"Wow, people actually use the door?" Persephone said by way of a greeting.

"Did Phoenix come to see you?" Sol asked. He stood in the doorway, his shoulders hunched awkwardly, uncomfortable in his body. His hair was scrambled from sleep, and his eyes were ringed with dark circles.

"Yeah, so?" Persephone beckoned him into the room. She sat up against her pillows, still clad only in the lingerie she had worn beneath her wedding dress. A night of tossing and turning had unwoven the intricate hairstyle of the day before, and her ginger locks now fell in flat, tangled curls over her shoulders. Her pale breasts spilled over the black lace of the lingerie. Her face was streaked with tear-trails of thick mascara.

"She's gone." Sol sat down on the vast bed, barely glancing at the lavishness that surrounded him. He didn't give a second glance to Persephone's state of undress, and his ignorance seemed deliberate. She could tell he was trying hard not to look at her body. The thought flickered through her mind for only a moment, before she was distracted again by her misery. Persephone wanted to wrap her arms around Sol, and bury her face in the safety of his chest. He was the last remnant of comfort in her disintegrating world.

"Huh?" She had little interest in Phoenix. All Persephone could think of was her own misfortune. She tucked her duvet around her legs, and hugged her knees to her chest, resting her chin on them sulkily.

"She ran away, Sphenya." Sol's eyes implored her to respond. Persephone maintained her indifferent silence.

116

"Where to?" she finally asked. "Not the Settlements, surely? She'd never go back there…"

"Why not?" Sol asked. "Her family's there."

"Her life was terrible."

"I don't know what she's told you, but it can't be true. Phoenix is the Settlement President's daughter."

"She lied to me!" Persephone was outraged. She had felt so privileged to have Phoenix confide in her, and now she knew the story was false. A memory resurfaced of the day they had visited the Settlements, how Phoenix had looked up at the screen in Red Square, and seen a video of the Settlement Presidents' Gathering. Persephone remembered the image of a man with brown skin and dark eyes. She remembered Tatiana's comment about Jakob, the 'intellectual' president of Tartarus Settlement. She tried to picture his face. Had he looked like Phoenix? They were not alike, but they shared enough features that she could believe they were related. "I helped her set the place on fire!" Persephone thumped her fist down, hard, against the bed, filled with horror at the crime she had been coerced to commit.

"You set the Settlements on fire?" Sol was impressed. "I can see Phoenix doing that, but you?" He laughed.

"She told me it was awful there." Persephone was ashamed of herself. She had believed her crime was for the greater good, that she was freeing the downtrodden from tyranny and oppression.

"She was right," Sol said, reflecting on the trauma of his own past. It was something he had never talked about. "It was worse than you could possibly imagine, Sphenn, but that wouldn't have been why Phoenix tried to burn it down. She'd have had her own reasons. We both know she's not the most compassionate person around, unless it suits her own interests."

"If she's not here, and she's probably not there, where would she have gone?" It was the pain of betrayal that motivated Persephone to care about Phoenix's whereabouts. If she had lied about the Settlements, what other truths could she have withheld?

"There is a third possibility," Sol suggested. "But it's unlikely."

"I don't think anything is unlikely where Phoenix is concerned."

"She could have gone to her mother."

"Isn't her mother in the Settlements?"

"No," he said. "Her mother was an actress here in Moscow before she married Mr Kashnikov. She ran away with another man when Phoenix was four years old. She could be with her."

"So she's fine? We have nothing to worry about."

"We have to find her."

"Why should we?" Persephone asked. Phoenix had lied to her, tricked her into being an accomplice to arson. She wasn't inclined to run off on a rescue mission. Persephone watched Sol with mascara-smeared eyes, her face painted in watercolour tears. She combed her hair back with her fingers, twisting it behind her head, and let it fall across her shoulders when she found nothing to tie it with.

"Because she'd do it for us."

*Would she?* Persephone thought. Phoenix tolerated Sol, on a good day.

"What about my marriage?" she asked. "I can't just up and leave any time I want. I have commitments now." She barely believed herself.

"Tell me, how did you spend your wedding night?" Sol asked.

"That's absolutely none of your business!"

"Alone? Yes, stay here with your husband. He'd miss you terribly." She was sure his anger went deeper than Phoenix's disappearance.

"He'd miss me more than he'd miss you," Persephone said under her breath. She regretted it the moment the words left her mouth. There was no reason for her to be cruel to Sol. She felt an invisible force pulling her away from her friends, making her hate them. She was relieved to find Sol hadn't heard her.

"Phoenix chose to leave," Persephone said firmly, turning from him so he wouldn't see the conflicted feelings that played out on her face. Her blue eyes flared with anger, the rings of smudged mascara branded across her face like war paint.

"She wants us to go running after her."

"Why?"

"It's the only way she knows how to deal with pain. If we find her, we prove we love her. If we stay here, she'll believe we don't."

"She betrayed me!" Persephone's strong resolve was fading fast, but she took a final stand.

"Have you never told a lie?" Sol asked. "I'll give you a few more days of wedded bliss before you have to make up your mind, but if you don't do this, Phoenix won't be the only friend you've lost."

✝

"Mum?" Phoenix asked. She knocked on an open door, and peered inside the dimly lit room to which it led. The wooden hut was situated in a small, muddy yard in a village thirty miles from Moscow. Phoenix's eyes met a vivid premonition of her future self as her mother appeared. The woman was the image of her daughter, altered only by the difference of age between them, and the hue of their skin.

She almost fell over from shock at the sight before her.

"Phoenix, can that possibly be you?" she asked. "You look just like me at your age, though a few shades darker."

"What greeting would be complete without some casual racism?"

Phoenix stood with her arms crossed, a glare upon her face. She was determined not to let her array of emotions show. It had been fourteen years since her mother left. Time had faded the memories, but not the pain of abandonment.

"Do you want to come in?" her mother asked. Phoenix nodded and stepped inside. "You grew up."

"Time flies when your mother deserts you."

"I'm surprised Jakob let you out of his clutches."

"He didn't," Phoenix said. "You can imagine what my life was like after you left. Or perhaps you can't, it was worse than anything he ever did to you. I was a shell of a person until two years ago, when I was kidnapped by the Tsar. He was a better parent to me than you or dad ever were. But he married my friend and stole her away from me. I didn't want to live there after that. I couldn't face another betrayal." Phoenix took pleasure in the subtle hint of guilt on her mother's face. It felt good to dig the knife in, twist it around and around, press it into the depths of the woman who abandoned her.

"I'm sorry, Phoenix."

"You're sorry? What do you expect me to say, that everything's fine now? It's not fine, and I don't forgive you. But I don't hate you yet, and I think I can even understand why you left. Except if I was in your situation, and I had a kid, I would've taken her with me." Phoenix's stormy blue-green eyes met her mother's identical ones. They stared each other out, waiting for the other to give in and apologise. Phoenix refused to forgive her mother, refused to let go of the past. She had been defined by the sixteen years she had spent in the Settlements; they had given her the strength of character she needed to survive, and all she wished was for them to be erased completely.

"I'm sorry," her mother eventually said. "I was twenty-three years old! I didn't know how to be a mother to you. I was trying to do what was best for you!"

"What was best for me? You knew my father was a monster, and you left me with him anyway! I was four years old, mum, *four years old*. I couldn't leave, I couldn't protect myself. You left me to suffer." Phoenix wrung her hands together in frustration, forcing herself to stay calm. She couldn't let her agony show. Not here, not now.

"If you hate me so much, why did you come?"

"I've nowhere else to go. There's nothing left for me in Moscow. Both my friends are in love with a psychopath—the same psychopath, might I add—which leaves only two people in the world to whom I have any connection. All I have is you and Dad, and I would take coward over evil any day."

"Are you planning to stay here?" her mother asked.

"I guess so." Something occurred to her then "If it's alright with your family."

"Oh, they'll understand."

"Do you have any more children?"

"Yes, two girls, both of them young." Her voice was emotionless as she dropped the bombshell.

Phoenix felt a sharp pang of emotion at her mother's words. In spite of fourteen years' worth of resentment, she thought they had a chance at reconciliation. How could they make amends if she had already been replaced, not once, but twice?

"Mama!" A girl of about nine years old ran through the door,

120

closely followed by a younger girl, and a middle-aged man, who brought with him the heady scent of cigars and liquor. Phoenix recognised him to be not only a rival for her mother's attention, but a threat to her own well-being. She knew his type all too well. He reminded her of her father, and of the Tsar, but a poor imitation. He lacked class and status. There was no mask to hide behind, no pretence of fitting into a civilised society. Phoenix had grown used to grandeur. After living in the palace for two years, she had forgotten the harsh reality of life outside of Moscow. Western Russia was a deeply impoverished country, and this was evident both in the presentation of her mother's home, and her mother's husband. Somewhere in the farthest reaches of her heart, Phoenix yearned for Moscow, for the Tsar's palace, for a home where the only security she had to worry about was emotional.

"Who's this, Katya?" asked the man. His accent was far stronger than the Muscovite one she had grown used to. Phoenix wondered how he couldn't figure out who she was, given the resemblance between mother and daughter.

"This is Phoenix, my eldest daughter," said her mother matter-of-factly. "Phoenix, this is my husband Yuri, and my daughters, Olga," she gestured to the elder, "and Irina," the younger.

Phoenix smiled insincerely, presenting a façade of obliviousness to the look of pure outrage on her stepfather's face. She wondered, for the first time in fourteen years, if it hadn't solely been her mother's choice to leave her behind.

Yuri grunted in her direction.

"It's lovely to meet you too," Phoenix said in an overly enthusiastic voice, extending her hand to shake his. Yuri looked confused. "Oh, I'm terribly sorry," she said. "It's an English custom, from the Settlements." Phoenix eyed her mother, letting her know this action had been no mistake. It was a reminder to Yuri that she had been there first, before him, and before these later additions to Katya's family.

"Phoenix is coming to live with us," Katya informed Yuri. Her voice was high and nervous.

"Isn't that wonderful?" Phoenix asked chirpily. "We're all going to be a family, finally. There's so much lost time to make up for, so many bridges to mend. But I'm sure we will all grow to love each other." She smiled at her younger sisters, avoiding the gazes of her mother and stepfather. The youngest girl, Irina, smiled back shyly. She had white-blonde hair, but otherwise shared the matrilineal features.

"I'm sure we'll... make things work." Katya said, less enthusiastic. "For now."

Yuri dragged his wife aside, speaking in a low voice. The strength of his accent and the pitch of his tone made it impossible for Phoenix to decipher his words, but she heard her mother's clearly.

"She's nearly an adult," Katya whispered. Yuri's thick hands clutched around her slim wrists, like shackles. "She'll be out of your way in no time. When she turns nineteen, we won't have any obligation towards her, and you won't have to put up with her any more. It's only eight months. I am her mother, and I don't have a choice.'

Phoenix pulled a section of her hair towards her mouth, straining for it to reach, trying to chew. It was tied up in a ponytail, and fell just short of her teeth. She sighed with irritation.

"Have you tried your nails?" Irina asked. "I bite mine when I'm nervous."

"What?" Phoenix asked.

"Your nails," Irina repeated. "You can't reach your hair."

"Oh," she said, taken aback. "I didn't realise I was doing it. Bad habit. Shouldn't chew hair. Or nails." After a moment of silence, she added "You're really smart, linking those two things together."

After an hour of searching, Persephone located the Tsar's bedroom. Her husband was absent, leaving her with time to take in the décor of the room they should have shared. The carpet bore the same shade of red as a pomegranate, as did the rumpled duvet on the grand bed. Little light came in through a window that overlooked the city. Flames glowed in the hearth, illuminating the area around them, and cast shadows onto the far walls of the room. Persephone was drawn out of her reverie by the emergence of the Tsar, entering through a door in the far right corner. He was dressed only in a thick, white towel that covered him from the waist down, leaving his muscular chest in plain view.

"Persephone!" he gasped, at the sight his wife standing before him.

"Good morning, Your Majesty." She curtsied, raising an eyebrow to show she was mocking him.

"Forgive me for not bowing," Haden said, "but I fear my towel would drop. What are you doing here?" He sat down on his bed, and looked at Persephone curiously. Her eyes were glued to his bare skin, to the tight, clenched muscles of his torso.

"Why did you marry me?" she asked. Her voice was calm and even, but her heart raced. A lifetime of servitude had made her believe it was not her place to question her superiors. But this was her husband; they were meant to be equals.

"I needed a wife," he said simply, smoothing back his wet, blond hair. Persephone couldn't help thinking of how different things would be now, had their wedding night gone as planned. This half-naked man in front of her would no longer be a mystery. She would know the feel of his body, the touch of his skin on hers. The tension of embarrassment built up as they eyed each other. There was no ease, no naturalness between them. They felt further apart from each other than they had when they were strangers.

"I'm not your wife, am I?" Persephone asked.

"How so?" Haden asked. "Did we not have a wedding a mere two ago?"

"Oh, we married," Persephone agreed, "but I'm hardly your wife! What do I say when people ask me about children? They'll blame me, you know. If I'm not pregnant soon, they'll say it's my fault, that I'm not a good enough wife, or a good enough Tsarina. I'll be the perfect person to persecute, because I'm young, and I'm foreign, and I'm from a Settlement! Nobody would consider that your perfect virgin bride is still a virgin. I gave up everything for you! I gave up my friends, my freedom—little as it was—my identity... And you won't even sleep with me?"

"Are you shouting at me because I didn't have sex with you?" The Tsar was deeply amused. A smirk hung upon his lips, taunting her. Persephone's eyes dropped to his chest, where his nipples met her gaze like a set of omniscient eyes.

123

"Yes. No. What the hell do you want from me, Haden? What's the point of marrying me if you don't even treat me like your wife?"

"I don't know how to answer you," Haden said sincerely. "We're as good as strangers, and we will be for a long time yet. Neither of us has fooled ourselves this marriage was a match based on love. Have no fear: our marriage will be consummated, Persephone, and you will carry my children. But I feel it's best to give it time, let it come naturally. I don't want to force myself on you; I don't want to make you do something you're not ready for. You're nineteen years old! You may have the body of a woman, but psychologically you are still a child. I don't want to cause any more harm to you than I already have."

"I want to." She looked directly into the heart of the glaciers that occupied his eyes. "I want to be with you as a wife should be with a husband. I want you to love me. I want you to treat me as a wife, and not as a stranger. After all I've given up for you, this is the least you could give me in return."

"We have a lifetime for this, Persephone. There's no hurry." He smiled tenderly, and patted the bed beside him, offering her a place to sit.

"Haden," she said, as she took a seat next to him. "You don't understand where I'm coming from on this. No one ever… touched me." She blushed at her own words, hastily adding "I don't just mean like that, it's so much more. I didn't have people to give me hugs and kisses, let alone anything else."

"I got that from your Virgin Bride speech," he said with a low chuckle.

"What I'm trying to say is that I grew up without any kind of physical affection. There was no one to even hold my hand, or pick me up when I fell. I never felt wanted. When I married you, I thought I'd finally have someone who could fill that emptiness, and give me the love I never had. I was silly to think it would be like that. This is an arranged marriage, after all. But I thought you could grow to love me."

"I will love you, Persephone," Haden promised, bringing his lips to her forehead and holding her close to him. She felt the warmth of his bare chest, reaching her through the thin fabric of her dress.

124

She wanted him more than she had ever wanted anything, more, even, than she wanted freedom. "I will love you more than I have ever loved another person," he said. "But love doesn't happen overnight. Love won't come when we consummate this marriage, though I do hope it comes before. Love will come when we least expect it. So for now, my wife, let us part as friends, and hope that is enough. I'll see you soon." He kissed her softly on her cheek, and whispered "You do amaze me, Persephone."

☦

When Persephone returned to her room, Sol was waiting for her. He sat stiffly on her bed, inspecting his fingernails. He looked up when she entered. The sight of his face was a welcome relief, in spite of how they had parted.

"Hey Sphenya, nice to see you dressed." He smiled slightly, to show he came in peace. His tone was soft, as was his gaze.

"Hey." She returned his smile, wishing to reverse the damage of the anger she had felt the during his last visit.

"I need a decision," he said.

"I'm sorry, Sol. I can't go. I feel like I finally have a chance to make my marriage work. I need to follow this through. I'm sorry."

"Fine, if that's what you want. I understand." His disappointment showed, in spite of his efforts to conceal it.

"I'm sorry, I—" She floundered, waving her hands in the air as if calling for divine intervention. "Give me one more week to make up my mind. Maybe I could go with you, and then come back..."

"Okay. I need to track down her mother anyway, find out where she lives." He patted her shoulder gently, his eyes filled with pity.

Persephone gave him a tight smile; her polarized desires left her torn. Sol and Phoenix were a package deal now, staying put came with a price. Her only option was to wait it out. In one more week, she would have a better idea of how her husband felt about her.

"You must be lonely," she said to Sol, "without her."

"She was all I had here, for so long," he said. "No matter what she does or says, I always forgive her. I know she cares about you,

125

Sphenn. She wouldn't have lied without a reason. She always has a reason."

"When I saw her I felt so angry," Persephone said. "I didn't even have a reason. I don't know how to forgive her. I don't know if I can forgive her. She doesn't trust me, yet she expects me to trust her, and believe in her stupid theories. She said all this stuff about Haden, and none of it made sense."

"That's Phoenix for you."

"I'm sick of being treated like I'm stupid and ignorant. Maybe I'm not smart like her, maybe I haven't read a zillion books, but that doesn't mean I'm dumb. I've survived this far, haven't I? Don't I get credit for that?"

"Phoenix is an intelligence snob," Sol said. "But it's not a reason to hate her. We've all been brought up differently. We're all children of different Settlements. Phoenix was raised away from everyone else, watching life through doors and windows. She learnt how to be human from reading books, Sphenn. She only understands how to be book-smart."

# Chapter Ten

Persephone decided to visit Haden again the next morning, to test the waters of their new-found understanding, and see what she could salvage of her marriage. A night of heavy thunder had bred a morning of light rain, which fell in a pool on the sill of the half-open window. Persephone buttoned up her white cotton dress, and pulled a thin scarlet sweater over her head, before plodding down the corridors to her husband's quarters.

"Haden?" she asked, knocking lightly on the thick, varnished wood of his bedroom door. Her foot jittered against the floor as she waited for him to answer.

"Persephone," he greeted her as he opened the door, a huge smile upon his face. "Come in!" Haden blinked in quick succession as she entered the room, his eyes followed her closely.

"Sit down." He directed her towards the bed. The deep-red duvet cover was tucked in tightly, with a stack of gold velvet cushions placed in neat formation above snowy-white pillows. Haden sat down beside her, leaving a few inches of deliberate space between them.

"I thought you might want to talk," said Persephone. "Yesterday felt like a breakthrough – talking with you alone. I thought we should do it again."

"I had the exact same thought." He gave her as warm a smile as his eyes allowed. "You're my wife and I know almost nothing about you." The Tsar let his hand fall into the empty space between them on the bed.

"You know everything about my life already," said Persephone, "I am sure." The thought made her uncomfortable. He was an enigma, whilst she was an open book.

"I don't mean your life, Persephone. I mean *you*. I don't need to know you grew up on a vineyard. I want to know the inner workings of your soul."

"Wow." Persephone was taken aback. There was a jarring possessiveness in the tone of his demand, and suddenly the idea of being close to him made her uncomfortable. "Even I don't know the inner workings of my soul, Haden. I don't even know if I have a soul."

A dark look crossed the Tsar's face.

"Sorry. I know you're religious, and souls are all part of the deal. But I don't know who I am yet. I can't share something with you when I haven't explored it myself." She reached out and patted his hand, which lay between them, cushioned by the creases of the duvet. "Let's start with something simpler."

"Okay," Haden laughed, rubbing the back of his neck. "Favourite colour?" he tried. "Favourite food? How many boys have you liked?"

"Grey," Persephone said, "deep grey – like clouds, intense and stormy!" Her face became more animated as the nervousness began to subside. "Grey; pomegranate; two."

"Pomegranate?" The Tsar raised an eyebrow. The corners of his mouth turned up a little.

"It was the beginning of the end." She squeezed his cool hand. "If I hadn't met you that day, nothing would've changed."

Haden nodded solemnly, then a spark caught in his eyes, and he asked "Two, huh? Who are these two boys?" His face broke into a mischievous grin "Or were they men?"

Persephone blushed scarlet. "I'm not saying!" she protested. She could hardly tell him that one was he, and the other Andrei. She wasn't sure if the latter counted, it had been nothing more than a brief attraction. She didn't dare mention Tatiana.

"Who?" he asked again, taking pleasure in her discomfort. "Who?" He nudged her with his elbow, testing her limits.

"It really isn't important." She laughed nervously, a shiver going up her spine.

"Was I one of them?" he whispered, leaning in so his lips almost touched her ear.

"Possibly."

Haden drew Persephone close to him then, his muscular body hard against her. The chiselled structure of his cheeks and jaw ensnared her eyes, demanding her attention. He was intoxicating, like mulled wine and wood smoke, like lightning storms in the dark of night. Haden had become a physical embodiment of everything intense that Persephone was yet to experience. He was a reminder that life was exciting, that thrills could be found in the most unexpected of places. She carefully placed her hands on his

128

shoulders, pulling him towards her, knowing that if she didn't act now, he would dominate her. It was her turn to be in control, to ensure her own desires were fulfilled.

"Are you ready to become my wife, Persephone?" Haden asked. His fingers traced patterns along the nape of her neck.

"Yes," she whispered, breathless. He kissed her urgently, his hands clawing at her back, drawing her to him; closer, closer, *closer!*

The Tsar pushed Persephone down onto the bed. He kissed her slowly, pausing only to tug her sweater over her head. He resumed their kisses as he undid the buttons of her white dress. His lips descended to her neck, his mouth hot and wet against her warm skin, moving further down until he reached her breasts. His soft caresses soon lost their gentility, and Persephone felt the sharp bite of her husband's teeth on her sensitive skin.

"Haden!" she yelped, jerking away from him. "That hurts! Stop right now!" She pushed him off her.

"I'm sorry," he said. "I lost myself there." Wilderness shone through the gloss of his eyes, the tight clench of his jaw betrayed the fragility of his self-control.

"Haden, can I ask you something?" Persephone tilted her head, to see his eyes. "Do you like to hurt me? This is the second time I've seen you get some kind of twisted pleasure out of making me feel pain."

"No, not at all," he said. "That's not it, Persephone. I just lose control sometimes. I forget I'm stronger than you."

"Stronger than me?" She laughed harshly, clenching her fists in frustration. "Why? Because you're a man, because you're so big and muscular, whilst I'm a weak little girl? You are not stronger than me, Haden. Don't think you can overpower me, because you can't!"

"Don't be so sensitive." He rested his hand on her shoulder; she shook it off immediately. "I didn't mean it as an insult, I just meant that I am a grown man, and you're—"

"I'm what? A *child*? You willingly married a child?" Her face betrayed her rage, cheeks burning a violent red.

"No," Haden said, stung. "You're not a child. But I am ten years your senior, and I am physically stronger than you. It is a matter of biology, not a battle of the sexes."

"Whatever." Persephone rose from the bed. She fastened her dress, and faced away from her husband. "You're right. We're not ready for this. We don't know each other well enough. This was a mistake." She turned to leave, tears spilling down onto her dress until the white fabric became transparent. She grabbed her sweater from the bed.

"Persephone, wait!" He reached for her arm, preventing her from moving. She was overcome, once again, with the sense that he could break her in an instant. Persephone's anger grew. She didn't have the will to move.

"Persephone, my darling, I am so sorry. I never meant to hurt you, and I never meant to insult your strength—" The bedroom door burst open, cutting him off before he could bring his apology to its conclusion.

"Your majesty!" gasped the young servant who crashed into the room. He stopped short when he saw Persephone. He turned awkwardly to Haden, who nodded once in response. "Your fruit laboratory has been vandalised," the young man said, discreetly brushing sweat from his brow. "The entire system has been damaged."

"I must go there immediately." The Tsar discarded his wife's arm, which he had held stiffly throughout this exchange. He sprinted from the room.

Persephone stared after him in disbelief. She stormed out of Haden's bedroom, biting back a scream of rage. She stomped her foot in anger, it met the plush carpet with a soft thump.

"Hello Sphenya." Sol intercepted her on her way back to her room. He wore a black turtleneck and black jeans. The gentle flush of his cheeks was the only hint of colour on him.

"I still have six days to decide!" Persephone snapped when she saw him. He stood in the hallway, blocking her path.

"How are you?" Sol asked good-naturedly.

"Terrible." Persephone attempted to push him out of her way. He caught her shoulders in his hands; his touch was far gentler than the Tsar's. He reached up and caressed her cheek with his thumb. She involuntarily burst into tears.

"It's okay," he said. "It's okay."

"I'm sorry, Solly." Persephone hugged him tightly. She squished her face into his chest. "I'm so sorry I was mean to you," she mumbled into the dense wool of his shirt. "You're the best person I know. You've always been there for me, and I've been such a crap friend to you. I'm sorry."

"You're not a bad friend, Sphenn." He wrapped his arms tighter around her. She wept into his chest. "What's brought this on?"

"You're all I have in this world. I'll never push you away ever again, I promise! You've never let me down, unlike some other people I know."

"Phoenix, or the Tsar?" Sol asked, resting his cheek against her forehead.

"Both of them – they're as bad as each other! Right now I'm most angry at the Tsar."

"What, you're not calling him Haden now?"

"Nope." She sniffed. "I have no reason to."

"Good," Sol said. "Phoenix and I found it irritating how you always had to emphasise the closeness of your bond."

"There is no bond!" Persephone said.

"That's what I like to hear!"

"Are you as angry with him as I am?" Persephone asked.

"Possibly," he said carefully.

"Why?"

"Let's not talk about it. I got my revenge."

"It was you, wasn't it?" she asked with excitement. "Who smashed up his stupid fruit?"

"Possibly," Sol said with a wicked grin. His straight teeth gleamed.

"Why?"

"It was our dear Phoenix's parting request."

"Why am I not surprised?" Persephone felt a stab of jealousy at Sol's words. She turned away, so he couldn't see the sadness in her eyes. She had always felt like Sol was hers, although he had known Phoenix first. Right now Persephone didn't want to share.

"I found a record of her mother, by the way." Sol led her down

131

the hallway, allowing her to pause every-so-often so she could angrily kick the places where red carpet met white walls.

"Oh?"

"She's married to a man named Yuri Lyubov. They have two kids, and live about thirty miles from here—"

"When are we leaving?" Persephone wanted to put as much distance as she could between herself and her husband.

"Are you coming with me?" Sol tilted his head to the side as he observed her.

"Anything is preferable to staying with the Tsar. Phoenix was right with all her ice jokes, that man is cold."

"We'll leave the day after tomorrow," said Sol. "We can get a train out of Moscow, and then go on by foot from there. We don't want to be too traceable. You know the Tsar will try to find us."

"He won't care if I leave."

"Is there something you want to talk about?"

"Not particularly, no."

"Sphenya." Sol squeezed her hand, pulling her to a halt outside her bedroom door. "You can talk to me, you know." His dark eyes were filled with concern.

"I just found out my husband's a total creep, okay?" Persephone was close to tears again. "As you know, we never did anything on our wedding night. And today, we were heading in that direction. Then he bit me."

"He bit you?" Sol asked. Persephone noticed his surprise was somewhat feigned; his thick eyebrows climbed a little too high up his forehead, and his mouth opened a little too wide. "Where exactly did he bite you?"

"In the, um, chest area," Persephone mumbled, refusing to look at him.

"The where?"

"You heard me!"

"I didn't," he said, making no effort to hide his amused expression. "Where did he bite you?"

Persephone gestured to her left breast. Her face turned a deep shade of beetroot. She didn't feel at all comfortable talking about this to Sol.

"I told him not to," she continued, "because I'm not into his

132

kinky crap, and then he said I'm weaker than him, and that it's a biological fact that he's stronger, because he's a man, and he's older than me. I mean, he was right in that sense, but that doesn't mean he should rub it in! Hasn't he ever heard of Feminism?"

"Whoa there, Phoenix!"

"Shut up. Anyway, as he was trying to talk his way out of being a misogynist prick, a guy came in and told him his stupid-ass fruit laboratory was broken into, as if it actually matters!"

"I love how you turn into Phoenix when you're angry." Sol laughed. "It must be hard," he added, "to be married to someone who doesn't have time for you, someone who doesn't love you."

"I don't love him, so it doesn't even matter."

"Would you be so angry if you didn't love him?" The discomfort in Sol's dark brown eyes made Persephone want to cry. She knew he was talking about his own experience of the Tsar as much as he was talking about hers.

"I don't love him. I hate him," she said. "He's stolen my freedom, stolen my entire life from me." She paused. "You love him, don't you? Phoenix told me." She reached for his hands. He shook off her touch.

"Phoenix should mind her own business." Sol's cheeks flushed an angry red.

"I thought she was always right?"

He refused to meet her gaze. "I'm not... It's not... This isn't what you think."

"You never know," Persephone said. "He might be better to you than he is to me. The whole misogynist prick thing wouldn't be an issue, because you're a guy."

"Regardless, I'm not gay."

Persephone didn't believe him. She knew Sol was hiding something from her. But Tatiana's warning rang like an alarm bell in her mind, and as much as she wished Sol would trust her, she understood why he didn't.

✝

Sunshine beat down upon the thick, black fabric of Phoenix's shirt, and reflected off her brown hair. She had woken in the dark, sweaty and sobbing from a familiar nightmare of her childhood demons. She ran outside, still in the black shirt and green leggings she had slept in, ran until she reached the forest, some two miles away. She climbed high up the branches of a sturdy tree, and watched the sun rise until it was high in the sky, choosing to return only when the pangs of hunger screamed louder than the war in her mind.

As the hard dust of the path merged with the drying, muddy yard of her new home, the peaceful silence of spring was broken by the too-familiar sounds of shouting and sobbing.

"Mum!" Phoenix screamed. She rushed through the door, just in time to see Yuri's fist crashing into her mother's face. "Stop!" she yelled, standing between her mother and her stepfather. Katya backed away slowly, leaving her daughter alone to face her punishment.

"Don't tell me what to do, little girl, or you'll be next," Yuri said. It wasn't yet noon, and his breath already stank of alcohol.

"Like I couldn't take you," she said. He punched her in the jaw. She kicked him hard in retaliation, her face stiff and resolute. She kicked him repeatedly, until he swerved away from her, and stormed out the door.

"Sit down," Phoenix told her mother.

"You shouldn't have seen that," Katya said. Her dark hair fell across her cheeks, obscuring her face from view.

"I've never seen one of your husbands hit you before, have I? I shouldn't've seen it, because it never should have happened! Yuri's evil, just like Dad was. You really pick them, don't you?" Phoenix opened the freezer and rifled through its drawers. The cold air numbed the pain in her jaw. She pulled out a bag of ice and wrapped it in a faded yellow tea towel.

"Put this where he hit you," she ordered Katya, handing her the icepack. "It'll help."

"Thanks."

"Why do you put up with that?" Phoenix asked. "I'm assuming it wasn't the first time?"

"I love him."

"Oh for f…" she trailed off, rolling her eyes and raising her hands towards the ceiling in a gesture of frustration. "Well *I* don't

134

love him, and I refuse to let him get away with it. How can you love someone who treats you that way?"

"You'll understand when you're older." Katya held the icepack to her cheek. The faint lines around her eyes had grown deeper.

"I won't." Phoenix was adamant. "I couldn't put up with it, not after the way Dad treated me. I'd leave, I couldn't deal with it. Not again. Never again. Being kidnapped was the best thing that ever happened to me! Mum, you've been through this before, five years of it, and you escaped! Why would you enter a second marriage with a violent man?"

"I still wonder how you came about," Katya said. "Your sense of justice… You're so different from both your parents." She pursed her lips, eyeing her daughter with something between jealousy and resentment.

"Thank the genetic lottery for that." Phoenix applied a block of ice to her own face. It had melted somewhat during the time she held it, and dripped cold water onto the floor. It was cool and slippery against her burning skin. The ice made her think of the Tsar. She wondered how Persephone was enjoying married life.

"I suppose it's a good thing," her mother said. "If you'd turned out like Jakob or I, you wouldn't have a chance at goodness."

"True."

"Why did you come here, Phoenix? I'm not fooled you returned out of love for me."

"No one cared about me any more," she said. "I wasn't important." It wasn't entirely a lie.

"You weren't the centre of attention?"

"Yeah, I suppose that was it."

"Maybe you're a little like me," Katya said. "When I was an actress – the most worshipped child star in all of Moscow, might I add! I appeared from nowhere at 16, and won the hearts of the entire city!" She smiled at the memory. "What was I saying? Oh yes, back when I was an actress, I always threatened to quit if I wasn't cast as the main role."

"That's why I'd never make it as an actress," Phoenix said. "I was born to be a side character, yet all I want is to be centre stage." She laughed harshly. "Also, I'm terrible at masking my opinions, it would be evident where a character ended and where I began."

135

She paused, collecting her thoughts. "I think we're different, Mum. We're an entirely different species. I can lie just as easily as you, but that's all I can do. I can change facts, not emotions."

# Chapter Eleven

A series of foul words escaped Persephone's lips in a breathless whisper as her foot struck a loose floorboard outside the Tsar's bedroom door. The resulting creak ricocheted off each one of her fragile nerves. She glared at the carpet beneath her, and wondered how such thick material could fail to conceal the noise of the floorboard.

When she was sure her footsteps hadn't awoken him, Persephone continued, placing her foot down each time with deliberation. Passing the Tsar's room had been the most nerve-wracking part of her escape so far, but she refused to feel relief until she was out of the palace entirely.

"Sphenn?" Sol met her at the foot of the stairs. "Are you ready?"

"I was born ready." Persephone walked past Sol, to the window at the far end of the hall. She stood by the sill, reaching out to touch the glass with her hand. She was dressed head-to-toe in grey, with a red rucksack hanging on one shoulder. Persephone thought of how much a life could change in 14 months.

"Will you miss this place?" Sol asked, joining her window-side reverie.

"In a way. The sweetest memories I've ever made rest between these walls."

"Here's to making more," said Sol. "If you can have the time of your life in a place like this, imagine the fun you can have when we hit the open road."

"It will be our grandest adventure yet!" she agreed. "But first," she dragged his arm around her shoulders, "we must escape!"

Sol let Persephone hug him for a moment, and released her so he could open the window. Cold, night air blasted their faces.

"You ready to start a new life?" she asked. Her heart raced; she was certain the Tsar would catch them.

"Always," Sol replied.

Persephone climbed onto the sill, and stepped out into the dark abyss of freedom.

"I can't believe we made it!" Persephone said, breathless, as they settled into their seats on the train. The vehicle jerked forward, and the thunder of the engine began to roar. The driver's voice crackled through the intercom, rattling off a list of unfamiliar city names, finishing with "final destination: Irkutsk".

"What did he just say?" Sol asked. His eyebrows furrowed in worry.

"Irkutsk? I think?"

"Irkutsk?" Sol repeated the name in confusion. "Unbelievable!" She watched him blankly.

"Irkutsk," Sol explained, "is in Eastern Russia. We're on the wrong train!"

"Eastern Russia? Are you kidding? We're going to Eastern Russia?" Persephone's voice was filled with panic.

"Calm down, Sphenn," Sol tried to reassure her. "We're not going to Irkutsk. We'll get off at the next stop, and we can find another train."

"We don't have money for another train," she said. "We're screwed."

"Then we'll walk," Sol decided. "It'll take us a few days, but our feet will get us there as good as any train."

"Okay." She inhaled deeply. "Okay. We can do this."

"Phoenix will laugh so hard when we tell her," Sol said. "She'd never end up on the wrong train."

"If only we were half the person Phoenix is." Persephone tried to keep the resentment from creeping into her voice.

"Okay, I need sleep." Sol yawned. "Are you alright to wake me when the train stops?"

"Sure." Persephone leant her head against the window, and set about watching the dark city pass by, illuminated by scatterings of light that soon turned to darkness. All she could see in the window now was the reflection of her own tired face. Sol soon fell into slumber, with his head buried in Persephone's shoulder. Two hours passed by in silence, save for the constant growl of the train's engine. Persephone was close to sleep herself when they finally pulled into the station.

"Sol." She shook him awake. "We're here," she glanced gloomily out the window, "wherever 'here' may be."

"Hmph," Sol groaned, rubbing his sleepy eyes as he stood up.

They departed the train, and stumbled across the deserted platform. There were no street lamps to illuminate their path, and mist hindered the grey light of early morning. The pavement was cracked, and Sol tripped as he took a step forward.

"Steady, steady." Persephone patted his arm. "Wake up, c'mon. You're practically sleepwalking."

"I'm tired," he complained.

"Let's get you some coffee," she said. "It's nearly 5 o'clock, there must be some kind of café opening soon."

"In what universe? This isn't Moscow, Sphenn. You'll be lucky to find somewhere open at 8 o'clock, let alone 5!"

"Fine!" Persephone said. "You go and sleep again. It's not like you slept the entire train journey! Look, Sol, you're not the only one who's tired. You chose to leave in the middle of the night, so deal with it." She marched away from him, to the alleyway that led from the train platform to the town high street. She didn't look to see if Sol followed.

"Greetings, my fair lady!" A man approached Persephone, disrupting her daydreams. She sat in the window booth of a small town's only café, her eyes glazing over as she stared into the depths of her coffee mug. It was their second day on the road, and Sol had disappeared to run some errands. They had bickered non-stop since the previous morning, and the reprieve from his company was more than welcome.

"Hi?" she said uncertainly. The man's voice was friendly, but she suspected he was teasing her.

"Forgive me for bothering you, but I could swear my eyes have had the pleasure of viewing your face before." She decided he was mocking her. "Do we know each other?" He was a tall man, almost as tall as the Tsar, with wavy, light-brown hair, and bright blue eyes filled with contagious warmth.

"No," Persephone said. "Sorry, we've never met. You must be thinking of someone else, I'm not from here. Sorry. Sorry." Caffeine and sleep deprivation had made her dizzy to the point she could hardly focus her eyes on the man's face.

"Three 'sorry's?" He laughed deep in his throat. "You must really regret not knowing me." His face broke out into a grin; dimples bloomed beneath the stubble on cheeks.

"No, sorry, I— Sorry, oh crap." She breathed in deeply, and blinked the haziness from her vision.

Their eyes met, and Persephone couldn't help laugh with him.

"Guilt complex?" he asked.

"No," she said. "I'm having one of those days where I get so lost in my own world, I can't focus on anything properly. I was trained to say sorry first, ask questions later." She swallowed the final mouthful of coffee. It was almost cold.

"I prefer it the other way around." He grinned, and settled into the seat across from her, without asking for permission.

"My, my, a real challenge." Her blue eyes glinted, teasing. She raised a solitary ginger eyebrow at him and tried to refrain from breaking into a smile.

"She looks like the Tsar's bride," said another young man, who came to join them. He was in his early twenties, with black hair and tanned skin.

"Yes, because Tsarina Persephone would be here." The young man rolled his eyes with exaggeration. He gave her a friendly pat on the hand, his skin lingering on hers for a moment too long. "Sorry about my brother – a situation where that word really is necessary!" He smiled. "You do look like the Tsarina," he added, "that must be who you remind me of. Her photo's on the front page of every newspaper I've seen today, and projected on the screen by the town hall."

"Oh, why is that?" Persephone asked. Her throat constricted as panic rose up within her. It was a struggle to force the words out of her dry mouth.

"She was kidnapped yesterday." He looked intently into her eyes. She returned his gaze with a hard stare. "Are you sure I don't know you from somewhere else? I can't shake the feeling we've met before. Grigory is right, you look a lot like the Tsarina. The resemblance is uncanny."

"Agreed," Grigory interjected. He took a newspaper from his bag, and held it up before Persephone's eyes. Her wedding photo

140

stared back at her, in black-and-white, a blown-up grainy image of her own face. "Very pretty," Grigory added. It didn't seem like a compliment. He made her feel uneasy. There was next to no family resemblance between him and his brother. Even their accents were unalike. "What's your name?"

*Oh crap,* Persephone thought. Her mind raced, searching for a name—any name—she could temporarily claim as her own.

"Sphenya!" she cried out triumphantly. "My name is Sphenya."

"I'm Grigory." He paused, pretending to mull over her answer. "Sphenya, you say? That sounds awfully similar to Persephone." This felt like an ambush.

She scowled. The young man came to her rescue. "Sphenya doesn't sound anything like Persephone. You'd have to compress half the syllables and switch some vowels. Don't make trouble with the nice lady." He smiled like he couldn't help it, a silly smile, plastered across his face every time he looked at her.

Persephone relaxed a little as she realised his interest in her was not suspicion, but flirtation.

"It's been lovely to meet you," he told her, rising to his feet. His smile deepened. "Truly a wild ride in such a short space of time." He bowed low. "Until we meet again."

"Weirdo," she said. Persephone found herself looking the man up and down as he and his brother departed. She couldn't help noticing his good posture, how his broad shoulders stood proud beneath the plaid fabric of his shirt. And the way his jeans flattered the firm muscles of his butt. Her eyes were glued to his retreating figure.

"Wait." The man turned around. "Sphenya? We have met before!"

Persephone looked at him blankly.

"Imagine me clean shaven, a little less tanned, perhaps surrounded by a stack of controversial literary volumes?"

"Drew, come on!" called Grigory.

Persephone didn't know how to respond. If she admitted to knowing Drew, it would link her back to Moscow.

"I must go," said Drew. "It was nice to see you again."

She smiled tightly, and didn't say a word.

As the café door closed, and Persephone returned to her senses, her mind began to race. Her pictures were on the front page of every newspaper, and most likely on every screen in every town across the country. Persephone knew it would be impossible to disappear. Leaving the palace had seemed the biggest hurdle to pass, but she suspected it was child's play compared to the challenge of staying hidden from the Tsar for the foreseeable future. Perhaps she would have been safer if she had gone to Irkutsk after all.

☦

"Sol!" Persephone hissed, grabbing his arm as he entered the café. She had waited by the door for the past five minutes, agitated; he was late. "Don't call me Persephone unless we're alone, okay?" Sol's eyes were wide, startled by the panic in her voice.

"Huh?" he asked, puzzled. His brow furrowed as he saw the fear on his friend's face.

"My dearest husband has all the newspapers saying I've been kidnapped. I'm completely fucked!"

"If you were 'completely fucked' in the first place," Sol said, "we wouldn't have this issue."

She hit him on the arm.

"Ow!" he protested.

"Sorry," said Persephone. "But Sol, call me Sphenya when we're in public. I don't want to be discovered as the Tsarina."

"Well, Sphenn, as your evil kidnapper, I shall make it my duty to protect your identity. However, there's a slight problem. You look shockingly like yourself!"

"I had no idea."

"First step: makeover," he decided, "second step: find Phoenix. Then we're all set."

"What are we going to do once we've found her? We can't go back to Moscow. There's nowhere else to go. We have no one, nothing. As much as we all resent him, the Tsar was responsible not only for bringing us together, but for keeping us together." A dark look crossed Persephone's face as she saw the extent of her husband's dominion. "He was our livelihood."

"Listen to yourself, Sphenn," Sol said. "He wasn't responsible for keeping us together, we were. He brought us together, but we

142

chose to be friends. Let's find Phoenix, and take it from there."

"Okay."

She squeezed Sol's clammy hand. He brought his arms up around her, a figure of safety, like the family she had never had.

"I love you, Solly," she whispered into his chest.

⸸

Persephone and Sol had set up camp for the night atop a grassy hill, some 25 miles out of Moscow. The cool twilit air caused the blades of soft, spring grass to dance across the fields.

Sol had gone in search of wood for the fire, leaving Persephone alone to reflect over the events of the day. She lay for some time in the grass, breathing in deep lungfuls of fresh, country air, trying to calm the thoughts that whirred around in her mind. She looked mournfully at the long waves of hair that hung down over her shoulders. She knew it had to go; her hair was too strong a signifier of her former identity. Persephone rooted through Sol's bag, and retrieved a pair of scissors. With shaking hands, she brought the blades to her hair.

"Sphenya?" Drew approached her, before she could cut a single lock of hair.

"Are you following me?" she asked.

"Of course not," he said. "You're the last person I expected to see twice in one day. Do you want help with that?" He gestured to her hair.

"No, thank you. I can do it," Persephone said. She wanted to minimise the time spent in his company.

"Are you sure? You won't be able to see when you cut the back."

"Alright, but please don't mess it up." Persephone handed him the scissors. "Sorry, I didn't mean to assume you couldn't cut hair just because you're a man."

"I never said I could cut hair." He held his lips tightly together in an effort not to laugh at the horror on her face.

"What?" she demanded.

"Just kidding," he assured her. "I've had lots of practice."

"Do you have sisters?"

143

"Not exactly. It was more a…" he paused for a moment, searching for a word. He muttered something to himself in what she noted was English. "Community!" he exclaimed triumphantly, upon finding the word in Russian. "I lived in a community. I've got steady hands, so everyone came to me to cut their hair." He held a hand out to show her its steadiness. "Do you trust me, Sphenya?" He shot her a winning smile.

"Not in the slightest, but I'm all out of options."

Drew positioned himself behind her, sitting cross-legged at her back, and poised the scissors to her hair.

"How short are we going?" he asked.

Persephone considered for a moment. Her hair had always been long, it was a part of her identity. Now it was time to discard that image.

"Short," she said. "Not too short." She held her hand at a point an inch above her shoulder. "Cut it to here."

"Don't be nervous. It's just hair, it'll grow back." He patted her arm reassuringly.

"I'm fine." She changed the subject quickly. "What brings you here?"

"You mean: why has sweet destiny brought us together twice in one day?" He snipped at her hair with the scissors as he spoke.

"I mean: why are you stalking me?" She brought his flair for drama right back down to earth.

"I, like you, am in search of a new life. I travel with a couple of like-minded friends." He paused a moment. "They're waiting on the main road. I came ahead to scout for somewhere to stop for the night." He moved to Persephone's side, and began to cut the hair beside her face. "We need a route suitable for a donkey and wagon. Two donkeys, if we're including Grigory."

"Were you planning on this spot?" She tried to sound casual.

"Is that a problem for you?"

She considered a moment. To admit it was a problem would increase any suspicion Drew already held about her identity. Yet if she let them stay, Persephone knew she would have to be on guard the entire time. She sensed Drew was as aware of this as she. But he seemed kind, and she didn't want to reject him. She also couldn't help noticing that his accent was different to how he spoke in Moscow, it was closer to Sol's now, and he had spoken to himself in English earlier. Persephone wondered if Drew, too, was a child of the Settlements.

"Sure." She forced a smile. "You can stay. So long as your donkey, I mean brother, doesn't accuse me of being the Tsarina again. If I knew I looked like her, I would've taken greater pains to change my image."

"Is that why I'm cutting all your hair off?" Drew asked.

"Amongst other reasons. I don't want to be mistaken for someone I'm not. Plus, I've had the same style for nineteen years. It's time for a change."

"Isn't the Tsarina also nineteen?" His tone was innocent, his question was not.

"I don't know. I take little interest in the Tsar or his wife. She's an idiot for marrying him." Persephone knew it was a risk to talk like this, but she couldn't leave it alone. She was compelled both to defend and condemn her choice of marriage. "Why would anyone in their right mind marry into such an institution?" It felt odd talking about herself like she was a stranger.

"He is the Tsar," Drew said.

"I don't see the appeal. I bet she ran away, too. He doesn't strike me as a loving husband." A stern voice inside Persephone's head warned her to stop running her mouth before she said something she would regret, but she couldn't help herself.

"Most likely," Drew said. "You're all done, my dear." He briefly touched her hair to admire his handiwork.

"Hey, *Sphenya.*" Sol returned with an armful of wood. He raised an eyebrow at Persephone's changed appearance. His gaze flitted nervously towards the stranger beside her.

"This is Drew." She introduced them to each other in Russian. "And this is Sol. Sol: Drew and his friends are going to set up camp here for the night. With us." Persephone gave Sol a hard look, daring him to speak. It had been tense between them throughout their journey, and she didn't quite trust him not to make things difficult.

"I will go and retrieve my fine companions," Drew announced. "I shall see you soon, my fair lady."

Sol snorted with laughter. As limited as his Russian was, he understood enough to be amused. Persephone pinched him hard.

"And my fair gentleman," Drew added, tipping a slight bow towards Sol. There was a hint of curiosity hidden behind the amusement in his dark blue eyes.

Persephone and Sol sat in silence, staring up at the first stars as they entered the dark blue sky. She sensed his thoughts were far away, and she couldn't shake the feeling he was keeping something from her. Sol had always been secretive, but it hadn't mattered so much when his silences were filled with Phoenix's constant chatter. Now that three had become two, it felt as if the silence between them stretched on forever, widening the rifts of their friendship until they stood on either side of a vast chasm, crying out for the other whom they could not reach.

Drew soon returned, joined by his companions. Persephone greeted him with a smile, as apprehension brewed silently inside her.

"Sphenya, Sol," he said, "this is Rozalina." He gestured to a tall woman in her early twenties. She had long black hair, brown eyes, and indigenous Siberian features. "And this is Grigory, who I'm sure you remember, Sphenya."

"Hi," Persephone said. Rozalina had a likeable air about her that she warmed to instantly. Grigory was another matter.

"It's freezing, isn't it?" he said, making himself comfortable by the fire.

"Do you mind if I sit here?" Drew asked, in polite contrast to his brother.

Persephone nodded her consent, and he took a seat beside her.

"Where are the two of you headed?" he asked. She noticed again the way his accent differed from that of his companions. He was not a native Russian, of that she was certain.

"We're going to see a friend," she told him. "I fell out with her, and I need to apologise. After that, I don't know. Where are you going?"

"Phoenix?" Drew asked. Persephone nodded. "We're going

to Estonia," he continued. "The Borderlands are common lands. They're free to farm, because most Estonians moved away during the Border Conflicts, twenty years ago."

"Estonia, as in the lawless lands?" Sol asked. Persephone couldn't help notice his shocked expression didn't seem quite genuine.

"Apparently they're very lawful," Drew said. "Estonia—and the Baltic Alliance as a whole—are far more progressive than Western Russia in every aspect of society. If they were lawless like people claim, why hasn't the Tsar successfully annexed them? The Baltic Alliance won the Border War against Western Russia, that's no mean feat."

"Why don't more people go there?" Persephone was intrigued that such a place could exist.

"Because," Grigory cut in before Drew could answer, "the Tsar can't risk losing his grip on power. He's spun his propaganda well enough for the majority of Western Russia to believe Estonia's a lawless, brutal country. He can't have people knowing there's fertile land up for grabs."

"Why?" Persephone asked. "If Western Russia is in such economic peril, why doesn't the Tsar make a trade deal with the Baltic Alliance? If these countries are as advanced as you say, surely it would be beneficial for Western Russia to work with them?"

"Food shortages are all part of the Tsar's mind-control," said Grigory. "It serves him better to have ninety-nine percent of the country living in poverty. Does that make sense, Sphenya?"

"Let's save talk of politics until we're all a little more awake," Drew said, a warning in his voice. The taunting undercurrent of his brother's question hadn't passed him by unnoticed, and he was quick to shut the topic down entirely. Persephone took this as proof that Drew was certain of her true identity, and he was no danger to her. At least for now.

# Chapter Twelve

"Can I go alone?" Persephone asked Sol, as they approached the village where Phoenix's mother lived. A sense of poverty permeated the area, emanating from the run-down wooden shacks and cottages. Persephone and Sol travelled with Drew, Grigory, and Rozalina. The extra company had eased some of the tension between them, if only because it allowed for them to avoid conversing with each other.

"Why don't you want me there?" Sol's tone was accusatory.

Persephone clenched her teeth in frustration. She took a deep breath and exhaled slowly.

"It's easier to solve a fight when it's two people," she said. "This is between me and her. Please let me do it alone."

"Fine," Sol said, as if it was anything but. "I'll wait with the others."

Persephone was riddled with nerves as she pushed open the gate to the yard of a small one-storey, wooden house on the outskirts of the village. The wood was rotting in places, and the house appeared to be on the verge of collapse. Phoenix had openly enjoyed the lap of luxury she had fallen into, and had a keen appreciation for the finer things in life. She couldn't be content living in this hovel.

Persephone stopped at the threshold. The hum of music wafted from the gap beneath the door. She hesitated a moment, and took a deep breath, before knocking lightly. There was no answer. She carefully turned the handle, letting the door swing open to reveal a dark room, with shadows cast upon the wooden walls.

The source of the music was Phoenix, who sang softly, accompanying herself on an out-of-tune guitar. She sat by the empty fireplace, facing away from the door.

"Hello," Persephone called out, loud enough to be heard above the music. She spoke the word in English, so Phoenix would know her identity before she turned to look.

"Well, well, well: Persephone, queen of the underworld," came the mocking reply. There was a cruel glint in her eyes, visible even in this dim light.

"Phoenix, I…" She was at a loss for words, unsure how to respond to her friend's malice.

"Skip the apologies, Sphenya, they're not my forte. Why are you here? What do you want?" Phoenix stood up. Shadows played across her face. Her features had grown harder. She had lost the girlish softness that used to parade itself in her sleek hair and neat clothing.

"I— I don't know," Persephone said. "I wasn't myself the last time we spoke. I don't know what came over me. I'm here to say sorry, and to beg to be your friend again." Her eyes were pleading.

"And what next?" There was venom in Phoenix's voice. "You go running back to your husband?"

"No."

"What, then?" Her expression mellowed a little, but anger still burned bright in her stormy eyes, and she folded her arms across her chest in a defensive posture.

"That depends," Persephone said. "Come with us, with me and Sol. We don't know where we're going, we don't have a plan. But it will be far away from here. We want to start a new life, away from the Tsar. Please come with us. We love you! We need you."

"No, Persephone. I'm sorry. I can't. I have obligations here." The darkness in Phoenix's voice intensified. She sounded much older than eighteen.

"Please!" Persephone begged.

"No." Her voice changed; it became desperate. "My mother's new husband is awful. He hits her. I can't leave her like she left me."

"Okay. I understand." She could have left it at that, and parted on peaceful terms. But friendship was nothing without honesty. "Can you tell me one thing, Phoenix?" Persephone asked. "Why did you lie to me about the Settlements? Sol told me the truth."

"Sol should keep his mouth shut." Phoenix's face was etched with fury, her hands tightened into fists.

"He says the same about you." Persephone wanted to say more, but she was stopped by the threat in her friend's fearful eyes.

"Sol doesn't know anything," Phoenix said. "My life was hell! He had no right."

"He didn't tell me much," Persephone said, mystified. "All he said was that your dad's the Settlement president."

"I keep forgetting you're not from around here." She relaxed a little.

"What's that got to do with anything?"

"Nothing that affects you." There was an acidic edge to her voice that Persephone had never heard before. It frightened her. Any fights they had had in the past were child's play compared to this. There was a depth of anger and hatred seething within Phoenix that could boil over at any moment, locked in only by her commitment to secrecy and self-preservation. In order to hold herself together, she had to shut Persephone out. Every lie she told, and every honest answer she avoided, was another nail in the coffin of their friendship. Persephone weighed the balance in her head, considered the love she felt for this girl, and held it up against her own needs. She couldn't keep pouring her heart into a vessel that resisted her. It was time to call it quits before the walls around her friend's heart crushed her completely.

"I'm leaving," Persephone decided.

Phoenix nodded, before springing towards her, and hugging her tightly.

"I am going to miss you, Sphenn. You have been the light of my life." Her face was a resolute mask, but the devastation in her voice told a different story. "I hope we meet again."

"We will, I promise." They clasped each other's hands, neither prepared to let the other go.

"Your hair's nice. It's different. I like it." She reached out and patted it lightly.

"I think I do too," Persephone said. "I needed a change."

"Don't we all?" Phoenix spoke more to the floor than to her friend. She took a shaky breath. "Goodbye, Sphenya." Her voice was ragged as she spoke. "Until we meet again." Phoenix gave Persephone one last rib-crushing hug, and let her go.


By the time Persephone made her way back to the dull patch of grass at the centre of the village, she was in floods of tears. Sol gave her a questioning look. She shook her head to indicate her failed mission, and walked off on her own. Drew followed her.

"What happened?" he asked, wrapping her into his strong arms for a hug. Persephone took a moment to reply, breathing in the warmth of his chest. There was a safety in his arms that felt like she had finally come home. She craved to be held like this, to be comforted solely by another's touch.

"She decided to stay," Persephone said, her face squashed against the soft fabric of his plaid shirt. It smelt like oranges.

"I'm sure she had a good reason." Drew rested his chin atop Persephone's head.

He stroked her shoulder gently as he hugged her. She wanted to sink into him and forget the world she was running from, forget the world she was running towards. "She did."

✝

Phoenix sat atop a precariously stacked pile of logs in the yard behind her mother's house. She stared mournfully into the distance, and chewed on her hair. Persephone's visit was the last thing she had expected, and it broke her heart to stay. Phoenix stomped her foot on the wood beneath her, resentment building within her. Why must she be the protector of a woman who had failed to protect her? Phoenix clenched her hands into fists. She wanted to scream, to shout, to smash something. She wanted to explode into a thousand tiny pieces.

"Phoenix?" came a male voice from behind her. Drew climbed over the fence and into the yard.

"What on earth are you doing here?" she asked. "I can just about fathom Persephone finding me, but both of you in one day?"

"Persephone? Do you mean Sphenya?" Drew nodded slowly to himself. There was a glimmer of curiosity in his eyes. She could almost see the speed of the thoughts whirring inside his brain.

"The one and only."

"I ran into her, in a cafe in god knows where. We've been travelling together since then. She's changed a lot since I last saw her, though I can't quite put my finger on how."

"Why did you leave?"

"I wanted a simpler life," he said. "I missed it."

"Poor Elizaveta," Phoenix said, "losing both her best staff in under a year."

"Fate is a cruel master."

"It certainly is."

Drew was silent for a moment. Then he said "I used to have a dog."

"So?" All Phoenix wanted was to forget Persephone's visit, forget she had had a chance to leave this hellish place. The longer Drew talked, the longer this pain dragged out. She had made a promise to herself, a promise to protect her mother, to right the wrongs of fourteen years ago. The abandoned could not become the abandoner.

"I loved him more than anything in the world," Drew continued. "He was a Samoyed, a beautiful dog..." His face creased into a nostalgic smile.

"The point being?"

"His name was Cerberus, and—"

"Cerberus? You've got to be kidding me."

"Cerberus used to bite me, all the time. My father told me I should get him put down – I was covered in tooth marks from head to toe. I loved Cerberus too much. As fate would have it, he died a year later." Drew patted her shoulder. She flinched and he hastily withdrew his hand. "But that's not the point, Phoenix."

"I would never have an animal killed," she said. "No matter how much he bit me."

"I'm with you on that one. How a man treats animals tells you a lot about his nature."

"Animals follow their instincts, they're not meant to live by our rules," Phoenix said. "Humans, though? Humans are evil. I often wonder why we deserve to survive."

"Did you come to a conclusion?"

"We don't, we were never meant to survive. Look what happened." She gestured around her. "This world... It used to be huge, yet the Earth tried to shake us off, tried to rid itself of these monsters that inhabit it. We destroyed half this planet, filled it with Dead Zones. And we're still here, clinging on, still living to fight another day. I hate being human. I hate it."

"What would you be?" Drew asked her. "If you could be a different type of creature?"

152

"I'd be an owl," she said. "Or an eagle. I want to fly. No," she paused to consider, "I'd be a phoenix, if I could. I'd be reborn from my own destruction. What would you be?"

"A dog." Phoenix nodded slowly. She could picture him as a dog, a mutt with shaggy brown fur, winning hearts with his placid temperament.

"Like the dog you made up?"

"Who says I made him up?" Drew asked in mock horror.

"Cerberus, really? It fits too perfectly."

"I never knew you were also a fan of Greek mythology."

"Not a fan," Phoenix said, "but I've certainly read about it. Cerberus guards the underworld. Persephone is the queen of the underworld. You do the maths."

"Smart."

"It's my one good quality."

"You can't protect your mother, Phoenix." Drew's tone grew serious as he cut to the chase. "It's her choice. Her situation is awful, but she's there with her eyes wide open."

"What would you know?" Phoenix asked. "You have no idea! This isn't the first time Mum's been with a man who's pure evil. When you're four years old, all you can do is watch. I'm older now; I can protect her the way she never protected me."

"Is that why you're here, because she left you with an abuser?" Drew asked. He took Phoenix's hand and looked firmly into her eyes. She didn't flinch when he touched her this time, she understood it was a reflex, his attempt to comfort her. "You're so young, Phoenix; it's not your responsibility to protect your mother. You have clearly suffered a lot at the hands of an abusive man – your father, I'm guessing. You have no obligation to stay in this place. She is your mother, not the other way around. You shouldn't have to protect her, Phoenix; it's her job to protect you."

"I know that," Phoenix said. "But I have a point to prove. She abandoned me when I was four years old, left me with the most evil man I've ever known. She left, and she didn't take me with her. I'm staying, to set an example. I'm not staying just for her, I'm staying for my little sisters. How do I know she won't abandon them?"

"I respect your decision," Drew said, "and I respect your

sacrifice. I'm sorry you have to deal with this."

"There's no value in pity. I made my choices." As he turned to leave, Phoenix called out "Hey, Drew! Can you give this to Sphenya for me?" She pulled a flame-shaped pendant from around her neck. It was fashioned from old, tattered metal, and hung on a length of braided, grey ribbon. "It's something to remember me by." She pushed her dark hair behind her ears, and stood a little straighter, forcing a false smile onto her face.

"I'll give it to her," Drew said, taking the pendant from her hand.

"Look after her for me?" Phoenix asked of him. "She needs someone to guide her; she's hopelessly naïve about the real world. Remind her to think before she makes stupid decisions. Her ambition can lead her astray at times." It took all her strength not to break down. "Tell her I love her. I'm a better person because of her."

"I'll tell her everything." He held his arms open to give her a parting hug, but she shook her head in response.

Phoenix watched as Drew departed. She felt the presence of tears, lurking in the corners of her eyes, and blinked them away hurriedly. This was not the time to cry.

"Persephone?" Drew called, when he was certain no one else was within earshot.

"Yeah?" She ran through the long grass towards him. "What is it?"

Realisation dawned across her face. The realisation turned to fear, then outright panic. Her eyes widened, and her pale face blanched to a deeper shade of milky white. Her mouth opened and closed.

"Drew," Persephone spoke hurriedly, her voice laced with terror. "Drew, you can't tell anyone, I beg you. This has to remain a secret, I can't go back! I'm sorry I lied to you, but please, please don't report me. I need a fresh chance, I need a future. I can't spend my life with him, I can't reduce myself to being the wife of a man who neither loves me nor cares for me. Please, Drew. Please

154

pretend for me!" Her breath came in shallow gasps, and her eyes held his with a panicked fervour.

"Your secret is safe with me, Persephone." He took her hand and gave it a squeeze. "Who am I to judge you? I respect you, and I respect your reasoning. I won't tell anyone. I promise."

"Are you even human?" she asked, allowing herself to laugh with relief. "You're just too perfect. I mean, you're a bit weird, and your sense of humour is rather odd, not to mention the fact you're dramatic in non-dramatic situations, and not dramatic at all in situations that would actually merit drama. You are mostly perfect."

"As lovely as your rant was," he smiled, "I do feel the need to point out the oxymoron of 'mostly perfect'."

"You know what I mean." She floundered, unsure how to express her point without digging herself further into a hole. "How did you know? I knew you suspected I was me, but what made you certain?"

Drew looked at Persephone, studied the fire in her eyes, brighter even than the flame-like hue of her hair. He had seen all kinds of beauty in his twenty-two years, but she was something else entirely.

"I went to see Phoenix," he said. Her hand was still cushioned within his own. He reached into his pocket with his free hand, and retrieved the pendant. "She gave me this to give to you." He passed it to Persephone, who glanced at it briefly before slipping it over her head. It slithered under the collar of her dress, lost beneath the fabric.

"She always wears that thing," Persephone said. "I barely noticed it because it was always there; it was as much a part of her as her brown hair or her all-knowing smirk."

"She also said to tell you she loves you, that you've made her a better person," Drew said. "And something about reminding you to be wise when making stupid decisions. Her word, not mine!"

Persephone laughed. "Of course she said that, that is so Phoenix. She can never be nice to me without insulting me." Her voice still bubbled with the nervous laugh of relief.

"Why did you run away, Persephone?" Drew asked.

"I shouldn't tell you so much about it." She glanced to make

155

sure no one was behind her. "I barely know you. I want to trust you, but it's better to be safe that sorry."

"What are you talking about?" he teased. "You're always sorry for something or other."

"You've completely got the wrong idea about me," she said. "I'm not sorry for anything."

"What a callous woman you are…" Their eyes met and he grinned.

"No, I just mean… Everything I regret, it's made me who I am. Why should I be sorry?"

"You always seem to be sorry for the little things."

"Well, you're always dramatic about the little things."

"I guess we're the perfect match."

Their eyes locked onto each other again. Drew dropped his gaze quickly.

"I'm sorry," he said. "I didn't mean it like that. I just talk sometimes, say things I shouldn't. Forgive me."

"There's nothing to forgive."

Drew sighed, embarrassed, searching for something to say to erase his slip. He settled for a change of subject.

"What are you going to do, now that Phoenix isn't coming with you? I presume you won't return to the Tsar?"

Persephone considered. Her eyebrows scrunched together in concentration. Drew watched her intently, flicking his eyes away before she could catch him staring.

"I can't go back to my husband," she said after some thought. "I have nowhere to go. I don't belong anywhere. I spent most of my life on a vineyard in Greece, then the Tsar brought me to Moscow. I've never known anything but captivity. Even freedom isn't free. I may not be imprisoned or enslaved, but my life is not my own. I have to hide my identity, and I can never marry again. But worst of all, I have no purpose, no reason to go forward. I've gotten myself into this huge mess, and there's no way out!" She clenched and unclenched her fists in frustration as she spoke.

"You could come with us," Drew said. The words escaped from his mouth before the thought had fully formed in his mind.

"To Estonia?" Persephone asked.

"Yes. No one would think to look for you there, and the chances of you finding someone to fall in love with in the scarcely populated Borderlands are second to zero, so that's two problems solved." He hoped she could be tempted by the small hope he had to offer her. He felt a responsibility for her, now that he knew her secret.

"What if I fell in love with you?" Persephone asked.

Drew looked down into her open, young face. There was such an air of innocence about her, yet he could tell she knew more of the world than he gave her credit for. He knew, in spite of his relentless conscience telling him otherwise, that he wanted her, wanted to know her.

"What if?" he whispered in response to Persephone's challenge.

"I'll come with you," she said suddenly. The air between them was tight and heavy. When their eyes met this time, he didn't look away.

"That's wonderful," said Drew.

Persephone gave him her brightest smile, her white teeth flashing in the midday sunshine, her dimples deepening with joy.

Drew hugged her on impulse. "To a bright, bright future," he said as they broke apart.

"The brightest," Persephone agreed.

"Will you come with us?" Persephone asked Sol, after she informed him of Drew's offer. They sat apart from the rest of the group, prolonging what could be their last moments of solitude together.

"No, Sphenn." Sol crushed her hopes in only two words. "I'm not made for adventure. If Phoenix won't come with us, I'm going back to Moscow."

"What about me?" Persephone couldn't believe what she was hearing. They had gone to such lengths to escape that city. "You're all I've got! If you stay here, I'll be all alone. I've lost everything, I can't lose you too!"

"Come back to Moscow, Sphenn," Sol said.

"You know I can't."

"I can't believe you've chosen these strangers over me. You won't survive alone, you know that. You need me!"

157

"I didn't choose them, Sol. I chose me. If I return to Moscow, Haden will find me. That city is full of cameras, this whole country is! If I go to Estonia with Drew and the others, I can start a new life. I can be free in a way I never will be in Western Russia."

"I can protect you."

"You know that's not true. Haden will destroy me."

"The Tsar will get what's coming to him. He'll lose his power soon, believe me."

"What do you mean?" She didn't like the certainty in his voice. "You sound like you're up to something."

"Let's just say I found his weak spot," Sol said with a cruel smile. He looked like a stranger now.

"Weak spot?" A thrill ran through her stomach at the prospect of bringing down the Tsar. She tried to ignore the savage glint in her friend's eyes.

Sol reached into his bag, and produced a collection of photographs. Persephone took them from his hand, apprehensive of what she would see. In the seconds before she caught sight of the images depicted, she imagined scenes of violence, cruelty— something terrible enough for the Tsar to be punished—and she would be free from her marriage.

Instead, she saw her husband lying naked in the arms of her friend.

"When did this happen?" Persephone asked, trying to swallow the stab of pain and jealousy that lurked in the passage of her throat, barely allowing words to pass. She didn't know what hurt more: that both men had betrayed her, or that Sol had kept it from her.

"The night before your wedding."

"Okay," Persephone said, "okay, so that happened. Wow. You learn something new every day." Tears prickled behind her eyes. It felt silly to cry, she had known her marriage wasn't real. But for Sol, of all people, to seduce her husband, heightened the betrayal.

"I did this for you, Persephone!" Sol said. "I did this for you, and me, and Phoenix. I let that man defile me, so we can have leverage over him. We can blackmail him with these photos. Or we can release them, and the public will turn against him!"

"I thought you were in love with him!" Persephone shouted,

losing her fragile grip on her temper.

"In love with him?" Sol snorted. "I'm not gay. I'm not a pervert like your husband."

"Do you have copies of these?" she asked. Anger seethed within her. She didn't know who Sol was any more.

"No, they're all I've got." He reached for the photos. Persephone snatched her hand away.

"I will keep hold of these, thank you very much." She made a snap decision. Regardless of her anger at the Tsar, she refused to let him be publicly shamed for his sexuality. "Listen to me, Sol," she took a step backwards, so he couldn't reach for the pictures again, "you will take your homophobic ass right out of my life, and you will leave both me and Phoenix alone. You will also leave my husband alone. You will stay out of all of our lives. What he does in private is no one's business but his. It is not your call to out him. Where is your humanity?"

"Where was his humanity when he stole me away from my family? He kidnapped me, he took me away from everyone I love! A man like that should not be Tsar."

"And a lowlife like you shouldn't be my friend. Get out of my sight. Now!"

"Sphenn, please!" Sol begged. "I did this for you! I did this to save you from your sham of a marriage."

"I don't need you to save me," Persephone said through gritted teeth. "I don't need you, or Haden, or Phoenix, or anyone else, to save me. I can save myself. Right now I am saving myself from you and your toxic hatred. You are not my friend any more. I told you to leave, so leave!"

"Fine," Sol spat. "But this is not over! You don't get to decide when our friendship ends. I will be back! You know you're being unreasonable, Sphenya. I would forgive my friends for anything. I would never cut someone out of my life like this!"

"I am not you."

"He deserves this. You know he does. Give me the pictures back!"

"No, he doesn't." She pulled a pack of matches out of her bag. "He deserves retribution for the way he treats his people, sure. But he doesn't deserve to be punished for being gay, Sol!"

159

"That man is a monster, how can you not see that?"

Persephone clamped the photos between her teeth and struck a match.

"If you believe that," she said, "then you are the monster." She held the flame up to the photographs, and watched the evidence of her husband's adultery disintegrate into ashes.

# Chapter Thirteen

Persephone sat with Drew, beside the final flickering flames of a campfire. Their companions had gone to bed, leaving them alone in the hour before night turned to morning. The world was silent, save for the sound of the crackling fire and the urgent beating of nervous hearts.

"How are you feeling?" Drew asked. His voice was soft in the near darkness, a comforting disruption to the solitude of Persephone's thoughts.

"I'm fine, I guess. I think I'm in shock." The earth beneath her hands was cold with night air, despite its proximity to the fire.

"It's okay to be sad," he said. "It's okay to be shocked, too. Losing friends is hard, and you lost two in one day."

"It was hard," Persephone said. Her voice caught in her throat. The ground seemed to sway beneath her. She closed her eyes and sucked in a deep breath.

"What's wrong?" Drew asked.

"I'm used to having them by my side, and they're gone. Just like that. There was no warning, no time to get used to their absence." Persephone hesitated, breathing deeply until her dizziness passed. "Sol and I had a fight, before he left. He wasn't who I thought he was, and I can't reconcile who he is with the person I chose as a friend." A slight sob escaped her. She bit down hard on her lip to stop herself from crying.

Drew took her hand, cupping it between his own. This slight caress sent tingles through her body, it made her want to burn with a fire she tried hard to conceal.

"Have you ever loved someone unconditionally?" Persephone asked. She looked down at their touching hands.

"No," he said. "There are always conditions on love, whether we see them at the time or not."

"I've only ever loved Phoenix and Sol," said Persephone. "I thought I loved them both unconditionally. After today, I don't know if that's true. I saw a side of Sol that I wish I hadn't seen. I don't know if it hurts so much because I love him, or because I don't. As for Phoenix, I can't help thinking if she really loved me, she wouldn't have stayed."

"Only you can know how you feel about Sol," said Drew. "But Phoenix loves you, I've heard her say so. Love looks different to different people. Do you want to talk about your fight with Sol?"

"I can't. It's not my secret to tell."

"I'm good with secrets. If you change your mind, I'm here."

"Why? You barely know me. Why do you care?"

"I've been travelling for the best part of seven years," Drew said. "It's a lonely life. You learn to make connections quickly, or not at all. It's true, I haven't known you long. But that doesn't mean I shouldn't care for you."

"Okay," Persephone said. "I'm so lost right now. I feel like I'm falling, continuously, and I know that soon I'll hit the ground. I thought Sol was there to catch me. But he failed me."

"Persephone," Drew said, "I know it's not the same, but my arms will be here to catch you, no matter how far you fall."

"Thank you." Persephone wondered if he knew she was falling at that moment. Right there, by the light of the fire, she almost felt brave enough to say it, to tell him he had given her hope when she thought all hope was lost. She rested her hand on his leg, heat radiated into her skin through the coarse denim of his jeans. Persephone looked briefly into Drew's eyes, and leaned in close. His breath was warm against her mouth, his lips millimetres away from her own.

"No." He turned away from her. "You're married to another man."

"Oh?" Hot tears burnt in her eyes as she realised the weight of his response. "You're saying I can't touch another man whilst I'm still married? I'll live the rest of my life alone." She fought hard against the sobs rising in her throat. "Let me ask you one thing." She looked directly into his eyes. "If I hadn't been married to another man, would you have let me kiss you?"

"I can't answer that." His whole face betrayed him.

"I should get some sleep." She stood up.

"I hope this doesn't make things awkward between us," Drew said. He reached his arm to touch her, and hastily withdrew it.

"Please forget it happened."

"Forget what happened?"

✝

Persephone didn't sleep at all that night. She lay wrapped in the soft blankets Sol had stolen from the Tsar's palace, now discoloured from nights spent sleeping on damp grass. The stars faded and the sun began to rise. The first person to wake was Drew. He walked towards her, his tall figure striding through the tangles of long grass, wet with the morning dew.

"Couldn't you sleep?" he asked, as Persephone stood up to meet him.

"Not at all." In spite of her best efforts to avoid his gaze, she found her eyes constantly drawn to him, she couldn't look away.

"I'm sorry."

"It's not your fault," she lied.

"I'm sorry about what happened. And I am truly sorry about what didn't happen."

"Forget it. I overreacted. It's not a big deal."

"We both know it is." He placed his hands on her hips. His touch was firm and commanding. She took a sharp intake of breath. "I don't know why you ran away from your husband. I should have followed my instincts, screw rationality"

"What did your instincts tell you?" Drew's closeness stole Persephone's breath from her. His index finger traced along the line of her lips, awakening in her a passion that didn't hurt, a passion that wasn't a shard of glass in her heart, but a gentle ache, a soft wearing away of the barriers she had so quickly constructed in the name of self-preservation.

"A beautiful girl tried to kiss me, and, in that moment, I should have kissed her, even if nothing could ever come of it."

"What do your instincts tell you now?" Her lips moved against his finger, her heart raced in her chest.

"They tell me to run as far away from you as I possibly can," Drew said. "I want to kiss you so much, I'll explode if I don't."

"It would be a shame if you exploded." Her whisper was barely audible now.

"Yes, an awful shame. If I kiss you now, Persephone, will you forgive me for the fact it can never happen again?"

She nodded.

163

"Good."

Drew leaned into the small space between them, so they were barely a centimetre apart. They looked into each other's eyes for a long moment, their lips so close they were almost touching, yet still not quite. The hairbreadth of space between them had the width of an ocean, and the depth of an abyss. Persephone knew the dam that would burst when they touched would be impossible to reseal.

Persephone took Drew's face in her hands, and brought his mouth to hers. His strong hands pressed firmly against her back, his warmth sent the chills of early morning into the distant shadows where they belonged. Her hands moved to his neck, pulling him closer to her, knowing that the moment she let go, she could never hold him again.

"Who knew committing treason could feel so good?" Drew asked, when he finally pulled away.

"Treason?" Persephone asked, alarmed.

"Kissing the Tsarina certainly qualifies as betraying the Tsar."

"I'm sorry," she said. "I know you have an issue with me saying sorry, but I am sorry."

"No," Drew said, "I'm the one who should be sorry. It won't happen again. I just needed to get it out of my system."

"Was that all it meant to you?" she asked, dismayed.

"It meant a lot more," he promised her. "But we both agreed it could never happen again."

"Of course," she said. "Never again."

"We should go and sort breakfast." Drew walked back to the ashes of the previous night's fire. Persephone followed at his heels.

"Do you think the others will be up soon?" she asked, as he lit the fire.

"Probably." His back was turned to her as he focused intently on his task. "We've got to be at the train station by late afternoon, and it's a good few hours walk from here, so if they're not up in an hour we'll have to wake them. They both sleep like the dead."

"No need to wake me." Grigory said in her ear. Persephone turned to face him, startled.

164

"Where did you spring from?" Drew asked.

"I've been up for hours!" Grigory said.

"You have?" Drew and Persephone asked in unison.

"I have!"

They stared at each other in horror, wondering how much he could have seen, and worse, how much he could have heard.

"What?" Grigory feigned a look of innocence. Persephone groaned inwardly. She knew what would happen. Grigory would mention it to Drew, and the guilt-riddled Drew would say it had been a mistake. Grigory would ask why. Drew would explain, and her cover would be blown. She knew Grigory wouldn't be able to keep his mouth shut for five minutes if he knew.

"You must be tired," Persephone said lamely.

"Not in the slightest," said Grigory. "You must be."

"I'm wide awake." She smiled at him, though her current plans involved wringing his neck. The grin stayed plastered to his face.

Drew gave his brother a warning look, and Persephone relaxed a little.

"Did you sleep well, brother dearest?" Grigory was enjoying himself.

"No," Drew said. "I had the strangest nightmare. The Tsar was overthrown, and I had to rule in his place. But you were my advisor, and led me into all kinds of trouble."

The mention of her husband caused a gnawing pain in Persephone's heart. She couldn't help thinking of all that she would lose because of that marriage. She refused to let her emotions show, not whilst Grigory watched her like a hawk.

✝

Haden dreamt of Persephone. In this dream, the Tsar was a young boy of three years old. His yellow-blonde hair was combed neatly in a centre parting, and his icy eyes were wide as he entered the library. Persephone stood by the tall floor-to-ceiling window, in the far corner of the room. She gazed out across the Moscow of Haden's childhood. The brightly coloured turrets of Saint Basil's Cathedral, rising up to the sky, seemed almost small across the great expanse of Red Square. Persephone turned to him, and it was not his bride whom he looked upon. The pumpkin colour of her hair turned to a rich, chocolate brown, and her eyes transformed until they were as icy as his own. It was not Haden's wife who stood before him, but Rhea: his mother.

"Haden, my darling!" she called out as he ran towards her. She spoke with Persephone's voice. "Come here," she said, scooping him up into her arms. "Come watch the city with me, my darling. This is your uncle's city, and one day it will be yours."

"Mine?" little Haden asked.

"Yes, darling," Rhea said. "Your big brother Poseidon is the heir to your father's throne, back home in the East, and your brother Zeus has set off to run a vineyard in Greece. You are all that's left for Western Russia, Haden, you will rule one day." It wasn't real, he knew the timeline didn't add up. Rhea was long dead by the time Zeus left for Greece. His mother's face was so real that Haden could believe it was a memory.

"I don't want to rule!" Haden said. He was older now, a nineteen-year-old man who had just been told his uncle was dying. "I never wanted this. I never wanted to inherit that god-awful country, Father. I want to be a scientist!"

Haden stood in his father's study, in a grand palace in Vladivostok, Eastern Russia.

"Haden," Kronus said sternly, "you do not belong here. You have lived in Western Russia since you were ten years old, since I learnt it wasn't safe for you to live here any more. Go back to your uncle, back to your country." He was taller than his son, with slick black hair, and deep lines carved into his cheeks. His eyes burned black as tourmaline.

"Listen to me, Father!" Haden's voice ripped through the air with an intensity he had never before been able to muster. "I. Do. Not. Want. To. Rule! I will be good, I promise. I won't do anything bad ever again, just let me come home. Please!"

"You have spent too long playing God, Haden," Kronus said. "Your lust for power is as insatiable as your mother's. At least once you are Tsar you will have an outlet for your eccentricities."

"Why can't Zeus inherit my uncle's throne? He is far older than I am. Let us trade places, let me go to Greece and live with Demeter, live with—"

166

"That is the last thing I would allow you to do," Kronus said, before the scene changed.

Haden was surrounded by a thick white mist that moved in tendrils, circling him, tangling him in a web. The mist began to form into a shape, a human figure, with long, ginger hair, and hands as cold as a corpse. Even in her state of demise, Haden longed to kiss Persephone. Yet as he brought his lips to hers, all he saw was his mother's face, a mask constantly flickering across his wife's.

Haden awoke, disgusted at the inner workings of his mind. He thought of Persephone, and shuddered. He wanted her with every cell of his being, but he knew that should they ever be together, he would consume her completely. She belonged to him in ways she would never understand. They couldn't truly coexist unless she accepted him as her maker, her God, her husband, her creator. He had designed everything about her. She was his. Completely.

☦

"You and Drew, huh?" Grigory asked.

They stood on the platform of a small train station in a village in the depths of rural Western Russia.

"I don't know what you're talking about," Persephone said curtly. Her eyes lingered on the dark metal rungs of the tracks. It was midday, and the sun burned hot in the sky, singeing Persephone's skin to a bright tomato-red.

"Funny." Grigory chewed gum as he spoke. "Drew said the exact same thing. You were kissing this morning, but you both deny it. Why could that be?"

The sound of his chewing grated on Persephone's nerves. She slowly inhaled and exhaled, focusing on her breath to keep the anger at bay.

"Maybe because you're married to another man?" Grigory suggested. "A very powerful man?" There was no spite in his question, but she could sense a hunger within him, a compulsion to unveil her secret. That hunger was more detrimental than spite.

"No," Persephone said frostily. Her mind raced. "I kissed your brother because he thought I was the Tsarina."

Grigory laughed. "I think you're the Tsarina, and you haven't kissed me."

"How surprising! A man thinks because a woman kisses one man she must kiss all others for the same reason!" Persephone said. "You want to know the difference between Drew's accusation and yours? He actually asked me. He asked me if I was the Tsarina, and I told him no. He didn't believe me. I kissed him to prove I wasn't a married woman. That's the end of it."

Grigory considered for a moment. "That does make sense, to some extent," he said. "But it doesn't explain why you're both so awkward about it. Any idiot can tell you like each other. Why deny it?"

"That's because of me." Persephone tried to think as fast as she was speaking. "I'm nineteen, for God's sake! I'm travelling to the middle of nowhere to start a new life with a bunch of people I hardly know. I like Drew, but I don't want to be tied to him forever, and I'm worried if I get with him now, that's what will happen."

"The train will arrive in a minute." Drew approached them. "Rozalina will need some help loading the donkey into the animal carriage. Maybe you could assist her, Grigory?"

Grigory shot Persephone one last suspicious look as he walked away.

"I'm sorry he keeps bothering you," Drew said.

"He asked about this morning," Persephone said in a low tone. "I had to tell him a story to shut him up."

"What kind of story?"

"I kept as close to the truth as possible. I told him I kissed you because you thought I was the Tsarina, and I did it to convince you I wasn't."

"What did he say to that?"

'He wasn't fooled. He asked why we were acting so awkward about it. I told him I don't want to be with you because I'm so young and I feel like if we get together now I would be stuck with you forever."

"Stuck with me?" Drew looked hurt.

"No, no!" Persephone said hurriedly. "Drew, I didn't mean it! I'd love to be stuck with you. But I had to say something to Grigory, because he's not going to let either of us live this down."

Persephone's words were drowned out by roar of the train as it pulled into the station.

"Come on." Drew grabbed her hand, and led her onto the train. Persephone looked around her. They were alone in a small carriage, empty of any seating. After a moment, the train began to move again with increasing speed, knocking them both backwards. They fell into a heap against the far wall of the carriage.

"Sorry." Persephone rolled off Drew and onto the hard floor.

"Don't apologise for that. I'd do anything to get you on top of me. Sorry," he added quickly. "That comment was deeply inappropriate. I beg for your forgiveness." His face clouded over, his mouth turned down into a frown.

"What are we gonna do, Drew?" Persephone asked. "I barely know you, I don't want to have feelings for you, but I do."

"Persephone," Drew said. "If things were different... But they're not. I can't be with you, not like this. I'm not that kind of man."

"Damn you and your morality," Persephone said. "Why did he have to come first? Why couldn't it have been you who took me out of that place?"

"What would we learn, if life gave us everything we wanted?"

"I would have learnt much more from you than I learnt from him." Persephone wrapped her arms around him, pressing her cheek against the soft fabric of his plaid shirt. "He taught me to be a prisoner. Drew, you could teach me how to love, how to be loved."

"Shh." Drew pressed a finger to Persephone's lips. "You break my heart with every word you say."

"These words have to be said! The universe needs to know how cruel it is! It can hear me, I know it can!"

"Is there any chance the Tsar would go for a nice, quick annulment?"

"There are plenty of grounds for one," Persephone said. "The marriage was never consummated. But who'd believe me over him?"

"You two... you never?" His eyes widened as it dawned on him, and he nodded slowly. "Ah, I hate him slightly less now."

"So my virginity makes me more valuable in your eyes?" Persephone asked.

"No," Drew said softly. "I'm glad you didn't have to be with

169

a man who didn't love you. Your virginity makes no difference to my feelings for you."

"Can we please change the subject?" Persephone asked, turning away to hide her crimson face. "I hate talking about it. Yet I was the one who brought it up. God, what's wrong with me?"

"Nothing is wrong with you." Drew took Persephone's chin in his hand, directing her face back towards him. "You have gone through a lot since marrying the Tsar, and you haven't been able to talk about it. Wanting to discuss this, it's a natural response. You can talk to me. About any of it, even the stuff that makes you blush. I want to be your friend, Persephone. Let me be that to you."

✝

The train travelled across vast expanses of Russian countryside, through green pastures, small villages, large towns, and forests that lasted for miles and miles. The journey finally concluded on a solitary platform at the very end of the line. They were the last passengers on the train.

"There's a story about this place," Drew told Persephone. The platform was surrounded by fields of drying grass. The uniformity of the land was broken only by a tiny white cottage a little way off, and a small cluster of trees beyond the cottage.

"A story?" Persephone asked. She couldn't imagine there would be any story to tell about a place as abandoned as this.

"A man and a woman fell in love," Drew said, "but they couldn't be together."

"Sounds familiar," Persephone said under her breath.

"So they decided to run away," he continued. "She promised to meet him here, at the end of the line, but she never showed. Every day he went to the station – there was a station here once. He even built a house near the tracks." Drew pointed to the small whitewashed cottage in the field beyond the platform. "He waited years for her, but she never came. Then one day, when he was an old, old man, he saw her: a woman, dressed all in white. There are two different versions of the story. One ends with her eventually coming to find him, after he waited here for sixty years. In the other, she's a ghost, who comes to ease him into the next life.

There's a song based on it too." Drew's voice was forlorn. "Hardly anyone comes this far on the train any more, there's no reason to. They say the house is haunted."

"How could she abandon him like that?" Persephone asked. "If I loved somebody, I could never leave them."

He bit his lip, looking away from her. "Maybe she was married," he said softly.

His words were like a punch to the gut.

"I want to see," she said. "I want to see the house."

"It's just a house, Sphenya."

"Then you'll have no problem with me seeing it."

Drew sighed. He smiled against his will. "You're very stubborn, aren't you?"

"According to Phoenix, it's the only personality trait I have." Persephone jumped over the faded-white picket fence, and into the field that surrounded the house.

"Wait for me!" Drew ran after her through the long grass.

Persephone ran to the door of the old, dilapidated house, and attempted to prise it open. It stayed firmly shut.

"It's locked," she said as Drew caught up with her, out of breath from the run.

"It won't be. There's no reason to lock an abandoned cottage in the middle of nowhere. It's probably just jammed. This door won't have been opened 70 years."

"That long?" she asked.

"That's how old the song is, give or take."

Drew shoved hard against the old wood, and the door swung open, letting out a gust of stale air. They exchanged a look, daring each other to be the first to cross the threshold. Persephone took a deep breath, and entered the one-room cottage. It was small, dark, and a strong smell of decay permeated the ancient air. She took a few moments to grow accustomed to the lack of light. Once she could see, she began to explore.

A double bed stood in the corner of the room. A chair and table, covered in cobwebs, were placed at the bed's end. Persephone's attention was caught by an old, gold-framed portrait above the mantel piece. Staring out from the canvass was a young woman, who couldn't have been much older than Persephone herself.

Chestnut-brown hair fell in cascades over her shoulders. Her crimson, rosebud lips demanded attention, and her narrow blue eyes surveyed the imposters with a life-like stare. A straight nose, and the slightest hint of dimples, completed the image before them.

"She looks like you," Drew said.

"No, she doesn't." It became imperative for Persephone that she must have no connection whatsoever to the woman in the portrait.

"She does. Her hair's a different colour, but the face is the same. Beautiful."

"The song?" Persephone asked. "Sing it to me."

"No," Drew said. "There's enough heartache between us. We don't need to take on their tragedy as well as our own. I'll sing it to you one day, when the wound isn't as fresh."

## Chapter Fourteen

The rough dirt road turned to mud beneath Phoenix's damp feet, as rain crashed down from the dark sky. Wind billowed through the trees, howling like werewolves at a full moon. She scowled up at the hostile sky, pushing her rain-soaked hair away from her eyes. Phoenix shivered with cold as she opened the door of her mother's house. The first strike of lightning flashed across the black night sky as she stomped across the threshold.

"Whereyoubeen?" slurred Yuri. Phoenix knelt in front of the fire to dry herself. His voice made her uneasy. He was a ticking time-bomb, waiting to go off, and she didn't want to be there when he exploded.

"Out." She stared into the yellow glow of the weak flames. "I was looking for Mum. She said she'd be back by now." Her mother's absence filled her with a sense of foreboding. Phoenix had been careful to avoid Yuri. Now the two were alone. The insecure, childlike part of her that she had fought to suppress yearned for her mother's presence, to protect her – as if Katya had ever been good at that.

"Don't call her that!" he yelled, startling her. By now, Phoenix was used to her stepfather's violent rages, yet she had not expected this, not tonight. Something about the intensity of the weather outside had lulled her into thinking home was a haven, albeit an unstable one. The stark reality of the situation hit her with a hard blow.

"She was mine before she was yours," Phoenix said. A voice in her head told her to breathe through the resentment and jealousy that boiled below the surface, but her impulsive nature got the better of her, and there was no going back.

"She never wanted you," Yuri told her. "She saw you for the filthy brat you are, and she left you." In this drunken state, her stepfather seemed more petulant than dangerous.

"She was pregnant, wasn't she?" Phoenix asked, as it dawned on her. "She must have miscarried, Olga and Irina are too young to fit the timeline. But she must have been pregnant. She wouldn't have left me for you otherwise." There was no spite in her voice now, she spoke with clarity, as she solved the mystery that had haunted her for over a decade.

"Wouldn't she?" Yuri asked. "What makes you so sure?"

"Simply the fact that my mother is a coward and my father is evil," Phoenix said. "You don't try to escape someone like him unless you've got a damn good reason. My mother barely has a self-preservation instinct, and, in spite of what she might say, she would never have left because of her undying, all-consuming love for you."

Yuri pounded his thick, meaty fist on the table. It echoed louder than the thunder outside. He took a swig from a nearby bottle of vodka.

"You stupid child," he growled.

"I'm not a child." Phoenix's laugh was bitter. "How could I still be a child when my mother stole my childhood from me?" She threw her hands up in frustration. "She stole everything from me." Her voice, which had fallen to a shaky whisper, suddenly rose again as she asked "Why do you hate me so much? Is it because I can defend myself, or because you hate people who aren't cowards like you?"

"Because you're just like your cunt of a father," Yuri yelled in triumphant response. He knew how to strike with his words, as well as his fists.

"I am nothing like my father!" Phoenix shouted, knocking over the table and running out into the storm, as hard sobs shook her body. She told herself it wasn't true, that Yuri had only said it to hurt her. She couldn't convince herself. Becoming her father was Phoenix's worst fear, and no matter how hard she tried to be good, to be kind, she found herself turning into him. There were moments when she had no compassion, no care for anyone but herself, and there were moments when all she could think of was the pursuit of cold intellect, of education over values, of knowledge over love. The sole gift he had bestowed her was her mind. She feared this gift would be her greatest curse, that she would lose her humanity, just as he had.

Phoenix walked briskly across the muddy ground of the small village's main street. It was late, but one building still had a light in the window: a building that served the triple role of pub, general store, and post office. She pushed open the door, brushing the tears

174

from her face, and took a seat at a table in the corner, waiting for the sobs that wracked her body to relent. When they finally did, she walked up to the bar.

"Hey, can I get a glass of wine please?" she asked, fishing in her pocket for the right change.

"How old are you?" asked the woman behind the counter.

"Eighteen."

"Do you have ID?" the woman asked. She sounded exasperated.

"No. You've met me, I'm Phoenix, Katya Lyubova's daughter."

"Phoenix?" the woman asked. "Phoenix Kashnikova?"

"Yes," she said cautiously. "Why's that?"

"A package came for you this morning," the woman said, before walking over to the closed post office in the far corner of the room. She returned with a small parcel, and handed it over.

Phoenix recognised Sol's slanted handwriting. She tore open the package. Inside, she found a letter, a bag of money, and a gun. Unfolding the letter, she read:

*Dear Phoenix,*

*You're probably wondering why I sent you money and a gun. I didn't rob any banks, I promise! I'll explain: from the beginning.*

*After you wouldn't come with me and Sphenya, we parted ways. She went with her friend (for want of a better word), Drew, to build a farm in the Estonian Borderlands, and I returned to Moscow. I had some business left to attend to, but once it is done I will join you, and the three of us can be together, where we belong.*

*Take the money, and go to Persephone. There's enough to get you to the Borderlands, and there should be enough left over to buy two train tickets to Tallinn. I sent the fruit samples to the Estonian Institute of Scientific Research, like you asked. We will destroy him, and we will be reunited.*

*You know what the gun is for. Use it to protect yourself.*

*Love,*

*Sol*

As her eyes skimmed over the final paragraph, tears flooded down Phoenix's cheeks and drenched her chest. After two years, she still hadn't warmed to Sol, but he was familiar, and his words

175

settled in a painful ache in the pit of her stomach. She missed Moscow, Persephone, Sol, and the bookshop. Phoenix almost missed the Tsar. She sobbed heavily, barely able to breathe through the pain in her heart. She went outside, where the morose weather mimicked her emotions. Soaked from top to bottom, Phoenix calculated her next move. She knew her time here was up: for better or for worse, she would leave tonight. She had no intention of living a quiet life in the Borderlands with Persephone. Estonia called out to Phoenix, but it wasn't the countryside she craved. Before departing from Moscow, she had directed Sol to send fruit samples from the Tsar's laboratory to a scientific institute in Tallinn. It was to this institute that she would go, when the time was right. First she must find Persephone, or her gateway to the Institute would be lost.

An hour's walk from the train tracks stood a cabin built from pine wood. A plaque hanging above the doorway read "the Haven" in 5 languages. Persephone read it in English and Russian, she presumed the first language was Estonian. The other two belonged to countries she did not know.

Rozalina knocked firmly on the door. There was no answer. Grigory motioned her out of the way, and turned the handle. The Haven was rustic, separated into two storeys, connected by a rough wooden staircase. Piles of wood surrounded a fireplace. A list was inscribed above the mantelpiece, but Persephone couldn't decipher the language.

"What does it say?" Grigory asked Drew.

"I can't read all of it," he said, "my Estonian isn't great. The gist is that it's a safe space for travellers to rest in, but not to make a home out of. It says do not outstay our welcome, and leave the place as we found it. It's the first building on the Estonian side of the border, built as a haven for persecuted Russians during the border conflicts."

Phoenix emerged in the doorway of her mother's house, soaking from the rain. She squeezed the water from her hair, and walked towards Yuri, who lurked in the shadows.

"Why do you say I'm like my father?" The words were a formality, she cared little for his answer. It was time for retribution, and she was no longer afraid.

Yuri took a moment to answer, as if it hurt his drunken brain to even think.

"Yougotyourmother'sstupidity," he slurred, "andhisarrogance."

Phoenix glared up at him, before stomping into the room she shared with her sisters, slamming the door behind her. It wasn't easy to be strong when every time Yuri opened his mouth he reminded her of her potential for weakness.

There was a leak in the corrugated tin roof, splashing cold rain onto Phoenix's makeshift bed. She sat down on the hard floor, hugging her knees close to her. Her sisters lay fast asleep in their own beds, ignorant of the thunder both outside and inside their home.

Yuri's voice reached through the door.

"You fucking bitch!" he yelled. "Come out here! Now!"

Phoenix slid the gun into her bra, hoping it wouldn't show or fall, and walked into the main room. Her stepfather punched her in the face upon entry.

"Bastard," she cursed, prodding tentatively at her nose. "You've improved your aim." She forced a smirk onto her face, refusing to let her fear become visible.

"We're alone." Yuri's voice was menacing. "Katya's out, and her brats are fast asleep. It's just you, and me. All alone." His laugh made Phoenix sick to her stomach.

"It's funny," she said, keeping her voice mocking, "people never come up with their own lines. I've heard that one, or, at least, variants of it, for my whole life. I lived to tell the tale. Nobody hurts me and gets away with it!" Even she knew it wasn't true. Everybody who hurt her had gotten away with it.

Yuri punched her in the chest, a rock-hard blow that barely missed the gun. She shuddered at his touch. The violent nature of the act prevented it from feeling like a violation. Her body wasn't a body, it was a battleground, and a punch to the breast was nothing but a wound of war.

"Who hurt you, Yuri Lyubov?" she asked. "Who made you into a monster?"

*Who made* me *into a monster?* Phoenix asked herself. She knew where this was going, knew how this night would end. She told herself to forgive, to have compassion for those who had no compassion for her.

*I am not my father*, whispered the voice in her head. *I am not bad, I am not cruel, I am not evil, I don't want to cause pain.*

*But what about justice?* asked that same voice.

Yuri punched her again, repeatedly, until he knocked her to the ground. When she lay helpless on the floor, he kicked her in the stomach. Phoenix hunched over, trying to make herself small, to lessen the pain. She was determined to keep from screaming. A small, pale face watched through the bedroom door, which now stood ajar: Irina.

Six years old, oval face, pointed chin, blue-green eyes... Only the white-blonde hair and pale skin distinguished her from Phoenix at that age. Suddenly it wasn't Irina she saw; it was herself as a child, watching her mother get beaten black and blue. Phoenix became aware of the ice-cold kiss of the gun against her warm breast. The chilling presence sent her fear and weakness running away into the night, and all she had left was her strength. She pressed her lips together, so no cry of pain could escape them. Phoenix stood up carefully, and pulled out the gun.

"Say you repent," she commanded, aiming the gun at Yuri's head. He spun around and saw the weapon in her hand. She trained it on his forehead, at the gap between his thick brown eyebrows.

"You wouldn't know how to use that thing," he said.

"Phoenix, don't!" Katya screamed as she came through the door, alarmed at the scene before her.

"You bitch!" Yuri thundered. "The little cunt attacked me!" He punched his wife in the face, his fist hitting her nose with a loud thump. Phoenix kept the gun firmly trained on the slick, sweaty surface of his forehead.

"Phoenix, no!" her mother repeated. Blood streamed from her broken nose.

"Shoot him," Irina whispered. "He hurt you, he hurt mama.

178

Shoot him."

Phoenix watched her little sister. Turmoil threatened to overtake her mind, limit her capacity for logic. If she crossed this line, there was no going back.

Phoenix looked at her stepfather, at the drunken, yellow pallor of his skin, at the thick hands that were capable only of causing pain. She hated him, but she wanted to hurt him, not kill him. All she wanted was peace. Tears of regret streamed down her cheeks with renewed fervour as her hands clutched the gun.

"Don't shoot him, Phoenix!" Katya yelled.

"Say you repent," Phoenix ordered. Her voice was like steel.

"No," said Yuri.

"Say I am not like my father." She was giving him a second chance, a way to end this without bloodshed.

"No."

"Say you will never do anything to hurt my mother again."

Yuri picked up Irina. "Put the gun down or I break her neck!"

The little girl shook fearfully in his arms.

"If you hurt her," Phoenix warned him, "I will shoot you in the hands and feet, and I will chop you into tiny little pieces."

"I mean it!" Yuri said.

"And I don't?" Phoenix laughed. It was the laugh of a madwoman. "What sort of man would kill his own daughter to save himself?" she asked. Madness turned to pain. She knew what sort of man did. She had met many incarnations of him in her short life: her father, the Tsar, and now Yuri. It was all too much. She couldn't go on. A tiny part of her wished she had the resolve to turn the gun upon herself. But that was not in her nature, it never had been. Phoenix had never been the type to end her own life when her problem could be solved by ending another's. A lifetime of abuse, of suffering in silence and craving revenge, had brought her to this point, and there would be no going back.

"Put the gun down, Phoenix!" Katya yelled as Yuri's hands tightened around Irina's neck.

"No." Phoenix squeezed the trigger. The shot rang out across the room. Lightning flashed outside, illuminating the darkened room. Yuri fell to the floor, blood seeping from the ugly hole in his head. Phoenix stared in horror at the gun in her hands. She threw

179

its heavy weight to the floor, and ran to the bedroom, bolting the door shut behind her. She began to sob, disgusted by the crime she had committed.

"Phoenix?" whispered Olga, who had woken at the noise. "What happened? Is Papa dead?"

"Shh," Phoenix said. Her voice sounded unnatural in her ears. "Go back to sleep."

She gathered her few possessions into a bag, and returned to the scene of her crime. Katya crouched by Yuri's body, sobbing over the small pool of blood. Irina stood by the door, watching her mother cry over her murdered father.

"Phoenix?" she asked softly.

"Shut up, Irina." Phoenix rushed to the door. Irina blocked her way.

"Where are you going?" the little girl asked.

"Get out of my way!" Phoenix lifted the child out of her path. She didn't look back.

The storm had cleared the air outside, but all she could smell was blood. Phoenix ran, ran for her life, for her future, ran because she knew any path out of here was the path to freedom. Her feet slipped continuously on the muddy tracks of the village, but mud soon turned to grass, and grass to the mossy floor of the forest, and relief was finally upon her. Phoenix fell to her hands and knees, and kissed the pine-needle-scented earth with religious fervour. Her tears mixed with the soft dirt, and here, alone in this black expanse of forest, she felt safe for the first time in her life. Tomorrow, Phoenix would have to come to terms with what she had done, but tonight, she allowed herself to consider the possibility that she had acted out of compassion, not vengeance, that she had killed to save lives, not purely to end one.

As Phoenix fell into a fitful sleep, her last thoughts were of Persephone, of the solace she would find in her absent friend.

# Chapter Fifteen

Persephone ran across the final metres of grassland, to the little white cottage by the end of the train line. She felt a connection to this tiny cottage, and the miserable story that haunted its single room. The door was open. She peered around its edge, into the gloom. Her eyes fixed on the portrait on the wall. Every time she came here she refused to look at it; it unsettled her deeply. The girl in the picture was so much like herself that it scared her to look.

When Persephone left the cottage, she noticed a figure standing on the train platform, watching her. At first she thought she had imagined it, but as she moved closer, she could see the person was familiar: slim, with dark hair. Light-brown skin, and a permanent half-smirk across her mouth. She wore black trousers and a dark green shirt, beneath a thick black jacket.

"Phoenix!" Persephone screamed. She ran at breakneck speed across the field and lifted her friend into an embrace, spinning her around until they were both dizzy.

"Sphenya." Phoenix hugged her tightly.

"How did you know where I was?" Persephone asked. They sat down on the hard concrete of the platform, their legs swinging out over the tracks.

"Solly Boy sent me a letter," Phoenix said. "He told me you'd gone to the Borderlands. I took the train here. I didn't expect to find you right by the train line."

"What about your mother?" Persephone wasn't sure it was wise to venture down this line of questioning. The mention of Sol had made her uncomfortable. She wasn't ready to broach the subject with Phoenix.

"I had to leave. Turns out she loved him after all. But it was too late by then." Phoenix fixed her eyes firmly on the metal rungs of the tracks.

"What was?"

"I did something bad. I don't want to talk about it." She fed strands of hair into the corner of her mouth and chewed them with intense concentration.

"Okay." Persephone knew better than to press her.

"So… You and Drew?" Phoenix changed the subject, her voice playful. "Typical that the only two people I don't utterly detest fall for each other.

"We're not together. I don't know what Sol told you, but we're not. He won't be with a married woman." She couldn't hide the bitterness in her voice. "Drew knows who I am, but the others don't, so try not to mention it to anyone – especially not Grigory, he's a complete prick."

"Like I would!"

"It was you who told Drew."

"I didn't know then, did I?"

The grass was soft beneath Persephone, and sunshine beamed down upon her closed eyelids. It was midday, and the residents of The Haven had taken a rest from building their new home. They sat in a wildflower meadow a few kilometres from The Haven, where they had laid the foundations for their house. Thick pine trees formed forests in the distance, a wall of darkness that bordered the sunny meadow.

"When your dog died," Phoenix asked Drew, "assuming he actually existed – did people realise how much you loved him?"

Persephone opened her eyes. She twisted the stalk of a blue flower around her finger absent-mindedly, only half listening to the conversation.

"No." Drew paused for a moment, to think up a response. "I came to see he wasn't good for me."

Persephone didn't realise what it meant until Drew spoke again.

"So your stepfather's dead?" he asked, sitting up straighter.

"Mm hm." Phoenix wouldn't meet Drew's gaze. She sat stiffly, with her limbs folded neatly together, as if they were trapped in an invisible cage.

"How did he die?"

"It was alcohol related."

Persephone watched her friend with suspicion. Phoenix had acted more evasive than usual since their reunion.

"Can I play this?" Phoenix gestured at a guitar by Drew's side.

"Only if you're good." It was Grigory who answered.

"I'm good," Phoenix said assuredly. She had taken an instant disliking to Grigory.

"Do you take requests?" Persephone tried to rid her mind of the possibility her friend was a murderer.

"If I know it."

"I'm not sure what it's called, but it's about a—"

"*End of the Line*," Drew said.

"How did you know?" Persephone asked him, their eyes met and they quickly looked away.

"I guessed."

"Get a room," Phoenix said under her breath. She watched the two of them with curiosity for a moment, then said "Yeah, I know it. It's an old song from the English Settlements. I'm surprised you've heard of it, Sphenya. I can't believe you know something I haven't taught you!"

"I don't. Drew mentioned it to me once. It was written about the train line near here."

"Oh," Phoenix said. She looked apprehensively from Persephone to Drew, then began to play a slow, bluesy tune. The ballad chronicled a doomed love affair from start to finish, laced with the refrain:

*"I will love you until the end of time*
*And I'll wait here forever*
*At the end of the line"*

Phoenix sang the final notes, and laid the guitar to rest at her side. Persephone stood up abruptly. She ran back to the Haven, up the stairs to the bedroom, where threw herself down on the bed and began to sob. It was only a matter of moments before a weight at the edge of the bed alerted her to Phoenix's presence.

"I'm so sorry, Sphenn," she said. "I didn't think. It's so obvious to me now. That song is completely you and Drew."

"I shouldn't have ever mentioned it," Persephone said into her pillow.

"Do you love him?"

"Sometimes I think I do, but I can't trust myself when it comes

183

to love. What would I know?"

Phoenix lay down beside Persephone and wrapped her arms around her.

"You do know about love," she said. "You love me, don't you? I never thought I could love anyone, or that anyone could love me. Then I met you, and you taught me how to love. Love doesn't have to be romantic. You can love Drew without wanting all that."

"But I do want 'all that', as you so eloquently put it," Persephone said. "I want romantic love. I don't know if I want it with Drew, but I want it someday. I want it so badly, and I can never have it, because I married the fucking Tsar!"

☦

Persephone woke in the early hours of the morning, and tugged her blankets tighter around her. She wasn't sure what had woken her. Perhaps it was the sound of a dog barking in the distance, or the first rays of sunlight, heralding daybreak. She was alone in the bedroom, and a light glowed at the foot of the staircase. Once her eyes adjusted, Persephone could see two figures sitting at the foot of the stairs: Drew, ruggedly handsome in a plaid shirt and jeans, and Phoenix, with a bulky green blanket wrapped around her shoulders. Grigory and Rozalina had gone to the nearest city, Narva, to pick up supplies for the house.

"I thought you might like this," said Drew, taking a book from his pocket, and handing it to Phoenix. He spoke in English. "It's a book of myths, in the old language. I've carried it around with me since I was fifteen."

"So why are you giving it to me?"

Persephone crawled across the floor to the top of the staircase, to get a better view.

"I'm not used to seeing you without a book in your hand, and you've read that letter from your friend so many times the paper's almost see-through."

Phoenix thumbed through the book. A half-smile twitched across her lips. "Greek myths. Of course."

"I lived in Greece for many years," Drew said. He took the book, and opened it to the front page. Persephone was too far away to see the handwritten inscription, but it silenced Phoenix. "I was interested in Greek mythology long before I met Persephone, you know that."

"She cares about you a lot." Phoenix glanced up the stairs. Persephone slid back into the shadows.

"She's married." Drew took the edge of the blanket, and lifted it around his own shoulders.

"On paper, that's it. She's not with her husband, she's not going back to him. You want her, she wants you, it's that simple."

"It's treason."

"Not here, it's not," Phoenix said. "The borderlands are a) technically part of Estonia, and b) do not have any laws. You're free to do what you like with Persephone, and there's nothing the Tsar can do to stop you."

"Adultery is morally wrong, I refuse to take part in it."

"I respect you for that. I respect people who live by their beliefs. I envy it, almost. Please don't break her heart. She's all I have in this world. I love her more than you will ever understand."

"She's your family, I get that. Why do you think I followed Roza and Grigory to the wilds of Estonia?"

"I would die for her. I probably will, given Sphenn's record of terrible decisions."

"You don't have to follow every emotional statement with an insult."

"Sorry, it must be my Sagittarius moon." Phoenix gave him an obnoxious smile, and tugged her blanket off his shoulders. "It must be killing you that you can't get her time of birth," she said as she stood up. "How are you going to psychoanalyse her if you can't find out her Venus is in Uranus?"

"Goodnight, Phoenix."

"Are you not going to sleep?" She hovered on the stairs, the blanket trailing on the ground behind her.

"I think I might go for a walk, watch the sunrise."

"Take this, it's cold." Phoenix dumped the blanket over his head. "Thanks for the book."

Persephone slammed her eyelids shut as Phoenix crawled into bed beside her. She lay stock still, curled into a corner against the wall.

185

"You're awake," Phoenix announced.

"How do you know?"

"You held your breath, and you're not snuggling me like you usually do."

"I don't snuggle," she said, wrapping her arms around her friend for warmth.

"You're doing it right now!"

"Well you always kick me when you're asleep."

"How much did you overhear?" Phoenix asked. Worry crept into her voice.

"He gave you a book," Persephone said. "You talked about me, and astrology. That was it."

"Okay."

"Phoenix?"

"Yup?"

"If there are no laws in the Borderlands does that mean there's nothing stopping me from being a bigamist?"

"You're nineteen! Do you really want a second husband already?"

"I'm serious. I don't mean now, but one day."

"Technically, yes," Phoenix said. "Realistically, no. There are no laws here, but there are also no churches or registry offices. If you wanted to remarry you would have to leave the Borderlands and either return to Western Russia, or go into Estonia proper. I don't know what the Estonian laws are, but I can't imagine they allow bigamy. You can't remarry. But if you can convince Drew to live in sin, you have a bright, bright future ahead of you."

"Great," Persephone said. "We can have a couple of bastards and be one great big illegitimate happy family."

"Why do you care about legitimacy?" Phoenix asked.

"I don't, not really," Persephone said. "I care about freedom. I don't feel free in a country where the law is against me."

"He might die young."

"Drew?"

"The Tsar."

"I don't wish him dead."

"Me neither."

"I don't know what I'm meant to do," Persephone said. "I have

186

my whole life to live, and I'm not free to live it."

"Freedom doesn't exist, not even free will."

"That's not a very atheistic thing to say."

"I'm not saying our actions are determined by an almighty God. I just think there are external factors: nature versus nurture, and all that."

"So you're saying I'm not responsible for all the stupid decisions I've made? It's my nature, or my upbringing that made me marry the Tsar, and I have no responsibility whatsoever? I'm just some robotic puppet, forced to carry out the actions it was programmed to do?"

Persephone heard a sharp intake of breath come from her friend. Phoenix didn't say anything. She wriggled out of Persephone's embrace, and sat up in bed. She fiddled with the edge of her blanket, folding it beneath her fingers with increasing speed. After a moment, she sank back down onto the bed, and opened her mouth to speak. No words came out.

"What?" Persephone asked.

"Nothing, it's nothing. But it could be something, something huge and important, but it's probably nothing, just a theory."

"Okay."

"What's it like?" Phoenix asked after a long time. "Being in love?"

"I don't know if I am in love," Persephone said.

"Okay, what's it like having all those feelings for someone? All the lovey-dovey butterflies-in-stomach-type feelings?"

"Are you trying to distract me?"

"No, I'm genuinely curious. I've never felt that way, ever. I think I might be immune to love."

"Some people are just made differently," Persephone said.

"Sometimes I think I am different," Phoenix said. "I don't know. I've never been in the right environment to explore that side of myself. I'll add it to the list of ways the Settlements messed me up."

"What happened there?" Persephone asked, squeezing Phoenix's hand in the darkness. Her own experience of being raised in the Settlements had been stifling, but she knew her friend had suffered something far worse. She felt a shudder run through

Phoenix's body.

"It's not something I choose to talk about," she said. "I don't want it to become a part of my identity."

"Someone hurt you, didn't they?" Persephone asked.

"Hurt is too small a word," she said. "They shook me to my core, swallowed me alive and regurgitated the frail, broken, mess I had become, only to devour me again. I can't tell you what happened, I refuse to relive it. I've fought my demons, and I've put them to rest as best I can. That's it. No going back."

"Would you consider telling someone else, though? Someone who could bring those people to justice?"

"Sphenn," Phoenix said, "no one cares. No one in Western Russia gives a fuck what happens inside the Settlements. A thousand people could have been buried alive, and no one outside would care in the slightest. There is no justice for the oppressed. We are not a civilised country, the Olympovski dynasty ensured that."

"What about in Estonia?" Persephone asked. "It's meant to be better here, isn't it? Couldn't you get help here?"

"The law doesn't work that way, Sphenn. It would be like if I committed murder in Western Russia, and was put on trial by the Estonian courts. It wouldn't happen. Each country deals with its own citizens' crimes."

"Did you commit murder in Western Russia? Is that why you're here in Estonia?" Persephone didn't know if she was ready for the truth.

"Yes," Phoenix whispered.

"Did you kill your stepfather?" Persephone felt the weight settle on her chest as she considered the magnitude of this information. She searched her heart for a sign of change, of fear or hatred towards her friend, but love and compassion stood there as strong as they had ever been.

"It was technically self-defence," Phoenix continued, speaking hastily now, her voice an urgent whisper. "He hit me, and he threatened to strangle my sister Irina. But that wasn't why I killed him. It was me. It was my awful nature. I chose to be cruel, I chose to be evil. I killed him and I don't regret it, and I know that makes me some kind of monster, but he was a monster too. I did the right thing. Some people don't belong in this world, Sphenn. I try to be good, I try so hard. He never tried."

# Chapter Sixteen

"Good morning Persephone." Phoenix said chirpily as she heard her friend's footsteps on the stairs. It was late morning, and Drew was already long gone. Phoenix stood by the table, slicing a loaf of dark rye bread.

"You never call me by my real name – even before I married the Tsar." Persephone eyed Phoenix with confusion, she knew something was wrong.

"Have some breakfast." She pushed a plate across the table towards her.

"What's going on?" Persephone asked through a mouthful of bread.

"Tell me everything that happened between you and the Tsar." Phoenix tied her hair away from her face, and grabbed a notebook and pencil from the windowsill. She held the pencil poised above the page, waiting for Persephone to speak.

"Why?"

"Just tell me, Sphenn! It's important."

"Fine," Persephone conceded. "You know all the stuff leading up to your departure."

"No, Sphenya," Phoenix said urgently. "I mean from the beginning. From the moment you met. Every interaction."

"We met at the Olympus vineyard in Greece. It was on a hill right near the border with the orange grove. I was staring out across the border, and–"

"Persephone," Phoenix interrupted, impatient. "You don't need to set the scene. I just want cold, hard facts, okay?"

"Being cold isn't in my nature."

"It's in his, and that's what matters right now. Tell me what happened."

"We met. We talked. He gave me half a pomegranate," Persephone began. She continued her tale in the same monotony of short sentences, a small rebellion against the tyrant Phoenix.

.

Phoenix scribbled notes as Persephone told her story. When she finally lapsed into silence, Phoenix began to think aloud. "So he freaked out the first time you kissed him? At first I thought

190

he was gay. I dismissed that theory because of that pornographic book I found in his library: it was mostly of women. Him biting you, there's something off about that. I'm not kink-shaming or anything, I'm just saying: you don't bite someone without their consent unless you have some serious issues. Knowing the Tsar, I'd say those issues are about control. And the fruit: he's done something to it, I know he has. I think he's using it to control people. But why does it work better on Sol than it does on you?" She was bursting with excitement at the opportunity to finally voice her thoughts, to tease out the theory that had been brewing. Her eyes sparkled.

"Phoenix, you're rambling," Persephone said.

"We're leaving."

"What?"

"Today. We're leaving today. We shouldn't have stayed here this long."

"What's going on?"

"Persephone, do you trust me?"

"Sporadically."

"You can't tell anyone where we're going. As far as they're concerned, we're going to visit Sol."

"Where are we going?"

"To Tallinn, to the Estonian Institute of Scientific Research. They can give you the answers I can't."


Phoenix slipped her feet into her shoes. She wore a clean, lilac T-shirt, tucked into a black, pleated skirt, and her hair was neatly combed. Her cheeks glowed with a hint of sunburnt red. Persephone lay sprawled on the bed, her shoes and bag resting by her side. She didn't want to leave.

"Oh stop being so miserable!" Phoenix took her arm and dragged her up off the bed. "I need to work out what game Old Icy's playing, and the only way I can do that is with an institute full of scientists at my back."

"Who says they'll help?" Persephone asked. She didn't want to leave The Haven. Ordinarily she would be impatient to return to the excitement of city life, to venture into an uncertain future.

But this time it was different, this time there were people she was scared to leave behind.

"It'll be a scientific phenomenon," said Phoenix. "Hell, if I believed in miracles I would think it was one of those. It goes beyond current levels of scientific knowledge. It shouldn't be possible."

"You're scaring me."

"Fear is just an excuse to hide away the moment life gets exciting." Phoenix perched on the windowsill, studying Persephone's face as though she were some scientific experiment instead of a human being.

"What do I have to do with a scientific phenomenon?" Persephone asked. She wished Phoenix would stop scrutinising her.

"Why don't you ask your husband?"

That evening, the girls were finally ready to leave The Haven. They hadn't spoken to each other since their dispute that morning. Phoenix was in good spirits. Excitement simmered within her, a steady sensation of warmth inside her stomach. She knew going to Tallinn, to the Estonian Institute of Scientific Research, would change her life. Science was Phoenix's one great love, and now, for the first time in her life, she would be surrounded by people who shared that love, people other than the Tsar.

For Persephone leaving meant further heartbreak. She couldn't shake the idea that Phoenix would lead her into a third instance of incarceration.

Their goodbyes were brief. Persephone gave Grigory and Rozalina a polite hug, whilst Phoenix and Drew said a more meaningful goodbye.

"Thanks for lending me this." Phoenix returned his book to him. "I won't be needing myths where I'm going."

"Where are you really going?" Drew asked in a low voice, so Grigory and Rozalina wouldn't hear him. "I know you love her too much to take her back to Moscow." His hands gripped Phoenix's shoulders. She wriggled out of his grasp. He meant well, but it was too much.

"I can't tell you."

"It's Springtime, Phoenix. Don't take her back to the underworld."

"You have to trust me. She does." Phoenix glanced back at Persephone. "She's a person, she's not living out some legend. He doesn't get to claim her back every year, she's with me now. Goodbye, Drew. You were my first real friend, I'm gonna miss you." He opened his arms, and she let herself surrender to the hug.

"Until we meet again, my favourite Firebird."

Persephone hovered a few feet away, unsure what to do. She had avoided Drew as best she could after Phoenix told him they were leaving.

"Can I hug you goodbye?" he asked, as he released Phoenix.

"Sure." His arms held her tight. His heart beat against her ear. Persephone breathed in the scent of oranges that clung to his plaid shirt, and wished she could turn back time.

"I love you, Persephone." His whisper tickled the top of her head. "I shouldn't, but I do."

She waited a moment, fighting the stubborn part of her that wanted to dig her heels in and stay. But in a choice between Drew and Phoenix, she would always choose Phoenix, just as she would choose the unknown over a peaceful life in this wild green place. As she hugged him tighter to her, Persephone said "It's too late, Drew." She looked away, but not quickly enough. There was no mistaking the hurt in his eyes.

"I love you," said Drew. "I love you, married or not."

Sadness pounded like an alarm bell through her bloodstream. She couldn't breathe, she couldn't think. But Persephone knew she couldn't change her mind now. "And I loved you," she said.

"Tell me one thing, Persephone." Drew leant his forehead against hers. He was so close they were breathing the same air. "Are you leaving because of me?"

"Don't flatter yourself."

"Hell hath no fury like a woman scorned. I should know that by now."

"It's not you, I promise it's not you."

"I'm just not reason enough for you to stay."

✝

Persephone marched away as fast as her legs would carry her. She and Phoenix were now out of sight of The Haven, walking briskly along the dry dirt road that ran through the fields.

"What happened with Drew?" she asked, seeing the tears upon her friend's face.

"Drew told me he loved me. I chose you."

"I'm so sorry, Persephone." Her stomach churned with guilt. Phoenix wondered again: when had she lost her humanity? "This is important. I can't tell you why until I know for sure, but believe me, it is important." She placed her hands firmly on Persephone's shoulders, and watched her with pleading eyes.

"I told him I didn't love him, Phoenix!" Her resolve cracked. "I lied to him because of your ridiculous theory. I've given up my one chance at love!"

"You didn't have a chance," Phoenix said. "Drew didn't want you until he knew you were leaving. Tell me, Sphenn, when have my theories ever been wrong?" She could hear the bitterness in her own voice, feel herself turning into the image of paternal cruelty she had strived so hard to erase. She continued in a gentler tone "I know you're upset right now, but—" She paused, to gauge how much it was safe to reveal. "I think the Tsar's using genetically modified fruit to control people, and I think, for some reason, it doesn't work properly on you."

"So?" Persephone asked glumly. Her husband was the least of her worries right now.

"So?" Phoenix was exasperated now. "He could control the entire nation!"

"Except you," Persephone said, her brain ticking slowly until the pieces came together in her mind. "You don't eat fruit. Is that why?"

"No. My fruit thing goes back a long way. Listen: this fruit made you and Sol love him. Sol still loves him. You don't. It doesn't work properly on you; it wears off quicker. I can't tell you the rest of my theory right now, but I am truly sorry about Drew."

"Sol doesn't love the Tsar," Persephone said. "He never did."

194

"How do you know?"

"It doesn't matter."

"Persephone," Phoenix said, "I've known Sol a lot longer than you have. He might not be in love with the Tsar anymore, but he certainly was a few months ago."

"Sol isn't gay, believe me."

"Did something happen between you two?" Phoenix narrowed her eyes. She didn't trust Sol as far as she could throw him, but seducing Persephone at her most vulnerable seemed low even for him.

"Not what you're thinking. We had a fight, he's not who I thought he was. But I can say with a hundred percent certainty he is not gay."

"It doesn't matter though, does it?" Phoenix said. "Because Sol didn't actually love the Tsar. The fruit made him think he did."

"The Tsar coerced Sol into loving him?"

"That's what I'm trying to say! I told Sol about the fruit a couple of days before your wedding. If he stopped eating it, then the feelings would have disappeared, and—"

"I believe you," Persephone cut across her. "The timing makes sense. I trust you."

✚

The train sped through the green eden of Estonian countryside. Already, the remnants of Russia and the Borderlands had been left behind. The Estonian train was silver, sleek, built to a higher standard than those of Western Russia. Through the train window, Persephone caught glimpses of Estonian landscape, of vibrant green fields, meadows strewn with wildflowers, thick forests of evergreen trees. The train passed through myriad villages and towns, none of which bore resemblance to the destitution of Western Russian habitation. In the space of a few hundred miles, the world had changed completely. The forests thickened as the train travelled further into the heart of Estonia. For miles around, the world was nothing but dark-green pine trees.

Excitement battled against misery, vying for Persephone's attention. A part of her had always yearned for freedom. She

195

hoped, in spite of her fears, that freedom was what she would find in Tallinn.

"Are you thinking about Drew?" Phoenix asked, breaking Persephone from her reverie.

"No, not really. But you are?"

"Yeah. How the tables have turned…" Phoenix forced herself to smile, wracked still by guilt. "I don't understand why you left the way you did. You didn't try to stay in contact. You didn't fight for him."

"I know I'll never see him again," Persephone said. Any quiet in her soul had vanished completely. "You tell me you've made some big scientific discovery that somehow centres on me. What are you doing with this discovery? You're taking it to a scientific-research institute! If you're right about whatever this is, they'll never leave us alone. And if you're wrong, then what? We have nowhere to go. What if the Tsar finds me? It doesn't matter if I love Drew. I'm never going to be with him."

"I've ruined your life, haven't I?" Phoenix's voice was saturated with distress. She leant her head against the window. The train had stopped in a station, and the world was momentarily still.

"I've done that on my own," Persephone said. "All because I was bored. God, why do I always make such awful decisions?"

"I'm the last person to champion predestination," Phoenix said, "but I think in your circumstance, perhaps there's a point to it." She faltered for a moment, considering her response carefully. "Sphenya, we don't always have control over our own lives. Sometimes our choices are chosen for us, and we don't have free will. That's how the world works, and you have been less fortunate than most in this respect. I hope you'll now have the freedom to choose."


It was night by the time the train pulled into Tallinn. The soft luminosity of city lights glowed against the window. Phoenix could see illuminated letters spelling out T.A.L.L.I.N.N. like flames against the darkening blue sky. The night was still light, even after sunset. Summer approached steadily, and the world refused to darken completely.

196

*Paradise,* Phoenix thought drowsily.

Persephone was curled against the window, fast asleep, her cheek squashed against the glass. Phoenix took a moment before rousing her, drinking in the sight of the city. This place belonged to her, before she took her first steps upon its ground. She wished she were here alone, wished she had the freedom to venture out into the twilit night, unencumbered by the oppressive force of company. But she was not here for herself.

"Sphenya." Phoenix shook her friend awake.

"Mmh, what?" Persephone woke with a start.

"We're here. We're in Tallinn."

# Chapter Seventeen

Phoenix bought a map of Tallinn inside the train station. Persephone followed dutifully as her friend led the way. A walled city stood upon a hill, its turreted towers pierced the clouded veil of the night sky. The buildings outside of the walls were more modern. Lights shone through their windows.

"This way," Phoenix said. She walked across the grass to the Old Town. Tallinn was unlike the cities Persephone was used to. It was cosy, like a small town, trapped in another era. She lagged behind Phoenix, taking in the sights. In Moscow she had been a prisoner, in the Borderlands she had been a runaway. But here, in Tallinn, Persephone didn't yet know who she was meant to be, and that freedom was the greatest luxury she could have wished for.

The Estonian Institute of Scientific Research was on the far side of the Old Town. Its outer buildings were metres away from Viru Gate. The main building was a small skyscraper, constituted of twenty-three floors, a few minutes' walk from the Old Town's edge. It was a remnant of the bleak Soviet era, lacking in the beauty of the Old Town's medieval architecture. The outer buildings ranged from two to six storeys tall, and stood around a courtyard at the centre of the complex, from which the tops of chestnut trees were visible against the night sky.

Phoenix and Persephone crossed the damp expanse of grass in front of the tallest building, and came to a revolving door. Phoenix strode through it confidently, and marched up to the unattended desk in the foyer. She rang the bell.

"Phoenix, it's late. Maybe we should come back tomorrow."

"We've travelled right across the country," came the sharp reply. "If they want us, they can have us now. There are plenty of things that can wait till tomorrow, this isn't one of them. Not when we've come so far."

"Are you scared I'll back out?" Persephone asked, as she took in her surroundings. The foyer was decorated all in white, save for the varnished wooden reception desk, and the dark bannister of a staircase at the room's rear.

"I'm scared I will." Phoenix repeatedly pinged the bell.

A man sidled down the staircase at the far end of the foyer. He was middle-aged, of medium height and round build. His bristly mouse-brown hair was close-cropped, and failed to disguise his receding hairline. Circular spectacles rimmed his grey eyes. His arm lingered on the bannister as he addressed Phoenix. Even in a foreign tongue, Persephone couldn't mistake the sarcastic tone of his voice.

Phoenix greeted him in slow Estonian, transforming from impatient girl to well-mannered woman. She smiled apologetically once she finished speaking.

"What's he saying?" The man's gaze shifted from Phoenix to Persephone.

"Miss Kashnikova and Ms Olympovskaya?" he asked in Russian. He looked from girl to girl, before coming to focus solely on Persephone.

"Yes!" Phoenix said, relieved. "You must be Dr Skryabin, we corresponded briefly. Forgive me, my Estonian is limited. I had to teach myself from books, and I fear my pronunciation is all wrong."

"You'll get better with practice," Dr Skryabin said. "You're significantly younger than I imagined, Miss Kashnikova." He turned back to Persephone as soon as he finished speaking.

"Does that lessen the merit of my discovery?" Phoenix stood up straighter. A troubled expression crossed her face. For the first time that evening, she seemed insecure.

"Quite the opposite. It increases the merit. Come, we have no time to waste."


"Can someone tell me what's going on here?" Persephone asked, as she followed Phoenix and Dr Skryabin through the stark white hallways of the Estonian Institute of Scientific Research.

They were too immersed in conversation to hear her.

"Now, Miss Kashnikova," said Dr Skryabin, "I've run some tests on the fruit samples that arrived from your friend in Moscow. The results will be ready tomorrow morning. They should have been prepared yesterday, but it's induction week. Every Autumn we take new students for our scientific education program. We hold a one-week training course for potential students at the end of May. Unfortunately, that clogs up the system, and means the well-oiled machine of efficiency does not run quite so smooth. Come this way." He led them through more identical bright white hallways, until they finally reached their destination.


The room reminded Phoenix of a dental practice she had visited shortly after the Tsar kidnapped her, right down to the reclining chair in the centre. The sterility of the white room promised a bright future.

"Ms Olympovskaya," Dr Skryabin began.

"Please, just use my first name," Persephone said hastily. She was unaccustomed to hearing her married surname.

"Persephone," he amended, "I will conduct a brief interview with you, to learn the nature of your condition, then I will run some tests – blood samples, x-rays, etc, to assess the situation. I'll explain everything to you once I am certain."

"Can't you tell me now?" Persephone asked.

"I don't believe it would be wise." Dr Skryabin's gaze drifted to Phoenix, as if asking for help.

"Sphenn," she said, "this could all be nothing. There's no point worrying about something that could be disproved within a matter of hours. Just relax, answer the questions, and breathe deeply. Think happy thoughts. You need to stop worrying."

"I'm only human."

"Persephone," Dr Skryabin resumed. "Do you have memories of your childhood?"

"Yes."

"How far do they date back?"

"I have memories from when I was a small child. My early memories all kind of blur together, nothing particularly memorable happened."

"Did you have any illnesses as a child?" Dr Skryabin asked.

"I've never been ill."

"Have you had any infections? Viruses? Coughs or colds?"

"I have never been ill. Ever. I've vomited from time to time, but only after eating something bad."

"Well aren't you just the picture of health," Phoenix said. She sat on the counter at the side of the room, swinging her legs in agitation.

"Do you menstruate regularly?" Dr Skryabin continued.

"What kind of a question is that?" Persephone asked.

"A basic medical one," Phoenix laughed.

"Oh." Persephone looked away, embarrassed. "Uh, yes. 5 days. Every 28 days."

"Like clockwork?" Dr Skryabin asked.

"Yes, there's just a tick, tick, tick inside my uterus." She didn't understand the purpose of these questions.

"How old were you when you first received fruit from the Tsar?"

"Seventeen."

"And what variety of fruit was this?"

"Pomegranate."

"What state of mind were you in during your time with the Tsar?"

"I had more than one state of mind," Persephone said tersely. "I was there for over a year."

"What *states* of mind were you in?" Dr Skryabin rephrased.

"I was relieved, I was scared, I was happy, I was angry. I'm not some automaton, Doctor. I felt many things during my time with Haden. A great many of those feelings weren't directed toward him at all. It was a time of growth, and a time of self-reflection. I experienced many emotions, I cannot specify. I felt; I don't know what I felt, but I felt."

"Did you feel love within that time?"

"Yes."

"Love for the Tsar?"

"Love for my friends. Love for myself, perhaps."

"You loved yourself?" She caught the well-disguised surprise in his voice. Persephone couldn't shake her sense of unease. She needed to know what this scientist wanted from her, why he asked her these questions. Her eyes scanned the room, searching for something to focus on, something to anchor her back to earth. The walls were white. The floor was tiled. A counter ran along one wall, where Phoenix still perched. A stainless steel kettle sat upon it, beside a jar of instant coffee. An unwashed mug rested beside it. Plants crowded the windowsill. All green, no flowers. Spider

201

plants, with long leaves hanging down. Untamed. Beside the plants was a framed photograph. A wedding picture. Dr Skryabin, and a man Persephone presumed was his husband. The scientist was human, after all. Another photo. Its subject was a cat, with dense, tabby fur. The frame was shaped in a love heart.

"Persephone?" He prompted. She hadn't answered his question.

"I loved who I had the potential to become."

"Did you have romantic feelings of any kind towards your husband?" There was still a look of bemusement upon his face as he watched her. Bemusement, or amazement.

"From time to time," she said. "We didn't marry for love. I do not love him, and I don't think I ever did. But I certainly wanted to try. I wanted to be loved, and I expected love from him. I didn't receive that love, or any pitiful substitution for it, so I left."

"Did you and the Tsar engage in sexual activity?"

"No, we did not."

"Whose choice was this?"

"Whose do you think it was?"

"He chose to abstain?" She could see his brain whirring, just like Phoenix's did when she was developing a theory.

"Yes."

"Was there any physical contact between you at all?"

"Yes. I kissed him, on our wedding night, and he freaked out about it. Then, a few days later, he kissed me. And then he bit me."

"Where did he bite you?"

"My breast." She couldn't meet his eyes. She didn't feel comfortable talking about this to a stranger.

"That's enough questions for now," Dr Skryabin decided. "I'll arrange some rooms for you girls to stay in for the duration of your time here. I'll run some tests on you in the morning."

"Right," Persephone said.

"Miss Kashnikova?" He crossed the room towards Phoenix.

"Yup?" She jumped down from the counter, and straightened her posture, as the scientist's attention came to rest on her once again.

"Your theories are sophisticated." Dr Skryabin glanced meaningfully at the back of Persephone's head. "How old are you?"

202

"Eighteen."

"You have a remarkable mind, particularly for someone of your age. Your letter was an intriguing read. I was sceptical at first, especially given that this is not my field of expertise. But you produced evidence, references, for a concept that is beyond the level of research at this centre, to the point that it would have been absurd for me to turn you down. If you are right, it would mean a great deal to the scientific community."

"All I did was recognise symptoms," Phoenix said. Her face shone with the praise.

"I've been thinking," Dr Skryabin continued. "Our degree program… Is it something you would perhaps be interested in?"

"Oh my gosh," Phoenix said. "That would be the most amazing thing ever. It would make my life!" The glow of excitement rapidly vanished from her face as she saw Persephone across the room. "It's not something I can agree to straight away. I need some time to think on it."

"You have an intriguing mind," the scientist said. "Don't let it go to waste. I would be happy to put in a good word for you, if you were to apply for a scholarship."

Phoenix's insides filled with butterflies, but she couldn't allow herself to be happy. The millstone of Persephone weighed heavy around her neck.

"I'll fetch someone to show you to your rooms," said Dr Skryabin.

Phoenix and Persephone didn't exchange a word in Dr Skryabin's absence. Persephone stood, arms folded, staring into space. Phoenix explored the room, glancing into every corner, eyeing up every object as if it held the secrets of the universe. This was where she belonged; she knew it was. Persephone would never be content here, particularly if Phoenix's theories were correct.

╫

The uncomfortable silence had almost reached its climax, when the door swung open.

"Hey!" said the boy who entered. He addressed them in Russian, so the girls knew Dr Skryabin had sent him. He had dark skin, and big brown eyes. Hair fell past his shoulders in thick dreadlocks. The warmth in his expression quickly banished the palpable hostility that had filled the room only moments before. "I'm Kai," he said. "I'm here to take you to your rooms."

"I'm Phoenix. This is my friend Persephone." The smile she had tried to conceal since Dr Skryabin's departure was back with a vengeance.

"I like your names." His easy grin was now somewhat shy. Phoenix couldn't help noticing the warmth of his deep brown eyes. He nodded politely to Persephone, before returning his gaze to her.

"Really?" she asked, almost tongue-tied.

"Yeah!" he enthused. "What's more badass than a bird that rises from its ashes?"

"One that doesn't burn in the first place," Phoenix said.

"You speak Russian," Persephone cut in.

"My family is Russian-Estonian," Kai said. "We speak Russian at home."

"So you're bilingual?" Phoenix asked.

"Currently," Kai said. "I tried to learn English when I was younger, but I failed. There are no native English speakers in Estonia."

"English is my first language!" Phoenix said. "Both of ours, actually. I'm half-Russian, so I'm fluent in both. I've been learning Estonian, but I only had the opportunity to learn it from books until now."

"Books... are great." Kai struggled to form a coherent sentence.

Persephone snorted from across the room. She had never seen someone so entranced by Phoenix.

☦

"What brought you here?" Kai asked Phoenix. Persephone was in her room, and the two were now alone. They sat on a wooden bench, under a cluster of cherry trees in the Institute's courtyard. Phoenix watched him whilst she tried to find a suitable answer. Kai was a tall young man, somewhat awkward in his strong build; he had not yet settled in the transition from boyhood to manhood.

There was a kindness in him that took Phoenix by surprise.

"I had a theory," she said. It was almost dark here. The night sky was clouded over; no light came from the heavens. Lamps were situated at the edges of the courtyard, but they cast only a dim shadow. "I wanted a scientific opinion on it, and I knew this was the go-to place for science."

Kai laughed. "The 'go-to place'? That is one way to put it. How old are you?" he asked.

"Eighteen. You?"

"I'll be nineteen in August."

"You look older. Are you here on induction week?" She could feel his knee, a hairbreadth away from hers, radiating warmth in the cold night. Phoenix moved a little on the bench, so they were no longer touching.

"Yeah, why?"

"Dr Skryabin suggested I apply to study here. He said he'd put in a good word for me."

"Are you going to take him up on it?" Kai's gaze shifted around her face, and he fiddled with the ends of his fingernails as he spoke.

"No," Phoenix said. "I want to. I want to more than I've ever wanted anything. But I can't leave Persephone. I'm all she's got."

"That's a shame. If Dr Skryabin wants you here, you must be smart as hell."

Phoenix laughed. "You could say that."

"Miss Kashnikova," Dr Skryabin addressed Phoenix the next morning. "You were right about the fruit." They sat at the table in his office.

"I was?" Phoenix asked. Her eyes glazed over as she stared pensively into her mug of tea. The implications of her theories had posed a danger to Persephone from day one, and now they were theories no more. It was too much for her to handle right now. She was thankful Persephone wasn't an early riser, as it gave Phoenix the time she needed to process the information.

"Yes," Dr Skryabin said, "genetically modified fruit. GMOs were banned in Western Russia early last century. As you suspected, this modification goes far beyond the norm. The fruit contains substances that manipulate both emotion and brain chemistry." His face was gravely serious. He took a large gulp of his coffee, before looking down at the sheet of test results that lay before him.

"Do you know what extent of control the fruit has?" Phoenix asked.

"Judging by the high level of foreign substances it contained, I'd say the impact is strong, particularly if a regular dosage was administered over an extended period of time. Which begs the question: why haven't they worked their magic on Persephone?"

"Do you think my theory about her is correct?" In spite of the gravity of the situation, Phoenix had always found a hint of excitement in her theory about Persephone. Now that the abstract of possibility was close to entering the realms of certainty, dread replaced excitement. Persephone was all Phoenix had left in the world. If the bond of friendship was broken, she had nothing.

"We won't know until I've run some tests on her," Dr Skryabin said cautiously. "It's beyond the findings of research in this field." His instinct told him the girl was correct, but he refused to speculate.

"But it's not impossible," Phoenix said. "I read books in the Tsar's library about some less-advanced prototypes, and if they were extended upon, I fully believe it's possible."

"We'll soon know. I'll do the tests later this morning, and we'll find out tomorrow."

"I'm worried how she'll react," Phoenix said. "She can be impulsive at times."

Dr Skryabin considered for a moment. He had always felt out of his depth when it came to giving advice, particularly to teenagers. In spite of many years of teaching, he had never found a way to connect with young minds; his students were a distant entity to him. The solitude of a laboratory was far preferable. He felt a connection to this girl, ever since the first letter she sent him. Her queries weren't in his field; she had contacted him because his name was Russian, and she wasn't fluent in Estonian. It was mere coincidence. Coincidence or not, he was determined to make her his protégée. He couldn't let such a mind go untrained.

"I'm sure she'll be safe here," he finally said.

"I have a bad feeling," said Phoenix. "I know Persephone, and I know autonomy is such an issue for her. If my theory is right, she's going to have the biggest existential crisis of her life. I don't know how she'll react. If I were in her position, I would fall apart – and I'm infinitely more accustomed to trauma than she is. We don't know how she's going to act. We don't know if there are unnatural parts of her nature that could suddenly reveal themselves. I've always thought her to be quite placid, but she's becoming more and more passionate. How do we know that's not leading to something?"

"We don't know," Dr Skryabin admitted. "This has always been the danger of science, Miss Kashnikova. When man plays God, there is an ever-present possibility that we shall all be plunged into hell. But if science started this, science can end this."

"What do you mean 'end this'?" Phoenix asked in panic. She had assumed Dr Skryabin would be her ally, but it occurred to her now that he could become her greatest enemy, if her theory were correct.

"I mean that if there is something wrong with her psychologically, there will be operations, there will be treatments. We'll find a way to fix her."

"She's not broken." Phoenix couldn't prevent the anger from penetrating her voice. "She's a person, just like you and me, and she will be treated as nothing less than that. She *feels*; she feels just as deeply as we do. No matter what the tests reveal, you cannot treat her as anything other than a human being. Do you understand?"

"Yes, of course." Phoenix breathed a sigh of relief. "I have met her, Miss Kashnikova, I have spoken with her. Externally, there is nothing to differentiate her from you or me. We will not do anything without her consent."

"If anything happens to her..." Phoenix didn't finish her sentence. She couldn't face the possibility that she had led Persephone into danger.

## Chapter Eighteen

"I'm a *what*?" asked a horror-struck Persephone, the following morning. Dr Skryabin had given Phoenix privacy to break the news. His office blurred before Persephone's eyes. She tried to focus on something solid. Plants! Plants! Cat picture! Plants! Coffee mug! They all spun. The world was upside down.

"Basically, a robot," Phoenix said gravely. Her blue-green eyes were weary as she brought them up to meet Persephone's. She didn't seem like the girl who had been her friend for a year. She was like a scientist now, dressed in an invisible lab coat that separated her from the world of ordinary people.

"You better tell me the complicated version, because I sure as hell don't believe the basic one." Persephone paced across the room, like an animal trapped in a cage. The floor continued to spin. She clung to the edge of the counter to prevent herself from falling.

"Sphenya, it's true," Phoenix said. "They've done about a thousand tests on you, not to mention the fruit."

Persephone spun around, turning to face her. "Who made me?" she asked. "If I am what you say I am, who made me? Clearly you know everything else, so you must know this." She didn't expect an answer.

"The Tsar," Phoenix said instantly. She didn't sugar-coat it, not when Persephone was already on the warpath.

"When he was ten years old?" she asked. "Yeah, right."

"He was a child prodigy, Persephone," Phoenix said, "inventing machines by the time he was five."

"Is that what I am, a machine?" It couldn't be true. She was a human, she had lived her whole life as a human, she could not be less than that.

"Of course not, Sphenn. You're human in almost every way." Phoenix tugged violently on her hair, forcing its ends into her mouth.

"Which ways am I not human?" Persephone was on the verge of tears. A whole life of feeling *other*, and suddenly *other* was what she had become.

"How you were made," Phoenix said, turning her back on

Persephone. "You weren't made like a human."

"Even I know there's more than one way to make a human," Persephone said. "What about test-tube babies? Are they robots too? They're not made the regular way." She refused to believe this absurdity.

"That's different. Even though they don't go through the normal... procedure, they're made from the same material."

"What am *I* made from?" Her face crumpled in defeat. It took all she had not to cry.

"To be honest, I don't know. The tests confirmed you have human DNA. But Dr Skryabin thinks this DNA didn't come from any parents. You're a clean slate."

"I don't have a family? Anywhere? Dead or alive?"

"We don't think it's likely." Her voice was hollow.

"What am I? What does 'robot' actually mean? What stops me from being human if I have human DNA? I am human, Phoenix; I have always been human. I love, I hate, I fear, I evolve. I have every human function. Why can't I be human?"

"Because you're *not*. Your brain isn't a human brain. Your heart may be flesh and blood, but your brain is closer to a computer. We can't choose how we're made."

"Or who we're made by."

Phoenix nodded solemnly, still facing the wall.

"Oh my God!" A sob of protestation slipped from Persephone. Phoenix turned around just in time to see her slide down the wall and onto the floor, hugging her knees close for protection. "I don't have a soul! I don't have a soul! I don't have a soul!" Fat tears rolled down her cheeks.

"You have more soul than anyone I know," Phoenix said. She wanted to go to Persephone, to comfort her somehow, but she was frozen where she stood.

"No, but I don't have a *soul*. I don't mean soul as in personality. I mean a real soul. Once I die, I'm gone forever. What's the point of living if you live and die, and that's it? How can I be good without a soul?" She wiped her nose on the sleeve of her dress.

"You really need to read up on Aristotle," Phoenix said. "The soul is our formal cause. It's our shape, our identifier. That's it. We're not these eternal beings. We're just us. We have reason, we have personality, we have morality. All of that, that's our soul."

"Can you stop being such an atheist for five minutes?" Persephone asked. "Why can't you believe in something outside of yourself? I'm not telling you God's real, and I'm not saying anything to threaten your closed-minded beliefs. I can't be just this. I need redemption, I need a future. I need to believe there's something special in all of us, because if there's not, why should I believe in anything at all?" She scrubbed the tears off her face with the hem of her dress, and stood up. "Why should I believe I'm a robot? You believe in science with a much stronger zeal than I have ever seen a person commit to religion. It suits you perfectly to pin me as a robot, because now I'll be your pet for life, the clueless guinea pig on whom you can test your abhorrent theories!"

"Come on, Persephone, you know I wouldn't lie to you!" Phoenix pleaded.

"You always lie to me. You lied about your childhood, and you lied about killing your stepfather!"

"I confessed that to you!" Phoenix's voice cracked with fury.

"Not your childhood though." Persephone dug the knife into Phoenix's most gaping wound. "You lie about your childhood, and you always will. It's the shield you hide behind, and it lets you get away with murder! As long as you're the victim of some unnamed abuse, you can never be blamed for your own wrongdoing! You're a liar Phoenix – you always have been. You're manipulative, and cruel, and condescending, and all you ever think about is yourself! You call me your friend, but you forget friendship is a two-way street. I don't belong to you, and I certainly don't belong to the Tsar. I gave up everything for you and your stupid theory. Drew loved me, and I abandoned him. For you."

"It's not a theory," Phoenix calmly explained. "A theory is a hypothesis that isn't proven. There is proof now. And I know what you've given up."

"No, you don't!" Now the floodgates of rage had opened, there was no going back. Every ounce of resentment Persephone had towards her friend became fuel for the projectile of word-vomit that threatened to escape her. "No one's ever loved you, Phoenix! How could you possibly know what I've given up, when you've never experienced anything like it?"

210

"Because I love you!" Phoenix shouted. She struggled to breathe, she could feel a panic attack coming on. "I love you more than anyone in this world, and I have effectively renounced our friendship by telling you the truth. I love you, and I have given you up by choice, just as you gave up Drew! And don't talk to me about victim complexes, because you've got a hell of a one yourself."

Phoenix shoved Persephone out of the way, and stormed out the door. Her pursuit of truth had backfired, she didn't know how to go on from here.

*But you knew*, she reminded herself, *you knew how she'd react. And you told her anyway.*

Phoenix found refuge in an empty corridor. She slumped against the wall, and cried until her eyes were red and puffy and her sleeves were soaked with tears. This was how she sat when Kai found her.

"Hey, are you okay?" he asked. He towered over her like a gentle giant. She stared at his shoes. Lilac socks peeked out from beneath the hem of his trouser legs.

"I'm great, thanks," she said. He wasn't fooled.

"What's wrong?" Kai sat down beside her on the floor. His brown eyes were filled with concern.

"Persephone told me no one's ever loved me," Phoenix said. She stared at the fabric of her trousers, pulled taut across her knees. She could feel the tears coming on again. She didn't want to cry in front of him.

"Do you believe that's true?" Kai asked gently. Phoenix could see her own pain reflected in his eyes. He gave her a comforting pat on the shoulder. She saw his hand coming with enough time to prepare herself, and didn't flinch at his touch.

"I don't know," she said. "My parents hate me, and my friend has transformed into the one-woman embodiment of the three Furies, so, right now, I'd say it's true." Phoenix breathed deeply in an effort to remain calm. "She's right. She's never right, and now she's right about the one thing that needs to be wrong."

"I'm sure she's not," Kai said. He put his arm around Phoenix's

211

shoulder. She gritted her teeth, and leant into him. It was a performance. She knew it was easier to let him comfort her in his way than to explain why she didn't like to be touched by strangers. The fabric of his purple shirt was soft against her face. "If she is, well, you've only been alive for eighteen years. I guarantee you, by the time you've lived another eighteen so many people will love you, you won't have enough room in your heart to love them all back."

"I doubt it." She faltered for a moment, before deciding he was safe to confide in. "How you see me, that's not really me. It's just a mask. I'm not how I seem. I'm messed up, and I'm weird, and wounded, and I've done terrible things. Who would love someone like that?"

"Phoenix," Kai said softly, "everybody deserves love, no matter what they've done." He paused, and took a deep breath. "We all wear a mask, Phoenix, believe me. I get scared, all the time. Talking to people gives me the fear. You're downright terrifying." He smiled to himself a little, as if he was in on a joke she couldn't understand.

"Why are you talking to me then?" Phoenix took the opportunity to wriggle out of the hug.

"Because I believe you're worth getting to know. I have to fight through my fear. Human connection is everything, it's what keeps us all alive. We're afraid because we have something to lose. That's why we put up walls and wear masks. If no one knows what matters to us, they can't take it away. Can I show you something?"

"You're not going to pull off your face to reveal what's beneath the mask, are you?" she asked.

"Not me," Kai said with a laugh. He took her hand and pulled her up off the floor, leading her to the lift.


"This part of the building's been around for a couple of centuries," he said as the lift ascended to the 22nd floor. "It was a hotel first, then the Russians commandeered it for surveillance back in the Soviet era. Now, it's the Estonian Institute of Scientific Research."

They walked up the flight of steps that led to the 23rd floor,

212

where the lift didn't reach. They stepped out onto a covered balcony, which offered a breathtaking view of the city below. It was a sunny day, but the wind was strong up here. It whipped Phoenix's hair away from her face and made her feel alive.

"See," Kai said, "this is Tallinn. The same place as down on the street. When you're close to people, they have a different view than when you're distant." He braided his dreadlocks into a thick plait to stop the wind from slapping them against his face.

"How are you so nice?" Everything about this boy was an alien phenomenon to her.

"I guess I was just brought up this way."

Phoenix inspected the view from the balcony – the rooftops of the city, and the deep green of the forests beyond. She loved Tallinn like no other place in this world. She loved all of Tallinn, whether she saw it from 23 storeys up, or from the ground on which it was built. Phoenix knew deep inside that Tallinn was where she belonged, where she could heal. She didn't want to leave. Now Persephone despised her, there was nothing to prevent her from staying here forever.

"Phoenix?" A familiar voice called her name as she reached the front entrance to the Estonian Institute of Scientific Research. She had spent much of the day wandering through the cobbled streets of Tallinn's medieval Old Town, searching for peace amidst the city's well-preserved heritage. If those buildings had stood for almost a thousand years, she too could survive. Flesh was superior to stone.

"Sol!" Phoenix screamed as she ran into his embrace. It had been two days since her fight with Persephone, and she felt lonelier than ever. "What are you doing here?"

He lifted her into the air and spun her around.

Sol restored her to the ground. He looked off into the distance. Phoenix eyed him with suspicion. She could tell he was running from something. She knew that evasive look in his eye all too well, it was the same expression she saw on her own face in the mirror.

"This was the address you told me to send the fruit to," said

Sol. "I figured you'd be here by now. You're a city girl, I knew you wouldn't last five minutes on a farm with Sphenya."

Phoenix's face fell at the mention of Persephone. She couldn't shake the feeling that by bringing her here, she had opened a can of worms that should have remained firmly closed.

"What's wrong?" Sol asked. Phoenix wasn't the only one who was suspicious. They watched each other like a hunter watching its prey. Beneath the pretence of friendship, they were the same adversaries they had always been. If she weren't so lonely, Phoenix would have tried to shake him off as soon as possible.

"We had a fight. I don't want to go into details."

"You can tell me anything. You know that, right?"

"Sure."

✝

"Persephone!" The sound of Sol's voice sent a shiver down her spine. He was the last person she expected to see here. She walked barefoot along a deserted stretch of Pirita beach, holding her shoes in her hand. Grey clouds hung low in the sky, spitting out rain arbitrarily. The sand was soft beneath her feet. Alone, in this quiet place where the world stood still, Persephone could let herself feel human. She had been at peace for the first time in days, until he approached her.

"How did you find me?" Persephone asked. She turned to face him. The wind whipped her hair across her eyes. Sol looked different than before. He was dressed in a suit, instead of his usual turtlenecks, and he had combed his hair to one side. The sight of him made her ache in the pit of her stomach.

"I asked Phoenix," he said.

"I didn't tell her where I was going. What, is she stalking me?" Persephone mustered up the last dregs of her strength. It took all she had not to scream at the sky and curse the names of every scientist at that institute. She hated science; she hated Phoenix; she hated this world.

"She asked her doctor friend. He told her."

"I can trust no one around here," Persephone said. Sol's brown eyes were as placid as a horse's, but she saw through his calm demeanour. "I told you to leave me alone. Why did you ignore me?"

"You can't just give up on a friendship," he said matter-of-factly. "I am never going to give up on you! You don't get to decide this is over."

"Sol," she said. "I don't want you in my life. You're not who I thought you were, you're not the kind of person I want to know. I wish we'd never met!"

"You can't say that, Sphenn. I love you, Sphenya. He's doing this to you, isn't he? He's controlling your mind again. You can't trust yourself, you know that. You need me; you need me to remind you how bad he was. You're not in your right mind!"

"Go fuck yourself!"

Persephone shoved past him and walked away from the beach. She found herself in a small grassy area, filled with a sporadic spread of trees. She hid behind a tree trunk and waited for Sol to disappear. Her heart thumped in her chest. Sol was no longer just a danger to the Tsar; he was a danger to her own wellbeing. If Phoenix told him why they were at the Institute, Persephone was sure he would use it to destroy her.

The grey skies of the previous day had given way to blue, spotted with fluffy white clouds. It was 10am on that late May morning, and Phoenix and Sol sat eating breakfast at the outside tables of a quaint little cafe in the centre of the Old Town. Persephone declined both of their invitations. Baskets of vibrant purple and orange flowers hung from hooks in the pink plastered walls of the building behind them.

"You still haven't told me what happened," Phoenix said. She stabbed a pastry with her knife, and looked up to meet Sol's gaze. "I know you're lying to me about something."

"I'm not lying." He took a swig of coffee to avoid saying more.

"You can't fool me, Solly boy. I'm the greatest liar of them all, I can spot the signs a mile off. Tell me, what happened when you left Sphenya? Where did you go?"

"I returned to Moscow," said Sol. A door creaked in the distance and made him jump. He looked behind him in fear.

"Calm down," Phoenix said. "It's just old creaky hinges. It's not going to kill you."

"Sure."

"What did you do in Moscow?"

"I had unfinished business."

"Since when did you have any business? I know you, Sol, you didn't have a life. You stayed in your room all day feeling sorry for yourself, and the only people you ever spoke to were Sphenya and I. You're lying, and I will get to the bottom of this or so help me!"

"Relax, you don't need to be so high strung."

"I'm high strung?" she asked in outrage. "You haven't stopped fidgeting since we got here! What are you afraid of?"

"No one. Nothing."

"Did you go back to the Tsar?"

"Why would I do that?"

"Sometimes we go back to people who aren't good to us, because they're familiar, they're all we know." Phoenix stuffed her mouth with pastry to stop herself from letting out a gasp of horror as her mind drifted back to the last time she saw her mother, to Yuri's body bleeding out on the floor.

"He isn't all I know. I had a life before him, I had a family!"

"You had a life? In the Settlements? Don't delude yourself."

"What would you know about the Settlements? You were bred in an ivory tower. You know nothing about how we lived." Fury flashed across his face. He quickly composed himself.

"And you know nothing about how I lived. You talk like it was some luxury! I guarantee I endured a hell worse than you could even dream of!" Phoenix clung to the edge of the table. Her hands shook.

"Come on," he said. "Let's not fight about this. We need to be a team, how else can we win Sphenya back?"

"She's not a prize. She'll come back to us when she's ready."

"She needs us."

"I don't think she does anymore. That's what I'm afraid of. Persephone could survive on her own, if she chose to. She's stubborn as hell, you know that."

"I don't think she's in her right mind."

216

"What do you mean?" Phoenix narrowed her eyes. Sol's face gave nothing away.

"She's acting crazy; she can't see what's right."

"Can you give me a particular example?"

"I did something, to help reunite us. She was so ungrateful. I sacrificed my dignity for her." He shuddered with disgust.

"I get that something weird happened between you two, but if you're going to be evasive there's no point discussing it. Excuse me; I have to go to the bathroom." She got up and headed inside the cafe. It was cooler here; the heat of the sun didn't reach into the old, stone building. Phoenix felt uneasy. She knew she couldn't coax an answer out of Sol unless he wanted to give it, and it was unlikely Persephone would tell her anything. Her instincts told her this was all about to blow up in her face.

✝

Haden watched as Phoenix walked inside the cafe. The boy was alone now. Sol fidgeted, turning his head in restless movements as if he knew he was being watched. Haden took a deep breath, and walked towards the boy. He slipped into the crowd so as not to be seen. Sol continued to look, panicked, in the wrong direction. There were no cameras here, on this quiet cobbled street; it was unlike any world Haden was used to. There was a sense of freedom, to exist in a place beyond the scope of the cameras' omnipresent eye. But the Tsar was used to being the watcher, and it unnerved him to walk in a world where he was not omniscient. If he didn't deal with the boy, the watcher would become the watched. After a lifetime of voyeurism, he would become the one who had to face the camera, the ridicule and prejudice of his citizens.

Sol jumped when he saw Haden. His face turned deathly white and his brown eyes were wide with fear.

It was a relief, to see the boy cower. Haden himself was almost shaking. He didn't have a plan. For the first time in his life, he was at a loss. There was no blueprint to follow, no rules for how to deal with the situation.

"What are you doing here?" Sol asked. His voice was tight in his throat. He spoke in English. Haden was fluent in the language,

217

it was his job as the Tsar to speak the language of the Settlers as well as that of his own people. But the words never tasted quite right. Russian felt like home in his mouth, and even after two decades of speaking it, English still felt like a mysterious stranger met in a dark alley on a winter night. He didn't trust the language; its words could never bend to his will like his native tongue.

"I'm here to make sure you keep your mouth shut," he finally said. "I am begging you."

Sol laughed cruelly. "You really are pathetic."

"If you go public," Haden said, "I will lose everything. I will lose my country. I could even lose my life. Do you want the weight of my death to rest on your conscience?"

"I would do a service to that country by telling them the truth," said Sol. He stood up from the table. "What they do with the information isn't my responsibility." A cruel look crossed his face. He was enjoying this.

"Why would you do it?" Haden asked. He watched the door nervously, waiting for Phoenix to re-emerge. "Why did you go to such lengths to destroy me?"

"You controlled my mind!" Sol burst out. "You made me feel disgusting things. You deserve to be punished."

Haden nodded slowly. "I never meant to hurt you," he said. "You were a variable. You and Phoenix both were. I had to know it worked."

"You controlled Phoenix too?" Sol seemed surprised. "She never loved you."

"Phoenix doesn't eat fruit," Haden said. "I thought she was an anomaly for a year." It was almost a relief to spill the secrets he had held so close, to talk through his methodology. He had spent a lifetime walking the tightrope between madman and genius. To talk about his experiments felt like a return to humanity, and at the same time a betrayal of his most private self. "The effects of the fruit were only ever intended for Persephone."

"You stole me from my home for your fucked up science experiment," Sol said. "You deserve what's coming to you." He reached into the pocket of his trousers and pulled out a gun.

A crude joke entered Haden's mind before the reality of the situation hit him. It had never occurred to him that Sol would resort to physical violence.

The street, which had been busy only moments before, was now empty. Phoenix had still not returned. They were alone, the Tsar and the blackmailer.

Haden took a step towards Sol. The boy was shorter than he was, and he hoped to intimidate him with his proximity. It was the only hope he had.

"What would you gain from my death?" he asked.

"Satisfaction," Sol replied.

"If you wanted me to satisfy you, all you had to do was ask." Haden couldn't help himself. He prayed his last words wouldn't be a sex joke. His eyes never left the gun in Sol's hand. He searched his brain for some form of solution or escape, but all that came to him was dark humour and bad jokes. He began to panic. There was no way out.

"Sol!" Phoenix came through the door, back out into the street. Haden seized this opportunity and reached for the gun. Sol fought him, but the Tsar was stronger. He grabbed the gun, and took a step backwards so he was out of reach. Adrenaline coursed through his veins.

Phoenix watched from the doorway, paralysed. She didn't intervene, or couldn't. Her eyes were fixed on the gun; her breath came in short gasps. She stared from Haden to Sol, tongue-tied.

"What are you going to do, shoot me?" Sol asked. He laughed.

Haden's blood boiled. He couldn't let that boy get away. It was self-defence, kill or be killed. This was the only solution. He looked from boy to girl – saw the terror upon Phoenix's face, and its absence on Sol's. He wished she would speak, he knew she would know what to do. She could find a way out for him. Phoenix did not move, she remained frozen and mute, hypnotised by the gun. Haden knew his fate was sealed. He could call it self-defence, convince himself his actions were just. Deep down he knew this was about power. He had to be dominant, he had to come out on top. If the Tsar couldn't keep his power, he was no use at all.

Haden looked his victim dead in the eye, and squeezed the trigger.

.

# Chapter Nineteen

Sol's body fell to the ground with a hard *thump!* Phoenix screamed, falling to her knees beside his warm corpse, her wide eyes transfixed by the bullet wound. She felt buried beneath a layer of concrete. It weighed heavy upon her, a mixture of despair and disbelief.

"Sol," she sobbed. "Sol, no, no, no. Don't leave me. Please don't leave me! I need you. You're all I've got! Sol, please!" Salty tears mixed with salty blood as Phoenix buried her living face in his dead one. She sobbed into his skin, slamming her fists hard against the blood-soaked cobbled street. Her knuckles stung from contact with the hard stones that scraped her skin, and soon her own blood mixed with Sol's.

Grief soon turned to anger. This was no time for crying, this was time for revenge. Phoenix slowly rose to her feet, but the Tsar was nowhere in sight. A crowd had gathered in the street, drawn by the sound of the gunshot and her screams. Police swarmed around. Phoenix had been oblivious to the buzz of life around her, fixated as she was on the figure of death. A police officer made her way to the scene of the crime. She towered over the girl's crouching form.

"My friend has been murdered," Phoenix said in Estonian. Her voice was little more than a choked whisper. "I was gone for two minutes. When I came back there was a man and a gun."

Phoenix spent the rest of the day in a Tallinn police station, where she endured the process of interviews and witness statements. She struggled through with her limited Estonian vocabulary. There were times when words failed her entirely. It was easier to lie in her first language, even easier in her second. Estonian was a minefield of words just out of reach and truths she didn't want to tell. Phoenix chose not to identify Sol's killer as the Tsar. She told the police a Russian stranger murdered her friend. Her rationale was that of all victims: she feared no one would believe her, and she herself would be blamed.

When Phoenix was finally finished with her statement, the police officer who had interviewed her asked "Is there anyone we can fetch to come and collect you? You shouldn't be alone at a time like this." Her fingers stood poised over a computer screen, ready to type. "No," Phoenix answered. "I'm all alone now. Sol was all I had." She broke down into tears.

"Where do you live?" the police officer asked. "I can arrange for someone to escort you home."

"I'm staying at the Estonian Institute of Scientific Research," Phoenix said. "I can get there myself." She rocked slowly backwards and forwards in her chair, unable to process the horror she had experienced.

"Miss Kashnikova, you have witnessed a traumatic event. I can't let you go home alone." The police officer's tone was sympathetic, and her blue eyes were kind. "You need someone to take care of you."

"Fine." Phoenix thought through her alternatives. She only knew three people in Tallinn, and Persephone wasn't an option. "Kai," she answered finally. "His name's Kai. He's also staying at the Estonian Institute of Scientific Research. I don't know his last name. He's just Kai."

"I'll send a message to the Institute," the police officer said. She tapped the glass computer screen, and spoke into it in rapid Estonian. Phoenix couldn't make out most of the words. The computer was far more advanced than any model she had seen; in ordinary circumstances she would be fascinated by it.

"Phoenix!" Kai immediately pulled her into a hug when he saw her. Her face was streaked with tears, and her eyelashes had formed into damp clumps around her puffy eyes. "Oh darling," he whispered, resting his chin on the top of her head. He hugged her tight against him. Phoenix was too numb to resist his touch; she fell into his arms, relieved to have someone to hold her. If it wasn't for his grip on her, she was sure she would fall to pieces.

"I'm sorry," Phoenix said. "They told me I needed someone to come, and I couldn't face Persephone. I don't know anyone here, it was either you or Dr Skryabin."

"Do you want to talk about it?" Kai asked gently. He took her hand in his as they left the police station.

"I don't know." Her voice broke on the final word. "I don't know what to do. Persephone hates me, Sol was all I had left. He's gone. I hate her. I hate her so badly. I hate her, and I hate the Tsar."

"The Tsar?" Kai asked, confused. His hand still held hers. It was warm and comforting, a tiny bud of life in the deserted abyss her world had become.

"The Tsar of Western Russia," Phoenix said, too exhausted to lie. "He killed Sol. I disappeared for two minutes, I came back, and he was there. There was a gun, and I— I couldn't move. He killed him, and it's my fault. The Tsar killed Sol because I didn't intervene."

"Phoenix," Kai said firmly, "this isn't your fault. Witnessing a crime doesn't make you the perpetrator. It was the Tsar who killed Sol, not you."

"You believe me?" she asked. Phoenix squeezed his hand. She wanted to drop to the ground, bury her face in the pavement and scream. Instead, she clung to the one human thing within reach.

"Why wouldn't I? You're friends with Persephone, the Tsarina. It's not impossible for you to know the Tsar."

"You're too good to be true," Phoenix said. "You're kind, and you're understanding, and you don't have a dark side. I'm convinced you're a figment of my imagination."

"We're all made differently. I'm as true as you are, and no more good." He gave her hand a gentle squeeze. "We're all made equal, Phoenix."

"Do you really believe that? I've met so many kinds of evil in my life, and so little good. Why shouldn't I hold you up on a pedestal, compared with all of that?"

"Because we're all human."

"That's debatable."

✝

When Phoenix reached the Institute, she knew she had to break the news to Persephone. Dread simmered within her as the lift drew her nearer to their rooms. She didn't know how to explain that both their worlds had shattered.

222

Phoenix knocked repeatedly on Persephone's door.

"What?" came the harsh reply. Persephone held the door with her hand, ready to slam it shut. Her eyes burned with fury.

"Sol's dead," Phoenix said bluntly.

"What do you mean, Sol's dead?" Persephone asked. Her voice faltered, and her hand dropped from the door. "I saw him yesterday. How can he be dead? This is Estonia, it's meant to be safe!"

"The Tsar... He was here, in Tallinn. He shot Sol. I saw the gun and I froze, all I could think of was Yuri. I couldn't move, I couldn't save him, this is all my—" She stopped midsentence. "No. No. It's all your fault. How could you marry that sadistic monster? What kind of evil possesses someone to play God and create the uncreatable? You may not be human, Persephone, and you may fucking hate me for telling you that, but you are a thousand times more human than that diabolical creature!"

"He can't be dead," Persephone said. Her face was emotionless. Phoenix couldn't understand why she wasn't crying or screaming or reacting like a normal human. A bitter thought in the back of her mind whispered *because she's not human.* She dismissed the thought instantly. This was not about Persephone's humanity, it was about whatever had happened between her and Sol.

"I saw the Tsar murder him." Phoenix's voice was stone cold. She broke into a fit of passion as the memory forced itself back into her brain. "He's dead. I felt his blood on my face. I felt his corpse. He's dead, and he's not coming back. You could have prevented this, you could have said no!"

"I didn't have a choice!" Persephone shouted. "If I said no, do you think he would have listened? No does not mean no to that man!"

"You should have fought," Phoenix said. "To die fighting is far better than dying as a side effect of another's apathy!"

"I fight, Phoenix. I fight all the time. Don't you ever accuse me of apathy, because that is certainly not a flaw of mine! How can you tell me I'm responsible, when only three days ago you told me my mind was controlled by the Tsar? I can't deal with your double standards. Not now, and not ever!"

"You're more emotional about my supposed double standards than about our friend's death," she said. It didn't make sense to her. Nothing made sense any more. "What did Sol possibly do to make you stop caring?"

"I do care," Persephone said. "Of course I care. He was my friend and I loved him, but it's not as black and white as that. I don't know how to feel about his death," the tears came hard and fast now, "because yesterday I almost wished it on him."

"How could you want that? When did you become such a monster?"

"I didn't want him dead," Persephone said. "I wanted him to permanently leave our lives. He was not a good person. You want him to be good because he was the first person who ever cared about you, and that makes you blind to what he really is."

"Just tell me what he did," Phoenix said. "Both of you skirt around the topic whenever I bring it up. If you're going to talk about him like he was terrible, you at least owe me the truth."

Persephone looked over Phoenix's shoulder into the hallway. There were people in the distance, not quite out of earshot.

"Come in," she said hurriedly, and shut the door behind them. "Do you remember when I told you I knew for certain Sol wasn't gay?" She paced back and forwards across her bedroom floor, focusing her gaze on the view from the window to avoid looking at her friend.

"I told you, it doesn't matter, because the fruit—"

"It does matter," Persephone said. "It matters because Sol was a homophobe."

"Okay," Phoenix said. She couldn't process the information. Every time she heard Sol's name she pictured his body lying dead on the ground. Things that would normally shock her paled in comparison to that. "Are you telling me you think bigots deserve to die?"

"No," Persephone said. "No, no. Of course not. I never once said Sol deserved to die. That was never what I meant." She paused, and sat down on the bed. She took hold of Phoenix's wrist, to make her sit down beside her. "When you told Sol about the fruit, he got angry at the Tsar. Angry for making him feel things that disgusted him. Angry for stealing him away from his family. Somehow, he knew the Tsar was bisexual. Sol set a honey trap. He seduced the Tsar, and had pictures taken. He planned to blackmail

224

the Tsar, or to release those photos to the public. You know what Western Russia is like, Phoenix! They couldn't have a gay Tsar. They would have killed him. I made Sol destroy the photos, but I don't think they were his only copy. I think that's why he returned to Moscow."

"I would rather the Tsar dead than Sol," Phoenix said. "I am not saying what he did was justified. It's awful and cruel, but don't you think the end justifies the means?"

"No!" Persephone said. "This is not about the Tsar and Sol as individual people, this is about what it represents! It's morally wrong to use someone's sexuality against them like that, to threaten to out them, especially in a country like Western Russia. It is wrong, regardless of who is involved. The end does not justify the means, not in this case."

"Normally I would agree with you. But this is the Tsar. He is an evil man, he controlled your mind, he controlled Sol's mind, he created you. He is a monster, Sphenn. Surely anything that brings him down is justified."

"This isn't about the Tsar!" Persephone burst out. "This is about Sol, and after knowing what Sol did, I could never trust him again."

"Sol would never hurt you," said Phoenix. "Sol loved you, he loved us both."

"Sol loved who he thought I was." Persephone took a deep breath. She stood up and began pacing again. "Would Sol have loved me if he knew I was a robot, if I was less than human?"

"It doesn't matter what you are, he would have loved you regardless."

"No, he wouldn't."

"Persephone..."

"The Tsar isn't the only one who's bisexual, Phoenix! Sol was as much a danger to me as he was to Haden. I am devastated he's dead – he was a good friend to me for a while. But he is not innocent in this. It was kill or be killed, and whilst I don't condone what Haden did, there is a part of me that understands it."

"This isn't about you." Phoenix stood up to leave. "Our friend is dead. I can't deal with you right now. His burial is on Sunday. The police are arranging it."

✝

It rained on the day of Sol's funeral: a slow, constant drizzle, pattering softly against the ground. There was no minister to officiate a ceremony, only two girls, one with hair of brown and one with hair of red, standing in the rain beside a coffin in the cold ground. Neither girl spoke, not to each other, and not to the corpse in the coffin. Persephone cried. Her tears flowed with the ease of the beautiful. Phoenix emancipated herself from emotion. She stared into the grave with her own brand of apathy. Persephone knelt to the ground and took a handful of wet earth; she gently released it into the grave. Phoenix mirrored the motion, and soon the grave was full. Persephone sobbed against the ground. Phoenix observed her with a formidable face of stone. The spluttering rain strengthened to a shower, soaking both girls' black garments.

"Phoenix," said a voice just above her ear. A warm hand slipped into her cold muddy one. Kai.

She didn't say a word to him, just squeezed his hand, comforted by his presence. With a final glare at Persephone, Phoenix turned away from the scene. They could fight later, now it was the time for remembrance, and the time to forget.

"I want to stay," Phoenix said to Kai as they left the cemetery. "I want to stay in Tallinn." They stepped out onto the road. She didn't look behind her to see if Persephone followed.

"I wish you would," he said. "You're a good friend."

"You've only known me since Tuesday," Phoenix reminded him. She felt numb.

"I feel like I've seen every side of you in that time." They crossed the road, to take shelter under the sloping roof that jutted out from a green, wooden house.

"You haven't." She clutched his hand tighter than before. "You haven't seen my good side. There is one, I promise."

"Tell me about it," he said. His voice was quiet against the cacophony of the pouring rain. "Tell me about your good side."

"I'm smart. I'm loyal, I'd fight to the death for someone I

226

loved. I'm independent, most of the time. Though I also have some codependent qualities. I'm a person of juxtapositions. Wow, I've veered away from the positive already." She leant back against the wall behind her, watching the rain splatter against the asphalt surface of the road. "I know how to be happy, is what I'm trying to say. I know how to smile, and I know how to live. In spite of everything. So if I don't stay here, don't worry about me. I know how to survive."

"Surviving isn't living."

"It's still preferable to dying." She held his gaze for a moment. Their proximity made her uncomfortable now. Phoenix could feel herself opening up to him. She wasn't ready for this closeness, not in the wake of recent events. She had lost the last two people she had let into her heart. She wasn't ready for a third casualty. "Come on, the rain's almost stopped. We should make a run for the Institute before it starts up again."

# Chapter Twenty
## *September*
### *2151*

It was hot inside the Estonian Institute of Scientific Research. Outside, the cold chill of autumn pierced through skin with merciless precision. Inside, the heating was turned up to a sweltering volume, and the swarm of new students sweated heavily as they waited for direction.

"Dr Skry, you gonna start or what?" asked a male voice. Kai glanced at the questioner, Erik, whom he remembered from induction week as a troublemaker and a prize idiot. Kai scanned the crowd of students, searching for the dark hair and seaweed eyes he so longed to see. He had resigned himself to the fact he wouldn't see her again. In spite of this, she had dominated his thoughts during the train ride from Tartu to Tallinn. This place had become synonymous with memories of Her, and he couldn't shake them from his thoughts, no matter how hard he tried.

"We're waiting on one more student," Dr Skryabin answered Erik. He adjusted his glasses as he spoke. The scientist was flustered, perhaps from the temperature, or the impatient flock of teenagers that surrounded him.

Hope sprang in Kai's heart – a heart that soon found the opportunity to skip a beat, as he looked up, over Dr Skryabin's shoulder.

"Sorry I'm late, Doctor! I came from the other side of town!" gasped a breathless Phoenix, crashing into the room. She hastily tied her hair above her head as her eyes searched the room for a familiar face. She let out a squeal of excitement when she saw him.

"Kashnikova, timing is important. I have taken a huge gamble on you. It would be appreciated if you returned the favour by learning the fine art of punctuality."

"I'm terribly sorry," she said. Kai grinned, and gestured for her to join him.

"Hi!" she mouthed in Russian, rushing over to him. To Kai's surprise, Phoenix threw her arms around his neck and gave him an enthusiastic hug.

"Hey," he whispered. He lifted her up, to relieve the pressure

228

from her tiptoes. He released her quickly when he caught Dr Skryabin's stern eye.

"Hey, yourself," she said. Her voice was warm and hushed. Her eyes locked onto his, ignoring the hustle and bustle of the room around them. There was a lightness about her that was absent the first time they met. The weight that crushed her had been removed from her shoulders.

"How've you been?" Kai asked.

"Great!" Phoenix said. "I worked in Tallinn all summer, at this crazy guest house in the Old Town. It was wonderful! I love this city so much, I'm free here. I feel like a different person." She paused, glancing behind her to make sure no one was listening. "Don't tell anyone I came here with Persephone, okay? That whole chapter of my life, it died with Sol. It's as dead to me as he is. How are you, anyway?" He had her full attention. It made Kai feel warm and nervous.

"Kashnikova, Chistikov!" Dr Skryabin interrupted their conversation. "Would you like to share your whispers with the rest of the room? It must be important, since you partook in this conversation instead of hearing the list of rules."

"I was listening to the rules!" Phoenix protested. "Can't a girl multitask? You missed rule number 5," she adopted a mocking tone, "No going into other students' bedrooms after curfew." She smiled sweetly.

"Indeed I did."

"It's a pretty stupid rule," Phoenix said. "We'll be in our twenties by the time we graduate. You can't really prevent people from getting it on with each other." She watched Dr Skryabin's face turn a deeper shade of red. Kai couldn't help laughing at her nerve. "What if we wanted to have late-night study sessions?" She watched the scientist like a cat watching a bird, ready to dig her claws in at the slightest hint of weakness.

"Now, where was I up to?" Dr Skryabin floundered, unsure how to respond to the girl's challenge.

"Rule number 7," Phoenix said helpfully. "10 o'clock curfew. Really the curfew rule should come before the rules relating to the curfew. It would make it easier to follow."

"Yes, Kashnikova, well done for reading the rule book." He

directed his next words to the other students. "I wish you all had the motivation for such research."

"I guess you're not going to follow rule number 5?" Kai whispered to a smug Phoenix.

"You'll always be welcome in my bedroom," she said. "Not like that, obviously," she added, when she saw the expression on Kai's face.


They spent the rest of the morning snatching moments of whispered conversation as Dr Skryabin conducted an extensive tour of the Institute's facilities. The scientist led them to the cafeteria, and continued to rattle off an extensive list of rules.

Phoenix leant towards Kai's ear and whispered "These rules are endless. Are they training us to be scientists or zombies?"

"With Skryabin, it could be either. He's had a thing about humanoid monsters, like zombies or robots, since induction week."

"Oh." Phoenix bit her lip as painful memories resurfaced. She forced herself to recover quickly. "Maybe he is one," she suggested. "Programmed to adjust his glasses every minute-and-a-half."

They got into line for the lunch queue; Kai chattered away to Phoenix. She soon deduced a problem, a chink in her well-oiled armour. The food was served by robots, who were programmed to give out balanced portions of healthy food. The peach slices on her plate gleamed with moisture. One was curved in the shape of a cruel mouth, taunting her. Phoenix followed Kai to a table, staring at the food on her tray. Her mouth searched for hair to chew, but her hair was all out of reach.

"What's wrong?" he asked, finally noticing the droop of her face, the mixture of fear and misery there.

"I've got a... thing about fruit," Phoenix said. The peaches glistened, wet from the juice they were preserved in. Her stomach flipped; she felt the tell-tale signs of her past coming back to haunt her. "I can't eat fruit, any fruit. It makes me really— It— I just can't."

"Hey, Phoenix, it's okay." He reached for her hand across the table.

"It's not," she said. It was the last thing she wanted to talk about.

Frustration brewed up inside her, and she knew if she didn't speak soon, her words would emerge in a scream or a sob. "You heard what they said when we came in, about balanced diets and all that. They'll put fruit on my plate at every meal. I can't— I can't cope with that. They're robots, it's not like I can ask them to make an exception for me, they're machines."

"How did this start?" Kai asked.

"I had a traumatic childhood," she said. "There are memories that involve fruit, and I can't eat it." She tried hard to breathe, but her breath came faster and faster, until she was nearly hyperventilating. "It brings it all back, and it makes me sick. I can't eat fruit without throwing up."

"Do you have PTSD?" he asked.

"I haven't fought any wars." Phoenix squeezed her eyes shut and forced herself to focus on her breath.

"You have internally. You're traumatised by what happened to you," he said. "Look at you, you just had a panic attack. It's natural for those traumatising memories to resurface when you're reminded of what happened. There is a solution to your immediate problem: you just need to see a doctor. They'll be able to give you a note so you don't have to have fruit. There's a code you can give the robots, it's what they do for people with allergies."

"Okay."

"You're not going to argue?" He was surprised.

"No. You're right. I should see a doctor."

"Okay, I'll come with you. We'll go tonight."

"You don't have to come," she said quickly.

"I'm not an idiot," Kai said, "I know you won't go if I don't come with you."

"Thanks for having faith in me."

"I don't know you well," he said. "But in the short time we've known each other, we've been through a lot. I want to trust you. You have a debilitating phobia of fruit, the solution is to see a doctor. What have you got to lose?"

She wanted to trust him, she couldn't find a reason not to trust him. But a lifetime of secrecy prevented her.

"My dignity, perhaps?" Phoenix stared into her fingernails as if they held the answers she sought. "Who in their right mind would

231

be scared of fruit?"

"What did the doctor say?" Kai asked as Phoenix walked out into the hallway. She had spent half an hour in the Institute's resident GP's office, and she was positively fuming.

She answered in Estonian, to make her imitation as accurate as possible. "Miss Kashnikova, you have no obvious allergy to fruit. Maybe you should see a therapist. Here, have a few vitamin pills because you're so unhealthy!" Fury emanated from Phoenix's pores, as if she was burning from the inside out. Buried deep beneath the fury was shame. She had allowed herself to be vulnerable. For the first time in her life, she had asked for help, only to be rejected.

"I thought it would help," Kai said. "I'm sorry."

"It's fine. I didn't expect anything less."

"Did she give you a note for the cafeteria?" he asked hopefully. She could see he felt bad. Kai's hands were firmly clasped, to stop himself from fidgeting, and he watched her with sad puppy-dog eyes.

"Yep, I got a code for the robots. She also recommended some therapists." Phoenix did not look thrilled by this prospect. "I rejected that offer, so don't you dare try to convince me."

"I didn't say a word," Kai said gently. "Come on."

"Where? I just want to go to bed."

"There's this place we call the Time Capsule. It's a collection of random junk from a hundred years ago, back when this place was a hotel. There's this room full of sofas where we used to gather during induction week. All the others will be there. It might take your mind off things."

"Hey, Kai!" called a female voice as they opened the door. The door was too narrow for them to enter side-by-side. Kai gestured for Phoenix to walk ahead of him. She was nervous, her new classmates felt like a hostile alien species.

"Who've you got with you?" asked the girl.

"This is Phoenix Kashnikova." Kai placed a reassuring hand on her shoulder as he introduced her.

"Oh," said the girl, whose name was Abi. Her dark-blonde hair was pulled back into a messy bun, and she wore an oversized black sweater. Something about her face reminded Phoenix of a warthog. "You're Skryabin's protégée, aren't you? I heard he put up quite a fight to get you your place."

"Well, I heard nothing about that," she answered coldly. Phoenix glared at Kai's hand on her shoulder. Before, his touch had felt comforting. Now, it seemed patronising.

The vast room was filled with students, lounging on antique sofas. A quick glance around the room told Phoenix that Kai was the only person here she wanted to know. Everyone looked so ordinary, and she couldn't handle their ordinariness, not after palaces and robots and royal brides. This was supposed to be her biggest adventure yet, but it terrified her. She hadn't been prepared for the people.

"How come you're here?" Abi asked. Phoenix had taken an instant dislike to Abi, and she couldn't help wanting to show her superiority. She was determined to prove she belonged here.

"Dr Skryabin offered me a place," she said with an insincere smile. "I was here in May, after I made a significant scientific discovery. He thought I had huge potential, enough to win me a full scholarship."

"What was this discovery?" Abi was unimpressed by this boast. Her curiosity was piqued, but the jealousy in her tone did not go unnoticed by Phoenix.

"It's not my place to say," she said. "Out of respect for the patient's privacy, I've opted for secrecy."

Abi snorted. She didn't believe anything Phoenix said.

"Shall we sit down?" Kai intervened. He gestured to the sofa opposite Abi.

"Are you two together?" someone asked as Phoenix sat down.

"Me and Kai?" She laughed. "No way!" Her laugh came out harsh and fake. She searched for an excuse to leave.

Kai, amused by her reaction, said "Come on sweetie, you can tell them." He stretched a lazy arm around her shoulders, laughing a little. He seemed different around his peers.

"Shut up." Phoenix kicked his leg in retaliation. The joke didn't feel funny to her.

"No," he said after a minute. He retracted his arm, and patted her hand gently in apology. "We barely know each other. But we're very good friends."

"Very good friends, who barely know each other?" Phoenix laughed. Her stomach tied itself in knots as other people gathered around them. She felt like a freak, or the star attraction of a zoo filled with deformed animals. The way the others looked at her made her feel physically marked as *different,* branded with ink she couldn't remove.

In the palace in Moscow, Persephone woke with a start. The room was white and sterile, unfamiliar. There were no windows. The room had two doors. One led to a bathroom, and the other was locked from the outside. Persephone twisted the tap in the bathroom sink, until icy-cold water spilled into her hands. She dabbed it onto her throbbing temples. Persephone knew with a dreadful sense of foreboding that she had been unconscious for more than a few hours or days, but it was not until she caught sight of her reflection in the bathroom mirror that she had an indication of how much time had passed. Her hair now fell past her shoulders, untangled in spite of the time she had spent asleep, but this was not the only part of her that had grown. Persephone wore a sheer white nightgown that clung to the curves of her body; beneath it, her abdomen had begun to swell. Persephone opened her mouth and let out a blood-curdling scream.

"Are you coming to the time capsule tonight?" Kai asked. They sat at the back of the classroom. It had been a long day, and both were nearing the end of their capacity for concentration.

Phoenix glanced up from her textbook. "Maybe. I don't know." She tapped her pencil absent-mindedly against her desk.

"Kashnikova! Chistikov! Why is it always the two of you who talk when I am speaking?" asked Dr Skryabin. He sighed with excessive melodrama, piercing Phoenix with his gaze, as if she were solely to blame. "Both of you can stay behind after the lesson and clean the classroom."

Phoenix pulled a face of protest, but stayed silent. She didn't go looking for trouble, yet somehow, it was always at her side.

"It was me talking, not Phoenix," Kai told Dr Skryabin. "Don't blame her. It's my fault."

"If Kashnikova were blameless, she wouldn't have responded," Dr Skryabin said simply. "I'll talk to you both once class is over."


When the lesson was finished, Phoenix and Kai lingered by their desks, waiting for Dr Skryabin to admonish them. He took his time to stack papers and tidy his desk, as if he were alone. They exchanged surreptitious glances, not daring to engage in another whispered conversation.

"Look, Doctor, Phoenix isn't at fault here," Kai began. Dr Skryabin finally turned his attention to the pair of them, as if he had only just remembered they were there.

"Perhaps not this time," he agreed. "Do you know why I kept you both behind?"

Phoenix opened her mouth to speak, but hastily shut it again.

"Go ahead, Kashnikova, hit me with the best you've got." His voice was teasing.

"You kept us here to punish us," she said. "Because we talk too much, which is disrespectful to you. But it seems like you hate me, so I don't know if that's the reason at all. Everyone says you put yourself on the line to get me a place here, which you wouldn't do if you hated me. It doesn't make sense. You knew what I was like from day one."

Dr Skryabin sighed, and looked from Phoenix to Kai. "You two are by far the most talented students we have had in many years, and I am genuinely glad you're friends. It will be useful to you in the future. Science isn't an industry built on talent, it is built on research, and research comes from discipline and patience. In order to progress to a higher level of scientific education, you must be dedicated, and I am struggling to see dedication in either of you. You're too distracted by each other. I understand you're at an age where education isn't your first priority, and that's natural. But it simply isn't good enough. Chistikov, can I please have a moment alone with Kashnikova?"

"Of course." Kai swiftly left the room.

"What am I going to do with you?" Dr Skryabin asked. He threw his face into his hands with existential weariness. "Kashnikova, you are an outstanding student, on paper. You achieved 100% on the past five tests, your practical examinations have been superb, and incredibly original. Your essays are also thought provoking, and I believe you have a greater understanding of the ethical issues of science than anyone else in this class, due to your relationship with Persephone. I can't understand why you're not taking your studies seriously during class." He paused. When he spoke again his tone was gentler. "Which area are you planning to specialise in?"

"Neuroscience," said Phoenix, "though I also have an interest in robotics. But I wouldn't study that. I don't think it's an area that should be advanced in. It's not ethical."

"Who is Estonia's leading researcher in the field of neuroscience?"

"You, I believe."

"Exactly," said Dr Skryabin. "This year, you have a number of teachers, because you are learning science as a broad subject. Next year, you will have fewer teachers, and learn in depth about specific areas. In third year, however, you will specialise, to prepare you for the industry placement you will undertake after graduation. You will have one supervisor for the majority of third year."

"And if I specialise in neuroscience, that supervisor will be you?" Phoenix began to cotton on. She glanced up at Dr Skryabin, her brow creased with worry as she recognised her mistake.

"Yes," he said. "I will be your academic mentor. I will also be responsible for writing the reference that will make or break your career. Do you understand why I'm frustrated with you, Kashnikova? I can foresee these next three years may be difficult. I have bet on you to the Institute's board, I promised them you would excel. You need to change your attitude, because I cannot risk you being anything less than the success I know you'll become." The passion in his voice surprised her. His eyes were intense, and he looked as though he wanted nothing more than to grab her by the shoulders and shake her until she listened.

"I don't try to be difficult," Phoenix said, "I promise. I just… I can't cope."

"What can't you cope with?" Dr Skryabin asked. He had predicted their conversation would end in Phoenix being forced to open up, but he hadn't imagined she would go through with it. She was secretive, she rarely trusted anyone, let alone him. He had forced her hand: it was speak or suffer, and she chose to speak.

"I can't cope with the people." She sat down on the edge of her desk. "I can cope with academia, I love it more than anything. I love learning, and I love science. It's who I am, this is where I belong. I am so grateful to you for everything you've done for me, please don't doubt that. But I can't deal with the social side of this." She gestured with her hands in frustration, wrangling an invisible ball of air. "I find myself hating people for the most trivial reasons. They're so boring, and shallow, and their interest in science is only superficial. The only person I like here is Kai, but I don't want to share him with all of them. Everyone loves him, because he's the nicest person ever. They're all friends with him. But he's my friend, and I don't want him being friends with them, because that means he's not with me. And I miss Persephone. I hate her guts, but I miss her. I'm self-sabotaging. My life would be easier if this all fell apart." She tugged at her hair, shoving it into her mouth, and chewed worriedly on its ends.

Dr Skryabin sat down on the desk opposite Phoenix, so they were eye-to-eye. He could see the pain in her face, the desolate look of someone who believes themselves to be lost beyond all hope.

"Listen, my girl," he said gently. "People are the hardest demons you will ever face. There's a reason people like us are drawn to science: it's a profession where we are either solitary researchers, or surrounded only by the smartest people."

"I don't like smart people," Phoenix said sulkily.

"Because you want to be the smartest?"

"I don't like any people."

"Except Kai?" Dr Skryabin pushed.

"Except Kai. And Persephone. I don't like Persephone sometimes. But I love her."

"Do you love Kai?"

"Loving people isn't worth the effort."

"You value him, though?"

"Of course I do."

"I value Kai too," Dr Skryabin said. "Kai is a nice, intelligent boy. He's the perfect companion for you. He's smart, but he's not a show-off, and he's not quite as smart as you, but near enough that you can't find any stupidity in him."

"He must be at least a bit stupid, if he's friends with all that lot," Phoenix said.

"Or smart," Dr Skryabin countered. "Kai knows they're not just his peers, they're his future colleagues. This may be the one area where he's smarter than you."

"Are you saying our success is determined by a popularity contest? We all know my future is fucked if that's the case!"

"Grow up, girl. Your classmates would like you if you gave them the chance. They admire you already – they can do that from a distance. You would have a lot more friends if you dared to let people in. You are a strong, independent, intelligent woman, and if you want to renounce the company of those you view as inferior, go ahead. Become the autonomous, mad genius that you are, and enjoy it. But I don't think you're ready for solitude, not at your age. There is a long road ahead. You need company, and you need love. Rely on Kai, Phoenix, rely on him, because he is the only person you've chosen for your equal. And rely on me, too, it's what I'm here for."

238

"You're here to listen to all my melodrama?"

"Yes, that's my job." He held her gaze with his pebble-like eyes. Phoenix couldn't remember the last time she had felt seen. Dr Skryabin saw her – the real her. He saw through the performance. Phoenix allowed herself to imagine a future, a future where she was on the other side of the desk. She didn't know how to be a peer, a classmate, a friend, but she could be a mentor. It occurred to her now that Dr Skryabin had a lot more to teach her than science, he also taught her that there was a place for her in this world, even if she had a lot of growing to do to get there.

"You're Estonia's leading researcher in the field of neuroscience."

"And I have chosen to teach, alongside my research. A large part of teaching is listening to melodrama. I didn't want brilliance, I wanted to help people learn, to show them the beauty of science."

"All my classmates, they don't see that beauty."

"They will by the time they're done," said Dr Skryabin. "You're at different stages in your evolution. You're an amphibian, whilst they're still in the water. You've lost your gills, you can breathe air. You can see this whole wide world, and they can only see their portion of it. By the end of their education, they will love science just as you do now."

"What about me?"

"You will evolve further. You will blossom into a talented scientist, and you will go far."

"Thank you," Phoenix said.

"Chistikov!" Dr Skryabin called. Kai re-entered the room. "Do you know why I wanted the two of you to clean this classroom?"

"Child labour is cheaper than cleaning staff?" Phoenix suggested.

"No," Dr Skryabin said. The glimmer in his eyes showed that her sarcastic manner was growing on him. "It's a reminder that you two have the potential to go far. If you waste that potential, there are a wealth of menial jobs waiting for you."

"How considerate," Phoenix said.

"I'll leave you to it," Dr Skryabin said as he vacated the room.

✠

"I'm sorry," Kai said when they were alone. "This is my fault."

"Don't be." Phoenix took a vacuum cleaner from the cupboard.

"It is my fault," Kai said. "I should know better than to start a conversation when he's talking. It never ends well." He tipped his head back against the wall, and let out a sigh.

"You know what? You're right, it's entirely your fault." Phoenix pushed the vacuum cleaner in his direction. "You can do this as punishment."

Kai didn't complain, he simply took it from her hands. Their fingers brushed slightly as the transaction took place.

"I'm kind of glad he got mad at us." Phoenix returned to her perched position on the edge of her desk. "He hit me with a few hard truths." She swung her legs slowly back and forth, lost in thought. "He thinks I'm wasting my potential."

"So you think I'm a little bit stupid, huh?" Kai asked. He smiled mischievously.

"You heard what I said?" Phoenix was horror-struck. "Oh my God, no, no, no. You weren't meant to hear any of that!" Her face felt like someone had lit a match beneath her skin. She shuddered with horror to think of what Kai could infer from her words.

"Thin walls." He grinned from ear to ear, amused by her discomfort.

"Crap, crap, crap, crap."

"Phoenix, calm down." He patted her shoulder. "You also said you valued me. That's what I'll take from it, not your remarks about my stupidity. I know which comments mean something."

"Why do you have to be so bloody perfect? You'll give me a bad name, honestly!"

Kai didn't answer. They cleaned the classroom in silence, but as Phoenix turned to leave, he said "You never did say whether you'd come to the time capsule or not."

"You heard what I said to Skryabin. I don't belong around those people. I don't fit."

"Amphibians still use the water," Kai said. "You may not need these people, but you can still use them."

"Are you suggesting manipulation?" Phoenix was shocked to hear these words from Kai.

"Have I come down from the pedestal yet?" Kai laughed. His

240

brown eyes were warm, and she wanted to rest in their glow. "It came out wrong. I wasn't telling you to chew them up and spit them out. All I meant was: friendships would be useful for you." He paused, choosing his words carefully. "You're my best friend, Phoenix, and I will always be here for you, but you need more than me. I can't be everything to you."

"I know that, and I'll make more of an effort, it's just…"

"What?"

"It's Abi. I can't stand her."

"Why?"

"She's—Whatever, she's your friend, and I won't say anything mean about her. I've been too quick to judge people here. I need to stop."

"We can go somewhere else. Just me and you?"

"There's nowhere to go. You know we're not allowed out at night."

"It's six o'clock. We'll be fine so long as we're back before curfew." Kai flashed a smile; his eyes lit up and melted her resistance. "We could go and get food."

"You know I can't say no to food!" Phoenix frowned. She didn't understand why she was so resistant to being alone with him. It wasn't the first time they had been outside of the Institute together. Now the act of going out into the city alone felt heavily weighted. Perhaps it was the knowledge that he had heard her conversation with Dr Skryabin, he knew how important he was to her.

"Come on then." Kai took her hand, and led her through the white corridors of the Institute, and out into the cold, evening air.

# Chapter Twenty Two

Phoenix's mood was reflective as she and Kai ambled through the snowy streets of Tallinn, venturing to the ancient, cobbled regions of the Old Town. The shops were closed at this hour, with wooden shutters fixed across their windowpanes. The only light came from lamps spread sporadically through the street.

"Where are we going?" Phoenix asked, as the paths narrowed and her feet slipped on the uneven surface. The world was peaceful here; this was the Tallinn she loved. The streets were silent, almost eerily so. Their footsteps were muffled by thick dunes of snow that reached up to her ankles. The world was empty, save for their two figures. Kai was carefree, walking with a skip in his stride, Phoenix walked slower, each step she took was placed deliberately.

"Do you like ice cream?" he asked.

"Who doesn't?"

"Some people don't in December," Kai said. "Might be something to do with the snow.'"

"Some people are idiots," said Phoenix. "So long as we go somewhere warm, I can handle cold food."

"That's exactly what I was thinking. There's this place on Lai street, they make the best ice cream."

"I know the place you mean," Phoenix said, "I worked down the street from there last summer, but never got around to going."

"So neuroscience, huh?" Kai asked as they turned from the alleyway into a broader street.

"You know you're not meant to use things you eavesdropped on as conversation starters, right?" Her eyes twinkled, in spite of herself. "And, yeah. Neuroscience. I've been thinking about it since I started here."

"I've been considering it too," Kai said.

"I guess we'll be stuck with each other for all our time here." The thought comforted her. Phoenix didn't like to think too far into the future, she knew it wasn't promised. Something about Kai made the future seem like a safe bet, a finish line that was almost in sight, a place to come home to.

"With each other, and with our good friend Dr Skryabin."

"I do like him, sometimes," Phoenix said. "I just don't think he likes me very much." They walked along the inside of the Old Town walls now, shadows dancing across their faces in the dim light cast by street lamps. "I like winding him up. Not the talking in class stuff—that's not deliberate—but the rest of it, my sarcastic answers to all his questions. He takes himself so seriously." She sighed. "I saw a different side of him tonight. He was kind to me. I respect him more. I've always respected him, but now I see him clearer. He's a good person."

"He is," Kai agreed, "and he wants what's best for us."

"Are you mad at him?" Phoenix asked. "Because he said you weren't as smart as me?"

"Why would I be mad about that?" Kai seemed surprised by her question.

"Aren't you threatened by it?"

"Of course not!" he said. "It's great being friends with someone smarter than me. I learn something new every time we talk; we always have interesting conversations. No matter how smart someone is, there will always be someone smarter."

"That's an interesting perspective." Phoenix laughed. "My point of view is more 'no one lives up to my standards, the world is populated with stupid.' Your attitude is refreshing." Snowflakes caught in her hair, and landed on the tip of her nose. She brushed the snow away; it melted on her fingertips.

"What you're really thinking is: 'I need to find the person who's smarter than me.' Am I right, or am I right?" His face held a look of pure affection; it felt alien to her. Her mind screamed *Not safe! Not safe! Not safe!* Phoenix didn't want to open this can of worms with Kai. If she let him in, he would become a liability to her. But he looked at her in a way she had never been looked at before, and in spite of her best efforts, she couldn't bring herself to look away.

"You know me too well, though you're actually the tiniest bit wrong."

"See, you are smarter."

"I know who the person is," she said. "The one who's smarter than me. It's the Tsar. He's done things I could never do, things I'd never want to do. He's the smartest person I've ever met, and he's evil. He's cruel. He has no morality, no ethics, not even the tiniest trace of a conscience. Intelligence isn't the be all and end all of virtue. I'm smarter than you, yet you're kinder than I could ever hope to be, just as the Tsar is smarter than me, but I have far more compassion than him."

"You continue to astound me."

"That's what I was going for." The air was heavy between them.

"Here we are." He opened the door to the café. The room was spacious, with wide windows, and tables and chairs cut from thick, light-coloured wood. Each table was adorned with a pale-pink tablecloth and a white candle. Kai headed to the counter to order, and Phoenix went to claim a table.

"You didn't answer my question," he reminded her. "Why neuroscience?"

"I'm interested in the brain," Phoenix said. "I know so many people who live without one, I'm curious how that works. What about you?"

"It's something I've always been interested in."

"Always, like since you were a foetus," she asked, "or more recent than that?"

"Since I was a foetus. Before my brain developed I knew I was interested in brains."

"With a comment like that, I really have to ask: did your brain develop at all?" She hit his hand lightly. He hit hers back, and they continued this back and forth until they both fell into a fit of giggles.

They were interrupted by the arrival of a waitress, carrying bowls of ice cream and a bottle of syrup.

"Thanks," Phoenix and Kai said simultaneously.

"Have you ever tried that stuff before?" Kai asked as Phoenix poured syrup into her bowl. "They like to experiment with new flavours here. Sometimes the results are... unique."

"Nope." She shook her head. "It's syrup. Have you ever heard of syrup that wasn't nice?"

At that moment, Phoenix caught a few words from the radio in the corner of the room:

"*The Tsar of Western Russia confirmed in a statement today that his wife, Tsarina Persephone, is in the second trimester of*

244

*pregnancy. The Tsarina was reported missing seven months ago. This is the first news of her since May, and sources have been unable to confirm when she was found. The Tsar has refused to comment."*

"Phoenix—" Kai started.

"This syrup is horrible!" Phoenix made it clear the subject was closed.

He squirted a little syrup onto his spoon to taste it. "It's like you," he said, after making a great show of swilling the syrup around in his mouth. "Sweet at first, then there's a bitter after-taste. I like it."

"Well, you would," she said under her breath. "I've never been sweet."

☦

They ended up at the Time Capsule after all. Phoenix had returned to her state of sullenness, submerged in melancholia at the thought of Persephone's betrayal. She wanted to avoid Kai's questions, and his pity. She figured a trip to the Time Capsule was her best hope at convincing him she was fine.

"Want a drink?" asked Abi. She lounged on a brown-corduroy sofa, tipsy and relaxed.

Phoenix nodded, and accepted a glass of wine. She downed it in one.

"Are you okay?" Abi asked. She sat up straighter, mildly concerned.

"Yup. Why wouldn't I be?"

"I've never seen you drink before."

"You've never seen me socialise before,"

"True." Abi nodded. "We do notice when you're not here."

"Why?" Phoenix prised the bottle of wine out of Abi's hand, and poured herself another glass. There was only one way she would get through this night: intoxicated. "I'm not... I'm not part of your group. I'm not part of anyone's group. I... am a lone wolf. I am an island. I need no one and no one needs me."

"What you are is a lightweight," Abi said. "I've never seen someone get drunk this quickly. And you are part of our group.

245

You have as much right to be here as anyone else."

Phoenix drank more wine, this time straight from the bottle. She gulped it down until the red liquid spilled over her lips and down the front of her shirt. It seeped into the black material, disguised by the darkness of the fabric.

"I thought you hated me." Alcohol made her honest.

"I don't hate you." Abi carefully removed the bottle of wine from Phoenix's grasp. "We're different people who want the same things. Maybe we're competitors, rivals, on occasion. But I don't hate you."

"That's very kind," Phoenix said.

A moment later, she felt a hand resting on her shoulder. She didn't have to look behind her to know it belonged to Kai. She shrugged his hand off her.

"I'm *fine*," she said.

"Sure you are." He sat down beside her on the sofa.

"I'm going to go and... talk to some people." Phoenix stood up abruptly, abandoning Abi and Kai. She meandered around the room for a while. The prospect of initiating a conversation with any of her classmates was daunting.

Phoenix spotted a stray bottle of vodka balancing precariously on the edge of an armchair. She made a beeline for it. Upon rescuing the vodka from its predicament, she took a large gulp, choked, and spat alcohol all over her shoes.

"Ugh," Phoenix groaned. The wine had gone to her head. She didn't want to be here, didn't want to be anywhere. The world was spinning. It was a relief when the floor welcomed her into its carpeted embrace.

"Are you okay?" A group of girls approached her. They leant down on the carpet beside her, reaching out their hands to help her up.

"I'm fine," Phoenix insisted. "I just wanna stay here. Don't wanna move. Moving is bad. Moving bad. Life bad. Everything bad." She rolled over, so her face was buried in the thick carpet.

"Let me get you some water," one of the girls offered. "You need to drink lots of water."

Phoenix shook her head, but when the girl returned with a glass of water, she accepted it gratefully. It felt good to be taken care of. The girls' mundane conversations were soothing to her ears. Phoenix rejoiced in the fact she didn't care an ounce for what they said. Boredom may kill the mind, but it eased her soul. As long as she numbed herself to thoughts of Persephone, the pain didn't reach her.

Kai observed Phoenix from a vantage point a few sofas away. She talked animatedly. It was a joy to watch, but he couldn't help wonder how much of this was really her. Alcohol transformed Phoenix: her eyes were alight, and her cheeks shined a glossy red. She was beautiful, but she didn't look real.

"Why don't you eat fruit?" asked Hanna, one of the girls who sat with Phoenix. Kai rushed over.

"Phoenix," he said, "I think you should go to bed now. Remember what Dr Skryabin said. You know he'll have your neck if you go to class hungover."

"But I'm having fun," Phoenix said.

*Really?* Kai thought. If Phoenix were sober, she would barely interact with anyone else in this room.

"He might suspend you," Kai said. "You don't want that." He was desperate. He couldn't watch her like this, he was overcome by the desire to protect her.

"Okay, okay, I'm coming!" she agreed grumpily.

"You'll thank me in the morning," Kai said. They stood alone in the lift. Phoenix could barely stay upright. "You don't want them knowing all your secrets. It's none of their business."

She considered his words for a moment.

"You're very nice to me," she mused. "Why is that?"

"We're friends."

"Are we friends?" she asked with sincerity. Sadness clouded her dark, impermeable eyes. "Or are we more than friends?" She voiced the question that had followed them both like a ghost all evening. Kai searched the solemnity of her eyes, looking into their blue-green depths. He told himself it was the strong wine talking, not Phoenix.

Kai didn't know what to tell her, so he stayed silent.

Phoenix didn't speak again until they were outside her room. "Come in," she said.

Kai shook his head. He didn't trust her or himself right now.

"Please?" she begged. Kai could see she was frustrated, desperate.

"It's not a good idea." He began to move away from her.

Phoenix grabbed his hand, and didn't let him go.

"Goodnight, Phoenix," Kai said firmly. In a moment of weakness, he bent down and kissed her cheek. She kissed his cheek in return. Her lips were warm and wet against his skin.

Phoenix kissed his face again. Her eyes were wild, like a feral kitten. When her lips touched his face, they were so close to his mouth that he felt the ghost of them against his own lips. Phoenix watched him determinedly for a moment, and finally planted her mouth firmly on his. The kiss was a shock. He knew it was coming, but it still took him by surprise. The softness, the passion, the way her thumbs stroked gentle lines across his face. It was a fantasy he had never let himself indulge in, and now it was real, she was real. Phoenix pushed him against the door, pressing her body as close as she could against his tall, firm frame. The air between them was thick and heavy. Kai couldn't believe that it was only alcohol causing this kiss. Before he knew what he was doing, he kissed her with an untamed passion he never knew he possessed. This was not a naïve young girl kissing him, it was a woman: a woman who knew what she wanted, and was desperate enough to ask for it. She desired him, he could feel it in her touch. Phoenix's fingers reached behind him to open the door. The sound of squeaking hinges returned him to his senses. Kai sighed wearily. He knew she was drunk, he knew her consent wouldn't count right now.

"Phoenix," he said, "we can't do this. Not tonight. You're drunk, you won't remember anything in the morning. It's not right." He wanted her, more than he had ever wanted anybody, but he refused to act on that desire.

"I don't care," she insisted. "I need you." Her mouth was a firm line. A lone eyelash had fallen onto her cheek, and the freckles dotted on her nose shone like a constellation of brown stars. Her face was still flushed with drunkenness.

"It's not right. I couldn't do that to you." He pressed his lips against her forehead. "I couldn't forgive myself."

"Why? Because you love me too much?" Phoenix said with a bitter laugh.

"Maybe." Kai placed his hands on her hips, and leant down to give her a gentle kiss. Her arms snaked around his neck. She kissed him desperately, driven by a primal instinct that went beyond thought and rationality.

Kai wanted to stay, to keep holding her. But he knew enough was enough. He withdrew himself from her embrace.

As he turned to leave, Phoenix grabbed his hand.

"Please don't leave me." She wrapped her arms tightly around him, and cuddled close to him like a small child.

"Phoenix—"

She stopped his words with her lips.

"I'm so lonely, Kai." She slowly kissed his neck. Her touch sent shivers down his spine. "I need you. Tonight, I really need you. Can't you just stay for five minutes?"

He nodded. Phoenix pulled him onto the bed. Her body was a grenade, ready to explode at any moment, and Kai would be collateral damage. Her touch made his body ache for something more than what he was prepared to let her give him. Phoenix took his hand, and guided it to her breast. Kai felt the soft flesh against his skin, too much to fit within one hand. He could feel his body responding to hers. Kai pulled away before they could go any further.

"Kai," Phoenix whispered. Her hands gently caressed his back, "I'm glad you're here."

"So am I," he said. His eyes scanned the room as he tried to distract himself from the allure of Her. The windowsill was lined neatly with books, the titles ranging from textbooks to novels, to classics that had been all but lost in time. Estonian books, Russian books, English books. All the shelves were also piled with books. He almost laughed as he realised how much smarter than him she must be.

"No," Phoenix sat up. "I don't mean here, in my bedroom, I mean here, in my life. You've been so good to me. I want you to know how great you are." She curled up next to him, whispering

"Please don't leave," as she passed out. Kai waited a moment, he knew this was the only time he would be this close to her. He drew her blanket around her, and kissed her warm cheek. He promised her "Of course I'll never leave."

Kai closed the door behind him, and returned to his own room. His mind was consumed with the events of the past twenty minutes: the feel of Phoenix's soft lips on his mouth, her body pressed so tightly against his own that he could feel every curve and angle. He ached for her.

The night dragged on and on, his mind occupied with the agony of adolescence. His whole body felt tense, as if the slightest movement would brush away the feel of her touch, the memory of her skin on his.

✝

"Hey," said Phoenix, when she approached Kai at lunch the next day. She held a cup of chocolate milk between both hands, and sucked long gulps of it periodically through a metal straw.

"Hey," he said. Flashbacks threatened to fracture his fragile composure. He couldn't look at her without remembering. His eyes were fixated on her lips, watching as they pursed around the straw in her mouth.

Phoenix gave him a shy smile. "Look, I'm a terrible drunk. Anything I say or do whilst I'm under the influence of alcohol, it means nothing." Her eyes were bloodshot and tired. She wore no makeup, and her hair was neatly brushed. She tucked it behind her ears, looked him dead in the eye, and continued speaking. "I don't remember much from last night, but if I did or said anything out of character, it was the wine, not me."

"Nothing happened." Kai decided in a split-second that lying was his best option.

"Good. I had this weird dream, and I was worried it might be based on fact. You know, sleepy drunk brain trying to make sense of reality?"

"What did you dream about?" Light shone through the windows of the cafeteria, glinting off Phoenix's dark hair, highlighting the angles of her high cheekbones. Kai was transfixed by her,

250

completely.

"It's kind of embarrassing," she admitted. Blood flooded to her cheeks.

"If it's any consolation, I dreamt of you too," he said. He didn't tell her that all his dreams had occurred during waking hours.

"I dreamt we were kissing," Phoenix said, "and you were kind of feeling me up." She blushed, her eyes flicking to his for a brief moment. "Then it was fifteen years later, and we were married. I turned into an actual phoenix. You were stroking my feathers. I could fly." She couldn't meet his eyes. "I was worried I might have kissed you last night. If I did, I want to know."

Kai considered the outcome. Honesty was the honourable option. "You kissed me."

Phoenix nodded slowly. She took a ragged breath, shaking her head slightly. In one abrupt movement, she shot up from her seat, and left without saying a word.

"Phoenix, wait!" Kai ran after her.

Phoenix sat curled up on a sofa in the Time Capsule. She had set a musical device to play sad songs, and she swayed slightly to the rhythm of the music. Her face was buried in her arm, the soft melodic hum did little to hide the sound of her sobs.

"Hey." Kai sat down beside her.

"Go away," Phoenix said. Her voice was choked with distress. She wiped her eyes with the cuff of her sleeve, and twisted her body around to face him. "I don't want to talk to you. I've ruined everything, I've made things weird between us."

"You haven't," he lied. Kai hugged her awkwardly. Her face was pressed close to his neck, she breathed in the scent of lavender shampoo. His skin was warm and soft against her. It felt good to be close to him, and she was terrified. Every instinct told her to run away.

"It is weird," she mumbled into his shoulder. "I can't look at you without thinking about us kissing, but I can't remember how it felt." Phoenix wriggled out of the hug, and folded her arms around her knees. "Tell me what happened?"

251

"I don't think that's a good idea, it'll just imprint false memories." He fumbled with the words, his discomfort evident.

Phoenix was a bomb, ready to explode. Kai's nearness overwhelmed her. She needed him, like she had never needed anyone before. It had not come out of nowhere, these feelings had bubbled below the surface for weeks. Feelings she was only used to knowing in fantasies. They were not unfamiliar, she had felt them in daydreams, lived them vicariously through characters in books. There was a world that had only existed in her mind, and now it threatened to overtake her body. It already had. This hidden part of her had unleashed itself, and she had no recollection of what it felt like.

"Kiss me then," she demanded.

"What?" Kai was taken aback.

"Please!" Phoenix begged. "This is driving me crazy. I hate not knowing; I hate not remembering my own experiences." She looked him in the eye, determined. "I won't be weird with you after, and I promise it won't ruin our friendship. Please, Kai. Do this for me."

"Okay." She knew he couldn't say no to her.

Kai inspected Phoenix, like he was unsure of how to begin. She sat incredibly still, riddled with nerves. He leaned in, and pressed his lips gently to hers. Phoenix's rigid body eased up at his touch. Intimacy did not come naturally to her body, but he made her feel comfortable, and safe. To Phoenix, sexuality had always been more of a fantasy than a reality. She didn't know how to turn thoughts into actions, how to share this part of herself she felt so distanced from. Her body had never felt like home. She was used to being an onlooker, watching her own body from the sidelines, seeing acts performed upon it, instead of making an active choice. It was different now. She wanted this, she wanted him to touch her, to kiss her, to do more than kiss her. Her whole body craved him. Kai kissed her with a gentle passion, and Phoenix reciprocated. At first, her kisses were nervous and hesitant, she had no idea what she was doing. Soon her hands were cupped around his face, holding him firmly in place, and her mouth was precise and certain in its movements. Kai wrapped his strong arms around Phoenix's waist, holding her tightly. Their kisses became stronger, desperate, they clutched at each other, pulling themselves closer and closer, as if all they desired was to merge with each other and become one.

"I'm sorry." Phoenix pulled away. Her lips were wet with saliva, and her hair was tousled from his roaming hands. "I shouldn't have asked you to do that. I don't know what I was thinking." She stood up hastily, and bolted from the room.

# Chapter Twenty Three

At the Tsar's palace in Moscow, Persephone awoke from a long period of unconsciousness. She rolled over onto her stomach, her mind hazy. Time passed and she became more alert. Something felt different to the last time she had woken. At first she couldn't place it, her brain was still foggy. Persephone searched her mind, trying to remember her previous experiences of waking from the drugged sleep. And then it hit her.

She began to weep with horror as realisation sank in. The room was dark, but she didn't need to see her reflection to know what was wrong. Persephone's hands searched the flatness of her belly as she sobbed into her pillow. Nothing made sense. She was no longer pregnant. Her mind had been obliterated again, and her baby had vanished from her womb. Persephone cried harder as it dawned on her that she may never meet her own child, her only true family. Anger hardened within her, and began to formulate into coherent thought. Every major moment of her existence involved the Tsar. If Phoenix was right, Persephone's life itself was owed to that man. She screamed at the top of her lungs, refusing to relent until a member of the palace staff came running through the door. It was a relief to scream, to reclaim her voice after so many months of silence. Persephone's roars reverberated around the dark room until the door burst open.

"Your Majesty, is everything alright?" asked the servant who entered. "Are you in pain?"

"I want to see my husband," Persephone said. "I don't care if the Earth is dissolving right under our feet, I need to see him now!"

"Of course, your majesty." The servant bowed and left the room. He didn't switch off the light as he exited. Persephone's prison was now illuminated. It was a different room to her last time here: smaller, claustrophobic, the same sterile white as the room Dr Skryabin had examined her in at the Estonian Institute of Scientific Research. It wasn't hard to imagine surgeons cutting her open within the prison cell of these walls.

Hours passed before the Tsar came. He wore a black button-down shirt and black slacks. His hair was neatly combed back. In his arms rested a baby. A fresh sob rose in Persephone's throat as she saw her daughter for the first time. She declined to acknowledge her husband's presence, for she knew the moment she looked upon his face, her resolve would collapse, and she would fall into the wretched wreck she had refrained from being for so long.

"Persephone," said the Tsar, "this is our daughter."

All words were lost when she saw the child in his arms: her child, his child, the future Tsarina of Western Russia. Tears streamed down Persephone's face as she stared at the baby girl – a chubby baby, with dark hair, and tiny fingers, wrapped in a pink, woollen blanket.

"She's beautiful, just like her mother." The Tsar sat down on the edge of Persephone's bed.

"Stay away from me!" She edged away from him, to the far corner of the room, where she huddled, half-hidden in shadows. She never wanted to lay eyes on him again, yet he held in his arms the most precious creature on Earth, and her only hopes of obtaining that creature were through an alliance with him.

"I want to hold her." Persephone's voice shook with tears and rage. "I want to hold my daughter."

"Her name is Melinoë," the Tsar said, as he approached his wife. He carefully transferred the baby into her arms. His closeness sickened her. She caught the stench of cigarettes on his breath, she choked as it filled her nostrils.

Persephone held her daughter close against her heart. Tears swelled in her eyes as she breathed in the sweet baby scent. She leant her forehead against Melinoë's soft brow, shielding her behind curtains of silky red hair, hiding both their faces from the Tsar.

"I love you so much," she whispered into Melinoë's cheek, nuzzling against her smooth skin until she was forced to come up for air. "I love you so much, my darling. I would turn this world upside down for you, I promise. I will be a mother you can rely on; I'll love you, my baby."

"I thought you would like to see her this once," said the Tsar.

"This once?" Persephone asked. "I'm not allowed to see my own daughter?" His words were illogical, surreal. Her brain refused to process them. This couldn't be a possibility, let alone a reality.

"You are not a good influence," the Tsar calmly informed her.

Persephone hugged the baby to her. "She's just as much mine as she is yours! More so. In case you don't remember, it was me who carried her for nine months, though I barely have any recollection of that!" Her fury threatened to escape its confines. If it wasn't for the baby in her arms, she would have clawed his face off with her fingernails.

"Forgive me, Persephone, for my lack of ovaries."

His arrogance made her want to slap him. Every cell of her being told her to end him, to steal his life from him the way he had stolen hers. Persephone knew she couldn't overpower him, and any attempt to harm him would only result in further pain for her. If she fought him, she would lose Melinoë for certain. This left her with only one option: she had to give in to him, relinquish her anger, give up her fight. It was the only chance she had to keep her daughter.

"I'll do anything." He had won. Persephone had given him everything. There was nothing left of her now that didn't belong to him. "I will do anything." Her voice was feeble as she begged him. "I will give you anything you want from me! I'll be your wife, I'll be your prisoner, I'll be your slave. I just want my daughter."

"There's nothing you can do to change my mind," the Tsar said. "From the moment I saw you at the ball, dancing with Tatiana's brother, I knew you would never truly be mine. I don't like to share."

"I'm not some object that belongs to any man who chooses to claim her," she burst out before she could stop herself. "I am alive, and I am aware. I have thoughts and feelings and I deserve autonomy! I am not your property, and I am no one else's. I don't care for Tatiana's brother, I can't even remember his name! I have no one left in this world, there is no one to share me with! I just want my daughter."

Melinoë's head snuggled into Persephone's breast, and she knew in that moment: she would do anything to keep her child.

"In the morning, you will start your journey back to Greece, where you will stay until your sanity restores itself. When I'm certain it's safe for you to return home to me, I will come and collect you, and we can be a family. We can even have more

256

children, if that is what you wish."

"Never!" Persephone screamed. "How can you think I would ever consent to be with you? You controlled my mind, you raped me whilst I was unconscious—and did God knows what else to me—and now you conspire to steal my child from me? I hate you, I hate you, I hate you!"

"I didn't rape you," the Tsar said matter-of-factly. "You yourself said you were unconscious. How can you possibly know what happened?"

"Oh, I don't know, perhaps because I'm holding our baby?"

"I do have some morality, Persephone."

"Forgive me for not believing you. With your track record, the idea of hearing truth from you seems far-fetched."

"When have I ever lied to you?" The Tsar asked. "I will let Melinoë stay with you for an hour or so, then I'll come and collect her."

"I would kill you, you know," she said. "If I could."

"Go ahead, I don't mind."

"Is that meant to make me feel sorry for you?" Persephone asked. "I know you. I know your nature, I know how evil you are. I will never forget what you did to me, and what you're doing to Melinoë. I will remember it until my dying day, and I promise I will be here to haunt you once I am gone! I won't let you live down your crimes. You are a despicable man, and the world will see that, and they will shun you like you deserve!"

"I will see you later, my darling," the Tsar said. He briefly kissed her cheek. Persephone slapped him hard across the face, and spat at his feet.

"I hate you," she said one final time as he departed from the room. Once he was gone, she scrubbed at her cheek, trying to remove every last trace of him from her. Persephone withdrew to her bed with Melinoë, and stared into her baby's eyes. She cried for the longest time. Persephone refused to return to Greece, to live a half-life, waiting for the Tsar to deem her sane enough to be a mother. She couldn't fight for Melinoë, not against as formidable an enemy as the Tsar, but she could fight for herself: reclaim her power and never relent to him.

"I will fight for you, my darling," she whispered to Melinoë, "but I'll fight on my own terms, and I will never give in to him. I will see you again, Mellie, I promise. I will see you when your father has been destroyed."

Persephone listened closely to the monotonous sounds of her guard's snores. This was the last night before they crossed the Dead Zones: her final chance to escape. As she crept softly on tip-toes to the door of her room, Persephone glanced once at the sleeping guard, and slowly turned the handle. She slid through the doorway, and sprinted down the hall. At the end of the hallway, she stopped. Voices and light drifted under the door of the end room. The hallway was wide, with soft blue carpet, and each windowsill bore a vase of carnations. This inn had the lowest security of all her previous prisons. She was kept in a room on the top floor, with slim windows and a guard, but that was nothing to her. There were no locked doors, no maze-like palace passages to navigate. Persephone headed to the nearest window—the ones in the hallway were far wider than those in her room—and unclasped the latch. She dumped the flower vase on the floor in an act of symbolic rebellion, and climbed onto the windowsill, breathing in the cool night air with sweet relief. After a deep inhalation of breath, she jumped out into the cold night.

It was a year since Persephone had last jumped from a window. She was overwhelmed by the sudden rush of air as she landed on the ground. This window-jump made her think of Phoenix. Persephone ran blindly into the darkness. Her legs wobbled beneath her, and sent spasms running through her. She laughed maniacally into the moonlit night, falling to her knees on the shore of a lake, and scooped up handfuls of sand. It trailed like dust through her fingers.

*This is freedom,* Persephone thought, as she scrubbed her legs with the coarse sand. The night was chilly, icy water lapped at her toes, and she was completely alone in this wide, wide world. There was no one to live for, no one to die for. No one to rely on. For the first time in her life, Persephone was completely free. When she finally rose from the comforting womb of the ground, reality began to set in, and loneliness quickly followed. She had no one to belong to, nowhere to go.

The Haven was unchanged from a year ago. Persephone sank down onto the wooden staircase, and watched the empty kitchen. It didn't feel like a haven now. It was a roof over her head, but she was as alone as she had been during her journey here. Two weeks of hiding on trains when she could, and walking as far as her weak legs would take her, praying she was headed in the right direction. The Haven was supposed to be her salvation, but there was no future for her here.

"Persephone." The door swung open. Drew looked like he had seen a ghost. "What are you doing here?" His plaid shirt was open at the front, and his sleeves were rolled up. Sweat glistened on his skin. His jeans were smeared with dirt, and he had pine needles sprinkled through his hair.

"I had nowhere to go." Persephone stood up. She ran into his arms before she could help herself.

The heady scent of sweat and pine needles filled her lungs as she buried her head in his chest. Drew clung to her. He kissed the top of her head, and finally released her.

"What are you doing here?" Persephone asked. "You don't still live here, the place is empty."

"I come here when the sun gets too hot, if I'm working on the edge of the farm. It's quicker than going home."

Persephone nodded.

"You don't look well," Drew said. "When was the last time you ate?"

"I had some water when I got here."

"That's not what I asked."

"I don't know," Persephone said. "Yesterday, maybe. It's hard to keep track, the days all blur together."

"Come home with me," said Drew. "Let me take care of you. You look like you're about to collapse."

"You don't have to do that. I'm fine."

"You're not fine, Sphenya. It's okay to not be fine."

Persephone didn't respond. She had to be fine, it was all that was left to her. If she let herself acknowledge her weakness, she would fall apart. 'Fine' was the closest thing she had to strength.

"We turned into that song, didn't we?" Drew said as they walked through the forest. "Without even realising it. I thought I was dead back there, and you were the Queen of the Underworld, come to take me to the afterlife."

"I'm never going to live down my name, am I?" Persephone asked. "All I want is lightness, but I can't escape the dark."

"The Greek Persephone wasn't just the Queen of the Underworld," said Drew. "She was also the Goddess of Spring. The darkness within you isn't something to fear. The Persephone myth was never about being consumed by evil, it was an allegory for growing up. The journey into the Underworld represents adolescence, and the time spent in the Underworld shows that we can't go back to being children, that we must find balance between childhood and adulthood."

"Really?" Persephone asked. "Because my, albeit vague, knowledge of the myth is that Persephone is kidnapped by her creepy uncle, eats a pomegranate that keeps her in his lair for half a year, and is forced to marry him."

"That is the literal story," Drew said, "but all Greek myths are metaphors. Every action and object has a meaning beyond the surface."

Persephone didn't reply.

"Why did you go back to him?" Drew asked, several minutes later. "I don't understand."

"I didn't," Persephone said. She had avoided the topic for as long as she could. "He drugged me." She struggled to get the words out. It was her first time saying it aloud. Her speech came out in short, sharp bursts, stopping and starting. She spoke faster and faster, saying the worlds as quick as she could. "He was in Tallinn, and he killed Sol, and it never occurred to us he'd have stuck around. Phoenix and I had a fight, I left her room, and that's the last thing I remember. I woke up months later, with almost no recollection of what had happened. I was his prisoner, and I

260

was pregnant. He drugged me, and he raped me, and he stole my daughter from me." She broke into a sob on the final word. Drew pulled her into a hug. Persephone wanted to find safety in him, for his arms to be a refuge from her pain and suffering. But he wasn't enough. It didn't matter that Drew was good, or that he loved her. Nothing mattered. He didn't understand what she had been through, and all the love in the world couldn't change that. Talking made it worse. The words didn't feel natural in her mouth. Her throat was dry and her tongue heavy.

"I could kill him." Drew's voice was filled with anguish. Persephone felt the rage that burned beneath him, hidden in the gentle touch of his hands as he stroked her hair. She knew his anger was directed at the Tsar, not her. But anger was an uncontrollable beast. Persephone knew passion was a monster, and it didn't matter that Drew's passion made him want to protect her. It could turn in an instant.

"He won't let me see her," Persephone said. "She's the only family I'll ever have, and I'll never know her. I can't exist like this! I can't be his custom-made punching bag. I can't cope. He may have designed me to live for him, but I refuse. I'm not his property, I don't owe him anything. I am my own person, and I deserve the same liberties as everyone else. I deserve to raise my daughter." She wept into the warm skin of his neck, wrapping her hands in the plaid flannel of his shirt. Crying didn't feel like a relief, it felt like a performance. Crying was how a human would react in this situation, so she let herself cry.

"What do you mean she's the only family you'll ever have?" Drew held her chin up so he could look into her eyes.

Persephone sighed. She had told him everything, except the catalyst for it all. "I'm, kind of, a robot." It sounded ridiculous. "I'm a robot. I do not have human parents, and I should not be able to breed with humans. I don't understand how Melinoë exists, and there's no guarantee I could conceive again."

"A robot?" he asked. "Okay."

"You're saying 'okay'? Really?" She laughed at the absurdity. "I'm serious. I am a robot, created by my psychopathic misogynist husband, who was apparently a child-prodigy scientist with a penchant for creating humanoid life forms. I'm a robot! I'm not human. I am a monster, a machine. I'm not real, I'm not alive. I'm a fucking computer!" Her voice tore through the air, brittle in her ears. Persephone didn't feel human any more.

"Persephone," said Drew, "I don't care if you're a robot, or a fairy, or the literal Queen of the Underworld, ruling an army of zombies. You are the most human person I know."

"You did hear me say I was a robot, right?" She couldn't stop laughing – bitter, hysterical laughter that verged on sobs. Life was a joke, and Persephone was the punchline. This time when she cried, it didn't feel like a performance. "He made me. I can deal with being a robot, barely. I can't deal with being created by him. He is effectively my father, and my mother, and my God, not to mention the fact he's my husband. It's like he's tried to be my whole world. And he's still failing. God, he must hate me!"

"I don't think he sees it as hate," Drew said. "He may even see it as love."

"He's never said he loved me. He's awful to me, he has been for our entire marriage."

"I know that," Drew said, "but I think in his twisted reality, he's devoted to you. Not in a good way, not in a healthy way. He's obsessed with you, he idolises you. That's not love, but he may think it is."

"He also controlled my mind with genetically modified fruit." Persephone had forgotten to include this detail in her explanation.

"He did what?" Drew was horrified.

"From the day I first met him, he was controlling my mind. Months of my life belonged to him. Even in retrospect, I don't know which decisions were my own, and which were his. He treated me like a puppet, and I can't shake the feeling of being controlled, like I have no influence over my own will. I feel like I've lost my way, but I never had my own way to begin with."

"You do now," Drew said. "I know you can't be free of him, that he'll still haunt you. But he can't control you now. You're here, you're safe. I won't let him hurt you again."

"You don't know that," Persephone said. "You can't protect me. I can't rely on you, I can't rely on anyone. I have to protect myself."

# Chapter Twenty Four

Persephone hadn't seen Drew's house since she had helped lay down its foundations. It was large, built from thick slabs of Estonian pine wood. Standing at three-storeys tall, it would have appeared formidable if not for the wide scope of its windows, and the trio of love hearts carved into the wood above the doorway.

"Guess who I've found?" Drew called out as he opened the door. Rozalina and Grigory emerged from a room on the left.

"Sphenya!" Rozalina screamed. She ran over to Persephone and lifted her in the air, spinning her around. Grigory stayed where he stood, observing the reunion with amusement. "We've all missed you so much!"

"Really?" Persephone asked. It was hard to focus on these people. The sole thought that occupied her mind was that this house was the first place she had ever set foot in that felt like a home. No white walls, no grandeur, just love hearts carved above a doorway, and woven blue rugs resting on wooden floors.

"It's so good to have you back," Rozalina said. "You belong here, just like we do."

✝

It was almost midnight by the time they went to bed. Rozalina had talked with Persephone for hours. Drew had stayed silent beside her and held her with loving arms. Persephone hadn't confided in Rozalina about the Tsar. She told herself it was because Grigory was listening. Or because the more she spoke it out loud, the more real it would become.

"I feel like I've hardly seen you today," Drew said, as Persephone sat down on his bed. "I thought Roza would never give you up."

"Well, I'm quite the novelty," Persephone said. "I'm sure she'll be bored of me by tomorrow. Then you can have me all to yourself."

"Is that so?" Drew sat down beside her, and wrapped his arms around her waist.

"You've got me all to yourself right now, too," she said. Conflicting feelings reverberated through her body as she felt the steadiness of his hands on her hips. She hadn't meant to say it, but once the words were out, it seemed like the perfect solution. Persephone had to prove to herself she was human, that she had free will. It was the only way to silence her demons.

"Persephone?" Drew asked. "Am I right to infer innuendo from those words? You don't have to do this. You know that, don't you?"

"I know I don't," she said. "Believe me, I know that. But I want to."

"I don't want to make things worse for you."

"You could never make things worse. You are one of the only things getting me through this. I've lost so much, I've lost my friends, I've lost my daughter. But I still have you. So yes, you were right to infer innuendo from my words."

Persephone kissed him slowly, pushing him down onto the mattress beneath them. She felt his heart beating against her fingertips as she carefully unbuttoned his shirt. Up until this point, he had lain, almost unresponsive, beneath her. He sat up, his arms tightening around her. Drew kissed Persephone passionately, rolling over so she was beneath him on the bed. He threw his shirt onto the varnished wooden boards of the floor. Persephone's legs wrapped around Drew, her hands clung to his back. He was warm, alive, and human. As he held her, Persephone searched her body for a sign of difference, something to mark her as separate. She had seen robots, in Estonia they were as common as dogs. She was not a robot, she knew she wasn't. Drew made her feel human, at least within her body. But her body was human, it was her mind that wasn't. Persephone looked into his dark blue eyes, saw the warmth within them, the fire that burnt solely for her. It was too much. The warmth she saw turned cold, and her mind was consumed by ice.

"Drew," Persephone said, "stop. Please stop."

"Of course." He rolled off of her. "I'm sorry, Persephone. You're not ready for this. We shouldn't have."

"No," she said. "I want this, I do. But I keep thinking about him, and I can't stop it. I feel like he's still controlling my mind. I know it's not possible, because I haven't had his stupid fruit in a year, but I can't shake the feeling that my mind isn't my own. He's imprinted on the back of my eyelids, and I can't remove his image. Every time I close my eyes, I see him, I see him vividly, as if he's right here."

"You were unconscious for most of your pregnancy," Drew said. "He must have had a way of getting nutrients into you during that time. Is there a chance he could have fed the fruit to you intravenously?"

Persephone shuddered. "Oh my God. He must've given me a lot. Phoenix said the fruit doesn't work properly on me because I'm a robot. If it's still affecting me now… God, I can't cope with this, I can't cope." Tears sprang in her eyes, and she cuddled into the warmth of Drew's chest.

"Persephone," he whispered into her hair, "you can fight this. You are fighting this. You're strong, he can't control you. If he could, would you be here with me now? He may have created the raw materials of you, but he did not make you the person you are. You are kind, and you are brave, and you are loving. Those traits are all you. You are strong, and you will only get stronger. You can fight any remnants of the fruit that remain in your system, just as you can fight the memory of him. He can't own you unless you let him."

"I just want to get Melinoë back," Persephone said. "As long as he has custody of her, he has control over me."

"You'll get her back," Drew said. "We'll find a way."

"He's the Tsar, for God's sake! He's not answerable to anybody. He can do whatever the hell he wants, and get away with it. He has all the power, and I have none. I don't want him raising my daughter, because God only knows what kind of monster he'll raise her to become. I don't trust him. I don't trust him to be a father, I don't trust him to look after her. I don't even trust him to love her, I don't believe he's capable of it."

"If there's one thing we know," said Drew, "it's that the Tsar wanted Melinoë to exist. There's a reason behind all of this. Maybe if we can figure out his reasoning, we can find a way to get her back."

"It's obvious, isn't it?" Persephone said. "He needs an heir. And he knew I would never be with him willingly. There's something that doesn't make sense in all this, something I'm missing, and I don't know what it is. Something doesn't fit."

"He wouldn't touch you on your wedding night," Drew remembered.

"Maybe he prefers his girls unconscious?" Persephone said. "But you're right; I think that is what I was thinking of. He's a man of extremes: everything about him is defined by immaculate control, and when he loses control, he loses it completely. I don't feel like he lost control, not this time. He might have, I have no memory, but it feels planned, it feels staged. He needs Melinoë, because she means I will be permanently tied to him. I still can't understand why he wants me though. He created me, but why does that make me special? Maybe it's not about me at all. Maybe we've been thinking about this wrong the whole time."

"Maybe it's about him," Drew suggested. "You, Melinoë, Sol, everyone caught up in this... Maybe you're all just collateral damage. He is clearly a troubled man, a dangerous man, and—"

"And I'm just a fly in his web? All the pain he caused me was an accident?"

"It's possible."

"I confronted him," said Persephone. "He told me he didn't rape me, he told me he had 'some morality.' He's lying, I know he's lying, but I also feel like I can't trust myself. What if I wasn't unconscious the whole time? I think I was, because I have no memories. If he was controlling me with the fruit, maybe I was conscious, and I don't remember? Oh God, what if I consented? Is that worse? Is it not equally awful, if he did indeed rape my mind in order to not rape my body? He said he has morality, but how can I believe that? How can anything about him be moral when he controlled my mind?"

"If the fruit doesn't work on you for long periods of time, doesn't that mean it couldn't wipe your memory?"

Persephone nodded slowly. "I guess so. I don't know what to believe any more."

"Believe in yourself," Drew said. "That's all you can do."

"I believe in everybody, that's my problem. I believed in Phoenix, and she let me down, I believed in Sol, and he wasn't who I thought he was. Hell, I even believed in the Tsar. I believed that by marrying him, I could help him be better. Look where that got me."

Drew didn't respond. He cuddled her to him, resting his face in the curve of her neck. The night passed in silence. Persephone lay awake, staring up at the stars through the skylight in the ceiling, listening to the soft patter of rain on glass, and the gentle rise and fall of Drew's breathing. If her mind had tormented her whilst Drew was awake, it was unstoppable now he was asleep. Alone with her thoughts, Persephone drifted back to the dilemma of Melinoë. How could she get her baby back?

"Drew." She shook him awake.

"Persephone?" he asked. "Are you okay?"

"Yes," she said. "I couldn't sleep."

"Do you want to talk?" Drew asked. His voice was slow, he had yet to shake off the sluggishness of sleep.

"No," she told him.

*I want oblivion*, Persephone thought.

"Talking is getting me nowhere," she said. "I just want you." Her finger traced a line down the length of his chest, her lips travelled with slow urgency across the base of his neck.

"Oh," Drew said. "Persephone, are you sure you want to do this?" Moonlight shone through the window, casting shadows across his face.

"Yes," she said. "This time, I'm certain."

"Just remember, you're calling the shots here. Whenever you want to stop, we'll stop."

"Thank you."

Drew moved to kiss her, his hands gliding over the soft flesh of her stomach. Persephone held his face in her hands, feeling the stubble on his cheek, the rough skin of his palms, the tenderness of his touch. Everything about him was real. There were no illusions. She knew, with each quickening heartbeat, that she was in safe hands. He wouldn't hurt her, he wouldn't break her. He was a stranger, an entire world she had yet to know. His hands caressed her thighs, and his mouth made her body shiver. In Drew's arms, with their bodies moving as one, Persephone saw it wasn't oblivion she craved, it was life, with all the fire and agony that came with it. She wanted to live, to love, to feel everything that defined her as human. And here, in the quiet moment where night turned to morning, she was human in a way she had never been before.

Fiery streaks of pink burned through the dark sky as the first hints of dawn hailed a new day, and Persephone, with wide eyes and tousled hair, lying in the arms of her lover, dared herself to believe the world could be good again.

✝

Persephone froze as she reached the foot of the staircase. She stopped dead as the familiar voice washed over her. The Tsar was here, in Drew's house. His voice strangled her like bindweed, caught her in a trap she was powerless to escape. It took all her strength to breathe, to put one foot in front of the other, to let her heart continue beating. When she entered the kitchen, Persephone saw with relief that her husband's voice came only from the radio. Drew pressed a finger to his lips, motioning for silence, and gestured for Persephone to sit down. She listened with horror to the words on the radio.

"*It hurts me,*" said the Tsar, "*to separate a mother from her child. The bond between mother and infant is the strongest connection known to our species. But my wife is mentally unstable. Whilst I believe a child should be with their mother, I do not feel it is safe for my daughter, Melinoë, to be raised by a woman who suffers from such fragility of mind. My duty as a father comes before my duty as a husband. I must protect Melinoë from Persephone's impassioned rages and bouts of violent insanity.*"

"I'm going to kill him," Persephone said. "I am actually going to kill him!"

"I want to kill him too," said Drew. "We'll toss a coin for it when the time comes."

"Impassioned rages?" Persephone muttered to herself. "I'm 'impassioned' because he stole my fucking child from me. I hate him, I hate him so much! I— Oh my God, he's right!" Persephone clenched her fists, her face screwed up in horror. "He's right: I am impassioned, and I do rage. What good does it do, when he can tell the whole world my fight is futile?"

"I don't know how to answer that," Drew said. "There's nothing I can say to make things better."

They ate in silence. Persephone stared glumly at her food. Her

268

thoughts drifted into melancholy daydreams, guided by solitary words snatched from the news report on the radio. The Tsar's speech had ended, followed now by an item on riots over food shortages.

"That's it!" Persephone whispered. She knew how to get her daughter back!

"Drew?" she asked softly. "If you loved someone, what would you do to protect them?"

"I'd do whatever it takes," he said. The sadness in his eyes told her he knew who she was choosing to sacrifice.

"I have to fight for Melinoë," Persephone said. "I can't trust the Tsar. I can't trust him to look after her. What's he going to do? Feed her genetically modified breast milk so he can control her before she's even old enough to think? I can't risk him hurting her."

"I understand, Persephone." Drew caressed the back of her hand with his thumb. "I love you, and I will wait for you. You'll get Melinoë back, and then you can return to me. I will be a husband to you, in everything but law, and I'll be a father to her; I'll love her as if she were my own."

"I wish I could turn back time," Persephone said. "I wish I'd known you before I ever knew him. I wish I had been more daring, I wish I'd looked near, rather than looking so far. I wish I'd never left Greece. My life would have been simple, and it would have been boring, but it wouldn't hurt like this."

"Remember yourself, Persephone," Drew said. "You were born to hold the flags of revolution high in the air. You were born to fight. When he created you, he never could've known how truly special you are."

"I don't feel special," Persephone said. "I feel broken. But broken or not, I'm going to get my baby back."

"What's your next move?"

"Phoenix. I need Phoenix. But I don't know where she is. I haven't seen her in almost a year, she could be anywhere in the world by now."

"She could be," Drew said, "but she isn't. She's a student at the Estonian Institute of Scientific Research."

# Chapter Twenty Five

"Phoenix!" Kai called to her down the hallway.

"What?" She spun around to face him. Her hair was pushed back by a pair of protective goggles, and her face was smeared with ash.

"Have you spent all morning in the lab?" he asked.

"Yeah," she said. "It hasn't exploded properly, though there were a few bursts of flame. I also made it do something new. Come on, I'll show you." She dragged him by the hand back down the corridor from which he had come. They soon entered a laboratory, a room decorated in the same sterile white as the majority of the Institute. Phoenix walked over to a square marble work surface in the centre of the room.

"Look." She reached into the cardboard box that rested on the counter. She lifted out a tiny purple bird, which she proceeded to carry over to the sink. Phoenix fed the bird a spoonful of bright pink paste. She took several steps back, watching as a lava-like substance spewed from the bird's mouth.

Kai grinned. "Hey, Syrup," he said, "it's a volcanic phoenix! You created yourself!"

"Can you please stop calling me Syrup? It's getting old now, Kai. It's been five months, it's not funny any more. And I am not volcanic!"

"Sorry Syrup."

"If you don't watch out, I'll— Oh my god, it's on fire! It's finally doing it!" Phoenix rushed over to the sink to watch as the bird burst into flames. Phoenix and Kai clasped each other's hands as the bird's fiery remains burned down into ash. They stood still, waiting to see if the bird would rise, living, from it's ashes, proving Phoenix had succeeded in creating her namesake. The minutes passed by, and it seemed the experiment had failed. Just as she was about to give up hope, a compact, purple wing emerged from the ashes, soon followed by the rest of the bird, which flapped its wings, and spewed lava all over the sink.

"That was the best thing ever!" Phoenix threw her arms around Kai's neck. "That was amazing! That was... Wow. We created that!"

"You created that," he corrected. He lifted her into the air, throwing her over his shoulder. "You're a genius, Syrup."

"Why stop at calling me Syrup?" Phoenix asked, feeling somewhat dizzy. "There's a whole world of names you could call me."

"I'm more worried about what you're going to call me if I don't put you down soon."

"Nah," she said. "I like it up here. I can see what the world would look like if I were tall."

"You're upside down."

"Yeah, but I've got such a great view from here." Phoenix's breath caught in her throat. The heady combination of pride at her invention, blood rushing through her upside-down body, and Kai's hands on her waist made her lightheaded, and the world spun.

"I'm putting you down now."

"Go ahead." His hands were gentle as he carefully released her from his hold.

It was only when Phoenix was restored to the ground that they noticed the woman standing in the doorway.


Persephone took in the sight of her old friend. Phoenix looked different; her hair was longer, thick and wavy, reaching past her shoulders. She wore a white lab coat over blue dungarees.

"I'll leave you girls alone," said the boy, who Persephone vaguely remembered from the last time she was here. He had had dreadlocks before; now his hair was short and curly. He also wore a lab coat, and the light blue of his button-down shirt complemented the dark blue denim of Phoenix's dungarees. They looked like a matching set of scientist dolls.

"You slept with the man who killed Sol!" Phoenix yelled the moment the door was closed. She spoke in English now they were alone. "I can't believe even you would do something that fucked up."

"Phoenix, I—" Persephone floundered. The hatred in Phoenix's eyes was not a spur-of-the-moment reaction, it had been boiling slowly for months, and Persephone knew she couldn't dispel it with a few words.

271

"Can explain?" The slight smirk of disdain was no longer a permanent feature, but it made a comeback as she spoke.

"I can explain, if you'd only listen!" Persephone snapped. "I knew I shouldn't have come back here. I'm just wasting my time."

"Time belongs to no one," Phoenix said. "You're not wasting your time, you're wasting time in general. Let's hear your attempt to explain your way out of this. Go on, I'm looking forward to it. You never were good at making up excuses. Give me your best shot."

"When I left your room after we had that fight," Persephone said, "someone hit me over the head from behind. He must have knocked me out and drugged me. I woke up months later, and I was pregnant. The Tsar raped me, Phoenix. I would never be with him willingly."

"Oh God, Sphenn," Phoenix said. "I'm so sorry. I— I'm sorry. I should've known you wouldn't go back to him."

"But you thought I did. You thought I would return to a man as despicable as the Tsar? Honestly, Phoenix, what do you take me for?"

"Sphenya, I'm sorry," Phoenix cried. "I didn't know what to think. You disappeared, and I thought you'd gone back to Drew, but you hadn't. Then I heard on the radio that you were pregnant, and I just assumed—"

"Stop crying, Phoenix! It happened to me, not you."

"I'm sorry." She wiped her tears away with the sleeve of her lab coat.

"After everything we know about the Tsar, you didn't consider this?" Persephone asked. "You chose to think the worst of me. He doesn't have a history of respecting people's boundaries. Remember how he controlled my mind?"

"I can't make up for not believing in you," said Phoenix. "All I can do is say sorry." She paused, composed herself. "Your daughter, who named her?" Her voice changed as she spoke.

"The Tsar, I guess," Persephone said. "He kept me unconscious for most of the pregnancy. I wasn't awake for her birth, or the six weeks after."

"This is like... Oh, how do I explain it to you?"

"Are you calling me stupid again?"

"No, I'm saying you don't know much about Greek mythology."

"I know enough."

"Greek Persephone had a daughter called Melinoë. I think the Tsar is trying to re-enact the myth. God knows, if Western Russian food prices don't go down soon, he'll literally be ruler of the dead."

"That's what I wanted to talk to you about," Persephone said "Tell me about the situation in Western Russia. The people are staging riots, right?"

"I haven't set foot in Western Russia in a year," said Phoenix. "It's not my home any more. But yes, to my knowledge." She was only half interested.

"If fuel was added to their fire, would they start a full-scale uprising?"

"Yes," Phoenix said. "Hell, if enough of them supported it, they'd even be able to overthrow the Tsar." The comment was careless, as though she didn't realise the significance of her words.

"Thanks, you've been a great help," Persephone said. "I'll let you get back to your life now." She turned to leave.

"Persephone, wait!" Phoenix grabbed her arm. "You didn't just come here to ask me that."

"I did."

"Look, I know you're mentally unstable and everything," she rolled her eyes, "but whatever you came here for must be important. Last time we spoke, you hated me." Her face belonged to a stranger. Her features were softer than a year ago, but beneath skin and flesh, she was hard as stone.

"I didn't hate you," Persephone said. "I could never hate you. I was just upset about the Drew thing, and the robot thing, and Sol."

"What changed?" Phoenix scooped the purple bird up from the sink, and ran her fingers along the down of its neck, stroking gently.

"I had a lot of time to think," Persephone said. "I can't change who I am, I can't change who Sol was, and I can't raise the dead."

"You never know." Phoenix said. "We don't yet know what your spooky robot powers are."

"I saw Drew," Persephone added. "I stayed with him for a couple of days, before I came here."

"Ooh, how was that?" Phoenix asked. Her eyes sparkled with

273

the gleam of curiosity.

Persephone smiled shyly. "It was great. Seeing him again, that is."

"I'm sure it was." Phoenix smirked. "Were Grigory and Rozalina still there? I went to visit last summer, and Grigory was thankfully absent at the time. It was good to see them again. It was how I imagine it would be to visit distant extended family."

"That was how I felt," Persephone agreed. "It was the closest to family I've ever had, apart from you." She changed the subject. "Do the Western Russian rebels have a leader?" She tried to sound casual.

"I dunno," Phoenix said. "These people, they're peasants, city workers. They're powerful together, there's no doubt about that. But their lives are hard enough already, it would take a lot to make them rebel. They need someone to motivate them, to rile them up, make them brave enough to fight back against the system that oppresses them. Right now, they're not united. Western Russia is huge, and its people aren't trained – they probably can't even use a gun." Persephone could see now that Phoenix's obliviousness had been an act. "Look, Sphenya, I'm sure you're familiar with the fact I'm not stupid. I know you're up to something, and it begs the question: why the hell do you want to be a rebel leader?"

Persephone burned under the ridicule of Phoenix's gaze. "He won't let me see my daughter," she said.

"So you thought you could exploit the Russian people's cause? Because you're not allowed custody of the daughter you had with the man who raped you?" There was no mistaking the venom in Phoenix's voice. Even she could see she had spoken out of line. Her mouth opened and closed like she was trying to say something, but she couldn't speak. She watched Persephone with remorseful eyes.

"Your mother left you when you were little," Persephone reminded her.

"The situations are hardly alike." She chewed on a lock of hair, her eyes flitting worriedly around the room.

"You grew up knowing your own mother didn't fight for you, that she left you with someone who wasn't a suitable parent. Look how it affected you!"

"What do you know about my dad?" Fear flamed in Phoenix's eyes. Her fingertips eased through the feathers of the bird in her hand, a fruitless effort to calm herself.

"I know nothing," Persephone said, frustrated. "You've kept me in the dark. You clearly don't trust me with whatever happened. I tell you everything, I trust you with the darkest parts of myself, with the worst things that've happened to me, and I'm still not good enough for you! You do a disappearing act whenever you don't get your own way, yet I still trust you. That's why I'm here! I need your help, Phoenix."

"It's human exploitation."

"So you care, when humans are involved?" Persephone asked bitterly. She was on the verge of tears. "I guess you don't care when I'm exploited, because I'm not human? It was fine for you to drag me here, test me for something I didn't want to know about? To tell me my whole existence was a lie… Yeah, that was fine, but if I try to coordinate my fight with that of others, to work for mutual justice, that's exploitation?"

"Sphenya—"

"You told me these people need a leader. Wouldn't it be a laugh in the Tsar's face if it was his very own Tsarina?"

"Look, Sphenn," Phoenix said, "even if the rebels win, it doesn't mean you'll get your daughter back. She's the heir to the throne, she'll be shot in the name of 'just in case'. That's what happens when a country rebels. It happened in the 1917 revolution, and it will happen in this one." Her face was earnest.

"I'll make sure she's given amnesty," Persephone said. She was desperate.

"You don't understand. Melinoë's very existence is a huge threat to rebellion, because she ensures the next generation of autocracy. And the term amnesty doesn't quite apply, seeing as she's, what, two months old? She hasn't committed any crimes. Sphenya, they're probably sitting around a campfire plotting ways to kill her right as we speak."

"I shouldn't have come here," Persephone said, distressed. All she could think of was the innocence in her baby's face, the softness of her cheeks, those tiny hands with fingers curled into little fists.

"In order for them to spare her," Phoenix said, "you'd have to make a deal they couldn't resist. And you'd have no hope of winning unless you had both the Baltic Alliance, and this Institute, on your side. The Tsar's a genius, and in order to battle that, you'd need a whole lot of geniuses. You need to make the Baltic governments think a war with Western Russia would be beneficial to them, which it wouldn't be. You're going to need help. There are rebel sympathisers in Estonia, people with Western Russian connections. You need to get them on side."

"Are you saying you'll help me?" Persephone looked quizzically at the girl who had once been her best friend.

"I don't know if help is the right word," Phoenix said cautiously. "I don't know if there's anything I can actually do to help. I can guide you, I can help you make the right decisions, that's all." She was calmer now. This side of her was alien to Persephone.

"Why?"

"Because I miss you, idiot, and I don't want you to leave again. I know I've got Kai, and he's great, but it's not the same. Things have been a bit weird between us since December." A blush crept over Phoenix's face. "I got drunk, kissed him, and couldn't remember it the next day." She paused, shaking her head slightly at the memory. "Screw the excuses, you're my best friend. If I have to plan a revolution to keep you around, then so be it!"

Persephone hugged her. "So you kissed Kai, huh?"

"It's not like it sounds. I was drunk. I don't know what happened. I thought I had better self-control than that."

"You don't remember any of it?" This type of conversation was new for them. Persephone had never thought of Phoenix being sexually active. She couldn't imagine her trusting anyone enough to let them close to her.

"Kai told me the next day. I should have seen it coming. I still don't know what came over me. Things have been a tiny bit awkward ever since." Persephone remembered the electricity between them when she had arrived. 'Awkward' was not the word she would have used to describe it.

"I think everyone has kisses they wish they could forget. I'd gladly forget my first."

"The Tsar? Ew, that's gross. Oh Sphenn, I shouldn't have told you that story. I didn't even think about the similarities."

"Phoenix, calm down, it's completely different. You don't need to apologise for talking about it to me. It's not the same situation. Plus, I wasn't talking about the Tsar."

"The Tsar wasn't your first kiss?" Phoenix was surprised. "Who was it then?"

"Tatiana," Persephone said.

Phoenix's jaw dropped. "Oh," she said. "Tatiana? As in: Tatiana?"

"Are you shocked because I kissed a girl, or shocked because of who it was?"

"Definitely the latter," Phoenix said. "I'm also surprised you managed to keep a secret from me for that long. I'm impressed."

"She told me not to tell anyone," Persephone said. "Western Russia's homophobia, and all that."

Phoenix nodded. "Makes sense. Sphenn, speaking of... this kinda thing. I owe you an apology. For how I reacted when you told me you were bisexual. Sol was dead, and that was all I could think about. But I am sorry. I should have done better, I should have supported you."

"You've apologised to me twice today. That's two times more than you've apologised in the whole time I've known you." Persephone didn't want to talk about it. Sol, or her sexuality. It was easier to be stoic, to lock her feelings far away where they couldn't hurt her.

"I've changed."

"You're not the only one."

# Chapter Twenty Six

It was a brief journey from the Institute to the venue of the meeting Phoenix had arranged: a building in Tallinn's Rotermann Quarter. The light of the waning moon was blocked by thick clouds, and no street lamps shone at this late hour.

Phoenix directed Persephone to a building on their left. Its sleek, wooden exterior was perforated by wide glass windows.

"This was not what I expected," Persephone said.

"What did you think it'd be like?" Phoenix asked.

"I don't know. This doesn't feel right. There's no hardship, there's nothing to make people fight. This place looks posh."

"War is an industry," said Phoenix. "It's not about justice, it's about money. I don't like it either, but this is how it works. Come on."

Phoenix rang the doorbell, and stepped back

A woman answered the door. She was six feet tall, of muscular build; Persephone guessed she was a bodyguard. The woman asked a question in Estonian, and Phoenix retrieved her student ID from her pocket in response.

Persephone couldn't decipher a word of the conversation. She looked from Phoenix to the bodyguard, and back again as the lyrical language washed through her ears. Finally, the bodyguard stepped aside and let them pass.

"This feels wrong," Persephone said as they mounted a flight of stairs. The steps were carpeted in purple, and the walls shone a reflective black, like a sinister mirror alongside the banister.

"Stop complaining," Phoenix said. "If you think this is bad, remember the Tsar's palace. The leaders of war profit, whilst the fighters die. It's almost enough to make me a pacifist. This is how the world is. You chose it."

"It makes my skin crawl!" Persephone said. "How can this Deripaska woman claim she sympathises with Western Russian poverty, when she lives in luxury?"

"Persephone," Phoenix said, "grow up. After everything that's happened to you, how can you be this naïve? People take and take and take, because they're allowed to, because they get away with it. No side is good in a war, each has an agenda. You've chosen one corrupt cause over another, because it benefits you. Learn to deal with it."

"I don't know how to do that."

"Shut up, play nice, do what you came here to do. I have classes in the morning, and I don't want to have stayed up half the night for no reason. Get your shit together, okay?"

"Okay."

Phoenix knocked on the door. It reflected their image back to them. Persephone stared at the misery in her own face. She hardly recognised herself now.

A voice called from behind the door. She spoke Estonian. Persephone could only make out a few words, not enough to understand.

Phoenix opened the door. Both girls stared in outrage and awe at the room before them: it was gargantuan in width and length, furnished with red sofas and soft, black carpets. In an armchair by the window, reclined a blonde, middle-aged woman. A tall glass of red wine rested on the windowsill beside her. Phoenix said something in Estonian, to which Ms Deripaska responded in Russian.

"You are Phoenix Kashnikova and Persephone Olympovskaya?" she asked.

"Yes." Phoenix barely masked her contempt. In spite of her chastisement of Persephone, she shared her friend's principles.

"I am Mariana Deripaska. I was told you had something for me, Kashnikova. It seems you've brought me a Tsarina."

"A Tsarina? I've brought you *the* Tsarina."

"My daughter is the Tsesarevna," Mariana said. "This girl is of no use to me. Husbands don't talk."

Persephone inspected the woman again: long glossy blonde hair; cloudy blue eyes; oval face. She knew those features.

"Your daughter," Persephone asked, "is she Tatiana?" The world was too small, she felt it closing in upon her.

"Yes," said Mariana. "Of course, you two must know each other." Her expression gave nothing away.

"We go way back," Persephone said. "Right back to before I married the Tsar, so let me correct you on a few things. Firstly, her husband is the Tsesarevich, he is not on the throne. Secondly, he is the Tsesarevich of Eastern Russia, so isn't likely to have any useful information. Thirdly, I'm not here to become an informant. I want—"

"Basically," Phoenix cut in, "your little orchestrated uprisings, if they can even be called that, are going to fail. You're lacking the magical component that makes revolutions work: a leader. You need someone who'll stop at nothing to bring down the Tsar."

"You want her to be our leader?" Mariana cast her eyes down the length of Persephone. She was unimpressed by what she saw.

"I think she'd be perfect." Phoenix gave Persephone a reassuring smile.

"That makes one of us," Mariana said. "I will not trust my life's work to an incompetent twenty-year-old."

"Persephone is the bravest person I know," Phoenix said. "She may be young, but she is far more intelligent than you give her credit for. More than that, she is idealistic! She wants to make this world a better place. She's a survivor. Persephone has the power to incite hope, she has the power to make people fight. If you don't trust her with a position of power, trust her to be the voice of the revolution, the face of the revolution."

"What did he do to you?" Mariana directed her question to Persephone. "Take a mistress?"

"He emotionally blackmailed me into marrying him, killed my friend, raped me whilst I was unconscious, and won't let me see my own child." She rattled off the list without emotion. Mariana watched her with a withering look. Persephone knew she had to stand her ground now, there would be no second chances.

"A grudge like that will last you a lifetime." Mariana's face broke into a slow smile.

"They say *hell hath no fury like a woman scorned.*"

"That sounds like something my son would say." Mariana's voice was wistful. Her façade began to show the marks of age and wear.

"Your son?" Persephone asked. "I met him once."

"You did?" Mariana's face brightened a little.

"At a masked ball," Persephone said. "The night I got engaged. His name's Andrei, isn't it? He was a terrible flirt, but we got on well."

"Persephone, try to remember why we're here." Phoenix was impatient. Her eyes flickered anxiously between Mariana and Persephone.

By the end of the night, Persephone had managed to secure another meeting, and she felt a weight lifted from her shoulders.

"Are you planning to write to Drew any time soon?" Phoenix asked as they walked the brief journey back through the dark streets to the Institute.

"I was waiting till I had something to write about, though now there's plenty to say. Why?"

"Oh, I was just wondering." Something in Phoenix's voice made it seem like she was looking for trouble. "Do you have his address? His last name? All the things a letter needs to make it to the right person?"

"No, I haven't," Persephone said. "I never thought about what the address would be, and I've never asked what his last name is. There's so much I don't know about him."

"I've got his address, when you want it."

"Sphenya!"

Persephone wondered how many times she had woken to the sound of Phoenix's voice. She pulled the covers over her head, but the other girl pulled them right off. Bright sunshine streamed through the windows, reaching down to the floor of Phoenix's room, where Persephone slept. It blinded her mercilessly.

"We really need to get you your own room," said Phoenix. She stood above Persephone, hands on hips, looming over her.

Persephone buried her face in her pillow.

Phoenix sat down on the edge of her bed. She poked Persephone's shoulder with her big toe. "The Tsar just passed a law banning international trade. Western Russia is no longer receiving imports from Eastern Russia or Greece. People are not happy."

"Unhappy people lead to riots."

"Precisely."

"What does this mean for the Tsar?" Persephone took Phoenix's hairbrush from the bedside table, and tugged it through her messy hair.

"Food prices will be sky high," she said, "so people will riot, and—whether as a result of violence or starvation—a lot of Western Russian citizens will die."

"No they won't," Persephone said. Something seemed wrong about this new law, and she hadn't been able to put her finger on it until this moment. Now she had no doubt what her husband's motives were. "He knows there's a war coming, and he knows his people are divided."

"So he starves them to death?" Phoenix asked, unimpressed.

"No, he feeds them. He *feeds* them, and that will ensure they fight for him. He's going to feed them his fruit."

Phoenix was taken aback. This was the first time Persephone had managed to connect the dots quicker than she could. It rubbed her up the wrong way.

"I guess so," Phoenix said.

"He has vast amounts of fruit. It wouldn't be designed just to make the occasional unsuspecting teenager fall in love with him," Persephone mused. "He's probably been planning this for a while."

☦

"Mariana wants to see you tonight," Phoenix whispered at lunch the next day. "Same time, same place. I can't come with you."

"Why not?" Persephone shuddered at the thought of walking through the city on her own at such a late hour. Mariana's place was only a few minutes walk from the Institute, but it was not a journey she wished to make alone.

"Some planet or other is visible for the first time in a century," Phoenix said. "Kai wants me to stay up all night stargazing with him." Phoenix was particularly chirpy today, Persephone was sure it must have something to do with Kai.

"Oh, right," she said. "Where is he anyway? Don't you two normally sit together at lunch?" Persephone was intrigued by their friendship. Kai brought out a side of Phoenix she had never seen before.

"Last time I saw him, he was with that awful Abi. He said he'd meet me here."

They ate in silence for a few minutes, before Kai appeared with a girl. She had dirty-blonde hair and a wide-set face. Persephone assumed this was the 'awful' Abi that Phoenix liked to complain about.

"Hi Abi, Kai." Phoenix looked annoyed. The smug expression on Abi's face told Persephone all she needed to know. There was a war between these two girls, and Kai was the prize they fought for.

Abi said something in Estonian, kissed Kai on the mouth, and ran over to the cutlery dispenser on the far side of the cafeteria.

Phoenix looked like someone had punched her.

"Are you two together?" There was no mistaking the deadly cocktail of disgust and fury in her voice.

"Yes." Kai couldn't meet her eyes. "I was going to tell you. It just happened."

"I'm so happy for you," Phoenix said in a tone that implied anything but. She took a mouthful of pear from her plate, not realising what she was eating. A fit of choking ensued, and she ran.

"I better go check she's okay." Persephone ran after Phoenix. She found her in a toilet down the hall, throwing up.

"You okay?" Persephone tapped lightly on the cubicle door.

Phoenix emerged a few moments later. She bent over the sink and splashed herself with water. Her face was streaked with tears.

"Is there anything I can get you?" Persephone asked gently.

"Coffee," Phoenix croaked. "Black, no sugar."

Persephone rushed back to the cafeteria. A cursory glance towards the tables told her Kai had disappeared. Abi sat alone. When Persephone returned to the toilets, Phoenix sat on the floor next to the row of sinks, sobbing into her hands. It was a pitiful sight.

"Thank you." She took the coffee and gulped it down. "I'm not crying over Kai."

"I never said you were." Persephone sat down beside her. "What are you crying about?"

"Memories." Phoenix stared into the cracks between the black-and-white chequered tiles of the floor, as if the water stains and scuff marks held the answers of how to repair her broken heart. "Do you ever feel like you can't exist? Like you physically don't belong in this world?" She leant her head back against the sink.

"I've felt like that my whole life."

"I wasn't born to be real," Phoenix said. "I wish I was a character in a book. Then I wouldn't hurt so much." She hugged her legs to her.

"I know it hurts right now, and you feel betrayed—"

"I told you, I'm not crying about Kai!" Phoenix protested.

"You love him," Persephone said. "I'm not saying you love him like that, but anyone with eyes can see you love him. It hurts you to see him with Abi, because it means he's not yours any more."

"He'll always be mine," Phoenix said. She buried her face in her hands again, horrified by how much she had revealed. "Gosh, I don't mean like that. I don't have romantic feelings for Kai. I don't, I don't, I don't." There was a wild lucidity in the directness of her gaze. "But I need him. I need him so much. He knows my soul, Sphenya. He saw me for exactly what I am, he accepted me. I don't understand why he's given up on me."

"He hasn't given up on you, he's just…. Oh, I don't know. He likes you, Phoenix. He really, really likes you, and you've been pretending you don't like him for so long that he's started to believe it. He's acting out to make a point, it's what people do."

"I hate people."

"Is that why your best friend's a robot?"

"Probably. Wait, are you accepting that now?"

"I don't have any reason not to. I'd believe anything of the Tsar. It doesn't change me. I've always been who I am, I have always been human in everything but name. I have lived, and I have loved, and I have become a mother. I know what it means to be human, and it's not something I will ever renounce."

"Even though it hurts so much?" Phoenix asked. She placed the end of one of her plaits in her mouth, before remembering she had vomited. "Ugh." She rinsed her hair under the cold water from the sink.

"Even though it hurts so much," Persephone said. "Being alive is hell. Even the parts that are meant to be good. We're taught to aspire to love, and what good does it do us? Love's left you crying on a bathroom floor."

"I don't think you can call it love unless it goes both ways,"

284

said Phoenix. "Otherwise you're only loving your idea of a person. What if I'm not capable of real love? What if I'm like the Tsar?"

"You are nothing like the Tsar!" Persephone crushed Phoenix into a tight hug. "You are good, you are so good. You've been hurt really bad, and you've had a crisis of faith, but that does not mean you are bad. Do you hear me? Anyone who makes you feel anything less than empowered is not worth it."

"Kai does make me feel empowered," Phoenix said. "I'm not saying I love him in that way, I don't know if I do. But he does empower me. When I'm with him, I don't feel so broken."

"That's a good step. The next stage is to feel like that on your own. You have to love yourself more than you love him. And Phoenix, don't hate Abi, even if she's as awful as you say she is. You can hate her for her faults, you can hate her for that smug look on her face, but don't hate her for being with Kai, and don't hate her for being a woman."

"When did you get so wise?"

"I think it's always been there."

"It hasn't. When I first met you, you were dumb as anything."

"True."

"You were like 'what are Settlements?' 'What's a Tsar?' It was hilarious."

"Sol always said you were an intelligence snob."

"Ooh, I bet he did!" Phoenix paused. "Is it okay that I miss him sometimes?"

"Of course it is," Persephone said. "He was your friend. No matter what else he's done, it doesn't undo the friendship you had."

"We were barely friends. I couldn't stand him until he was dead. God, I'm a terrible person! Do you ever miss him?"

"It's complicated. There are times when I remember some happy moment, like it's frozen in time. I miss what we used to have. Then I remember he would've been disgusted by me if he'd known everything. Our friendship was a lie, his death doesn't change that."

"Do you think he would've changed his mind? If he knew you were bi? If he saw it from that personal level, the perspective of someone he loved?"

"No," Persephone said. "Even if it would've made a difference eventually, I never owed him that. It's not my responsibility to make him less of a bigot. I don't want to spend my life having to convince people I'm normal." She shook her head slightly. "I guess I don't have much of a choice in that, now I'm a robot."

Persephone's head twisted around involuntarily as she hurried towards the Rotermann quarter. It was a five-minute walk from the Institute to Mariana's headquarters. When Phoenix had accompanied her here, the journey was over before it began. Persephone's legs shook and her heart raced in her chest. Her shoes clacked against the pavement. She was alone. She knew she was alone. If someone was behind her she would hear them. The night was cloudless, and the weak light from the moon illuminated her path. Persephone reasoned with herself. Tallinn was safe, there was nothing to be afraid of. No one here wanted to hurt her.

A figure moved in the shadows. Persephone screamed. She wanted to run, but fear paralysed her. The figure ran at the sound of her voice. She saw now that it was too small to be a man. It was a large, red fox. Persephone collapsed to her knees and wept into her hands. She sucked air into her lungs. There wasn't enough air in the world for her to breathe. The gravel beneath her knees clawed at her skin, but she couldn't move.

A door opened in the building in front of her. A tall woman approached her. She said a few words in Estonian, and offered her hand to Persephone.

"I'm sorry," Persephone said in Russian. The woman shook her head slightly. "It was a fox." She tried to mime a fox. "Fox?" she tried in English. The woman continued to shake her head.

The woman stepped under the glow of a street lamp, and Persephone recognised her. Mariana's bodyguard.

"Mariana," Persephone said. "Mariana Deripaska." She searched for the words in Estonian. "I'm here for Mariana Deripaska."

The bodyguard muttered something in Estonian, and let Persephone into the building.

"Persephone," Mariana said curtly, upon the girl's arrival. She wore a dark-red dress, buttoned up to her throat. Her hair was neatly pinned back into a bun. It was the middle of the night and she was perfectly put together. Persephone wondered if the woman ever slept.

"Mariana." They eyed each other warily, sizing the other up. It was the bowing of lionesses. Both kept their cool, but each growled below the surface.

"I've got a proposition for you, Tsarina," Mariana said. Her lips were painted in a red matte lipstick, the colour of drying blood.

"Care to elaborate?" Persephone's face was streaked with tears, and waves of panic continued to reverberate through her body.

"Sit down." Mariana directed her to the sofa by the window. She looked like Tatiana in this light. Older, harder, but the image of her daughter nonetheless. The kiss with Tatiana was a can of worms Persephone hadn't let herself open in a long time. Here in Estonia, she was free to explore that part of herself. But there was Drew. Even if there wasn't, Melinoë had to be her focus right now. So she had locked the memory up and thrown away the key. Until she met Mariana. "I presume you've heard about the new law?"

"Yes." Persephone clasped her hands tightly in her lap. She focused on the view of the Institute through the window. It was easier than looking at Mariana.

"What does your husband think he's playing at?" Mariana paced back and forth in front of the window. The sound of her heels on the floor set Persephone's nerves on edge.

"He uses genetically modified fruit to control people's minds." She smiled sweetly when Mariana finally deigned to look at her. The power was in her hands now. "He's going to feed the population of Western Russia with genetically modified food to subdue them, or force them to fight for him."

"Really now?" Mariana was intrigued. "You're proving useful after all." The lines around her mouth creased into the faintest hint of a smile.

"I have my moments."

"I want you to do a speech." Mariana stopped pacing, and stood in front of Persephone, her arms folded across her chest.

"A speech?"

"If you want to be the voice of this revolution, people need to know who you are. Think of this as your audition. You will have three days to write it. I know you don't speak Estonian, so you will have to do it in Russian. We will broadcast live to Western Russia, and use a translator for the Estonian broadcast. It will do you good to remember this is live, and public." Mariana paused. Her arms came to rest limply at her sides. "Every mother loses their child at some point. I'm certain I lost both of mine a long time ago. Even if you move the Earth for them—even if they're yours for a while—they'll leave you in the end. Only fight this war if it's for you. Don't do it for your daughter."

"My daughter's happiness is my own, Mariana," Persephone said. "Let's not make this personal. When you have a child, it's your duty to put them first, no matter the cost to yourself. My motivations don't affect you. I am fighting for your cause."

"How did it go?" Phoenix asked the next day. They sat on the grass under the flowering-cherry trees in the Institute's courtyard, warming themselves in the late afternoon sun. Persephone stretched out her legs, her bare toes pushing through the blades of green grass into the moist earth beneath.

"Mariana wants me to give a speech," Persephone said. "In two days from now. It will be broadcast on the radio, and all the screens in Western Russia. I have to tell people about the fruit." Persephone plucked a fallen blossom from the ground, and spun it between her fingers until the bruised pink petals became a blur.

"Oh great." Phoenix munched mournfully on a large bar of chocolate. She had barely heard a word her friend said.

"How did it go with Kai last night?" Persephone sensed the cause of her anxiety.

"Great." Phoenix forced a smile. "We talked. All night. Which is exactly what you do with your female best friend the very same day you get a girlfriend..." She broke off another chunk of chocolate and popped it into her mouth. "We're not going to let anything get in the way of our friendship. Not even her." Her hair was styled neatly in French plaits, and she wore all black, like she was in mourning. "It's bullshit! He's Kai, he's sweet and kind and a decent human being, and she has the world's biggest superiority complex and thinks she's oh so smart, when she's plain average! She thinks she's better than me. No one is better than me. I'm not jealous, I'm stating a fact."

"You are jealous. You as good as admitted it yesterday."

"I don't want to be with him, if that's what you're asking."

"Don't you? Not even a little bit?"

"He keeps trying to explain to me why I should give her a chance."

"Why? Because she's his girlfriend?"

"Surprisingly, no. His reasons were valid, that's the problem. She has all these dreams and goals, just like the rest of us. She wants to go to Eastern Russia, where her family's from, and start a Science for Equality movement, teach Russian women to work in scientific fields, as a way to end their oppression. She's honourable."

"I thought you hated her because you thought she's average?" Persephone asked. "Now do you hate her because Kai thinks she's your equal?"

"He said they talk." Phoenix wrinkled her nose in disgust. Crumbs of chocolate had melted around her mouth, and the petulant expression she wore made her look like a small child.

"That's generally what people do in relationships," Persephone pointed out.

"I could have dealt with it if it was just physical. But if he's with her to talk? Talking is our thing, why does he need her for that?"

"Phoenix," Persephone said, "I don't know the answer to that. Have you tried asking Kai?"

"I can't do that, not with our history." Her hands scrunched into a tight ball of frustration. When she unclasped them, her knuckles were bitten with deep, red fingernail dents.

"I think if you kissed him when you were drunk—and asked him to kiss you again when you were sober—deep down, there's a part of you that wants to be with Kai."

"I just want to be loved." Phoenix hid her face from Persephone. "I don't mean loved as a friend. I mean *loved*. I want to know

289

I've got someone by my side for life, someone who won't leave me, won't abandon me, won't abuse me, won't give me up when someone better comes along. Kai proved he's not that person. He chose Abi."

"Phoenix." Persephone sat up and took hold of Phoenix's hands. "You talk about finding someone who won't abandon you, but what about you abandoning them? Kai loves you, it's obvious. But you run away whenever you feel uncomfortable, and he knows that. He's not going to fight for you, because you've never fought for him."

"He loves me?" Phoenix asked. Her face lit up involuntarily. She composed herself quickly; the flash of joy would hardly have registered if Persephone hadn't known to look for it.

"If the only thing you heard is that Kai loves you, I don't think you're ready to love him. You have to learn to stick around, to stay when the going gets tough. No one's going to give themselves to someone they can't rely on. Kai isn't going to save you, Phoenix. You've got to save yourself. I have a speech to write. I'll see you later." Persephone rose from the ground, leaving Phoenix alone under the trees. The grass was soft beneath her bare feet. She had almost reached the door when Phoenix called out to her.

"Sphenya, wait! Do you want me to help you write the speech? I know more about the Tsar and the history of his reign than you do."

"Sure," Persephone said, "but I don't want to hear a single word about Kai or Abi. Once this speech is written, I'll listen to all of your problems, but right now, I have to do something for me and Melinoë. That is what I need to focus on."

# Chapter Twenty Seven

Haden lay back in his favourite red-velvet armchair, by the wall of windows in the library. His head pounded. The faint scent of chamomile wafted from the mug of tea that rested, just out of reach, on the coffee table beside him. He let his eyes droop shut, and fell peacefully into a meditative state, where he drifted in and out of sleep with ease.

It began with white noise. The radio coughed and spluttered until it found its frequency. Haden cursed as he searched for the source of the disruption. It had been a quiet morning. The onset of this blinding headache had made him cancel all his meetings, and he had let himself relax for the first time in months. Haden twisted the knob on the radio, but it wouldn't turn off. The noise grew to a crescendo. His head felt like it was infested with tiny, hammer-wielding goblins, hitting him over and over. Just as he thought he couldn't take it any more, the noise stopped. For a moment, there was silence.

Her face arrested the Tsar's gaze as her voice washed over him. From his vantage point at the window, he could see the closer screens in Red Square. Persephone looked healthier than the last time he had seen her. Her glossy hair was pulled back into a high ponytail, and her porcelain skin had caught the sun, adding a welcome flush of red to her otherwise pallid complexion. She wore no makeup, and her blue eyes were youthful and solemn. He liked her Russian speaking voice, it was pleasant to the ear. So pleasant that he forgot to take notice of the words she spoke as the radio blasted them into the room.

Cold dread settled over Haden as he finally snatched a few words from her eloquent speech. He heard the words 'fruit,' 'rape,' 'mind control,' 'daughter.' Panic seized him. Haden wanted to smash the radio into the floor, fling it through the window and watch it shatter on the ground below. He wanted to scream, shout loud enough to defend his honour. He loved her, in spite of it all. He loved her as she lied about him.

Persephone stood on a platform outside Tallinn's town hall.

The words flowed from her mouth in Russian, a jumbled mess that untangled themselves on her tongue and came out smooth. She was frozen with fear as she spoke. Persephone's mind wasn't in a city square in Tallinn, it was in Moscow. She imagined the Tsar reacting to her words, and felt as though her heart had stopped. Panic overwhelmed her.

Persephone held a picture of Melinoë in her mind's eye, she let herself find strength in her daughter's image. Fire flowed through her veins. The Tsar would pay for what he had done, she had the power to make him pay. Persephone's voice grew louder, and the last trace of fragility left her. The crowd stood before her like the eyes of Medusa, and turned her to stone.


Phoenix hated crowds. Phoenix hated people, full stop. This crowd didn't jostle her like the Moscow marketplace crowds she was used to. The stillness was worse; it leached the energy from her, clung to her skin like a filmy layer of oil. If the crowd moved, she could elbow them, push people out of her way, fight back against the claustrophobia that overwhelmed her. This crowd stood like statues, and she wanted to take a giant hammer and smash them to pieces. Phoenix hid in the back, away from the microphones and the cameras. She didn't want to be seen, didn't want her face and location to be broadcast on every screen in Western Russia. The Tsar wasn't the only enemy that would be watching.


Haden dragged the heavy curtains closed. He fumbled in the dark for a lamp switch. He couldn't turn off the radio, but at least he could hide her face from view. The lamp light bounced off the curtains and carpet, and the library glowed an eerie red.

"Orlov!" Haden yelled to his butler through the door. "Fetch me Vasiliev. Now!" He paused. "Send him to the nursery."

The Tsar unbuttoned the top of his shirt. His collar was a noose around his neck, strangling him with every breath he tried to take. Haden lifted a key from the table, and vacated the library. He took the stairs two at a time; his feet barely touched the ground.

"Leave," he ordered the nanny as he entered the nursery. She scurried away without acknowledging him. The radio on the windowsill silently taunted him, its antenna pointing to the sky like a finger flipping him off.

Haden rushed over to Melinoë's crib and lifted her into his arms. He kissed his daughter's head, and sank down into the rocking chair by the window. She stirred in her sleep, and snuggled into his chest.

"Your Majesty." Vasiliev bowed as he entered the room. He had been in the Tsar's service since the beginning of his reign, and was the closest thing Haden had to a confidante.

"You heard?" Haden stroked Melinoë's tiny hand as he spoke. Her skin was warm and smooth, he reminded himself what he was fighting for.

Vasiliev nodded. "Yes, Your Majesty. Do you have a plan?"

"Yes," Haden lied. "Of course I have a plan."

Melinoë stirred in his arms. He shushed her gently, and began to rock in the chair.

"I need vegetables," he said. "Vegetables, grains. Bread, pre-packaged food."

"What about the fruit?" Vasiliev pulled the window shut and turned the key in the lock. "You can never be too careful," he said, his eyes now fixed on the door.

"The fruit..." Haden thought for a moment. "We can still use it. Put it in ice cream, yoghurt, whatever other desserts normally contain fruit. The way Persephone talked you'd think I intended to hand out baskets of strawberries on the street. People may fear fresh fruit, but no one reads the ingredients on pre-packaged food."

"Good plan, Your Majesty."

"Vasiliev?" Haden asked, before he could help himself.

"Yes, Your Majesty?"

"Are you afraid of me?"

"Do you want me to be?" Their eyes met for a moment. Haden shook his head slightly, and turned away. He couldn't afford to be vulnerable now. "I respect you, Your Majesty," Vasiliev said carefully. "I don't fear you, because you haven't given me reason to."

"Switch off the screens," Haden ordered. "Every screen in Western Russia, switch them off. Unplug them. There will be no

293

screens, no radio, nothing for her to hack. I refuse to let Persephone use my media against me again. Western Russia will remain in media blackout for the foreseeable future. Anyone who refuses to comply is an enemy of the state, punish them accordingly."

╪

"The good news," Phoenix said to Persephone two days later, "is that Estonia overwhelmingly supports your cause." They sat on a secluded stretch of stony beach behind Linnahall, the Baltic Sea lapping at their toes. This was not a conversation for the Institute, where anyone could overhear.

"What's the bad news?" Persephone threw pebbles into the murky green sea. She had been restless since her speech, impatient for results, for proof that her words had been a catalyst for change.

"It's not necessarily bad news," Phoenix said. "Western Russia has a complete media blackout. The Tsar wouldn't do that if he wasn't scared."

"But?"

"But, there's no way to know what effect your speech had on the Western Russian people. Estonia can't go to war against Western Russia. It's laughable. Estonia is tiny. The Baltic Alliance is tiny."

"It was all for nothing?" Persephone asked, deflated.

"Don't talk like that," Phoenix said, "I didn't raise you to be a quitter."

"You didn't raise me."

"Fair point," Phoenix said. "You were raised by what, half of Greece?" A slow smile spread across her face.

"Your point being?"

"Who did the Tsar just ban all trade with?" Phoenix jumped up from the ground. "Estonia can't win a war against Western Russia. The Baltic Alliance can't win a war against Western Russia. But if the Baltic Alliance joined forces with Greece..."

"We'd have a chance?"

"Bingo."

"That's great and all," Persephone said, "but you're forgetting one little obstacle. We're nineteen and twenty years old, and neither of us is even an Estonian citizen. Why on Earth is anyone

294

going to go to war on our say-so?"

"You had to choose now, of all moments, to be come a realist?" Phoenix rolled her eyes, and extended a hand to lift Persephone up from the rock she sat on. "Why do you think I wanted you to get cosy with Mariana?"

"Because she's such a pleasant human being?" Persephone followed Phoenix along the beach. The stones cut the soles of her feet. She stopped still to put her shoes back on.

"Ask her to introduce you to the Estonian president. Mariana has connections, big connections, and not just to the Russian monarchy. Her ex-husband was the president of an English Settlement in Eastern Russia."

"So?" Persephone hurried to keep up with Phoenix, who walked briskly ahead of her, talking at a hundred miles an hour.

"You're not of this world, are you Sphenya?" Phoenix sighed dramatically, and turned around to face her. "Settlement presidents hold a lot of sway, they're effectively part of the nobility, especially in Eastern Russia."

"You said he's her ex," Persephone pointed out. Phoenix looked like she was about to spontaneously combust.

"He was," she said through gritted teeth. "He's been dead for years, his brother is president now. Even so, he's uncle to Mariana's kids – Tatiana, who you know, and the other one. What was his name? It started with a D or something, didn't it?"

"Andrei," Persephone said. "An A is hardly a D."

"They're closer than you'd think." The cutting quality in Phoenix's voice made Persephone think she was up to something. "Focus, Sphenn. Word from Western Russia is that the Tsar is supplying food, but it's bread, grain, vegetables. Not fruit."

"Shit! Do you think it might be genetically modified?"

"Do I think, huh? This is the Tsar, Sphenya. Haven't you noticed a pattern in everything he's done? He always gets his own way. Always. One speech is totally going to quash his quest for world domination!"

"God, what is with you today? I don't want to be around you when you're like this."

"I've had a tough day." Phoenix turned away, and stared out towards the sea.

"Do you want to talk about it?" Persephone knew it was no use. Phoenix was all for deep and meaningful conversations, unless they were about herself. Her shoulders were hunched over, and the faintest sound of sobs drifted through the air.

"It's nothing," she said finally. "Family stuff."

"What family stuff?" Persephone rarely heard Phoenix mention her family, except to say they were evil or dysfunctional. "Has something happened?"

"It's nothing," Phoenix repeated. "Just a stupid letter."

"What was the letter about?" Persephone asked. Phoenix slumped down onto the grassy ledge behind her. She rocked herself back and forth, breathing in short gasps. "Who sent it?"

Phoenix buried her face in her hands, swaying where she sat, submerged in a bubble of crisis.

"My student ID," she whispered, pulling the grass up by its roots and twisting it violently around her fingers. "I— I was wearing my student ID around my neck. The cameras... I must have been on camera. He— He must have seen the Institute's logo. He knows where I am." Phoenix cried harder. She buried her face in the grass and slammed her fists against the ground.

"Phoenix!" Persephone grabbed her wrists to stop her from hurting herself.

"Don't touch me!" Phoenix screamed. She slapped Persephone hard across the face on instinct. "I'm sorry," she said. "I'm so, so sorry Sphenn. I didn't mean to hurt you."

"It's okay," Persephone said. "It's okay. But you have to tell me what's going on."

Phoenix reached into her pocket, and pulled out a small, black envelope, from which she retrieved a photograph. A young child, six or seven years old, lay strapped to an operating table. Her blue shirt was torn open, and a bloody wound ran diagonally across the length of her abdomen. The girl's eyes were squeezed shut in agony, but Persephone recognised her face. Scrawled on the back of the photograph were the words "I know where you are."

Phoenix stood up slowly. She lifted her shirt to reveal a scar that matched the wound in the photograph. "Spot the difference."

"Who did this to you?" Persephone asked. "Who sent you this photo?"

"My father. See where I got my charming personality?"

"This is no time for sarcasm," Persephone said. "We need to do something. He's threatening you!"

"This is my reality. I've lived with it my whole life, you can't swoop in and save me, it doesn't work like that, believe me."

"You need to tell me what's going on Phoenix. I'm serious!"

"It's none of your business." She snatched the photograph from Persephone's hands, and tore it into pieces, her eyes wild with terror. "I don't need your help, and I don't need you!"

# Chapter Twenty Eight

The May heat had burned out by evening. It climaxed in a tumultuous storm of thunder and lightning. Persephone stood alone in Tallinn's Town Hall Square, a solitary figure soaked by the unexpected onslaught of rain. This empty square had been full two days ago, packed with an audience that had stood here just for her. There had been a point, during her speech, where time had stopped, and she had held the world within the palm of her hands. Persephone was powerful, then. Now she felt powerless. The image of Phoenix as a wounded child was burned into her brain. Melinoë wasn't the only child Persephone would go to war for; she was determined to find justice for Phoenix.

Laughter drifted across the square. In the twilight, she saw two figures running from the rain, to find shelter under the arch of the town hall. She didn't recognise them at first. The rain and the setting sun merged into an orange haze that blurred everything around her.

"Persephone!" It was Kai. His companion was Abi. "What are you doing here? You're soaked through!"

"That makes three of us." Persephone joined them under the arches. A bench was built into the whitewashed wall of the town hall. She sat and watched the rain splashing off the cobblestones in the square. "I needed some fresh air. I didn't notice the storm clouds until it was too late."

"Where's Phoenix?" Kai couldn't help asking. "You two are usually joined at the hip." He had a nice demeanour, in spite of the puppydog eyes that grew mournful every time he looked in Phoenix's direction. His face was wide and oval, a pleasant shape. His skin was brown, and his face was framed with tightly-curled black hair. Kai was good-looking, in an unassuming way. When Persephone first met him he still looked like a boy, now he had the face of a man. Stubble crept across his cheeks, hiding the lines of his dimples, except when he smiled. He smiled a lot, especially around Phoenix.

"Back at the Institute, I guess," Persephone said. "She's not in a good place."

"Is she okay?" Kai asked. "Has something happened?"

Persephone glanced briefly at Abi. "It's not my place to say. She needs a friend, and she made it clear she didn't want to talk to me."

"What are we going to do with her?" Kai didn't try to hide his concern.

Abi muttered something under her breath in Estonian. He didn't hear her.

"Abi?" Inspiration struck Persephone.

"Yes?" she asked in Russian, suspicious.

"I wanted to talk to you about something."

"In that case," Kai said, "I might go and check on Phoenix. I don't like the thought of her being alone when she's sad."

"Oh yes," Abi said with a voice of steel. "Go ahead."

Kai sprinted out into the rain. Thunder roared in the sky above.

"She doesn't even have to call and he goes running." Abi sank down onto the bench beside Persephone. Her blonde hair fell in damp tangles over her shoulders, and her face was slick with rain.

"It doesn't feel fair, does it?" Persephone asked.

"What would you know?"

"I don't know what it's like to be you, but I have an inkling as to what Kai's feeling right now. It's hard to be loyal to two people."

"Loyal?" Abi snorted. "Is that some kind of euphemism? Save me the tact, Persephone. He's in love with her, you don't need to sugar-coat it. What did you want to talk to me about? Or was that just an excuse so Kai could go run after Kashnikova?"

"Of course not," Persephone assured her. "Phoenix said Kai told her you want to start this Science for Equality movement in Eastern Russia."

"She mentioned that?" Abi's eyes lit up, and the sourness vanished from her face. She sat up straighter.

"Yes."

"I heard your speech, you know." Abi's demeanour grew warmer, and she turned to face Persephone. "You dropped so many truth bombs, and remained composed whilst talking about the worst experience of your life. I'm in awe of you."

"Thanks," Persephone said. She was ambivalent towards her speech. The words didn't feel like they belonged to her. Standing in front of that crowd was like being naked. Telling them her story was a step further than that. It was like carving away her skin, showing them her blood and bones and muscles, carefully prying her organs out of her body and letting the crowd hold them. Persephone's blood was her own, her organs were her own, but they were the parts of herself she didn't get to see. The words may have been hers, but the feel of them was as alien and unfamiliar to her as her heart or her intestines.

"He's using science to control people," Abi said, when Persephone didn't stir from her silence. "I want to use it to liberate people. To liberate women. Education brings freedom, it brings autonomy, and prospects, and purpose. My mother nearly died giving birth to me. My father was a rich factory owner, and he could afford to send her to a hospital in the city. I was born with a birth defect, and no doctor in either of the Russian countries could cure me. So my mother brought me here, to the world's leading scientific research institute. I lived here for the first ten years of my life because it was too dangerous to travel home. I don't know if you know much Estonian history, but I was born two years after the border war. It was a miracle my mother managed to get me into the country; for a long time it was impossible to smuggle me out. I could have died so many times, but when I look back all I can think about is my privilege. Many women in Eastern Russia don't have that luxury, their babies would have died. Education shouldn't be reserved for people in cities, or people with money. It needs to be accessible in rural areas. For me, it's more than that. I grew up in this Institute, I had this community of scientists, the students here were my babysitters...When I finally came home, I felt like an alien. I had no community, my homeland was foreign to me. I hated Eastern Russia for so long, I looked down on the people, the country. I left as soon as I was old enough."

"What changed?" Persephone asked.

"The day I moved back to Estonia," Abi said, "was the loneliest day of my life. My aunts used to cook together, all crowded into the kitchen, bickering and gossiping. It was chaotic, I hated it. I remember sitting in the Institute's cafeteria on my first day, and it hit me that I wouldn't help cook my own food for the next three years of my life. I don't like cooking. I don't like gossiping either. My aunts always existed in this separate world to me. I couldn't put my finger on why this felt like such a loss."

"You missed the sense of community," Persephone said. "I get that."

"It took me months to see it. It was December, I was going home for Christmas in a couple of weeks. We were all in the Time Capsule, and Phoenix was drunk. She lay on the floor, and half the girls in our year crowded around her. They brought her water, took care of her. It was this small, silly thing, and to me it was utterly profound. You see, women don't exist in a vacuum. We work together, we support each other. That's why education equality can change the world. Each woman you liberate is part of a whole community of other women. It's a domino effect."

"Okay, now it's my turn to be in awe of you," Persephone said. "I want to apologise, I think I was given the wrong idea about you."

"I don't hate her, you know," Abi said. "I should, I suppose. My boyfriend's in love with her. But I don't. I admire her. I don't like her. She's moody, and antisocial, and she's a total teacher's pet – you should see the way Skryabin fawns over her! But I don't hate her; I respect her."

"I don't see why you do it to yourself," said Persephone. "You're smart, and you're a champion of women's rights... I don't get why you're in a relationship with a guy who loves someone else."
"I'm letting myself believe the fantasy," said Abi. "If it were anyone else, I'd dump him and move on. But Kai's different. He's not like other guys."

"Isn't he?" Persephone asked. "He may have good intentions, but he's breaking two girls' hearts at once. That isn't fair, and it isn't kind."

"I couldn't bear it," Abi said. "If I broke up with him, how long would it take him to get with her? Half an hour?"

"More like half a decade," Persephone said. "Phoenix has a prickly shell, she doesn't let people in easily."

"I'm an idiot, aren't I?"

"Love makes idiots out of us all."

301

Phoenix lay in bed, curled up into a protective ball. Her ears were tuned to the music of the formidable storm outside. The warm glow from her bedside lamp illuminated the pages of the novel in her hand, and each of her senses lulled her into a protective cocoon. The scent of the storm soothed her, and the sweet taste of fresh air slipped through the open window and onto her tongue. Change was coming, and the forceful might of this dark rainy night came embedded with promise: promise of redemption, and promise of retribution. Her eyes grew heavy as she read, her lids drooping with the calls of sleep and the peace that slumber would bring. The words of her book warmed her heart, they burnt alongside it, and she chose to read a while longer.

The gentle thump of a fist on her door roused her from the comfort of fiction. She ignored it. The knocking continued.

"Go away!" Phoenix called. "I don't want to see anyone."

"Come on, Syrup, let me in."

Kai! She wanted to curse him and hug him. He was the cause of her distress, but he was also the balm for it. The heart had always seemed funny like that, how it could only be soothed by its own poison.

"Please leave me alone," she begged. "I can't deal with you right now."

"Persephone sent me. She said you were upset." His voice was concerned.

Phoenix groaned.

Kai opened the door. His clothes were soaking wet, and rainwater glistened on his hair and eyelashes.

"What is this ocean I see before me?" Phoenix asked. "Who drowned Kai?"

"Persephone said you needed someone to talk to. I was in the Old Town, and it was raining like mad. I ran all the way here."

"There's a towel in the bathroom." Phoenix buried her face in her pillow as he walked to the other room. She felt the gravitational pull from him, even when they were separated by a wall. It was too much. Her love for him had grown from a pain in the pit of her stomach, to a void that would absorb her entire universe if she let it. She ached for him, and it destroyed her.

Kai emerged from Phoenix's bathroom, a large, purple towel

wrapped around his shoulders like a cape. His face was still slick with rain, and his eyebrows held the remnants of rivers. She wanted nothing more than to nuzzle against his soft, wet skin, to find a home in the man who had run to her through the storm.

"So," he sat beside her on the bed, "what's up?"

"Nothing." She resumed her novel.

"What're you reading?" He craned his neck to see the book in her hands. The cover remained hidden from his view.

"*Jane Eyre*," Phoenix said, a little more responsive now. "It's three-hundred-years-old, and it's still relevant. I first read it when I was sixteen. I was a freshly minted Muscovite who knew nothing of the world, but I had my books. I hadn't been exposed to many novels until the Tsar took me. *Jane Eyre* wasn't my first love, but reading it struck a chord, opened my heart to possibilities I'd never considered before. It's such an intense study of the human condition. This book taught me what it means to be a woman."

"Suffering through unrequited love?" Kai asked. "If that's all it means to be a woman, I'm glad I'm a man."

"It was requited." An involuntary burst of sweetness bloomed in Phoenix's heart to know Kai had read her favourite novel. "Rochester loved Jane the whole time, he just never told her. He strung her along, made her believe he was engaged to someone else, all to make her jealous enough to react. But she didn't give him that satisfaction; she stuck to her principles, even when it meant losing him."

"Can you lose someone you never had?"

"Certainly," Phoenix said. "You can lose your idea of someone, the person they were to you. You can lose the parts of yourself you gave to them. And you can lose your self-respect, because you find yourself thinking all these thoughts that you have no right to think, wondering about what-ifs, and forget about the awful reality."

"You're not this sad over a book, are you?" Kai asked.

"Why not? Books have been far more constant to me than people," Phoenix said. "I'm not sad, anyway. Sad is such a pitifully small word. I'm devastated, I'm terrified. My world continues to implode upon me, and all my control has vanished." She paused. "Something happened, earlier. I was reminded of events from my past I want to forget, and I'm so, so scared."

"Oh sweetie." Kai cuddled her to him. "I'm sorry. I'm so sorry. You can talk to me, you know. You can talk about any of it."

"No, I can't," Phoenix whispered, her voice breaking. Tears dampened her eyes, and she snuggled into Kai. She felt like she belonged here. She could tell herself they were just friends, that there was nothing wrong with him hugging her – after all, she had lain like this with Persephone on many occasions. But this was different, the quickening beats of their hearts and the way her breath caught in her throat were testaments to that.

"Why not?" Kai asked.

"Because this is wrong," Phoenix said forcefully. Her back stiffened against him, her body was no longer warm or yielding. "You have a girlfriend, Kai. You can't cuddle me, and call me by terms of endearment, and then go running back to Abi the moment we're apart. We can tell ourselves we're just friends, we can pretend every time you touch me it's completely innocent. But I can feel every part of your body pressed against every part of mine, and I know we fit together in a way that is not pure, or innocent, or acceptable."

"Oh God, Phoenix." Kai loosened his embrace. "I'm so sorry! I didn't mean to make you uncomfortable."

Phoenix heaved a sigh of frustration. He had misunderstood her. Discomfort was not the issue. Lying in his arms, she felt more comfortable than she had in her whole life. That was the problem.

"Kai," she said, "you're not making me feel weird, that's not what I'm saying. What I'm trying to say is: we have this habit of acting like a couple, and I find it a bit odd, given that you have a girlfriend."

"Phoenix—" he began.

"It's true, isn't it? You can't talk your way out of this one."

"Phoenix, can you please turn around? I feel like I'm talking to your back."

"You come around this side. I'm comfortable as I am."

"You're going to drive me mad one day, you know," Kai said. He climbed over her, onto the other side of the bed.

"That was not what I meant!" she protested. "You could've walked around, like a normal person, but no, you had to prove my point. Stop stalling, Kai." His brown eyes held her with a challenging stare. Kai had always been kind to her, a safe pillow to fall back on when the rest of the world rejected her. Phoenix could see the error in that habit: her reliance on Kai had made him invincible to her process of deconstruction. He had become perfect to her, and now that he showed the first signs of being human, she hardly recognised him. The hardness in his eyes was met with an equal fervour from her own. He saw she wasn't going to let the subject drop.

"You're right, Syrup," he said gently, and all traces of animosity vanished.

"Don't go calling me Syrup again," Phoenix said half-heartedly.

"I was stalling," Kai continued. "I love you, Phoenix."

"You what?" She hardly dared to breathe.

"I love you," he repeated. "You're my best friend. I apologise if you feel I've blurred some lines, that was never my intention. We've had such different upbringings, I was brought up to think love and affection could make everything better, and—"

"And I was brought up to think everyone has an ulterior motive," Phoenix finished. "I'm sorry, Kai. I'm sorry for being all—"

"Syrupy?"

"Shut up. Don't finish my sentences."

"You finished mine."

"If you don't want me to apologise…"

"I don't. I wasn't asking for an apology, I was trying to apologise to you. I didn't think about how you must feel. You were already upset about something, and I've gone and made it worse."

"You didn't make it worse by cuddling me," Phoenix said. "That part was nice. I give you full permission to resume the snuggling. However, I keep thinking about Abi, and how she'd react if she saw us like this."

An impatient knocking on the door interrupted before Kai could respond.

"Kai, are you in there?" It was Abi.

"Speak of the Devil," Phoenix muttered as Kai went to the door.

"Hey, Abi," he said. They were awkward in each other's presence, they both knew he shouldn't be here.

"Can we talk, please?" Abi asked. Her gaze rested on the figure of Phoenix, who lay face down on the bed, ignoring her. "Alone?"

Kai shifted awkwardly from foot to foot.

"Yeah," he said, "of course – Phoenix, I'll be back soon."

Kai closed the door behind him, and Phoenix was alone once again. She hit her foot against her mattress in frustration. She wanted to tear the clouds from the sky, wrap them around her heart to dampen the burning agony that consumed her. Love wasn't meant to feel like this, wasn't meant to burn, and bleed, and boil. Love should be the feeling of arms around her, not the questioning of the motives behind them.

Kai was gone for a long time, and Phoenix wondered whether he planned to return. Sleep was almost upon her when his knocking hand alerted her to his presence outside her door.

"You can come in," she called out.

"Hey," he said. She noticed he had changed his clothes. The damp garments were gone, replaced by a grey long-sleeved T-shirt and a pair of black sweatpants. Kai looked both hopeful and deflated. His hair was damp and fuzzy, sticking out at odd angles like he had run his hands through it too many times.

"Sorry I was gone so long," he said "I needed a shower, I had to clear my head."

"You didn't need to come back," Phoenix said.

"Oh, I needed that more than anything else." He stood awkwardly in the doorway.

"What did that— I mean, what did Abi want?" Phoenix asked. She sat up against her pillows, and pulled her blanket over her knees for comfort.

"To break up with me," Kai said. He took a deep breath. "I'm glad she did. I liked her, but I didn't like her in the right way. She was my friend, and I'm sad because I've lost a friend, but I'm not sad she broke up with me. I'd rather lose her than you, and I feel like I lose you a hundred times each day." He fiddled with his hands as he spoke. "You were right when you said I was behaving inappropriately towards you. There's a bond between us that I can't always understand, I know you and you know me. You light up my world. Every day, I feel as though I haven't truly woken until I've looked in your eyes, seen the way they sparkle—"

"Kai, are you saying—"

"Kashnikova! Chistikov!" Dr Skryabin appeared behind Kai.

306

"What on earth do you think you're doing?"

"Having an important conversation," Kai said.

"Kashnikova," Dr Skryabin continued, "I thought you were familiar with rule number 5?"

"Oh crap," said Phoenix. "Technically, we haven't broken any rules, Doctor. Kai's not in my room, he's in the doorway."

"His feet are two inches over the threshold," Dr Skryabin said. "Chistikov." He focused his attention on Kai. "Now would be a good time for you to leg it back to your own room, and hope I forget all about this."

"Yes, Doctor. Of course. Goodnight, Dr Skryabin. Goodnight, Phoenix."

"Did I interrupt something?" Dr Skryabin asked when he and Phoenix were alone.

"Surely rule number 5 applies to teachers too. Your foot is right where Kai's was."

"Kashnikova..." Dr Skryabin tailed off as he noticed Persephone's bedding on the floor. "What's with all the blankets?" he asked.

"Persephone's back," Phoenix said. "She hasn't got anywhere to live, so I let her stay here. It doesn't break any rules, I checked. She has nowhere else to go."

"You should've asked for a room for her when she arrived," Dr Skryabin said. "The Institute has a long history of providing accommodation for asylum seekers. I heard Persephone's speech on the radio, but I didn't realise she was back in Tallinn. I must admit I was intrigued by her pregnancy; it shouldn't be possible for her species to breed with a human. Let alone under those circumstances."

"Well, the Tsar has his ways and means. He wanted that baby, that's certain."

"So it seems."

"Why are you patrolling the halls at night?"

"I saw young Chistikov entering the female corridor, and thought it curious. I assumed it had something to do with his girlfriend—"

"Ex-girlfriend."

"I assure you, if I had discovered him in her room they would both have been suitably punished. However, it was in your room that I found him, which seemed curious to me, until I overheard your conversation."

"How much did you hear?"

"He said your eyes sparkle, Kashnikova." Dr Skryabin chuckled to himself. It took all of the self-control Phoenix had to refrain from throwing her pillow at him. "That statement is only going one place, and that place is not friendship."

"I beg to differ. I notice Persephone's eyes sparkle, and I don't have romantic feelings for her." Wind howled outside; it slammed the window open-and-closed with an incessant *Thump! Thump! Thump!*

"All I'm saying, Kashnikova, is: be discreet."

"What?"

"Be discreet, and be safe." Dr Skryabin's face took on a pink glow as he spoke. Phoenix wasn't sure who was more embarrassed, him or her.

"Oh my gosh, Doctor! What are you implying?"

"Goodnight, Kashnikova."

"Goodnight, Dr Skryabin." Her face scrunched up as she cringed at the awkward interaction. Phoenix shook her head slightly, trying to rid the thought from her mind.

Within minutes of Dr Skryabin's leaving, Kai returned. He made sure to close the door carefully behind him.

"Phoenix," he said, breathless. "Sorry, I know we'll be in trouble if he catches me here, but I need to talk to you." His face was earnest.

"He doesn't have a problem with you being here," Phoenix said. "He just told me to be 'discreet'. He's got the wrong end of the stick about what you're doing in here, but he doesn't even have a problem with *that*—which both shocks, and worries me, might I add—so I don't think he's too bothered about us talking."

"That's good," Kai said, "because—"

"Kai," Phoenix interrupted, "shut up. You're about to say something in the heat of the moment, because you're all mixed up about Abi, and I don't want you to say the thing you're going to say. Not right now. We both need some space from each other, space to find ourselves."

"Do you want me to leave?" Kai's dark eyes wilted like old flowers. He half-turned towards the door.

"No, not tonight. Tonight I want you to stay, stay and hold me. I just don't want to talk, at least, not about her, or us, or any of that."

"Okay."

"I've never seen you this sad," Phoenix said. The sight of him made her heart hurt, she wanted to take his pain away, restore him to the smiling boy she had grown to love.

"I'm not sad," he promised her. "I'm reflective. Do you ever think about your life, and where you want to be in ten years' time?"

"I could never be certain of the future," Phoenix said. "I used to think I'd die young. Then I thought I'd stay in Moscow forever. Now I've got a career to aspire to, I have prospects. But I still don't know what the future holds. I somehow think I'm going to spend my life being Persephone's lapdog, giving up everything for her over and over again." Phoenix let out a harsh laugh as she fell back against her pillows.

"Do you resent her?" Kai asked.

"Never. Come on, lie down with me. Don't stand there all night."

"Won't Persephone be due back soon?"

"Not yet," Phoenix said.

Kai nodded. He walked, trance-like, to Phoenix's bed, and lay down beside her. She snuggled into him, let him hold her in his arms. Here, she was safe. Safe from her father, safe from photographs in black envelopes, safe from friends who would drag her off to war. Phoenix's breathing synchronised with Kai's, their hearts beat in harmony. They were on the brink right now, on the border between childhood and adulthood. They had tipped over tonight. For the first time, they met with the honesty of adulthood, and all childish masks were removed. Something intangible and irrevocable had changed between them, there was no going back.

"I love you," Phoenix murmured into Kai's shoulder when she was sure he was asleep.

# Chapter Twenty Nine

Persephone didn't knock when she reached the inner sanctum of Mariana's headquarters. Her hair was wet from the rain, and fell in tangled curls over her shoulders. She was breathless and exhilarated as ideas bubbled into thoughts, and thoughts into plans. Persephone finally knew where she had been going wrong, and in that moment, she felt unstoppable.

"What do you want?" Mariana asked, as she noticed the young woman in the doorway. "I didn't request you."

"I've been thinking," Persephone began. "We've gone about this the wrong way."

Mariana's impatience was evident in her gaze. "Who benefits from whatever hare-brained plan you've concocted this time, lover boy or the Kashnikova girl? Come sit by the fire, for goodness sake. You look like a drowned kitten."

"Meow."

"I always found ginger cats made far more noise than any other shade. It seems their human counterparts are the same." She pulled the window firmly shut, and motioned for Persephone to sit.

"Why did you think I'd be doing this for Drew?" She sat cross-legged on the floor by the fire. It was the end of Spring, far too late in the year to pass days sitting by the hearth. Persephone suspected Mariana only kept the fire burning for aesthetic reasons.

"Drew?" A peculiar look passed across her face. "Is that the name of your lover?"

"Yes." Persephone couldn't recall having mentioned him to her during their previous meetings. She wondered if Phoenix had said something.

"Why, you ask? Because you're prepared to start a war for a daughter you don't know. I've seen the measures you go to for people you love."

Persephone didn't respond.

"Tell me about this Drew." Mariana sat down in the chair across from Persephone. Firelight glowed on the elder woman's face, dancing across the lines of her wrinkles. She could have been attractive, had she been kind. There was something about the shape of her brow, the neatness of her nose, that Persephone warmed to.

In this light, she looked familiar. The harshness was momentarily lost, and a gentler side revealed itself, previously hidden behind the steel mask of politics.

"Why do you want to know?" Persephone asked. She knew Mariana dealt in information, it didn't feel wise to tell her about Drew.

"I want to know what kind of man you fall for."

"That's personal." Persephone sought to change the subject. She had come here for a reason. "This war shouldn't be fought by Estonia. This is a war for the Western Russian people. We can't go in and fight a war on their behalf, we need to work together, we need solidarity."

"You can't win a war unless war is declared," Mariana said. "If you think a bunch of peasants can defeat your husband, you're deluded."

"Phoenix wants me to meet with the Estonian president. She said you would be able to arrange it."

"I can never figure out, with you and Phoenix, who is the puppet and who is the puppeteer."

"Oh save your insinuations! I am here to do business with you, and I would be thankful if you could refrain from commenting on my personal life. Now, the president."

"I will contact Birgit tomorrow," Mariana said.

"You're on first-name terms with the president?"

"Does that surprise you?"

"I don't even know her last name."

"Her name is Birgit Poska. She has been president for three years, and has two years remaining in office. Is there any more information you need?"

"One condition of this meeting," Persephone said. "We meet alone."

"You don't speak Estonian."

"I'll find a way. I need to do this without you, without Phoenix, without anyone who doubts me. I must sell myself to her, and I can't do that with your unfounded negativity."

"You sold yourself long ago, girl."

311

Darkness thickened around the silhouette of the Institute when Persephone returned. Light glowed through the glass doors of the lobby. All else was blackness. There was no receptionist on duty at this time of night, and Persephone ventured into the building with continued solitude. Her shoes clapped softly against the thin, brown carpet of the floor. The Institute was peaceful at this hour, it seemed less like a centre for scientific research, and more like a hotel. The Institute would never feel like home, not to Persephone. She couldn't stand the minimalist whiteness of the walls, the scientists in lab coats, the constant sense that everyone in this place had a purpose except her. She craved the normality she had never known; longed for a house, rather than a skyscraper; a normal person for a spouse, instead of a Tsar; a normal career, other than that of Hopeful Revolutionary.

When Persephone reached Phoenix's room, she was shocked to find her slumbering friend was not alone. Phoenix and Kai lay in each other's arms, a tangle of limbs and hair and sleeping faces. There was no impropriety in the scene before her, yet Persephone felt like she had stumbled upon something far more intimate than cuddling. Phoenix's face was buried in the crook of Kai's elbow, her arms wrapped tightly around his waist; her legs were interwoven with his. This closeness between them confirmed Persephone's suspicions: Phoenix was in love with Kai. This wasn't just love, this was trust, something that had been previously unreachable for Phoenix.

Persephone took a step back, closing the door silently behind her, and meandered dazedly through the corridor, unsure where to spend the remainder of the night. She wandered through the hallways of the Institute, barely conscious of the darkness around her.

*I would be gold to these people,* Persephone thought. *If they knew what I was, they would kill to get their hands on me, run tests on me, create more of me. They only treat me as human because they assume I am one.*

There were four people in the world who knew of Persephone's true species, and only one had no connection to science. She trusted Phoenix not to harm her intentionally, but she didn't trust Dr Skryabin. She didn't trust anyone who could benefit from

312

exploiting her.

A door opened down the corridor, and Persephone recognised this particular stretch of hall from her first visit to the Institute. Dr Skryabin emerged from his office.

"Persephone," he greeted her. "I heard you were back."

"I can't stay away," she said. "From Phoenix, that is, not all the poking and prodding, or the needles and tests. Not to mention the life-changing revelations about my identity." She smiled to show she spoke good-naturedly, but it came out as a grimace. She still felt the pang of those needles. It was dehumanising to be treated as an object of science, and her resentment lingered.

"I am sorry," Dr Skryabin said. "You are an exciting prospect for any scientist, but for a neuroscientist like myself, you are the Holy Grail. Seeing the effects of a robotic brain in a human body is truly fascinating. I'm sorry for forgetting your humanity."

"You weren't the only one," Persephone reminded him. "It wasn't you who sent me here, who suspected what I was and sent me to an institute of scientific research, of all places! I've subdued my resentment towards her because I love her so much, but I'm angry. Sorry, it's past midnight, you don't need to hear my word-vomit."

"Persephone," Dr Skryabin's tone was paternal. "I'm happy to listen to your 'word-vomit.' You are my patient. Everything you tell me is confidential."

"You won't tell Phoenix?"

"I doubt she would listen." She could see from his smile that he adored Phoenix. "She is particularly selective when it comes to taking advice."

"She's selective when it comes to anything."

"I hear you've been staying in her room," Dr Skryabin said conversationally.

"She told me it didn't break any rules," Persephone said. "Not directly, at least."

"It would be better if we provided you with your own room. Girls of your ages need privacy."

"You know, don't you?" Something in his face told her he had witnessed the intimacy between Phoenix and Kai.

"That a certain young gentlemen is in her room right now?" Dr

Skryabin chuckled. "I'm surprised it took them this long."

"They're not doing anything," Persephone assured him. "They were just cuddling. I came in, and they were asleep, all snuggled up together."

"How did that make you feel?" Dr Skryabin asked.

"It made me miss Drew – my boyfriend, or whatever he is."

"You felt jealous?"

"Frustrated." It was good to talk. "Phoenix trusts Kai more than she does me, even after everything we've been through together. I need her to love me. I need her to love me, so I know she won't turn on me. I'm scared she'll become like the Tsar, that she'll see me as nothing but a robot, a creature to be manipulated."

"But you're more than that, aren't you?" Dr Skryabin's questions were leading.

"The way I see it," Persephone fumbled for the right words, "is that none of us is 'made' as a finished article. You're all born, as babies, and—although you may not be blank slates—you've got a lot of developing left, which has nothing to do with DNA. I may not have been born a human, but I've been raised as one. I couldn't live like a robot now if I tried. It's not who I am, it's not my nature. I am human, even if I'm the only one who believes it."

"It certainly poses interesting questions about nature and nurture," said Dr Skryabin. "We should talk more on this sometime. Come, I'll find you a room."

"Isn't it a bit late at night to be arranging that?"

"No, no. There are plenty of spare rooms. We'll go and get the keys now, and I can do the paperwork in the morning. We have always provided accommodation for those in need. You certainly qualify."

"Dr Skryabin?" Persephone asked hesitantly. "If my brain is a computer, does that mean it can be programmed like one? Could you install the Estonian language into my brain?"

# Chapter Thirty

The world was hazy. Persephone was neither awake nor asleep; the white room blurred grey beneath her half-closed eyelids, and the back of her head felt numb. Music played softly in her ears, so she couldn't hear the sounds of Dr Skryabin installing software into her brain. She wouldn't let him put her under general anaesthetic; Persephone didn't trust him enough to be unconscious. The haziness began to pass. At first, it was slow, like the cells in her brain were stirring awake after a long sleep, growing warmer and warmer until they burned. Persephone screamed. Her mind was on fire. The pain struck through her like lightning, an incessant attack that she had no way to strike back against or evade. The pain ravaged her until she lost consciousness.

"Persephone." She woke to the sound of Dr Skryabin's voice. "Persephone, can you hear me?" Something about him sounded different, the texture of his words didn't match the cadence of his Russian speaking voice.

"Did it work?" Persephone asked. Her head throbbed, and her throat was dry and itchy.

"You asked me in Estonian," Dr Skryabin said. "Here." He handed her a glass of water.

Persephone nodded slowly, and gulped down mouthfuls of water.

"Do you feel different?" he asked.

She shook her head.

"I'm a robot," Persephone whispered. The word felt tangy and acidic in her mouth, unnatural. She wanted to carve its ghost out of her tongue, gargle soapy water until all evidence of it was gone. "I'm a robot," she repeated. This time the word came out as a sob. "I'm not human, my brain is a computer. I don't understand. I don't understand. I don't understand! How do I think? How do I feel? I'm a computer! How does my body connect to my mind when one is flesh and blood and the other is a machine? Nothing about me is natural!"

"I don't know," Dr Skryabin said. He stood by the window now, with his back turned to her. "I'm a neuroscientist, Persephone. I study brains, not computers. Your brain is a hybrid of those two things. All I know is that, on a surface level, it functions like a human brain. I could do more tests on you, but they would be invasive. Do you want my advice?"

"So long it doesn't involve you hacking into my brain."

"Live your life, Persephone. You don't need to learn the ins and outs of what you are, unless it will bring you peace. You have so many other battles ahead of you, don't go to war against yourself."

Birgit Poska watched Persephone from across her immaculate desk. The President was a tall woman, and sat straight as a skyscraper. Her blonde hair was tied back in a ponytail, and the gaze of her green eyes pierced with precision. In spite of this, she had a warmth about her. The slight curve of her lips froze her face in a permanent half-smile, and her cheeks glowed with the faintest hint of raspberry pink.

"What brings you here?" Birgit asked. "I heard your speech, that's all I have to go on. Mariana told me very little about you."

Persephone sat up straight, preparing to pitch. "As you know, I am the Tsarina of Western Russia. I want to bring down the Tsar."

"I'm not sure how I can help you with that."

"The Baltic Alliance could declare war against Western Russia." Persephone expected Birgit to laugh at her. The President didn't laugh, she sat in silence, observing the young woman in front of her.

"We can't win a war against Western Russia," Birgit finally said. "I heard your speech; the Tsar has done enough to warrant foreign intervention. If he has found a way to control his own citizens' minds, no one is safe. However, the Baltic Alliance is too small. We simply don't have a large enough army." She spoke without agenda. Birgit inhabited a world of logic and facts, where the sway of emotion and ideology was not powerful enough to fuel a fire.

"We don't," Persephone said, "but we could. If we were allied with Greece." She held her breath, and watched Birgit's face in anticipation.

"It's an interesting idea." The President nodded slowly. "Greece won't have taken kindly to the Tsar banning international trade."

"I'm sure they'll be looking for a new trading partner. This could benefit the Baltic Alliance." The air in the room was too warm. Persephone wanted to take off her cardigan, but she already felt naked under the directness of Birgit's gaze. She rolled up her sleeves as a compromise.

"You do understand I can't make this decision on my own?" Birgit asked. "I must reach an agreement with the Latvian and Lithuanian presidents before anything else can happen. Your war is a long shot, Persephone. Don't get your hopes up."

✝

June passed by in a blur. Persephone's experience of Tallinn changed now that she could speak and understand Estonian. She was no longer reliant on Phoenix to communicate for her, and her world expanded. Her life filled up with the simple pleasures of making chitchat with shopkeepers, riding on trams and knowing their destination, eavesdropping on strangers' conversations in crowded streets. It wasn't enough to keep the bad thoughts at bay, but it held them off for minutes or hours at a time, and that was the best Persephone could hope for right now.

When July came, her world changed.

"Why is she still involved?" Persephone whispered to Birgit. They sat side-by-side on Mariana's sofa. It was midday on the 1st of July, and blinding sunlight shone through the large windows.

"We're going to war," Birgit told her. The words settled on Persephone's shoulders. She didn't know how to feel. Her wish had been granted, and the quiet world she had become accustomed to disintegrated beneath her feet. "The Baltic Alliance and Greece will declare war on Western Russia within the next few weeks."

"That doesn't answer my question," Persephone said. She lowered her voice further to make sure Mariana couldn't hear her from across the room. "I don't need her help anymore."

"There is still a complete media blackout in Western Russia," Birgit said. "Mariana has contacts on the inside. Without her, we

317

have no way to coordinate with the Western Russian rebels."

"Let me go to Western Russia." The words left Persephone's mouth before she stopped to consider their significance. "Mariana's spies might be able to provide information, but we need more than that. We need the Russian people to fight, otherwise this isn't a war, it's an invasion."

"Persephone," said Birgit, "if you go to Western Russia, I can't protect you. You will be in the Tsar's territory. It's not safe."

"Screw safe. This is a war, Ms Poska, I have no intention of waiting safely on the sidelines. I wasn't in Western Russia when the Tsar drugged me and kidnapped me, I was right here in Estonia, staying in the same building I live in now. He knows where I am. You said it yourself; Western Russia has a complete media blackout. He won't know I'm there."

"Do you have a brain?" Mariana sat down in the chair by the window.

"No, actually." Persephone glared. "I don't have a brain at all, there's a computer in my head that makes all my decisions for me. It's why I'm so stupid." She wondered how Mariana would respond if she knew the truth.

"A media blackout doesn't mean the cameras are switched off," Birgit cut in. "Every minute you spend in Moscow is another nail in your coffin. You poked a sleeping wolf when you did your speech, and luckily for you there were no repercussions. When we declare war, you're not just poking that wolf; you're locking yourself in a cage with it."

"One day," Persephone said. "That's all I need in Moscow. One day." A memory flickered in the back of her mind, a conversation in the bookshop shortly after her engagement. "There's someone I need to see. After that, I will stick to small towns, places where the Tsar's presence isn't so strong."

"You're a fool," said Mariana.

"Let me give you some advice, Persephone," said Birgit. Her tone was kind, but her words punched with their usual directness. "There are a lot of people in your life who should have given you this advice, and in holding back, they have failed you. Stop being so impulsive. Stop making decisions when you're emotional, stop taking extreme measures without thinking them through. You need

318

a plan, you need to be methodical, and you need to be objective. If you don't learn to control your impulses, you will get yourself killed."

"Have a little faith." Persephone stood up to leave. "This isn't a suicide mission. I know what I'm doing; I know how to win this war. I am going to Western Russia, and you can't stop me."

"You're right," Birgit said, "I can't stop you. But I also can't let you put yourself in harm's way." She indulged in one of her frequent silences. Mariana opened her mouth to speak, and Birgit silenced her with the motion of her hand. "I have an idea."

+

"Mariana?" Phoenix snorted. "Your chaperone is Mariana?" She lay sprawled out on Persephone's bed, with her legs kicked back in the air. In moments like this, she looked like the girl she used to be in Moscow – lively and exuberant, a ray of sunshine wrapped around her dark and damaged core.

"Oh, not just Mariana." Persephone didn't try to conceal the disgust on her face. She had drawn the short straw, and she had no desire to pretend otherwise. "There's going to be a whole strategy team following me around the country, because I'm so incapable of making my own decisions."

"Where was this strategy team two years ago?" Phoenix laughed. "You could have avoided marrying the Tsar entirely!"

"Hilarious." Persephone flopped onto the end of the bed. She buried her face sulkily into the duvet. The air was warm and clammy, and the fabric was uncomfortable against her face. She rolled onto her back and glared at the ceiling.

"You gonna see Drew?" Phoenix asked. "Before you cross the border?"

"I hadn't thought about it. It would be nice to see him again. Maybe I will, if my stalkers let me."

Phoenix sat up. Her face was serious now. "I don't think it's a good idea. Not with Mariana and all them glued to your side. Some worlds aren't meant to collide."

"I'm hardly going to introduce them," Persephone said. "I could drop Mariana and her people at the Haven, and go to Drew's alone."

"I'll tell you now that it's a bad idea."

"Why did you suggest it then?"

"I didn't. I was making sure you had enough common sense to keep Mariana far away from him." There was a warning in her voice that Persephone didn't understand. She wondered what Phoenix knew about Mariana.

"Whatever."

"Sphenn?"

"Yes."

"I love you."

"I love you too."

Phoenix crawled across the bed and pulled Persephone into a hug. "Please be careful."

✝

The woods were peaceful. Light-green moss covered the black earth like a fuzzy blanket, and beetles crawled across the soft ground. Twigs crackled beneath Persephone's feet with each step she took, and birds chirped in the distance. Drew was on the other side of these woods. Drew, and Rozalina, and Grigory; remnants of another life. She could run to him, let him hold her in his arms and pretend life was simple and safe. Persephone entertained the thought for a moment, remembered the feel of his hands on her skin, the unmistakable affection in his eyes every time he looked at her. It was a choice; Drew had always been a choice. A choice she had never chosen.

Persephone walked back towards the Haven. It was better for everyone that Drew didn't know she was here.

"Persephone?" Drew stood outside the Haven. "What are you doing here?" He wore a tight grey T-shirt, the colour of cloudy skies. His hair had grown out, and fell in waves a couple of inches above his shoulders, more blond than brown in the bright summer light.

"Hey," she said. It wasn't a relief to see him. His presence was a weight on her shoulders that she couldn't shake off. "I'm sorry I

320

didn't tell you I was coming. I'm only here for one night."

"One night? What would bring you back to the Borderlands for—?"

Before Drew could finish his sentence, Mariana emerged from the doorway. She stopped short at the sight of the man in front of her. Neither said a word. Their eyes locked onto each other. The energy overwhelmed Persephone, who stood halfway between them. She couldn't read Drew; he wore an expression she had never seen on him before, like fear and defiance had coiled together inside his cells, changing the familiar landscape of his face. Mariana began to speak, but Drew cut in before she had a chance.

"Who is this woman?" he asked. "What is she doing here?" The faint lines around his mouth deepened. He was a wild animal, defending his territory. There was war in Drew's eyes, where before Persephone had only ever seen peace.

"This is Mariana Deripaska," Persephone said. "Mariana, this is Drew. Drew, I'm going to see Elizaveta. I think she can help me bring down the Tsar."

Drew watched Mariana with suspicion. His gaze returned to Persephone when he spoke. "I don't know what you've planned." He looked at her as if she was the only person in the world. "What I do know is that Elizaveta gives great advice, she was like the mother I never had. You're going in the right direction."

The door of the Haven slammed behind them. When Persephone looked around, Mariana was gone.

"God I needed to hear that." Persephone reached out for Drew's hand. The heaviness lifted, she was glad to see him now. "You're the only person who hasn't told me I'm stupid or impulsive."

Drew smiled to himself. "Oh, you're definitely impulsive, there's no doubt about that. But you've gotten this far. Look at what you've survived. I've never been a gambling man, but I'd place all my bets on you, Persephone."

"Come with me." His hand was like an anchor, rooting her to the ground. Solid, reliable, human. She wasn't ready to leave him behind again.

Drew looked from Persephone to the door of the Haven. "I'm sorry," he said. "I love you, but there are some things I can't go back to."

He kissed her softly on the lips, and the world stopped. Persephone tangled her hands in his long hair, and pulled him towards her. She had forgotten this sweetness.

"I love you too," she said when they broke apart.

# Chapter Thirty One

The bookshop was frozen in time. Persephone watched as ghosts of her former self rested on the windowsill, sat by the fireplace, lurked behind the furthest shelves. She barely recognised the girl she was back then, the hopes she had had, the decisions she had made. Persephone wondered: if she were to do her life over, as the woman she was now, whether she would have the courage to say no to the Tsar's proposal.

"Persephone?" Elizaveta emerged from the door of her office. She looked older now. The creases around her green eyes had deepened, and she wore the face of a woman who had seen too much of the world. Her black hair was plaited away from her face, and she wore no makeup. She looked bare, raw, human in the most powerful way. "I'm so glad you're alive! Can I give you a hug?"

Persephone nodded. She couldn't stop smiling as Elizaveta enveloped her in the comfort of her arms. Elizaveta's hug was warm and firm, she hugged Persephone like an old friend, not an acquaintance she had met a handful of times. Her gaze was maternal, and it made Persephone want to weep.

"Why did you think I was dead?" Persephone asked when they separated. She followed Elizaveta to the window seat.

"There's been a media blackout for months; no one knows what to think. It wasn't a stretch to presume the reason the news stopped was because the Tsar wanted to cover up your death."

"You're saying everyone in Western Russia thinks I'm dead?" Persephone considered the implications of this for her war. She had sneaked out of her room that morning, before Mariana and the strategy team awoke. She wondered how much Mariana knew of her rumoured death.

"Not everyone," Elizaveta said. She glanced out the window at the sparsely peopled street below. "But it's certainly flavour of the month for conspiracy theorists."

"You haven't asked why I'm here," Persephone said. Her eyes drifted around the shop as she spoke. It was surreal to be back.

"Why are you here?"

"I remembered something you said to me, when I got engaged."

"You'll have to remind me," Elizaveta said. "It's been a long time, my memory isn't that good."

"You told me I don't have to fight alone. You said to build a solidarity network of women I could rely on."

A small smile crossed Elizaveta's face. "A lot has changed since you've been gone, but I stand by that advice."

"I'm going to war against the Tsar." Persephone watched Elizaveta closely. She expected a strong reaction, but all the woman did was nod. "Greece and the Baltic Alliance will declare war on Western Russia, to protect its citizens from the Tsar and his genetically modified fruit. But I need more. This country can't be a pawn in this, a plaything for Greece and the Baltics to divvy up between them when the war is won. I feel like that's the direction this is going in. I don't want a war, Elizaveta, I want a revolution, and that has to come from the Western Russian people."

"And that's why you're back?"

"I don't want to sit safely in Estonia and pull strings behind the scenes; I'm not that kind of person. I want to talk to the Western Russian people. I want solidarity, I don't want to exploit them. I am not just fighting for my daughter: I am fighting for all our daughters."

"Revolution doesn't happen inside this bookstore," Elizaveta said regretfully. "No matter how much I want it to. We're privileged people playing at politics. When I was younger, I thought I was going to change the world. Now I'm old and weary, and the world has changed without me having a hand in it. If you want a revolution, you need to talk to the people who suffer most under the Tsar's regime, and I can guarantee you won't find them in this bookshop."

"You're right," Persephone said. "I didn't expect to find them here. I came for you. I need an advisor, someone to tell me the truth, to stop me from being impulsive. I was given an advisor—a whole team of them—and I don't trust a single one. They don't have Western Russia's best interests at heart. I need you, I trust you."

Elizaveta took her time to answer. She looked wistfully around the shop, letting her eyes linger on the shelves, the floor, the ceiling. Eventually she said "Okay. Maybe it's not too late to change the world."

324

✝

Life on the road invigorated Persephone. In the months she had spent in Estonia, Western Russia had mutated into an a nightmare state in her mind. She forgot the nuances of the country, all she saw was a dictatorship. Now Western Russia was laid out before her, a world of dark-green forests and flowing rivers, crowded trains and quiet conversations.

Mariana snapped at her heels like an unpleasant chihuahua; she had grown more irritable since their night at the Haven. The strategy team were Mariana's people, and they made it clear they didn't trust Persephone as far as they could collectively throw her. Elizaveta was Persephone's sole ally here.

"Any word from Moscow?" Persephone asked Mariana. They sat in a bustling teashop in a basement in Saint Petersburg. The shop was furnished with antique sofas and vibrant blue woven rugs; tall glasses steamed with fresh mint tea.

"No." Mariana was cold, colder than usual. "My sources have nothing."

"The Tsar knows war is coming," Elizaveta said in a low voice.

"It sounds like you need new sources," Persephone said to Mariana, before she could stop herself. "Go on." She nodded to Elizaveta.

"I went down to the docks," she said. "I met a handful of sailors who've just arrived from Moscow, and they said the city's on lockdown. It's near impossible to get in or out without a travel permit. The Tsar's grip is tighter than ever."

"Oh please," Mariana cut in. "Tatiana said nothing has changed since we left."

"With all due respect, Mariana, your daughter is the Tsar's sister-in-law, I hardly think she's a reliable source. If you want to know how the Tsar is treating his citizens, talk to common people."

"With all due respect, Elizaveta, you do not have the authority to tell me whether or not I can trust my own children."

"I beg to differ."

Mariana scowled, and picked up her glass of tea. She held it in her hand for a moment, and looked from the scalding green liquid to Elizaveta and back, as if weighing up her options. Her wrist jerked slightly, the tea began to spill. Persephone carefully removed the glass from Mariana's hand before she could pour it over Elizaveta's head.

"I don't know what's gotten into you two," she said, "but you're meant to be stopping me from making rash decisions, and right now you're acting like children. Grow up, or go home. I have a war to win, and I don't have time to deal with your petty rivalry."

# Chapter Thirty Two

Phoenix lay on the grass under the out-of-bloom cherry trees, cushioned by the soft earth beneath her. It was late August, and humid heat bore down on Tallinn, reducing the city to a sweaty sauna. The courtyard was Phoenix's favourite place in the Institute, a green oasis where she could ground herself when her mind got lost in the world of theories and experiments.

"Syrup!" Kai called from the other side of the courtyard. He ran across the grass towards her. "God I've missed you." He sat down beside Phoenix. A smile crept onto her face at the sight of him. His absence had lurked quietly in the pit of her stomach all summer. Now he was close enough to touch.

"I've missed you," she said. "Persephone's been away for weeks, it's so quiet here without her. I've spent far too much time talking to Dr Skryabin. Now I have you back, and all wrongs have been righted." Her words came out in a fast gabble. She had so much to say to him, and not enough time. "It's so hot out here, isn't it? What was it like in Tartu?"

"Even hotter," he said. "This weather is getting worse! We're going to melt out here. I feel like I'm on fire." His eyes feasted on her.

"Same," Phoenix said. "I don't think it's the weather."

"Are you saying…?" he asked.

"I'm ready to talk about it." She sat up straighter. "I'm ready to talk about us. But the timing is wrong again. I made a commitment over the summer, and I can't back out of it. I won't back out of it. I'm leaving here. Tomorrow."

"What?" Kai sat bolt upright with shock. "You're leaving? Tomorrow?"

"I joined the army." Phoenix couldn't look at him. She fiddled with the grass beneath her, twisting and tugging until each green blade tore from its roots.

"I know you have a personal vendetta against the Tsar," Kai said. "I know you feel obligated to fight in this war. I know how much it matters to you." Phoenix felt herself clamming up at his words, locking the doors to her heart that she had been ready to open. She knew what came next, she knew he would try to convince her to stay. "You don't need to go, Phoenix; not at this stage. Not when you already have PTSD."

"After all the violence I've suffered, war will be nothing to me," Phoenix said.

"That's what I'm afraid of. I know you, Phoenix. I know where you're soft, where you're sweet, where you're vulnerable. I don't want you to lose your goodness."

"You don't understand what it means to be a victim," Phoenix said. "You don't know the pain of passivity. For the first time in my life, I have a chance to fight back!"

"It wasn't the Tsar who hurt you, and it certainly wasn't the Western Russian people. I love you, Phoenix. I know I've said it before, but I don't mean as a friend. We've been dancing around this for months, trying to hide our feelings for each other – or simply avoiding them. Hear me now: I love you. I don't want us to be just friends."

"I love you too," she said, so fast Kai could hardly understand her words. Everything she had been afraid to say was out in the open. A part of her knew their friendship was meant to culminate in this. It was inevitable. Phoenix had never been one to believe in fate, the concept unsettled her. But Kai was more than a series of choices she had made, he had to be.

"So why leave?" he asked.

"Because I'm scared!" Phoenix said. "I can't handle this, I can't handle loving you. I can't handle feeling safe. I can't let myself trust you! You were with Abi. You chose her. I've got issues when it comes to stuff like this. Intimacy isn't something that comes lightly to me. I thought I was ready to be with you, because I want it so much. Maybe I am ready, I don't know. I'm not running away this time, Kai, you have to know that. I'm running to something. I have to fight, I need to know I have power over my own life and my own body. Can you at least understand that?"

"Of course." Kai put an arm around her as he spoke. Phoenix felt his closeness like an electric shock. He had always been affectionate with her, touched her too casually. Now every movement had meaning, every gesture was a promise. The fire within her was no longer confined, and it burned: oh, how it burned! The blaze transcended love and transcended desire, it was a flame that had finally found oxygen, and it spread with the freedom of wildfire. Phoenix leant her forehead against Kai's so their noses touched. She felt the faint brush of his lips against her cheek. Her hands travelled over his shoulders and journeyed up to his face, tracing the shapes of his features, marking them as her own. Phoenix held Kai's face in her hands, and saw how easily he could become her whole world. This love could be enough for her, it could nourish her through the agony of life, heal her better than any magic or medicine. But who would she be, if she tied her happiness to Kai? Phoenix was ready to give her heart, and even her body, but not her identity. She leant in to kiss him, knowing this time may be the last. His embrace tightened around her. She felt the warmth of his mouth on hers, the desperation in his touch, the insatiability of their combined need for each other.

"I love you," he said again when they finally broke apart. "I love you so much." Tears glistened in his eyes. "I wish we could stay like this forever."

"So do I," Phoenix said. "But we can't. I'm still leaving tomorrow." She refrained from tears herself, but her heart cried with Kai.

"What about your education?" he asked.

"I've been studying all summer," Phoenix said. "I've got a three-month head start, and I can do the rest when I come back."

"What does Skryabin think?" Kai asked. "He wouldn't let his prize pupil go to war. He'd never risk losing you, not when he fought so hard for you to get that scholarship."

"He's not happy about it," Phoenix said. "He feels like I've betrayed him. He bet on me, you know? He convinced the Institute's board to let me in with no formal education; he promised them the risk would pay off. Now I've gone and thrown that back in his face. Skryabin isn't stopping me, Kai. He's mad at me, and he's confused, and he thinks I'm an idiot, but he knows I'm *his* idiot. He's invested so much time and care into me, he knows I never planned for this. You say you love me, Kai, this is your opportunity to prove it. Let me go. Let me go for now, and I promise I'll come back to you. I can't stay here."

"Why can't you stay?" Phoenix could see the agony in Kai's eyes, it was too much to bear. She wished she had left without saying goodbye. "I know it's too late now. You've already made your decision, I respect that. I respect you." He paused. "Is there anything I could've done differently? If I'd loved you sooner, loved you harder, supported you more… Did I ever have the power to prevent this?"

"No, darling. You couldn't have done anything. This isn't about you. It's not even about me, not really. I'm not fighting this war because I believe in a cause, or because I feel like I owe it to Persephone. Those are reasons, certainly, but they're not *the* reason. You know me, Kai, you know how selfish I am. It's self-preservation. I told you I wasn't running away, but I lied. I am running, but I'm not running from here, or from you, or even from myself. I'm running because I don't feel safe here. There's someone who hurt me, and I can't stand up to him… I don't know how to stand up to him. I thought I was safe, thought he'd forgotten me, but he hasn't. That night, three months ago, the night Abi broke up with you – I'd had a letter that day, from him. He knows where I am, Kai, and I just want to be safe."

"Who is he?" Kai leant his forehead against hers, so all he could see was her face.

"My father." Phoenix trembled as she spoke. A faint wave of relief ebbed at her heart, lapped at the metal bars that had surrounded it for so long. The act of naming her trauma, no matter how vaguely she labelled it, was a declaration of liberation. Relief disappeared as quickly as it arose. Phoenix cursed herself for being so naïve. No matter how much she confided, she could never undo the pain she had endured.

"You're not going to tell me, are you?" Kai asked. His breath tickled her cheek as he spoke.

"Not right now," she said. "I will tell you one day. I promise. I've never told anyone what he did to me, not even Sphenya. My wounds are safely guarded, I couldn't bear to share them, not before I'm ready."

"Of course." When their lips met this time, there were no butterflies, no fiery sparks to light up heavenly skies, but there was warmth in Phoenix's heart, warmth far sweeter than any fire, for this heat didn't burn. Kai kissed her passionately, softly, his fingers pressed against the yielding flesh of her hips. She knew this kiss was a distraction, a way of stopping time and hiding from the inevitable, but she didn't care. Phoenix chose to drown in the comfort Kai gave her, because she knew how soon it would end.

"We need to talk," he whispered against her cheek.

"No, not now." She pulled his arms around her, and locked her mouth firmly with his. Now wasn't the time for talking, now was the time for kissing, embracing, loving. Now was the time for living, because Death lurked in the shadows, waiting to claim its prey.

"My sweet, sweet Syrup," Kai murmured into her hair, "You will come home to me, to this, I know you will."

The train rattled slowly through the dark night. Everyone in the carriage was fast asleep, save for Phoenix. She lay back against her seat, watching the image of her own face cast upon the window by the dimmed light of a lamp. Her appearance had changed dramatically since her last train journey, over a year ago. Her dark hair hung past her shoulders, and the gaunt wilderness of her face had long since given way to soft, rounded cheeks and sparkling eyes. The panther had become a house-cat. Now she felt like a mewling kitten, wandering on wobbling legs to fight battles way beyond her years. Tears burned behind her eyes, and Phoenix wished she could turn back time.

"Stupid girl," she whispered, burying her face in the back of the seat in front of her. "Stupid, stupid, stupid girl." Certain that all others in the vicinity were submerged in slumber, she allowed herself to sob. Phoenix cried long and hard, consumed by the weight of her decision. There was no going back.

The first rays of morning shone through the windows of the train as it pulled up to the platform at its destination. The journey was long – the train had picked up recruits from even the smallest towns and villages of Estonia and Latvia. The military training centre was a vast building in the south of Latvia, constructed from

331

wood of the region's native pine trees. As she stood in its shadow, Phoenix couldn't help thinking of the Tartarus settlement. The scale and proportions of the training centre mirrored the prison that had confined her for so long. Her head hurt from a night of crying, and the skin around her eyes was dry and itchy.

A hand lightly tapped her shoulder. Phoenix spun round at the unexpected touch.

"Hey stranger!" said the woman in front of her.

"Oh my gosh, Sphenya!" Phoenix flung her arms around Persephone's neck. "I haven't seen you in so long! What are you doing here? I've missed you so much!"

Persephone laughed at her friend's exuberance. "I'm here to train," she said as Phoenix released her from the embrace.

"I thought you were running around Western Russia with Mariana?"

"I was," Persephone said. "The strategy team want a unit on the ground, to report back to them. They're all way past their physical prime, so I volunteered. I figured it was the only way to shake them off once and for all. I also suggested they recruit you. I hope you don't mind, but I thought we'd both be happier if we were together."

"Yes!" Phoenix said. "Yes, definitely! I missed you."

Persephone nodded in agreement. The long red locks of her ponytail bounced from the movement of her head. Her sapphire-blue eyes glowed with joy. She didn't look human on days like this, when the sun brought out the orange hue of her hair, and her eyes were too bright to be real. She passed as human because no one knew otherwise. "I'm so glad we're together again. I missed you like crazy. I feel like I'm a different person now, Phoenix. I'm not a little girl any more. I'm not damaged, or bruised, or broken, at least, not completely. I'm a woman now. I have a purpose, I feel whole. I think maybe you and I are equals now. I know I'm not smart like you are, but I am intelligent. In a different way."

"We've always been equals," Phoenix said. She hugged her friend again.

"Ouch, can't breathe!" Persephone protested. "Can't hug and walk at same time. Doesn't work."

"Sorry." She let her go. "Sphenn, there has never been any

doubt that you and I are equals. We don't have to be the same to have the same worth."

"You've changed your tune. You frequently used to tell me I was stupid."

"I was wrong to do that. I treated you like you were dumb just because you weren't educated. I shouldn't have done that. I've changed too, Sphenn. I know where I belong, and I want to go back there. I'm not going to throw that all away. I'm going to fight to live, not fight to die."

"I can't believe you left the Institute," Persephone said. "I didn't think you'd give up your education for anything." She walked differently now. There was a confidence in the sway of her hips that hadn't been there before. She was a woman who knew her power.

"Neither did I, but this is something I need to do. I'm scared— I'm completely terrified—but I can't go back on my decision now."

"I can't help wondering if I did the right thing," Persephone said. "Encouraging Estonia to go to war. I don't believe in war, I don't believe killing is right. But I've never felt as good as I do now. I'm fighting for something, Phoenix, and I've never had a chance to fight before." Her pale skin was almost translucent in this light; ethereal, alien. Phoenix used to think Persephone was beautiful; that label didn't fit any more. She was something else entirely, like she had been transported from another world.

"This isn't fighting, Sphenn. This is merely the preparation for it. Fighting won't feel good at all. We're going to have to kill people. Even if we hate them, even if we mean to kill them, even if it's the right thing, it's not something that can ever be shaken off. War is meant to be different to murder, war is meant to be just, but every time a life is taken... They are still a person, still someone who is wanted and needed and loved. We're never going to forgive ourselves for this."

"I'm hoping we won't have to kill," Persephone said. "Our unit is here to assess, not to fight – unless we have to. I know it's naïve, but I hope I can come out of this war without blood on my hands."

"Won't we still be killing by proxy?" Phoenix asked. "You started this war, Persephone. We may all have blood on our hands, but you will be drowning in it."

"I know." A sob rose in her throat. "I know, and I hate myself for it. But survival is about the lies we tell ourselves, so let me lie, let me pretend I'm not as evil as I truly am." The light changed, and her face was human again.

"You're not evil, Sphenn," Phoenix said firmly. "War is, but perhaps it's a necessary evil. We're fighting for a just cause, and even if fighting is wrong, it's not as wrong as what we're fighting against. We'll live with our actions, because we have to. We'll forgive ourselves, because this isn't just a war. This is a revolution. There will be blood on our hands, Persephone, but we can use that blood to paint a better world."

�﹢

The cold November air cut through Persephone like a knife. It was early morning, and the sky was dark. Dim yellow lights cut through the foggy haze in the training centre's grounds. Persephone had risen earlier than required, to snatch a few moments of solitude before another day of training. She hated the routine here, the constant company. She missed Western Russia, the wide-open spaces, the days passed on trains with Elizaveta by her side.

"Persephone Olympovskaya?" asked a soldier as he came towards her. A messenger bag hung across his side, and she recognised the postal service logo stamped upon it.

"Yes," she said, "that's me."

"There's a letter for you."

"Thank you." She supplied a wan smile, and took the letter from his gloved hands. She slid her finger under the envelope's seal, prising apart the cold, hard glue, and retrieved the letter from inside. Persephone glanced at the front of the envelope: the letter was forwarded from the Institute.

*Dear Persephone,* it read. *I can't do this any more. Something changed between us, that day at the Haven. I'm not the man you think I am. I wish I was better, I wish I could step up and be the man you need me to be, but I'm not him. I love you, I will always love you, but this is too much. Not all wars can be won, Sphenya. I'm sorry.*

*Drew D*

Persephone flung the letter onto the snow-streaked ground, and stomped it into the frozen mud. Drew hadn't written her a single letter in the months they had spent apart, and now he wrote her this? Something didn't seem right. Persephone wanted to scream. She wanted to tear up the Earth and the sky, and incinerate them until they were reduced to ashes. Months of training in the military arts of discipline and restraint forced her to swallow her heartbreak. She would mourn this loss later, when the war was won. For now, she would fight on, for Melinoë, for a better world. She refused to let his betrayal define her, no matter how her heart ached for Drew. She still had Phoenix. Persephone would let that be enough for her.

She retrieved the letter, now filthy with exposure to dirt and snow, from the frigid ground, and walked calmly back to her dormitory. Phoenix was awake by now. She sat on her bunk bed, swinging her legs over its side, a melancholy expression painted on her face. Persephone climbed up beside her, and handed over the letter. Phoenix's eyes darted across the page, scanning its contents. She put an arm around Persephone's shoulders and watched her with sad eyes.

"A war is probably a bit much payback for Drew," she said. "I think a small uprising will suffice."

Persephone scrunched the paper between her fingers, crushing it like a skull.

"I feel like he's hiding something from me," she whispered. Everyone else in the dormitory was still fast asleep.

"We all hide things," Phoenix said, "whether they be our past, or our intentions, or our own nature. It doesn't mean he doesn't love you. He's lost you, Sphenya, and you've lost him. It hurts, and I know how your heart must bleed, but we have to keep moving forward. Onwards and upwards: it's the only choice we have."

"I thought he was a good man," Persephone said. Uninvited tears streamed from her eyes. "I thought he'd never hurt me." Drew was more than her first love, he was the first man she had trusted after the Tsar. His betrayal was visceral, it sliced right through her and left her heart in jagged shards.

"He's still a good man," Phoenix said. "He's one of the better ones. But he's human, just like the rest of us."

"Not all of us."

"Even you are human, Sphenya." Phoenix leant into her shoulder. "You're human in nature. The thing about us humans is that we can never reach perfection, it's an indefinable concept. Drew is a good man, but he's still flawed. This isn't the first time he's broken your heart. Maybe he's doing it to protect you, or to protect himself. Don't tie yourself in knots trying to understand his motivation. Only he can answer the questions you're asking yourself."

Persephone unscrunched the letter and smoothed it out against the surface of her leg. The reverse side faced her now. In the centre of the page was were smudges from a pencil's eraser. She squinted to make out the ghost of pencil marks on the now-blank paper.

"What is it?" Phoenix asked.

"Look," Persephone said. "He wrote something else. I can't make it out."

"Gimme." Phoenix took the letter, and held it close to her face. "I'm still betting on you," she said. "It says 'I'm still betting on you.'"

# Chapter Thirty Three

It had been years since Mariana had both of her children under the same roof. Mother, daughter, and son were now reunited, in a grand apartment in Moscow. Tatiana lay on the sofa, chewing cherry-flavoured gummy bears and staring petulantly at the ceiling. Andrei paced back and forth by the window, ill at ease in his fitted suit.

"Are you ever going to cut that hair?" Tatiana asked her brother. His hair nearly reached his shoulders now. His skin was tanned, and his muscles were accentuated after years of manual labour. He looked like a god from the books of Greek myths he used to read as a child.

"I'll cut my hair when I join the army," Andrei shot back.

"You will stay far away from my war if you know what's good for you." Mariana held a glass of red wine in her hand. It took all her self-control not to down it in one. Andrei had been a sweet child, but he had grown into a passionate and idealistic man. He didn't listen to his mother like he used to.

"It's not your war," Andrei said. "It's Persephone's."

"Oh come on!" Tatiana's mouth was clogged with half-chewed gummy bears, and her words came out garbled. "You met her for like five minutes, two years ago. Even I know her better than you do, and you don't see me running off to fight in a doomed war."

"I'm not fighting for Persephone," Andrei said. "I'm fighting to bring down the Tsar."

Mariana raised an eyebrow at him; he chose to ignore her. Her son had been a stranger for a long time, she had grown accustomed to the ache of his absence. When she saw him again, it tore the wound right open, and she couldn't reseal it. If Mariana wasn't careful, Andrei would cause her to bleed out entirely.

"Drei," Tatiana said, "if you want to kill a Russian monarch, I have the perfect candidate for you. Get rid of my husband, and I'll be eternally grateful." She smiled sweetly. "Pretty please?"

"How am I related to you?" Andrei burst out. "Either of you. I don't belong here, I never should have come back. Tatiana, maybe your husband would like you more if you stopped running off with Delinov. Mother, I will see you on the battlefield." Andrei stormed

337

out of the room.

"Have I missed something?" Tatiana asked.

"Who's Delinov?" Mariana's eyes lingered on the door through which Andrei departed.

"No one," Tatiana said hurriedly.

"You will be a Tsarina one day," Mariana told her daughter. "I caught you the second-most powerful man in Eastern Russia, you should be more grateful."

"You should've dyed my hair brown and changed my name to Rhea," Tatiana said, "then I wouldn't have had to settle for second best."

☦

It was a bitter winter. Persephone and Phoenix were holed up in a military building near the Eastern Russian border, kept far away from the fighting by Mariana's strategy team, who curbed Persephone's impulsive nature by moving her about between isolated locations. Her frustration grew daily, and if it wasn't for the icy Russian winter, she would have jumped from a window long ago.

"I hate this!" Phoenix moaned. She lay on the floor by the fire in Persephone's bedroom, reading a letter from Kai for the thirtieth time, with a gloomy expression on her face. "I wanted to fight, not be trapped in Siberia or wherever the fuck we are."

"I don't want to be here any more than you do," Persephone said.

"They have Estonian technology," said Phoenix. "It's kept under lock and key, but luckily for us, I happen to be a genius, and know how to pick locks."

"What kind of technology?" Persephone swigged red wine straight from the bottle, and crawled over to join Phoenix by the fire. "War tech? Something we could use to blow up this place?"

"Better."

"Something to kill the Tsar?"

"Okay I've gotten your hopes up." Phoenix took the wine from Persephone and gulped it down. "Communication technology."

"What use is that? Mariana's abandoned us here, even

Elizaveta's disappeared off the face of the earth. She was meant to be on our side!"

"It's not Mariana we need to reach," Phoenix said with a smug glint in her eye. She drank another mouthful of wine, and continued. Her lips were stained with deep purple-red. "We're going to go above her head, and contact Birgit."

"God I love you," Persephone said. "You, my dear enabling friend, have offered me my first impulsive decision in months. I would literally marry you right now if it wasn't for my dreadful husband." The wine had gone to her head long ago, and she began to cackle maniacally.

"If you'd married me, your life would be so much easier." Phoenix nodded solemnly. "C'mon, we have a president to call."

✝

"Persephone?" The upper half of Birgit's body was projected onto the white wall in front of them. Persephone and Phoenix sat cross-legged atop the table in the conference room. "It's the middle of the night. What's wrong?" Her voice was sleepy, and her eyes were smudged with faded mascara. Birgit's blouse was creased, and strands of hair had fallen loose from her ponytail.

"Mariana's locked us up in the middle of fucking nowhere," Phoenix said. She downed the remainder of the wine. "This is Persephone's war, and she hasn't been allowed anywhere near it."

"Are you drunk?" Birgit asked.

"Absolutely," Phoenix said. She nodded sagely. "Very drunk. But I'm right, you know I'm right. Mariana is a leech and she's stealing—"

"Shh." Persephone patted her shoulder to calm her down. "Listen," she directed her words to Birgit, "you told me Mariana would advise me. She hasn't done that. It's February, and I have been kept in the dark since November. You need to tell me what's going on, you need to get me out of here. If you don't, I will self-destruct. You think you've seen Impulsive Persephone? Think again. If you do not get me out of here right now, I will burn this place to the ground. Do you hear me?"

"Persephone," Birgit said calmly, "do not speak to me like that.

I don't respond to threats."

"What do you respond to?" Phoenix asked. "We will play by your rules, if you tell us what they are."

"I'll have a word with Mariana," Birgit said. "Persephone, your strategy team are meant to work with you, not against you. You'll be returned to Moscow as soon as I can arrange transport for you both."

"Thank you," Persephone said with relief.

"Get some sleep, girls. And please drink some water!"

"Wait," Persephone said. "What's going on with the war? I haven't heard anything in months."

"Elizaveta will explain when you reach Moscow," was all Birgit said before the projection disappeared.

✝

"I always feel like a fugitive in this city," Persephone whispered to Phoenix as they slipped through the door of a freight train, and into a deserted station on the outskirts of Moscow. "Every time I come or go, it's under cover of darkness."

"You're lucky we got in at all," Phoenix said. "Come, Elizaveta's apartment is this way."

They exited the station and crept down a dingy alleyway. A smashed security camera dangled from a wire in the wall. Persephone yelped as a fox darted across their path.

"Shhh!" Phoenix hissed. "Keep quiet, pull your hood up, don't draw attention to yourself. The media blackout doesn't mean we're not being filmed."

Persephone screamed again, and Phoenix slapped her hard across the back of her head.

"Sphenya, what did I just say?"

Persephone continued to scream. She pointed to the darkened wasteland beyond the alley. As Phoenix took a step closer, she saw frozen corpses strewn across the snowy ground. Persephone subdued her screams to mewling whimpers. She shook with cold and terror. Phoenix darted towards the nearest body, and knelt down beside it.

"Come here," she said. Persephone stayed put. "Sphenn!

340

They're Russian."

"We're in Moscow. Of course they are."

"No," Phoenix said. "His uniform is Estonian. But look." She pushed the torn sleeve back from the dead soldier's wrist. "His tattoo is Russian, Western Russian army."

"What does that mean?" Persephone couldn't think straight. Corpses loomed in the shadowland before her. She wanted to turn on her heel and run far, far away. There was no running now. Persephone couldn't run from this, the destruction before her was a product of her own choices; she was responsible for these deaths.

"I don't know." Phoenix stood up. "Perhaps he defected to fight against the Tsar. Perhaps these are all the Tsar's men and they're framing the Estonians. Either way, they're all dead. Come, we need to find Elizaveta. We need to know what's going on."

"We have to stop," Persephone said when the field of corpses was far behind them.

"If we stop, he'll catch us." Phoenix didn't slow down. "Moscow isn't safe anymore – if it ever was." Weak stars shone down from the black night sky. The light pollution wasn't strong enough to dim them entirely.

"I don't mean stop walking. We have to stop the war."

Phoenix didn't say a word. Persephone knew things were bad when Phoenix chose to stay silent.

"It was never meant to be like this," she continued. They walked along a deserted road, following the path of the tramlines.

"What the hell do you think war is, Sphenya?" Phoenix finally burst out. Camouflaged in her black jacket, she almost blended into the night. "On the Persephone Scale of Terrible Decisions, you've finally outdone marrying the Tsar. Congratulations!"

"Why didn't you stop me?" Tears pricked in Persephone's eyes as she was hit by the colossal weight of what she had done.

"Have you met me?" Phoenix laughed harshly. Her voice was a loud whisper. "I tried to burn down the Settlements, I killed my own stepfather! If you rely on me to be your moral compass, you will be exponentially screwed."

"Do you think I should end the war?" Persephone stopped walking. She slumped against a lamppost, exhausted and traumatised.

"You don't have that power." Phoenix stood mere inches away, her eyes intense even in the darkness. "I think you should finish what you started. Stop running away. You're never going to learn from your mistakes if you refuse to be held accountable. You screwed up, you did a terrible thing. Guess what: tomorrow is a new day. Make new choices, do better. Face the worst parts of yourself, accept that they're there, and learn to control them."

"What if I can't?" Persephone rested her head on Phoenix's shoulder.

"What do you mean?"

"All this time I thought it was him, the fruit, the mind control. What if it was me? What if there is some dark and twisted thing inside of me? I'm not human, Phoenix. If I lose my humanity, what's to say I'll ever get it back?

The door to Elizaveta's apartment swung open when Phoenix raised her hand to knock. She exchanged a glance of trepidation with Persephone, and crossed over the threshold. The room was chilly; a coldness permeated the air, sharp and brutal after the warmth of the hallway.

"Elizaveta?" Phoenix asked in a loud whisper. It was dark inside the apartment. She fumbled against the wall for the light switch. Persephone still stood in the hallway, her face as frozen as the corpses in the field. "Elizaveta?" A faint moan answered her from the depths of the darkness.

"Persephone," Phoenix said when her hand finally clapped against the light switch. "Come in, close the door, and whatever you do, do not scream."

"What's going on?" Persephone asked. She stepped into the apartment, and pulled the door shut behind her.

Phoenix crossed the room, to find the source of the voice. The apartment was neither large nor small. The kitchen and living room were open-plan, with deep-blue sofas facing the fireplace in the far wall. In the gap between two sofas, Phoenix saw a pale hand, with fingernails painted in fuchsia pink. She knew that hand, knew the sight of it curved around a pen, filling out paperwork, knew the hand stacking books, serving customers, handing her a paycheck.

"Elizaveta," she said again, and knelt to the floor beside the body. Blood seeped, pink and permeating, into the white rug beneath.

"Per... Perseph..." Elizaveta tried to speak. The long, black curls of her hair were matted with blood, and her face was contorted with pain.

"Sphenya," Phoenix called across the room. "She wants you. Come here!"

Persephone walked with slow, careful steps across the wooden floorboards. She was trance-like, her gaze fixed on the wall above the mantelpiece, refusing to look at the dying woman on the ground.

"Persephone." Elizaveta tried to sit up, but barely managed to raise her head. "You stop the chaos. You're— The end of the line. Rea—" The final word died with Elizaveta. Phoenix held the dead woman's hand in her own. Silent tears streamed down her cheeks. Persephone didn't move, didn't react. Phoenix kissed Elizaveta's forehead, and closed the lids over her eyes.

"Okay," she said, and stood up. Phoenix didn't let herself mourn, not here, not now. She took a baby-blue blanket from the sofa, and covered Elizaveta's body. "I don't know how to hide a body!" she said suddenly. The words felt ridiculous in her mouth. "I killed a man, and I don't know how to hide a body."

"Why are we hiding her?" Persephone asked finally. She fingered the flame-shaped pendant around her neck, digging the metal into her skin.

"We can't exactly go to the police," Phoenix said. "You'd be walking right into the Tsar's hands. Whoever killed Elizaveta did it to send a message to you. We need to bury her, and we need a plan."

"We need to stop the war," Persephone said. "She said stop the chaos, she said this is the end of the line. Do you know what that means? It means I have to stop the war."

"You think that's what she meant?" Phoenix walked towards a door in the far corner of the room.

"It had to be. What are you doing?"

"Checking it's all clear."

343

Before Phoenix could touch the door, it swung open, to reveal a man standing before her. He was tall, with light-brown hair shaved close to his head. He wore the blue uniform of the royal guard.

Drew didn't look like himself. He was a stranger, with stranger's hair and a stranger's clothing. His kind, lively face was haunted and worn. Phoenix didn't know what to say or do, she couldn't process his presence here.

Persephone finally broke out of her trance, and snapped into action. She stalked across the room, pushed past Phoenix, and slapped Drew hard across the face. She looked from him to the body, and understood.

"You killed her," she whispered. "You killed Elizaveta!" Her voice crescendoed to a scream. "You killed Elizaveta," she looked up and down the length of him, saw the uniform that was burned into her brain from that day in Red Square so many years ago, "and you're working for the Tsar!"

"Persephone, stop shouting!" Phoenix hissed. "You're going to get all of us killed if you don't learn to shut up."

"He killed her!" Persephone was hysterical. She couldn't breathe. Her body jerked out in half-formed movements, unable to contain her rage and frustration. "He killed her, Phoenix!"

"No, I didn't," Drew said. "She was like that when I found her. I heard voices in the staircase, and hid in here."

"I don't believe you," Persephone said.

Phoenix wedged her way into the gap between them. "Come," she said, and gestured to the bedroom. "Sit down. Drew, you're going to tell us what happened. Sphenya, you're going to be quiet, or I will have to gag you. If you want to kill half this country, that's your prerogative, but I refuse to let you kill me with your recklessness."

Drew and Persephone sat down on Elizaveta's bed. Phoenix stood by the window, and looked out into the darkness below.

"You're working for the Tsar," Persephone repeated. "You betrayed me."

Drew shook his head, and buried his face in his hands. Phoenix had never seen him this defeated. She wanted to run across the room and throw her arms around him, protect him from Persephone and the world. He was her first real friend. She knew him, the good

344

and the bad in him. She knew he hadn't killed Elizaveta, and she knew that, whatever his reason for wearing that uniform, he would never work for the Tsar.

"Moscow isn't safe." He looked Persephone in the eyes as he spoke. She turned away from his gaze. "It's safer for me, because I have connections here. There are ways for me to come and go as I please, but if I were to use those connections, it would be a betrayal to you. I wanted to fight in your war, Persephone. But it's not your war anymore, we all know whose work this is. So I wear this uniform as a disguise, to walk the streets freely without being questioned."

"What do you know about Mariana?" Persephone asked.

Drew laughed. He couldn't help it. Phoenix watched him closely. Even now, she knew he wouldn't tell.

"You're a puppet," he said. "She's hiding behind your face, calling this your war. You're not the only puppet here. Have you spoken to a Muscovite since being back?"

"We only got back tonight," Phoenix said. "Why?"

"They're not in their right mind," Drew said. "They're zombies. I've never seen this city so loyal to the Tsar, and I know it's not of their own volition."

"He's using mind control?" Phoenix asked.

"I'm certain of it."

"I have to stop the war!" Persephone sank down onto the bed. Drew reached out to touch her, but pulled his hand away at the last moment. "I did this to stop him, and it's made him attack the minds of an entire city – probably an entire country! Elizaveta is right. I have to stop the chaos. This is it, this is the end of the line. It ends with me."

"Persephone," Drew said. "She wasn't talking about the war."

"What do you mean?"

"*End of the Line*. Don't you remember?"

"The song," Phoenix said. "Of course!"

"Am I missing something?" Persephone asked.

"*End of the Line* is about the wife of Tsar Khaos," Phoenix said. "The first generation of the Olympovski dynasty."

# Chapter Thirty Four

Persephone woke in Elizaveta's bed, curled up with Phoenix and Drew for warmth. They hadn't been able to find the heating switch. Drew's arm stretched across Phoenix, so his hand rested on Persephone's waist. She wanted to shake him off. Trusting him had burned her too many times before.

"Sphenn," Phoenix said as she woke. She wriggled out of Drew's sleepy embrace, and sat up against the headboard.

"I still don't trust him," Persephone whispered.

"I do."

The dim light of morning crept through the window, illuminating the calender on the wall.

"I want to change it," Phoenix said. "It's silly, I know. She'll never see March, but it feels wrong to leave her trapped in February, frozen in time."

"It's March 1st?"

"Mm hm."

"Melinoë is a year old today. My baby isn't a baby anymore. I've missed a whole year of her life!" Persephone swallowed the lump in her throat. Her powerlessness weighed down on her like the world on Atlas' shoulders. It was her burden to bear, and crying wouldn't change that. "She's here, in this city, barely two miles away from me. What's to stop me breaking into the palace and stealing her back from him? I could do it, I could take her back. She's mine, she doesn't belong to him!"

"Persephone," it was Drew who answered, woken by the increasing volume of her voice. "Don't do it. Don't walk into his trap."

"Why should I take advice from you? You're a liar, and a traitor."

"I'm sorry I hurt you. If I could turn back time and make different choices, believe me, I would."

"I don't want you here," Persephone said. "You should leave."

"He has nowhere to go either," Phoenix cut in.

"Go back to the Borderlands, and stay away from my war."

"It's not your war anymore," Drew said. "It's Mariana's. You are reckless and impulsive, and because of this, powerful people have taken advantage of you."

"Don't you dare victim-blame me!"

"He's not victim-blaming," Phoenix said. "I think you were right last night, about the parts of you that aren't human. You are good, and kind, and loving, but you don't see the bigger picture when you make decisions. It's one thing to marry the Tsar, that was your own life you were throwing away. But this war—"

"We're not condemning the war," Drew said. "If you had better advisors, more input... If it were you in control, instead of Mariana, it would have turned out different, I do believe that. This war is a catastrophe, Persephone. It has caused more damage to Western Russia than the Tsar's regime ever did. You have good intentions, and a good heart, but everywhere you go you leave chaos in your wake."

"Are you saying I'm a monster?" His words cut into her gut like a knife, twisting around, tearing through her insides. Her greatest fear had come true. Persephone's humanity had slipped through her fingertips and she hadn't even noticed.

Drew didn't speak. He reached for Persephone's hand, and held it, warm and steady.

"Yes," Phoenix said bluntly. "You're the worst kind of monster, because you don't see the damage you've caused. There's no point sugar-coating it. You can't be good just because you want to be good. Goodness comes from the choices you make, the actions you take. You've failed yourself."

"What do I do? How do I be better?" Persephone buried her face in Phoenix's lap as her world imploded.

"We go back to the Institute. We test you, we find out exactly what you are, so you can learn how to live with it."

"I don't want more tests, I don't want to be poked and prodded and dehumanised."

"I'll make sure it doesn't happen," Phoenix promised. "I will be with you every step of the way. No matter what you are or what you do, you will always be human to me."

"What about the war?" Drew asked.

"You're not going to like this," Phoenix said. "As you pointed out, this isn't Persephone's war anymore, it's Mariana's. If we want to stop the war, we have to go through her."

"I don't want to do this," Drew said as they stood outside the door of Mariana's Moscow house. He still wore the uniform of the royal guard. Persephone wore a headscarf around her hair, and a hooded black jacket. She looked a cross between a babushka and the grim reaper. Phoenix was paranoid about the Tsar finding them; Persephone was too defeated to care.

"Fine," Phoenix said. "I understand. Give me the key, and wait by the river. We'll come get you when we're done."

"Why do you have a key to Mariana's apartment?" Persephone asked. "What is your relationship to her? What the hell kind of hold does she have on you? Don't think I didn't notice the way she looked at you when you met at The Haven. Are you in love with her? Is that why you wrote that letter? Did you leave me for her?"

"No," Drew said. "Of course not."

"Honestly, she's old enough to be your—"

"She is!" Drew shouted, cutting Persephone off. "My name is Andrei Deripaska. Mariana Deripaska is my mother! Are you happy now? Do you understand why I want nothing to do with her?"

Persephone didn't merit his confession with a verbal response. She stormed past him towards the riverbank, and leant over the railing. She wanted to scream into the icy water. Every time she breathed, the world got smaller. Mariana and Tatiana and Drew were a family, a family connected to the Tsar. There was no place in the world where she could be free of her husband's influence. Not even a place in her own mind. Persephone was the monster he had created, and she wanted to tear herself apart, smash every inch of her robot brain until it was only shattered parts, and all that remained of her was human.

"Sphenya," Phoenix said gently. "Don't be too hard on him."

"You knew, didn't you?" Persephone asked. "You knew all along."

"Yes. I'm sorry. It wasn't my secret to tell."

"Okay."

"You have every right to be angry with me. I would be angry

if I were you. But Drew and I come from a different world. You don't have a family, Persephone, you don't know how messy and complicated they can be. Loyalty isn't a black-and-white matter."

"Okay. Let's go. We need to talk to Mariana. Drew can go jump in the river for all I care, I have a war to end."

☦

"Oh dear God," said Mariana when the three walked into her living room. It was early morning, and she wore blue-and-white-striped pyjamas. Persephone had never seen her look so human. "I see you escaped your babysitters. Andrei, why are you wearing that uniform?"

"Mariana," Persephone said with as much calm as she could muster. "You will stop taking my war hostage. You will talk to Birgit, and get her to arrange a ceasefire with the Tsar."

"Now why would I do that?"

"If you don't," Drew said, "We will tell all of Eastern Russia that their Tsesarevna has a child with a bartender named Delinov."

"Tatiana what?" Mariana breathed heavily through her nose, trying to to cling onto the last fragments of her self-control.

"His name's Blayk," Drew said conversationally. He sat down on an armchair opposite his mother. Looking at them now, Persephone could see the family resemblance, the light hair and full lips. But Drew's face had always been animated, whilst Mariana's remained a mask. "He's growing up so fast. Your first grandchild, and you never knew... I suppose it would destroy Tatiana's reputation – and her husband's."

"You wouldn't dare."

"He wouldn't," Phoenix said. "Drew wouldn't destroy someone's life like that. But me? I owe you nothing. End the war, or Tatiana's little secret will be a secret no more. And that's just Tatiana...wait till we start airing the skeletons in your closet."

"I have no skeletons," Mariana said coldly.

"Oh don't you?" Phoenix laughed. "You're forgetting who I am, Ms Deripaska. My father is the president of Tartarus Settlement, I've heard the whispers of what went down in Eastern Russia. I know why you were forced to leave your husband. Your daughter's

349

infidelities are nothing compared to your own."

"Fine. I will speak to Birgit. But if you breathe a word of this ever again, I will personally make your life hell. Do we understand each other?"

The ceasefire announcement came the day they returned to Tallinn. Persephone sobbed when she heard it on the radio. She wasn't sure if she cried from relief, or heartbreak. It was one thing to accept the monster inside her, but another to come to terms with the fact she would never get her daughter back. It had all been for nothing. The war, the destruction, the loss of her humanity.

Phoenix was asleep as the train approached Tallinn. Persephone and Drew sat across from each other, staring out the window in silence.

"The letter." Drew broached the subject they had both avoided for a week. "She made me send it. I hoped you would see the hidden message on the other side, and know I didn't mean it."

"Oh, you're betting on me, huh?" Persephone laughed bitterly. "Right now it feels like you're betting against me, it feels like the whole world is."

"What I'm trying to say is, my feelings for you didn't change or go away. I love you, Persephone, and I am asking you to give me a second chance. I love you, I have never loved someone like I love you."

"Love isn't enough, not for us. It's like we're this beautiful painting, sitting in a dusty room, and if you look at the picture long enough, you forget you have to deal with the reality of its surroundings!"

"Then we should just draw pictures in the dust."

The streets of Tallinn hadn't changed in the months since Persephone had left. The cobblestones of the Old Town were unchanged by time, the road from Viru Gate to the Institute was the same as it had always been. But her heart was heavier. She closed her eyes and saw frozen corpses in a Western Russian field, Elizaveta's blood soaking into the white rug on her floor.

Persephone sat now in Birgit's office.

"The Tsar agreed to a ceasefire immediately," the President said. "This war was worse for him than for us."

"He controlled the minds of every person in Moscow!" Persephone burst out. "Don't act like this was a loss for him."

"I asked him about the soldiers in Estonian uniform," Birgit said. "He knew nothing. I don't think he was lying."

"I can't believe you trust him!"

"Persephone, we can't solve every mystery. Wartime is chaos, things happen that governments have no knowledge of, or control over."

The word chaos tugged at her mind. Elizaveta's final words were another mystery she couldn't solve. Persephone had played the *End of the Line* song over and over in her head, searching for clues, but came up blank.

"What matters is that it's over," Persephone said. "I wish I'd done better, instead of leading five countries into a war that none of us could ever win."

"Do you want some advice?" Birgit asked.

"No, but I could probably use it."

"The custody of your daughter, it's a matter for you and your husband to resolve between yourselves. Keep it between the two of you, it's the only way to minimise the collateral damage."

"I can't fight him on my own," Persephone said. "He's the Tsar, I'm barely a person. This is not an even playing field."

"Then you have no choice but to accept defeat."

## Chapter Thirty Five
*Two months later*

The Institute's computer room was a grand affair. Sleek, high-tech machines were set out in row upon row as far as the eye could see. The one thing the room did not have to offer was privacy. Phoenix unplugged a computer from its socket, and dragged it into a cleaning-supply closet. The walls were lined with shelves made from dark-brown wood, filled with cloths and paint and bottles of surface cleaner. She perched precariously on a counter, and began her mission. It took hours for her to crack the code. Once she was in, there was a wealth of material to sift through.

Phoenix stared at the dates on the screen; something didn't add up. She fast-forwarded through a few-days' worth of footage to make certain. Still nothing. She clicked on another camera, and encountered the last sight she had expected to see.

"Sphenya!" Phoenix ran at break-neck speed down the hallway. "Persephone!"

"What?" Persephone asked as she came around the corner. Phoenix was doubled over and out of breath, she had run halfway across the Institute.

"There's something you need to see." She dragged her friend to the closet where she had left the computer. "Melinoë was conceived in June, right?" Phoenix clicked hurriedly at the computer.

"How would I know?" Persephone asked. "I was unconscious. Why are you asking me this?"

"Conscious or not," Phoenix said, "it would've been within a small window of time. Melinoë was born on March 1st, and you were kidnapped on the 1st of June. That's nine months apart." She shifted the computer screen so Persephone could see. "I had a plan to turn the Western Russian public against the Tsar. I hacked into the Palace's surveillance footage, and—"

"You what?" Persephone asked in absolute horror.

"If we had indisputable evidence he raped you, we could turn his citizens against him." Phoenix said the words matter-of-factly, whilst Persephone stared at her as if she were a monster.

"Phoenix." Persephone was close to tears. Her eyes were wide with terror and her breath was ragged. "I don't want to see that. I don't want to think about that. I just want to forget."

"You need to see this." Phoenix ignored her. "I don't think the Tsar raped you."

"I don't understand." Persephone's hands clenched into fists. "He raped me, Phoenix. I didn't consent. I never consented, I—"

Phoenix clicked again, and a video popped up onto the screen. Persephone lay unconscious on a table. Her eyes were closed, and her pink lips were slightly parted. There was no sign of life here, she could easily have been a corpse. Her face was as pale as the white cotton dress that covered her. The Tsar stood over his wife, dressed all in black, as if the lines between good and evil were so clear-cut they could be shown in a choice of clothing. In his hand was a syringe, with the letter M written on it in purple marker.

Phoenix adjusted the volume, and his voice became audible.

"I'm sorry to do this to you," he said, and kissed her gently on the forehead. He carefully injected the syringe's long needle into the flesh of her belly. A pensive expression crossed his face, and he stroked Persephone's hair, before lifting her off the table. The Tsar carried Persephone over his shoulder, where she hung limp as a fabric doll, and departed from the room. Phoenix stopped the video.

"There's no footage of any sexual act between you two," she said, "consensual or otherwise. I think Melinoë was conceived by artificial insemination."

"That's not how it works," Persephone pointed out, "even I know that. There're no syringes involved."

"This is the Tsar," Phoenix said. "He does things differently. Perhaps he created Melinoë the same way he created you, but decided to have her grow inside you, rather than in any other kind of vessel."

"So she's not really my daughter?" Persephone asked.

"Oh no, I think he would've used your DNA, and his own, as some warped way of sanctifying your union. I just don't think there was any sex involved in her conception."

"Why? Why would he do that?"

Phoenix climbed up onto the edge of the counter. "The only answer I can come up with is that he wanted to keep you 'pure.' He holds you up on a pedestal, Sphenya. He thinks you're this

353

creature of ethereal beauty that mustn't be tarnished. He doesn't see you as human. You're an object he's scared to break."

"That's so fucked up."

"Do you remember that day in the library?" Phoenix asked. "He and his father... They were talking about you, I think. Tsar Kronus said something like 'Rhea's death was no excuse for that absurdity.' The Tsar made you to replace his mother."

"Can this get any more perverted?"

"It's not just you and him, is it? I fit in there somewhere." Phoenix paused for a moment, calculating. "The reason I hate the Tsar is because he reminds me of my father – that coldness, that genius-minus-morality. I didn't want to live through it again. I couldn't. Even though the Tsar never touched me, even though he helped me rebuild myself in so many ways, I always believed he had the potential to hurt me."

"I've been meaning to ask," Persephone began tentatively, "you've never told me what happened to you when you were young. Did your father sexually abuse you?"

"No," Phoenix said. She squeezed Persephone's hand. "It's perhaps the only thing he didn't do. He tortured me – in so many ways. There were only two parts of my life where he didn't abuse me: my sexuality, and my education."

"Does it make it better?" Persephone asked. "That he didn't violate you completely?"

"I've asked myself that question so many times." Phoenix rocked slowly back and forth where she sat. "I've never come to an answer. On the one hand, yes, of course, of course it makes it better. But on the other hand, to say that would devalue the immense pain he caused me. He did violate me completely, he just found inventive ways to do it."

"I frequently told myself," Persephone said, "that if the Tsar hadn't raped me, I'd be able to forgive him, that it would have made a difference to his evil. And now, now it's a reality, I no longer know what to think. Does it make him less evil because he only raped my mind? He stole my free will, he stole my thoughts, perverted my opinions, impregnated me without my consent. Even if I'd had a chance to consent, what kind of consent could it have been? He used me, against my will, and I don't know how I'm meant to think of that any more. In some ways it was easier when I believed he had abused me physically, because it was something people understood. We are a society that knows rape, but not mind control, a society that cares little for the suffering of any victim, let alone a victim of mental mistreatment. It was literally just in my mind."

"I can't give you answers, Sphenn," Phoenix took both Persephone's hands in her own. "But I do know how you're feeling. This is why I don't tell people about my past: I'm terrified my suffering will be invalidated. All we can do is fight back. Hopefully once we have answers about what you are, and how your brain functions, you will at least have some kind of closure. Dr Skryabin has finished developing the exploratory test, we can do it tomorrow."

☦

"Can we talk?" Persephone asked Drew. He sat alone at a table in the Institute's cafeteria, coffee in one hand a book in the other.

"Of course," he said. He closed his book, and downed the last of his coffee. "Anytime."

"I meant now." She felt awkward to be alone with him. He reminded her of a future she no longer hoped for. He was a living ghost that continued to haunt her. But she was seized by the compulsion to tell him what would happen tomorrow, in case she didn't come back from it. "Let's take a walk."

They left the Institute in silence. Persephone was unsure of where to begin. Every time she tried to speak, the words never quite left her mouth.

"We have a lot to talk about," Drew said. By this time they climbed the steps of the Linnahall ruins, which overlooked the dark-blue sea. The sky was cloudy, and a sea breeze blew softly through the air. "It's hard to know where to begin."

"You read my mind," Persephone said. "So let's start at the beginning." She wanted to make peace, but peace seemed too futile a goal in the pursuit of truth. "Let's start from the first time you lied to me. You knew who I was the whole time, didn't you?"

"I didn't know for sure." Drew sat down on the steps, and

355

looked off into the distance. "You wore a mask when we met at the ball, I didn't recognise you from the bookshop. The next time we met, you were familiar but I couldn't place you. Grigory said you looked like the Tsarina, and I had a hunch. You told me your name was Sphenya, and I began to wonder if the girl from the ball and the girl from the bookshop were the same person."

Persephone sat down beside him, careful to avoid the fragments of shattered green glass bottles that littered the steps. "Grigory's not your real brother, is he?"

"He's not my blood brother, no. I met him and Rozalina when I was in Greece. We worked together, picking oranges. Grigory and I decided to become brothers, because we had both forsaken our own families. It was never intended as a lie." He spoke softly, his voice heavy with regret.

"I wish you'd told me the truth," she said. "From the beginning."

"So do I," said Drew. "We both lied, Persephone. If we'd been honest from the start, we'd've never stood a chance. My sister is married to your brother-in-law. We're both tied up in that messy family. It was so much simpler to know you as a stranger. I knew we could never marry, so my real identity wouldn't be an issue."

"Until I began working with your mother."

"Fate has a way of destroying the dreams of mortals," Drew said gravely.

"I miss your melodrama," Persephone said. "I miss you." She reached for his hand.

"I never had an easy relationship with my mother," Drew continued. "I grew up in Eastern Russia, in the Settlement, with my father. Tatiana was raised in Eastern Russian high society by my mother. We were a divided family, after the divorce. My father was a good man, I learnt my finer qualities from him." Drew smiled sadly, remembering. "He died young, and my uncle took over the Settlement. My mother wanted me to live with her, and I did for a little while. I hated it. Before long, Tatiana was married off, and it was just the two of us. I left home the day I turned sixteen, and travelled to Greece, where I met my true family."

"Why did you go to Moscow?" Persephone asked.

"Tatiana wrote to me," Drew said. "She told me our mother had disappeared off the face of the Earth. I came home because I was scared my mother was dead. As soon as I was back in the country, she reappeared, and I took that as my cue to leave. Roza and Grigory were still in Greece, and I refused to stay in Vladivostok and be my mother's plaything, so I went to Moscow. I guess my mother must have moved to Estonia around that time, though I had no idea. I got a job in Elizaveta's shop, and a year later I met you." He grazed her hand with his thumb. "Now you know how our epic tale began."

"I wish I was ready," Persephone said. "To draw pictures in the dust." She removed her hand from his, and brought her hands to her face. She didn't want him to see the expression that played across her features. "I do love you, I don't think I'll ever stop. But it's infinitely more complicated than that."

"I know," Drew said. "Obviously my heart is shattered on the floor right now," his eyes glinted with dramatic flare, "but I will strive to survive the crushing weight of your rejection."

"Shut up." Persephone laughed. "It's not personal."

"Sure it's not."

"I can't make you a priority right now. I don't want to. I have to live my own life. There are parts of myself I'll never learn about if I'm in a relationship with you. This isn't about our history, or all the times you lied to me. It's about the present, not the past."

"Phoenix told me what you're doing tomorrow."

"That surprises me."

"You always forget she was my friend first."

"I'll make an effort to remember."

"Are you scared? Of what you may discover about yourself?"

"Of course I am. There is something inhuman inside me, and I've tried to deny that for more than a year of my life. It's terrifying to face it. At the same time, I feel this sense of freedom. This is the final frontier. I've spent my life searching for an identity, searching for where I belong. After tomorrow, I'll finally know who I am. That, or I'll get permanent brain damage."

"Is there anything you would change?" Drew asked. "If you could go back and do things differently?"

"I'd be more careful in my choice of husband, that's for certain. And I would stay far away from Mariana. But the rest of it? No. This war was a disaster, but I had to fight for Melinoë. I went about it wrong, I know that now. I still wouldn't take it back. Every failure, every bad decision I made taught me who I am, it gave me an identity. I wouldn't go backwards even if I could."

# Chapter Thirty Six

"Good morning," Persephone said, as she entered Dr Skryabin's office. Bright, May sunshine blazed through the windows, shining on the white-tiled wall. The spider plants on the windowsill had begun to wilt; the ends of their leaves were brown and crunchy.

"You sound awfully chirpy for someone who's about to have her brain dismantled," Phoenix said. She sat on the counter top, swinging her legs. Her hair was styled in two immaculate plaits, and her black shoes were so clean they sparkled.

"Dismantled?" Persephone asked. "He's going to take my brain apart?" She stared at Dr Skryabin in horror.

"She's joking," he said. "We're going to look at the connection between your brain and your body, as well as attempting to explore how your brain works. Your brain is, for all intents and purposes, a computer. But it functions within your body in the same manner as a human brain, and that is the part that is most curious. There are many advanced robots in the world, particularly here in Estonia, you are not unusual because you are a robot. You're unusual because you are human flesh and blood merged with the mind of a machine."

"I'm not a machine," Persephone whispered.

"Are you ready?" Dr Skryabin asked.

Persephone nodded slowly. She wondered if it was too late to back out. Dr Skryabin attached the wires to her head, and she thought of the pain his last experiment on her had caused, the blinding fire of the Estonian language as it was installed into her brain. This memory was the last thing Persephone was aware of before her whole body went numb. The blood drained from her face, and her skin turned a ghostly white. Her lips were now a lifeless purple, and she slumped back in her chair, eyes glazed over.

"Persephone?" Dr Skryabin asked.

"Must. Kill," said Persephone, in a monosyllabic, computerised voice.

"What the—" Phoenix didn't have a chance to finish her sentence. The door burst open, and six Western Russian police officers stood before her.

"Phoenix Kashnikova." The nearest police officer clipped her wrists into handcuffs, "You are under arrest for the murder of Yuri Lyubov. You do not have to speak, but anything you do say can and will be used against you in court."

Panic burned inside her. The police officers didn't notice Persephone, didn't hear the repeated refrain of "Must kill." It was all Phoenix could hear.

"I'm sorry, officers," she said in a calm, uncharacteristically sweet voice. Her Russian was slow, like she wasn't a native speaker. "There must be some mistake. I'm not Phoenix Kashnikova. My name is Nikhelaina Skryabina. I live here with my uncle." She gestured to Dr Skryabin, who stepped forward, towards the police officers. "Phoenix Kashnikova died in Moscow last February."

"Whatever your name is, you're coming with us."

Phoenix stared at the white wall of her jail cell. There was no furniture, only an ominous white door. White had been a colour of safety, of sterile scientific laboratories. Here it was the colour of fear. It was four days since she had been dragged here. Four nights of fitful sleep on a cold concrete floor. Four days of solitary confinement. No one believed her story, all they saw was a desperate girl who thought she could get away with murder, lying her way out of culpability.

"Kashnikova!" yelled a guard. "You've got a visitor."

Phoenix glanced up half-heartedly. She was in a Moscow jail cell, no one should be visiting her here. No one she wanted to see. Panic seized her. There were three people left in Western Russia who knew she existed. The thought of any of them coming here sent chills down her spine.

"Hey Syrup," said the last voice Phoenix expected to hear.

"Kai!" She ran to him as he came through the door. "How did you get here?"

"I got a train." He hugged her.

"I'm so glad you're here," she said in Estonian. She glanced at the door, and whispered in his ear "Be careful what you say, you never know who's listening."

360

"I've been so worried about you." He hugged her tighter.

"Have your seen Persephone? Is she okay?" She turned to the door again, paranoid.

"Right now," Kai said, "we need to focus on getting you out of here. Skryabin's going to be a witness for you. He stayed in Tallinn, for Persephone's sake, but he's recorded a testimony."

Phoenix felt a surge of gratitude towards Dr Skryabin. He had come through for her when it mattered. He was prepared to lie in court for her, and risk his career for her. Phoenix's eyes filled with tears.

"Hey, Syrup, it's okay." Kai hugged her as she started to cry. "I'm going to get you out of here, I promise."

Phoenix nodded, but she couldn't stop crying. She hated crying in front of other people, but she couldn't control herself. She was consumed by fear. If she went to prison, all her education would be wasted, everything she had fought so hard for would be gone.

"You're going to be okay." Kai tried to wipe away her tears, but the feel of his hands on her face only made Phoenix cry harder. "I promise."

"Time's up!" yelled the guard.

Kai's words reverberated in Phoenix's head as she was led into the courtroom by two prison guards. *"You're going to be okay. You're going to be okay. You're going to be okay."*

Panels of dark wood adorned the walls of the stately room; matching wooden benches were lined up on either side of an aisle. A smell of musk and old perfume permeated the thick air. Most of the back seats were empty, though a number of members of the public sat, watching, from the front and middle rows. Phoenix looked past them, searching for emptiness, for blankness. Her eyes landed on another face. The face itself wasn't familiar, but Phoenix had learnt by now not to be fooled that a man's face was a true indicator of his identity. She recognised the yellow-blond hair, and she was sure she saw the gleam of ice in his faraway eyes.

*"You're going to be okay. You're going to be okay. You're going to be okay."*

361

This had to be the Tsar's doing. It had been two years since Phoenix murdered Yuri. She was here because someone had orchestrated it, of that she was certain.

"*You're going to be okay. You're going to be okay. You're going to be okay. I promise. I promise. I promise. I promise. I promise. I promise.*"

Phoenix felt as though someone had walked over her grave. All hope was lost, her fate was sealed. She forced herself to switch off the part of her mind that cared, as her charge was read. This wasn't personal, it was business. She knew that, knew this must be the Tsar's attempt to separate she and Persephone. It was all clear now, this was a sham trial. The case could be open and closed, if they used DNA evidence to determine her true identity. If her mother had wanted to prosecute her, she would have done so two years ago.

Phoenix watched her mother take to the stand. The woman's presence cut through her like a knife. Another abandonment, after all these years.

"Katya Lyubova, do you hereby swear to tell the truth, the whole truth, and nothing but the truth?"

"Yes."

"Mrs Lyubova," asked the prosecutor, "what happened on the night of your husband's murder?"

"I was out, visiting friends." Katya didn't take her eyes off Phoenix as she spoke. "I came home to find Phoenix pointing a gun at Yuri. I begged her not to shoot him. My daughter killed my husband in an act of cold-blooded murder."

"There has been some dispute as to whether or not the girl arrested is Phoenix Kashnikova," continued the prosecutor. "Is this girl your daughter?"

"Yes."

"I want to go on the stand," Phoenix whispered to her court-appointed lawyer, an ageing woman named Vasilisa Kovaleva.

"We haven't prepared for that," she warned.

"I don't care. I need to fight this."

"Later," she said. Ms Kovaleva turned to Katya and asked "Is it true, Mrs Lyubova, that you have not seen your daughter Phoenix in two years? How can you be certain this girl is not an unfortunate lookalike?"

"Just look at her!" Katya said. "She is the image of me, if a few shades darker. I know my daughter, and she is a smart girl. She is prodigious genius at its worst. Phoenix is smart enough to think her way out of a murder trial. You're a fool to underestimate her."

Phoenix tried not to let her hatred show. Killing Yuri had been a last resort, a desperate act to protect her mother.

The next witness was Dr Skryabin, via a video testimony. He confirmed that Phoenix was Nikhelaina Skryabina, his niece. She began to relax a little, Skryabin was in her corner. He would keep her safe.

"Jakob Kashnikov, do you swear to tell the truth, the whole truth, and nothing but the truth?"

"Yes," said the voice that haunted her nightmares. Phoenix didn't hear another word her father said. She couldn't bear to look at him. She focused her eyes on the man in the back row, the man she presumed was the Tsar. She felt safer with him there. He, the man who had abused her best friend, was the very man who had saved her from her own abuser. Phoenix knew no matter what cruel things the Tsar did, he wouldn't let her father hurt her again. Their eyes met for a moment, and he nodded once, as though he had read her mind. Phoenix swivelled her head back around to the front of the courtroom; she refused to meet her father's gaze. He lurked in the corner of her eye, an abyss that would suck the soul right out of her if she dared to look in his direction. He was the monster that lived under her bed, the personification of primal terror that had haunted her for two decades.

Phoenix turned around again, this time looking at Kai, who sat on a bench two rows behind her. The agony in his eyes mirrored that in hers, and it was all she could do not to sob. She focused on her breaths, breathing in the love she felt for Kai, the feeling of warmth that bloomed within her every time they touched. Phoenix knew she was loved, knew she mattered, yet that love felt like a drop in the ocean compared to the tremendous fear that submerged her when she dared to raise her eyes to meet her father's.

"Are you ready to take to the stand?" Ms Kovaleva whispered to Phoenix.

She gave a shaky nod in return.

✝

As Phoenix swore on The Bible, she wondered how sacred such a vow could be, to someone who didn't believe in God.

"I don't have much to say." Phoenix projected her voice, so the Tsar could hear her in the back row of the courtroom. "Everybody else has already said it – whatever 'it' may be. It's not right for a person to be sent to prison without being allowed a chance to provide testament of their truth. I didn't commit this crime, and I'm not Phoenix Kashnikova. She died long ago. It is my innocence that gives me the clarity to speak today, to stand up for myself, a self who has been wrongly accused – and also, to stand up for Phoenix. Phoenix was the best friend I have ever had. We knew each other inside out, and my mind was the only one to whom she entrusted her darkest secrets." Her eyes scanned the room, passing over her mother, her father, and the Tsar, finally coming to rest on Kai. As long as he was there, she could do this, she could announce publicly the crimes of which she had been victim, release the secrets she had held so tightly to her chest. "Phoenix was not a criminal." She breathed in and out, in and out, deeper and deeper, until she could force the words to lift themselves from her mouth. "I remember one day, Phoenix received a letter—a threat—from her father. She wasn't the same after that, she was a girl who'd been broken by this world, and it was then that she confided in me. Phoenix was a victim of abuse. Her mother abandoned her when she has four years old, and for the subsequent twelve years, her father tortured her, and—"

"This isn't Phoenix!" Katya's voice ripped through the air, halting Phoenix mid-sentence. "This girl is no daughter of mine."

Victory did not taste sweet like Phoenix had imagined. There was no clear path for relief to sweep in. She was consumed by the indisputable fact that her mother had let her down again. Katya had stolen her daughter's childhood, stolen her rights, her freedoms. And now, the thief crept in once more, to take the only precious thing that remained to Phoenix: her voice.

"I am not Phoenix," she shouted over her mother. "I am not Phoenix, and I have attested to that repeatedly, and now her own mother confirms it! But it wasn't my identity I spoke of, it was Phoenix's! These people, her parents, they destroyed her. Her mother neglected her, and her father abused her. He took her humanity from her, and if you choose to ignore this evidence, then you have done the same! Phoenix may be dead, but she was not the only victim in this country. Oh no, she was a member of a rapidly growing population, and you cannot call yourselves upholders of the law if you only provide justice to those who suit you!"

"Silence!" commanded the judge. "Silence in this court! Mrs Lyubova, are you one hundred percent certain this girl is not your daughter Phoenix?"

"Yes," Katya said.

"Case dismissed. Miss Skryabina, you are hereby free to go."

# Chapter Thirty Seven

Phoenix stood, alone in the lobby of the courthouse, waiting for Kai. She had been taken to sign some papers, and he had waited behind in the courtroom, to make sure her parents were gone and the coast was clear. Phoenix's hands trembled with anxiety, even though the case was over and she was safe. What was safe, any more? The three people who had damaged her were together under one roof, and it had shaken her completely. She wished Kai would return sooner, wished he were there to hold her, to make her feel safe again.

"I told you we would meet again, child," said the menacing voice of her father. He sounded like squashed slugs, strangled kittens, and nails on a chalkboard was all she could think – his presence reduced her to childlike similes, and she couldn't bring herself into adulthood, break out from the cycle of victimhood. Speaking out against him had been of little cure, because who, in that room of so many people, had listened? Who had believed her? It had been only those who loved her who had listened, and they all knew her for a liar on at least one count. Any truth she now told would be met with scepticism. Phoenix wanted to run, ached for movement, to free herself from the paralysis that restricted her.

"Go away!" Her words came out in a choked whisper.

"We should have brought you some fruit, it would have closed the case far sooner."

"Then they could see how sick and twisted you are!" Phoenix spat as she found her voice. She had never spoken against her father to his face – she had screamed, and cried, and sobbed, certainly, but never challenged him with words.

"What's happening?" Kai asked as he approached Phoenix. He stood behind Jakob, and didn't recognise him immediately. "Who is this?"

Jakob Kashnikov turned around. "See the familial resemblance," he said in Russian. "Observe. Engross yourself. It doesn't meet the eye immediately, not now she's fattened up, but it is fascinating to watch. The brightest plants can grow stunted, given the right circumstances." Jakob was a tall man. His dark hair was slicked back with oil, and a beard grew on his face like ivy creeping up a building. The black pits that masqueraded as his eyes were portals straight into hell.

"Are you okay?" Kai asked Phoenix. He ignored her father.

She stood still, speechless.

"Come on," he said gently, taking her hand and leading her away.

After a moment, Phoenix spun around. "I'm not stunted, you arrogant cunt!" she yelled. "I have grown better than you ever will!" She clung tightly to Kai's hand as they walked away. The sound of footsteps behind them was inaudible; there was no warning, only that moment of fateful horror when Phoenix realised what had happened, felt Kai's hand slip from hers as he fell to the ground. Jakob yanked locks of Phoenix's dark hair into his hands, pulling her away from Kai, who had fallen unconscious from the heavy blow to his head. There was no chance for Phoenix to fight back as she was dragged away.

Phoenix cowered in her childhood bedroom. Her mind raced through the reel of memories that had led her to this point. Her room was untouched by the fire, as, she soon learned, was most of the building. That which had burned had been rebuilt. This fortress looked defeat in the face and laughed. Phoenix wished it had all burnt down, wished her father was mere ashes in the cold, damp ground. Wishes were no use now. They couldn't undo her torment, or turn back time to protect her from the wounds of the past.

"You must be hungry." Her father's voice was a stealthy assassin, it struck her before he entered the room.

Phoenix shook her head, as angry as she was terrified. Angry at herself, for being a victim. She was utterly helpless, trapped in a waking version of her recurring nightmare.

"You will eat." Jakob pressed a button on the wall, which opened to a kitchen filled with plates of fruit. Juice soaked into the cracks of the chipped pottery.

"No," Phoenix said. Every inch of her body ached to scream, to release the animal within. But she refused to show him her weakness. "I'm twenty years old," she pleaded, "you can't make me do this any more. You have no hold over me. I am no longer the terrified little girl you abused and tortured! I refuse to be the stoic martyr who never fought back."

"You can choose: you will eat fruit, or you will take a trip to the knife room."

"No," Phoenix screamed. "No, no. No! I'll eat it, I'll eat it!"

With shaking legs, Phoenix stepped slowly into the kitchen. The fruit stood in mountains before her, sliced with surgical precision.

"Eat," Jakob commanded.

The sight of the fruit made her stomach somersault with trepidation. Juice glinted in ominous droplets, ready to catch in her throat, sing a siren song to the contents of her stomach until they launched themselves to the floor in surrender.

Phoenix took a stray banana from the far end of the counter, and slowly stripped it of its peel. She lifted it to her lips, and bit into the soft goo of its flesh. It was overripe, brown and mushy. The first mouthful was bearable, she swallowed without difficulty. The second mouthful was harder.

"Eat," Jakob bellowed in her ear. He rarely lost his temper. Her father was a violent man, but he was cold and clinical. Crimes of passion were as alien to him as kindness. "Eat!"

Phoenix shoved the rest of the banana into her mouth, and scooped up slices of watermelon. She forced them into her mouth, swallowed without chewing. The seeds triggered her gag reflex, and the familiar gush of vomit rose from her stomach. Phoenix turned to face her father. Jakob grabbed her by the hair, and took a handful of blackberries from a bowl on the bench. He pushed the fruit into her mouth. Dark purple juice dripped down her chin. Phoenix sank her teeth into her father's hand, until the sweetness of the fruit mingled with the salty taste of blood.

The scalding water of the shower burnt Phoenix's stiff body like the breath of a dragon. Tears streamed, unpreventable, down her face as she convulsed on the tiled floor. The weight of realisation crushed her, smashed her further with each bombshell that dropped on her mind. She was trapped, again, and this time there was no escape. No one was coming to save her. She was all alone. Alone with the sandpaper feeling in her throat, alone with the saliva that kept on rising up no matter how hard she tried to swallow it back, alone with the thoughts that burrowed through the defences of her mind and told her *you're going to die this time.* The mass of fruit gurgled in her stomach as she wept, a reminder of her own powerlessness. Phoenix shoved two fingers into her mouth, forcing them down her throat, further and further until the acidic lumps of vomit spewed from her lips. She clawed at the stained white tiles beneath her, watching as the contents of her stomach swirled down the drain.

"Phoenix?"

She was sure she imagined Kai's voice.

"Phoenix?" He repeated.

"Kai?" she whispered, her throat aching and raspy. Phoenix switched off the shower, and cautiously peeked around the curtain. Kai approached, holding up a towel to wrap around her.

"Oh my darling." He lifted her up into his arms.

"How did you get here?" she asked, dazed. "This place is a fortress."

"I tried to break in. When that failed, I waited till the guard shift switched over, and watched them type the entry password into the keypad. Once I was inside, it was fairly easy to find you."

Phoenix didn't speak. She buried her face in his shoulder, sobbing hard against the fabric of his shirt, clinging to him like a child. Her mouth still tasted of vomit.

"We need to talk," he said.

"We do."

"I understand if you aren't ready to talk right now, and I'll give you time, I promise. But we can't go on like this, with all these secrets. You were in danger today, and I had no idea. I couldn't protect you."

"I'll tell you everything," she said. It was suddenly important that her story was shared; it couldn't die with her.

Phoenix dressed quickly, and sat down on the bed.

"My mother was an actress in Moscow." She took Kai's hand and stroked it as she spoke. "She married my father when she was eighteen years old. I was born a year later. My earliest memory was my father hitting her. She left when I was four. My mother abandoned me with him, with this monster. And that," she swallowed hard, "that was when he began to hurt me. It wasn't the first time he'd hit me, but this was different. My father was inventive with his tortures. He used to make me eat fruit, so much of it I was sick." Phoenix looked into Kai's eyes, her grip on his hand tightened. "It was dehumanising. I had no control over my own body, over my own reflexes. He would force me to eat, to eat so much I would vomit. By the time I left here, when I was sixteen, I wasn't sure whether the vomiting was a reflex any longer, or a chosen act of dissent. I found myself forcing it, pushing for it to happen, so I was in control." She pressed her lips together to suppress a cry, doubling over as the waves of traumatic memories washed through her. "The fruit wasn't the worst of it, not by far. My dad also had this place he called the 'knife room' – you don't need to be a whiz at etymology to guess what it contained. I was forced to stand there for hours at a time, whilst knives rained down around me. If I moved even slightly…" Phoenix slid up her shirt to reveal the long, diagonal scar across her abdomen. "When I was sixteen, things started to look up. I was kidnapped by the Tsar. I don't think I would have survived much longer otherwise. The Tsar saved my life. We never spoke of it—we barely spoke at all—but he saved me. That man, that despicable Frankenstein of a man…he dragged me from the depths of hell and gave me a chance to start again. It's hard to believe now, but the Tsar was good to me. He sent me to the best doctors and dentists in all of Western Russia. My teeth were fixed, and everything about me glossed and glowed. I was pristine, on the outside. I healed considerably. I was bright, I read books, and learnt about science, and it made things better. For the first time in my life, I was happy. I flourished. A year later, I met Persephone, and shortly after that, my story converged with yours. You know the rest. I'm back here, again, and I'm so scared. I can't reconcile who I thought I had become with who I am when I'm here. I feel like a small child again, and I don't want to be a child. I want to be an adult, I want to grow up, I want to live in a world where I have control."

Kai didn't respond. He pressed his lips thoughtfully against Phoenix's temple, and rocked her gently.

"I know what you're wondering," she said. "I killed him, Kai. I killed my stepdad."

She expected him to veer violently away from her, to be disgusted, to forget he loved her.

Kai held her, still.

"I know, Phoenix," he said gently. "You wouldn't have lied otherwise."

"Do you hate me?" she asked timidly.

"Of course I don't hate you." There was a hint of reservation in Kai's voice that set Phoenix on edge. "I have opinions about this, of course I do. It goes against everything I believe in. You killed someone, Phoenix, you made a decision to end another person's life, and that's a level of power none of us should be allowed."

"I'm not the all-powerful sadist you think I am," she said. "I killed him because none of us had any power while he was alive. I wasn't playing God, Kai, I was trying to save my family."

"That's not what I meant," Kai said calmly. "What I'm trying to say is: this is hard for me. I could never condone what you did, because, to me, it's intrinsically wrong. I love you, and I need to validate your feelings, but I can't validate your actions." She could see he was struggling. Kai may have worn the body of a man, but beneath it he was still an anxious young boy, out of his depth, trapped in a whirlpool he had no hope of swimming through.

"I don't regret killing him." Phoenix raised her eyes up to Kai's in a challenge. "Yuri Lyubov was not a good man. He hurt my mother, and he threatened to kill my sister."

"I didn't know you had a sister," Kai said.

"I have two. They're little, and practically strangers to me. I killed him to protect people. I made a choice, and it saved more lives than it ended! I'm not proud of what I did, but I would do it again and again, because it was the right thing to do." Phoenix stood up abruptly, storming off into the bathroom. The differences between she and Kai had never been more evident. Loving him seemed so futile now, when he couldn't comprehend her torment, couldn't see clearly the affliction with which she had been cursed. Arms closed around her, and Phoenix's thoughts numbed in her mind. She was too afraid to consider the implications of Kai's view, she couldn't lose him now.

"Phoenix," he said behind her. "I love you, no matter what. I'm horrified you killed someone, and you have to allow me to feel that horror. You must believe me, Phoenix: I don't love you any less."

Kai moved around, so he stood in front of her.

"I really thought you hated me," Phoenix said quietly. "I couldn't bear for you to hate me."

Kai didn't respond.

"What are you thinking?" Phoenix asked, slipping her hands into his. "You're giving me that stare, like you can see right through me, and I never know what it means."

"I was wondering what it's like to be you." He laced his fingers through hers and pulled her closer to him.

"It's not too great," she said, "and that's the understatement of the century."

"I wish I could fix things for you. You've lived through so much pain, and I don't know how to make it better."

"You already have," Phoenix said. "You've given me hope. You can't underestimate how much you've done for me, Kai. Remember that day, two years ago, when I'd had a fight with Sphenya, and you made me feel better? I was so miserable, and you spoke to me, and made my sad little face light up. You got me, somehow. Everyone in my life has been so selfish; you're the opposite. You've become a part of me."

Kai kissed her gently. He lifted her up, and carried her over to the bed. Her arms snaked around him, tightening him within her embrace. Phoenix felt the warm urgency of Kai's mouth as it kissed hers. She was overcome by the need within him, within herself. Something had changed between them, they were no longer just a boy and a girl, no longer two people who loved each other. She had told him her truth—a truth that shattered and devastated her, continuously broke her down, ground her to a coarse dust—and he had loved her still. The bridge of which they had stood on either side for years had been swept away, but the white rushing water was no longer a threat. They had become one with the current, they no longer needed distance, or safety, or stability. Phoenix's heart pounded as Kai laid her down on the bed. His hands were warm as they slid up under her shirt, and his mouth was hot and frantic on hers. The intensity of his touch stilled her mind and awoke her body. She kissed him harder, blocking out the world, hiding in the safety of oblivion.

"Phoenix." Kai pulled away abruptly. "Can you hear footsteps?"

"I— What?" Phoenix sat up, pushing him off her frantically. "Kai! Get under the bed! Now!" she whispered, pulling her shirt down over her. The footsteps grew louder, nearer, closing in like an oppressive force.

"Child," said Jakob Kashnikov, "it's time to reacquaint you with the knife room."

"No," Phoenix whispered. "No. No!" They spoke in English, she knew Kai wouldn't understand a word they said.

Jakob grabbed her wrist, his fingers like a cold, steel cage around her warm skin. His touch made her stomach turn.

"No," she repeated as her father tried to drag her away.

"Let her go!" Kai sprang out from under the bed, and placed his hands protectively on Phoenix's shoulders.

"I will take your boyfriend there first," Jakob said. He continued to speak in English. "You will have your turn tonight."

"No!" Phoenix shouted. It seemed the only word available to her. She couldn't think, couldn't tie reality to the panic that spun her mind around. Kai's presence by her side made her brave enough to speak. So she said "No" repeatedly, until even that word failed her.

"I'll take him," Jakob stated.

Kai squeezed Phoenix's shoulders to soothe her.

"No!" said Phoenix. "You can do what you like to me." She looked her father in the eye, for perhaps the first time in her life. She stood up straighter, shrugging Kai's hands off her shoulders in a bid for autonomy. "Hurt me, hurt me as much as you need to. I'm used to it, I'm used to the monster you are. But if you lay a finger on Kai, I swear I will kill you!"

Jakob laughed mirthlessly, and punched his daughter in the face, knocking her to the hard floor. When Phoenix regained consciousness, she was alone.

# Chapter Thirty Eight

"Kai!" Phoenix screamed. She ran through the open door of her childhood bedroom, down the hallways where so many drops of her blood had been spilled. There was no time to think, to freeze in panic or wallow in the memories.

Jakob stood in the control room. He adjusted the dark green switches on the wall, beside the window into the knife room. He didn't see his daughter standing behind him. Phoenix hesitated at the door. She couldn't do this. Her father was the one opponent she couldn't bring herself to face, and she had to pass him to get to Kai.

*Kai!* He stood still as knives rained down, centimetres away from his stoic face. He wore a mask of stone: brave, resolute, determined. Phoenix suppressed a sob; she couldn't let him be a saint for her, die a martyr to her lost cause. This wasn't his destiny, such a cold and violent death. Phoenix's grave was marked by the sharp steel of a stone-coloured blade, determined the day she was born. If she was going down, she would go down fighting. Phoenix forced open the door to the control room, and sprinted past her father, into the knife room. Knives flew, angularly, towards her, like vicious birds pecking at a freshly-blooded carcass. Phoenix dodged them with well-versed skill, and ran to Kai. She grabbed his hands and yanked him through this war zone, to a safety of sorts. It was only when they collapsed through the control room door that Phoenix realised a knife had penetrated Kai's shoulder.

Jakob waited for them, with eyes as hard and dark as frozen blood. Phoenix kicked him hard. He grabbed a handful of her hair, and threw her to the ground. She screamed and yanked on his legs, trying to pull him down with her. Consumed as he was by his daughter's attack, Jakob didn't think to look behind him. Kai didn't make a sound as he pulled the knife from his shoulder. He crept across the room on silent feet, and plunged the blade deep into Jakob's back. Kai reached for Phoenix's hand and pulled her up from the floor. They ran.

☦

Phoenix took Kai to a hospital, and waited till he was sound asleep before she left. She took a train across the city, seized by a compulsion to visit the prison where she had first felt liberation. She bought a bottle of kvass from a street vendor, and stood in the shadow of the Tsar's palace, letting the fizzy drink wash over her tongue. The media blackout had ended with the war. The screens above her played reels of the Tsar signing the peace treaty with the Baltic Alliance, honouring fallen soldiers, commemorating those who fought bravely. The footage was months old. He looked older than she remembered. There were lines around his ice-blue eyes, and the corners of his mouth turned down in a frown. The Tsar looked defeated, he didn't look like the victor of this war. Phoenix walked closer to the palace walls. It was bitter-sweet to be back here. Even now, there were days when she missed her old life, the simplicity of a world that contained only she, Persephone, and Sol.

A blond man stood a little way off, looking up at the screens. His eyes were obscured by dark glasses, but she recognised his tall gait and the shape of his rigid shoulders. He could fool the citizens of Moscow with his disguises, but she saw right through him. Phoenix approached the man, in spite of herself.

"It's cold, for May," she said to him. Small talk had never been her strong point. "It's downright icy."

The man nodded in agreement. "I prefer it this way," he said. "I burn easily." She knew that voice. It comforted her, in a strange way. The Tsar had been the one constant in her life since she left the Settlement. There were months or years where his presence loomed, threatening, in the distance, at odds with the days and weeks where all she felt was gratitude for this man who had dragged her out of hell. Whether she hated him or was grateful to him, he had never abandoned her.

"What brings you to Red Square?" Phoenix asked.

"It's where I'm meant to be," the man said. He still didn't look at her. "What about you?"

"Moscow was my first home," Phoenix said. "I came to pay my respects. I don't intend to return."

"I envy you," said the man.

☦

375

"We didn't do this," Phoenix said when she saw Persephone. Her friend looked worse than before, almost lifeless. A gaunt face animated by an inhuman force. If Phoenix hadn't seen the transformation herself, she wouldn't have believed this was Persephone. "The program we used couldn't have done this."

"Must kill," said Persephone. "Must kill me. I will self-combust on November 1st. Must kill." Purple lines stood out on her cheeks. Her skin had sunk in on itself, and her eyes were black as coal.

"Oh, shut up, Sphenya!" Phoenix burst out. Fear rippled through her, she didn't know how to reverse the damage.

"She can't hear you," Drew said gently. He placed a comforting hand on Phoenix's shoulder. Dark circles had formed under his eyes, and a layer of stubble grew on his face. "I've been with her since you left. Nothing's going in, she can't hear anything."

"I think she can," Phoenix said. "At worst, the real Sphenya will be in some kind of coma. She can hear us, Drew, I know she can." She directed her next words to Persephone. "Who made you this way? Come on Sphenn, break free from this. Tell me who did this to you. It wasn't me, I promise."

"Hello, Phoenix." Persephone's monosyllabic, computerised tone grew deep and human, a man's voice. "I see you have realised this isn't your doing," the Tsar continued through Persephone's lips. "I haven't harmed Persephone. No permanent damage will be caused, if you can cure her before the first day of November. You have plenty of time. Did you think I would let you decimate my country, Phoenix? You know me better than that. I'm banking on our connection to get you out of this, my protégé. Good luck."

Drew and Dr Skryabin stared at Persephone, before turning their gaze to Phoenix. She paced across the room, ignoring them. This was too big a weight to carry, and they looked at her like she was their saviour.

"Must kill. Must kill," Persephone said with clockwork urgency.

"Shut the fuck up, Sphenya!" Phoenix snapped. "I'm trying to save you here."

"You don't think she's telling us the answer, do you?" Drew asked. "All she says is 'must kill.' What if that's what the Tsar means? What if you have to kill Persephone?"

376

"Over my dead body," she said. "Persephone will live a long, full life, and it will be like this never happened. I promise you, Drew, I am going to fix her."

"How can I help?" He watched her wearily. She wanted to tell him to go and sleep, take a break from caring for Persephone. She had known Drew long enough to know there wasn't any point in telling him what to do.

"You can look after her," Phoenix said. "She's not a machine. Persephone needs fresh air, sunlight, people to talk to her. We need to make sure there's still a person in there to save. Change her clothes, give her a shower, take her outside, and talk to her. Talk like she's Persephone, not the computerised robot he turned her into."

"Is she beyond saving?" Phoenix asked Dr Skryabin. She sat, perched on the worktop in his office. It was such a relief to be home. His office smelled like old coffee, a scent that Phoenix traced back to the stack of unwashed mugs piled high beside the sink. Dr Skryabin stood by the window, tending to his pet cat, who sulked inside a basket, with a bandage wrapped around its paw. If she had been less exhausted she would have made a snide remark, or asked about the existence of Bring Your Cat To Work Day – surely it couldn't be hygienic to have an animal running around the Institute. Today she was too defeated to care.

"There's no need to be dramatic, Kashnikova," said Dr Skryabin. "You underestimate the resources—the minds—we have at our fingertips"

"I'm so terrified of losing her," she said. "If we can't save her, I'll be to blame. I couldn't cope."

"It isn't your fault, Phoenix. You didn't do this to her, the Tsar did."

"How did he get in here?" she asked. "How can the fucking Tsar of Western fucking Russia break into the Estonian Institute of Scientific fucking Research without leaving a fucking trace?"

"Because he's got fucking superpowers," Dr Skryabin said with a small smile.

"I feel like I'm always a step behind," Phoenix said. "Everything is planned, and free will and free choice are just an illusion. I thought I was exempt from his mind games, that he and I were so alike he'd leave me alone – even if he tormented everyone else in my world."

"This is all going to be okay," Dr Skryabin said. He patted Phoenix's shoulder, and looked into her morose blue-green eyes. "The Tsar believes you're smart enough to solve this. If the two of you are so alike, this will be a puzzle only you or he could solve. Think, think outside the box."

"All I can think is that it's science," Phoenix said, "because it's our point of commonality. But that's too broad, and too simple, which makes me think the cure isn't scientific at all."

"This means there'll be a trigger of some kind. If we figure out the trigger, then we can mend her."

"I've gone through hell and back for her so many times," Phoenix said. "I love her to the ends of the Earth, but I sometimes wonder if my life wouldn't have been so much easier if she and I had never met."

"Do you think you would be happier?" Dr Skryabin asked.

"I don't know. I wouldn't be here. I'd probably still be in Moscow. I'd keep floating along. I wouldn't be happy, but I wouldn't be sad."

"I think you underestimate Persephone's impact on you." The cat jumped out of its basket, and limped towards Phoenix. She grudgingly patted its furry head.

"You do?"

"You are both special people, you need each other." Dr Skryabin lifted up the cat, and murmured affectionate words into its ear. He planted a kiss on the tip of its nose; it retaliated by licking his face.

"Because we don't belong in the real world?"

"Because the real world is a challenging place, and it's easier to navigate as a pair."

"Like you and that furball?" Phoenix asked.

"Precisely. Villem here is my very own Persephone."

Phoenix reached out to scratch Villem's chin, he snapped his teeth at her fingers. "Robots make better pets."

# Chapter Thirty Nine

"Miss Kashnikova," the Institute's receptionist stopped Phoenix as she came in through the front door. It was late, and the sky outside had long since grown dark. The Institute was heavy with the pressure of Persephone's condition. For the first time in two years, Phoenix didn't want to be there; she sneaked out of its confines every time she had the chance. "There was a delivery for you."

"For me?" Phoenix asked. She headed over to the reception desk. A large, white parcel rested on the counter. Her name and address were scrawled atop it in dark purple ink. "Thanks." She took the parcel under her arm and walked back towards the lift. She didn't recognise the handwriting, but the postmark was Russian.

When Phoenix reached her bedroom, she pried open the seal of the box, and pulled back the folds of cardboard. On a bed of purple velvet lay neat rows of red apples and pomegranates. Phoenix screamed when she saw the fruit. The light from her bedside lamp glinted off the dark-red skin of the fruit; it gleamed with malicious intent. There was only one person who could have sent this parcel. Phoenix knew the fruit was a warning from her father, a reminder that she would never be free of him. She inhaled sharply as she stared into the box, trying to remain calm in spite of the rising tide of panic that threatened to consume her. In this light, the fruit didn't look natural. It looked more like it had been carved from rubies than grown on a tree.

Phoenix flung her bedroom window wide open, and carried the box of fruit over. She heaved it out into the dark night, and watched as the blood-coloured fruits made their descent to the ground.

"Phoenix!" she heard her name called from below. "Phoenix!" It was Drew.

"What?" she called down.

"I can't hear you! Phoenix, come down here!"

She rushed out to meet him.

"What?" she asked. Drew stood by the door, his face animated with an unlikely combination of hope and fear.

"Phoenix," he said. "Where did this fruit come from? Why are you throwing it out the window?"

"My dad," she gasped, out of breath from the run. "It had to be from my dad! He's the only person who would send me fruit, and it had a Russian stamp. He's trying to intimidate me, I know he is, and—" She could barely get the words out.

"Phoenix," Drew interrupted. "Why would your dad send you pomegranates?"

"Because he uses fruit to torture me, and—"

"Pomegranates, Phoenix, pomegranates!" Drew took her shoulders in his hands; she was shaking with fear. He met her wild eyes; his fingertips were hard against her skin. "Your dad didn't send this."

"What do you mean? It had to have been him. I should have known he'd never let me escape!"

"Pomegranates, Russian stamp—" Drew spoke slowly and deliberately. "Phoenix! The fruit is from the Tsar."

Phoenix stopped shaking. She hit herself hard over the head. Her fear had been so overpowering she had forgot for a moment that Jakob Kashnikov wasn't the only man in Western Russia who used fruit as a tool for torture.

"Why would the Tsar send me fruit?" she asked. "He knows I don't eat— Oh my god, it's for Persephone! The fruit is the cure! We have to find all the fruit. But it'll be all smashed up... I've ruined our only chance at saving her." Phoenix was horror-struck; she buried her face in her hands and tried not to cry.

"Wait," Drew said. "If the Tsar sent the fruit, it'll be genetically modified. If we feed Persephone that fruit, he will be in control of her mind again. We can't do that to her. She'd never forgive us."

"It's the only option," Phoenix said. "If we don't give her the fruit, she will die."

"I think she'd prefer that."

"I don't care what she'd prefer. We will feed her the fruit, and then we will find a way to stop the mind control. I refuse to let Persephone die. I couldn't live if she was gone. We have to do this, we have to save her."

"Fine."

They scrambled about through the grass and bushes. Chunks of shattered apples and clumps of stray pomegranate seeds were strewn across the ground. Phoenix crawled on her hands and knees until they were bruised and bloody, discoloured with dirt and gravel and deep-red pomegranate juice.

"Come on," Phoenix said, when they had collected as much as they could salvage. She scooped up the box full of broken fruit. "Let's give this a wash, and save Persephone."


The fruit stilled Persephone. She ceased her urgent refrain of "must kill", and fell into a peaceful trance. The purple and black faded from her skin and eyes. Slowly she began to look like herself again. Persephone stayed in this placid state for days, silent and docile. Phoenix and Drew barely left her side.

"Moscow," Persephone said suddenly. "I have to go to Moscow."

"Sphenya!" Phoenix threw her arms around her friend's neck. "You're in there. I knew you weren't lost!"

"Take me to Haden," Persephone said. "I must destroy him." Her eyes were clear and lucid, and her voice was her own. She was a computer no more.

Phoenix and Drew exchanged a look of confusion.

"She's not in love with him?" Drew looked from Persephone to Phoenix and back. He hadn't expected this.

"I must end the Olympovski line," Persephone said with clarity. "I must tear Haden limb from limb. I must destroy him, and Melinoë." Her face was emotionless, and her voice calm. The more she spoke, the less human she seemed. It was like she was frozen, a statue of a woman carved from snow and ice.

"Drew," Phoenix said, her voice filled with fear, "I don't think the Tsar sent that fruit."

"It had to be him. There's no one else."

"The Tsar wouldn't do this to her, and Sphenya would never harm Melinoë. There's something else going on here." Phoenix watched Persephone with trepidation. There was something she was missing. No matter how hard she tried to see, something blocked her vision. "I know the Tsar. I know what he's capable of, I know how he works. I know him, and I know he didn't do this."

"Do you think it could be my mother?" Drew asked. "She wouldn't give up her schemes without a fight."

"No," Phoenix said. "Mariana is an opportunist, certainly, but she doesn't know Persephone's a robot. It has to be someone who knows what Sphenya is, knows about the fruit, and about the mythology. You said yourself it was significant they sent pomegranates. Pomegranates and apples. The significance of the apples must be Biblical. Persephone is Eve, she knew too much and now she is being punished. The pomegranates are from the Greek myth. The only person who could pull this off is the Tsar. It's his myth for God's sake! No one else would do this. I don't know what's going on. I'm all out of theories."

"Right now we must focus on saving Persephone," Drew said. "If the fruit is like the Tsar's fruit, it doesn't matter who sent it. You believed you were capable of curing her from his mind control, so you can cure her from this."

"I'm scared," Phoenix said. "Not only does Persephone have a new enemy we know nothing about, she has a common enemy with the Tsar. I could handle the Tsar. He was my equal, in a way. He was the devil I knew. I don't know how to save her from a stranger."

☨

Persephone lay on the reclining chair in Dr Skryabin's office. Her wrists and ankles were tied down, like she was going to be tortured. Phoenix didn't trust her, she didn't trust the thing inside of her. The Tsar's fruit had made Persephone inconsistent and irrational, but it had never made her want to commit murder.

"I need to get into her brain," Phoenix said when Dr Skryabin returned.

"She doesn't have a brain," he pointed out. "Not in the traditional sense."

"Exactly." Phoenix stalked back and forth across the room. She couldn't sit still. "You installed the Estonian language into her mind. Her brain is a computer. Whatever set her off when we tried to program her wasn't just mental, it was physical, it altered her body as well as her mind. This is different."

"Hold on," Dr Skryabin said. He looked down at the sheet of

paper in his hand. "The test results from the fruit are back. I ran it against the results from the Tsar's fruit I tested the first time you came here."

"And?"

"It's not the same."

"Is it more advanced, or?"

"They were made by two different people. If I had to hazard a guess, I would say this fruit was made by a copycat. A copycat who is far more advanced than the Tsar. The fruit contains foreign substances, but it's not genetically modified. This is something else entirely."

"Oh my god." Phoenix felt the earth collapse beneath her feet. Her gut had told her this wasn't the Tsar's doing, but she hadn't let herself consider the full implications of this. Persephone had a new enemy, an enemy more dangerous than the Tsar. "Okay," she said. "Okay. I need you to show me what you did when you installed Estonian in her brain."

Dr Skryabin nodded. He crossed the room and took wires from a drawer. He attached them to a small screen.

"Don't freak out," he said. Phoenix didn't understand what he meant. Dr Skryabin attached the wires to Persephone, and hooked them up to the screen. A blood-curdling scream tore from Persephone's lips, and she struggled against the restraints that held her down.

Phoenix tried to block out the noise. "Is that her brain?" She pointed to the image on the screen.

"Yes," Dr Skryabin said.

"Is there anything different from last time?"

"I don't know." He adjusted his glasses, and took a closer look. "Wait. Yes. Look there." A magenta light glowed in the far corner of the image, nestled between parts of Persephone's computer-brain.

"It's a virus!" Phoenix yelled. "The fruit is a computer virus!" She turned to Dr Skryabin in horror. "This was designed for her. Not for Persephone the Tsarina, or Persephone the person. This was designed for Persephone the robot! Whoever made this fruit knows exactly how her brain works."

"Let that be tomorrow's worry," Dr Skryabin said. He kept his eyes studiously focused on the screen. "I can run an anti-virus program, it should reverse the damage done."

"You can save her?" Tears of relief crawled from the corners of Phoenix's eyes.

"Yes." Dr Skryabin typed frantically on the screen. "I've set it in motion." He placed the screen down on the table, and pulled up a chair beside Persephone. "You should get some rest, Kashnikova. I'll find you when it's done."

"Wait," Phoenix said. Something didn't add up. "Why did you tell me not to worry?"

"You've spent your life worrying," Dr Skryabin said. He watched Persephone closely. "Each time one battle ends, you find a new one to fight. You can't live like this."

"You know something," Phoenix said. She was certain of it. "The first book I read about the less-advanced robot prototype came from this institute. You know something! You've known all along, haven't you? What's going on? Who are you really?"

"Phoenix." Dr Skryabin stood up, and took hold of her agitated wrists. Phoenix glared at him furiously. "Phoenix, calm down, you're being paranoid. I am not out to get you. Take a deep breath, and stop seeing conspiracies where there are none."

Phoenix watched him with frightened eyes. She didn't know what to believe any more.

"Phoenix!" Persephone struggled against her restraints. "Phoenix! What's going on? Why am I tied here? You promised you wouldn't hurt me!"

"Persephone!" Phoenix wrenched herself from Dr Skryabin's grasp, and untied Persephone from the chair. "Sphenya, I wasn't hurting you. I would never hurt you! I can't tell you what's going on, because I don't know. I don't know who did this to you. All I know is it wasn't the Tsar."

The end of the year 2153 came to Tallinn quietly. The last days of December crept by in a blur, and before Phoenix and Persephone knew it, another year of their lives had slipped by.

While most of the city celebrated in style, Phoenix and

Persephone found themselves in the courtyard of the Estonian Institute of Scientific Research on that New Year's Eve. Silver fairylights hung from the trees, glimmering majestically in the dark night.

"How come you're not at the party?" Phoenix asked.

"Drunk scientists aren't really my crowd," Persephone said. It was cold on the bench where she sat, and she shivered in her velvet dress.

"I'm sure this wasn't the only party you were invited to," Phoenix said, a sly glint in her eye. "I do recall an invitation from a certain Birgit Poska lying on your dresser."

"Perhaps drunk politicians aren't my crowd either." Persephone wanted to avoid the topic of Birgit. "Plus, we don't know who my enemies are. I figured it's best to stay away from that world."

"I couldn't see you with Birgit anyway," Phoenix said. "She's not Russian."

"What's that got to do with it?"

"You have a certain type." A mischievous smile crept across her face.

"No I don't!"

"You so do! Tall, blonde, rich, and Russian."

"That's not true!"

"The Tsar, Tatiana, Drew... Birgit's a solid 3 out of 4, so clearly it's the Russian part that makes the difference."

Persephone smacked Phoenix's arm, which only made her laugh harder. She tipped her head back and cackled into the dark sky.

"Why aren't you out partying anyway?"

"Many reasons," Phoenix said. "For a start, I despise humankind and hate large gatherings. Also, I have other plans." She folded her arms across her chest, and stared down at her shoes, avoiding Persephone's gaze.

"What kind of plans?"

"Nothing, plans with Kai."

"Oh." Persephone cottoned on to what she meant. "Those kind of plans. Certainly took you long enough."

"I knew I shouldn't have told you." Phoenix shook with embarrassment, and a deep-red blush spanned from the top of her head to the collar of her shirt.

"Oh, come on!" Persephone laughed. "It's getting late. You go and... get some. Try and do more than kissing when the clock strikes midnight!"

"You horrify me." Phoenix turned to leave.

"You're growing up so fast!"

"Please shut up!" As she walked away, Phoenix called out "Hey, Sphenn? I'm proud of you, you know. Three years ago, we'd never have talked like this. You'd be blushing harder than I am."

"We've grown a lot. And I'm proud of you too. You've come very far, Phoenix." Persephone snorted with laughter. "And you're about to come so much more..."

"If you don't shut up right now, I swear to god I will uninstall all three languages from your robot brain!"

"I'll see you in the morning, okay? I want all the details!"

"You're not getting any details!" Phoenix said. "Goodnight. Love you!"

"Love you too. Make sure you use protection!"

"Shut up, Sphenya" Phoenix yelled behind her as she ran across the courtyard to meet Kai at the door. Persephone watched them, laughing to herself at the sudden awkwardness between the couple as they hurried indoors.

✝

Persephone's path crossed with Drew's as she ventured outside the Institute on New Year's Day. It was a clear morning, and the air was sweet and fresh.

"Are you avoiding the hungover scientists too?" he asked. He had changed so much in the time she had known him, but today he looked like the man she had met in a bookshop more than three years ago. There was a lightness about him that she could never bring herself to walk away from. With him, the world was still.

"Something like that," she said.

"Great minds think alike." Persephone could see in his eyes that he was still in love with her. He had respected her wish to be friends, and she was grateful for that. But in moments like this, when the two were alone, she knew there was only so much time

386

before he would grow impatient with the platonic love she was prepared to give him. Their friendship could only last so long. "Shall we walk together?" he asked.

"If you wish. I might not be the best company this morning, my mind's all over the place."

They set off towards the Old Town.

"Is it anything I can help with?" Drew asked, ever the faithful follower. He wore a bulky navy-blue coat and black denim jeans. A grey scarf was wrapped carelessly around his neck.

"I'm trying to figure out what to do with my life now."

"That makes two of us." He was silent for a moment, before adding "I'm going back to the Borderlands. Next week."

"For good?" Persephone felt a pang in her heart at the thought of him leaving. She had grown to rely on him, even if she didn't want a romantic relationship.

"For good."

"Because of me?"

"Our time ran out, Persephone." He gently touched her arm. "Every story has an ending. I spent two years of my life holding out for a love I thought was meant to be. You told me you didn't want this, and I convinced myself I could change your mind. I didn't respect your decision, and I'm sorry for that. I'm leaving because it's best for us to be apart. At least for now."

"I'll miss you," she said. "I know that doesn't mean much now, and they're such flimsy words. But I will miss you, more than you could know."

"We can write to each other," Drew said.

"You know that's not the same."

"You were the love of my life. I don't think I'm the love of yours. One day you'll meet someone who makes you feel something I never could. You deserve the love you're holding out for."

"It was never personal," Persephone said. She took his hand, and held it to her heart. "I did love you. I still do. But every time we had a chance to settle down and be together, something was missing. Something within me. I'm not looking for a happily ever after, Drew. I'm looking for a purpose, a career, something to make me feel alive. Love just doesn't do it for me. I spent my whole life waiting to be loved, and when I finally fell in love I realised it wasn't enough. I am so sorry you became collateral damage in that."


Snow lay around Town Hall Square, and weak winter sunshine cast a shadow of the town-hall spire across the cobbled ground. The morning was cloudless, and the world was peaceful.

"I love this weather," Persephone broke the silence that had lasted between she and Drew for the past five minutes. "It's brutally cold, but it's so fresh. It truly feels like a new year. After this past one, I'm glad for it."

"This year will be better," Drew said. "You have your fresh start now. You can create a new life for yourself."

"I will. I owe it to myself."

Persephone breathed in the fresh, January air. She was filled with joy at the sudden sweetness of life. The square was still decorated with Christmas lights, and looked eerily beautiful on this snowy morning. Persephone shivered under the thick, white wool of her dress.

Until now, they had walked alone. The majority of the city was still sleeping off a night of New-Year's parties.

"I think we're being followed," Drew said quietly.

Persephone heard the sinister crunch of boots on snowy cobbles. She knew something was wrong, that this bubble of joy could be shattered in an instant. She spun around and met the icy blue gaze of the Tsar. Haden stopped a few metres away from them. Droplets of melted snow were caught in his hair, complementing the cold, winter chill of his eyes. "Leave us alone." Persephone stood in front of Drew. She didn't trust the wildness in the Tsar's eyes. Something told her he wasn't in his right mind.

"Why, my dear wife?" Haden asked. He was trance-like, watching her as if she was a ghost instead of a living woman.

"I may be your wife," Persephone said, "but that doesn't mean I don't hate your guts. You won, Haden. You won the war, you won Melinoë. Is it too much to ask that you leave me alone instead of gloating in your victory?"

"Melinoë's talking now," the Tsar said. He couldn't take his eyes off Persephone. He reached out towards her, but stopped himself.

"Her first word was *throne*. Her second was *tsarevna*. She has a much larger vocabulary now, though *mother* doesn't feature in it. Come back with me, Persephone. I'll give you another chance. Don't you want to see our daughter grow up?" He was desperate.

"I would rather die," Persephone said. "I will never come back to you. Not even for Melinoë."

"Please," Haden begged. "I can't live with the guilt of what I did to you. You have to give me another chance. If you have any goodness in your heart, you will come home to me." He reached for her hand and she jerked it away.

"Don't touch her!" Drew came between Persephone and the Tsar.

"Don't tell me what to do," said Haden.

"I'll tell you what I like," Drew said. "You've tortured Persephone beyond belief, you despicable cretin, and I refuse to let you harm her any more."

"I don't want to hurt her." Haden took a step back, away from Drew. "I just want her to come home."

"Western Russia is not her home," Drew said. "Her home is here, where she's loved."

"I can speak for myself!" Persephone cut in. "Drew, I don't need you to defend me. Haden, go fuck yourself. My life is worth more than two men fighting over me, so don't you dare get any ideas. I don't belong to either of you, and that's the end of it."

"I made you," Haden said. "Your connection to me is far greater than your infatuation with him. You know it in your heart, Persephone. You know we were made for each other!"

"You don't own me."

"Don't I? You owe me your life, your child's life, your friendship with Phoenix. Even your brief stint as a military strategist wouldn't have come about if you'd never met me. You haven't earnt a damn thing in your life Persephone. Everything you hold dear can be traced back to me."

Persephone punched him hard in the face. Haden reeled back as blood spurted from his nose. A moment later, he grabbed Persephone by the arm.

"Let go of me!" He didn't relent.

Drew prised Haden's arms off Persephone. The two men

389

wrestled on the snow-covered ground. Persephone tried to break them apart, but by the time she succeeded, Drew was unconscious.

The Tsar scrambled to his feet, bloody and battered.

Persephone launched her leg at him in a strategic kick, but it missed its mark. Her foot landed on something hard and metal in his pocket.

"Do you have a gun?" she asked.

"No, I'm just pleased to see you."

"Go fuck yourself."

Haden pulled the gun out from his pocket. He watched it distrustingly.

"Did you come here to kill me?" Persephone asked. It was almost a relief. She had lived an empty life for twenty-one years. Her life had been without purpose, now her death would match that.

"Don't worry," Haden said with a forced smile. "The gun was never for you."

"Who was it for?" she asked.

"The creator," he said. "The monster." He laughed ruefully. "The robot is more humane than the human. God is dead, and his creation is more heavenly than he could ever hope to be." He seemed far away. She wondered if he had taken drugs before coming here.

"Don't spew poetic crap at me," Persephone said. "I know you came here to kill me. That's the only way this could ever end."

"I'm not going to kill you." Haden stared down at the gun in his hand. "I could never do that. I love you."

"What would you know about love?" Persephone asked in disgust. Something had gripped her from the moment she saw the gun. It was a symbol of the fate she was rushing toward. This twenty-one-year trajectory of freedom versus confinement was always destined to culminate in this. She knew she could never be free as long as she and Haden both lived. He would never let her escape him for good. It all became clear now. There was a freedom in this final moment of checkmate. For the first time in her life, Persephone found something she could entirely claim as her own. "If you love me, Haden, punish yourself. Punish yourself, and kill me in cold blood, just like you created me." Blue fire burned in

390

her eyes, and her pumpkin-coloured hair shone in the winter light. She could do this, she knew she could. She could let go of this living realm, even if there was nothing after. Haden stared at her in horror. He never meant to install a self-destruct button in his favourite robot. Persephone did not want to die, suicidal thoughts were not in her nature. But she knew death was the only place she would be free of his claim on her life. She was prepared to die a martyr for her own freedom. It was all or nothing, the ultimate sacrifice. Destiny knows no compromise.

"Kill me," Persephone ordered. She was consumed, as if something had taken over her mind that she couldn't control. The words did not feel like her own. They belonged to something she never knew she had within her. "Rise above the nothing that you are, and kill me. Kill me for my ruined honour, kill me for betraying you, kill me because I'm your damned robotic creation. Kill me for whatever reason you please, but make sure I am dead! You don't deserve to live in a world where I exist. If you love me at all, Haden, pull that trigger and shoot me in the heart you created. All I am worth to this world is the power of my death!"

"Persephone, no!" Haden begged. He lifted the gun to his own temple. "I would sooner kill myself than kill you. There are two ways to end this. Let me die, let me end your suffering that way."

"No." Persephone was adamant. "This is how it must end." She felt like a puppet, a mouthpiece for some greater power. Her voice no longer belonged to her, but a thrill of exhilaration rushed through her body to know her life would finally be worth remembering. She tried to wrestle the gun from the Tsar's hand. Their fingers touched against the metal. Their eyes met.

"Persephone, no. Please, no."

"You're a coward," she said. "You yourself know I'm not human. You created my life, now end it."

The Tsar hesitated. This was what Persephone wanted him to do. But she would be gone forever. He couldn't face a world without her, not after the extremities they had lived through together.

Persephone looked her creator in the eyes, daring him to play God one last time, daring Frankenstein to kill his monster the way he was destined to do. In creating Persephone, the Tsar had blurred the line between human and robot until even he couldn't tell them apart. Persephone's existence was the purest form of chaos he had ever seen. Haden refused to accept the truth: he was always meant to end the impossible life he had created, he should have done so long ago.

Her husband's ice-like eyes were the last thing Persephone saw before she fell, face-first into the snow.

# Chapter Forty

The bullet hit Persephone in the back of the neck. It wormed its way through her long red hair, into the pale skin beneath, lodged itself inside her flesh and made a home between muscle and bones. There was no blood, no indication of a wound. Haden looked into Persephone's eyes before she came crashing to the ground. He never pulled the trigger.

The Tsar caught the glimpse of a ghost across the square. His own eyes reflected back at him. Chocolate-brown hair, streaked with grey, framed a face he had banished to the dregs of his memory. When he blinked, the spectre was gone, the mirage had dissolved into dust.

Haden fell to his knees beside his wife's corpse, and rolled her over to see her face. He refused to believe she was dead. Her heart did not beat, and her lungs did not breathe. The eyes that stared up at him were too accusatory to be lifeless. She saw him, he was certain. He leant his head against her soft thigh, and sobbed into her skin.

Haden caught sight of the ghost again, the ghost who had been gone for 25 years. Two women had turned the Tsar into the man he was today. One lay dead on the snowy ground before him, a bloodless corpse with living eyes. He sprinted across the square towards a hallucination of the other.

Phoenix woke in Kai's arms. The room was quiet, and the world was peaceful. She snuggled into him, relaxing in the warmth of his body. Her mind was still, and for the first time in as long as Phoenix could remember, she felt no fear or apprehension. All she felt was love. Her throat was dry from the wine she had drunk the night before. Phoenix slipped out of bed. The air was cold against her naked body, and she dressed in Kai's white shirt for warmth. The fabric was soft against her skin. Life was in high definition, every sense was heightened. Phoenix poured herself a glass of water from the tap in the bathroom, and stood by the window, looking out past the Rotermann Quarter to the sea. When she finished the water, Phoenix crawled back into bed. She kissed Kai's forehead, and lay beside him, watching him sleep.

A harsh knock on the door broke her out of the quiet. Kai woke with a start.

"What's going on?" he asked. His eyes were still half closed, and he wrapped his arms tighter around her.

"I don't know," Phoenix said. She slithered out of his arms, and grabbed her dress from the floor. She tugged it over her head and ran to the door.

Drew stood before her. His eyes were bloodshot, and his face was covered in cuts and bruises. It wasn't his injuries that shocked her, but the expression on the face beneath them.

"What happened?" Phoenix asked. She had never seen him look this devastated.

"It's Persephone," Drew said. His hands were cold as he placed them on her shoulders. Tears streamed from his eyes. His voice broke on the final word. "She's dead."

☦

Phoenix ran to Town Hall Square. The area was sealed off with police tape. No body lay on the ground. Only smears of blood, frozen pink on the white snow, unnatural in the blinding light of morning. She stared in shock at the sight before her, the place where her best friend was murdered.

Phoenix doubled over as sobs wracked her body. She howled into the eerie silence. Drew and Kai followed at her heels. They held her shoulders, stopped her from falling over. Their touch was firm, but Phoenix barely felt it. She barely felt anything. It began to snow. Thick, fluffy flakes landed on her hair. She shivered in her dress. She wore no coat and no underwear, and was entirely at the mercy of the elements. The winter cold cut through her body and she didn't care.

"There's nothing you can do for her here," Drew said gently. "She's gone. He killed her."

Phoenix dragged her feet against the ground as Kai and Drew gripped her arms, trying to carry her away. She knew who the killer was, knew the culpable man would get away with murder once more. A war raged within her mind. She sucked air into her lungs, tried to prevent the wild-animal roar from leaving her mouth. Her world had ended, and Phoenix Kashnikova did not dare to scream.

# The First Sign of Chaos...
*January*
*2070*

Khaos Olympovski rode into Moscow on a fine white stallion, like a spectre of a Russia that had all but been lost to history. 152 years after royal blood had been spilled on Siberian soil, a new Tsar emerged from his chrysalis.

The charred shells of two cars burned, several metres apart, in front of the entrance to the ransacked GUM department store in Red Square, as though they sensed the world no longer needed them, and had imploded in a fiery suicide pact. In the soot-stained slush between the vehicles, two musicians stood, playing jazz on a trumpet and guitar, serenading the flames that demolished the old world. A small crowd gathered around the musicians, watching in reverential silence.

Yann stood by the wall of the Kremlin, waiting in anticipation. At that moment, he was the most knowledgeable man in Moscow. The most knowledgeable woman eluded him, fled in the night with blueprints and a brain he couldn't hope to compete with. But Yann didn't need Taisiya now. Together, they had orchestrated the coming of a new epoch.

As the music wafted through the square, the clack of hoofs on cobblestones reached a slow crescendo. Yann looked up from his feet, and witnessed the sight of his wildest dreams: the Russian monarchy had been restored.

The horse came to a halt in front of the small crowd by the musicians. Tsar Khaos did not speak; he looked to Yann, who slowly approached him, and gestured for the young man to join the crowd.

"Is this all that's left of Russia?" asked the new Tsar. He looked around the expanse of the square, as if expecting a larger crowd to materialise from thin air. "Where are my people? Is this all that is left for me?" The fire in the burnt-out cars was nothing compared to the fire lit in Khaos's blue eyes. His hair was as red as an open flame, and a red flush spread across his cheeks. "Is this the empire I have returned to?" he thundered.

To the onlookers, he was a mere madman. Something in the

expression on Yann's pallid face caught the Tsar's eye, and an understanding passed between the two men.

"You know who I am," said Khaos. "You must serve me."

Yann shook his head. He was here to witness this abomination, not aid his personal antichrist as the new messiah.

"Tell them who I am," commanded Khaos Olympovski with regal authority.

Yann couldn't bring himself to look at the Tsar. He turned to the crowd, and spoke the words he would regret for the rest of his long life.

"This is Tsar Khaos Olympovski. He has come to end the war."

"Russia has been oppressed for too long," said Khaos. "The Russian Federation is on its knees. Do you bow to the 'great' alliance of a failed state and that ghastly island? America is burning, Britain is sinking. You look to them for power?" Khaos looked Yann directly in the eyes, and the fire that burned in the Tsar's gaze was a near spiritual sight to behold. "Russia is *ours* for the taking. Fuck the old system. You call this an empire?"

Khaos reached into the pocket of his snow-white coat. In his hand was a device Yann had never seen before. The new Tsar's arm swung back as he threw the device into the Kremlin's outer wall. The red bricks burst into blue flames. Unnatural blue, unlike anything Yann had seen in his life.


When Yann returned to Red Square two days later, there was mere ash where the Kremlin once stood. White ash, quickly covered by falling flakes of white snow. A clean slate.

The cobblestones of Red Square were brushed clean of snow. There were no burnt-out cars in sight, and rubbish no longer gathered in the entrance to the GUM store. Moscow was still a shell, with citizens hiding inside their homes like moles in the ground. But the exterior had begun to change.

In the centre of the square, the fiery-haired Tsar preached like a messiah. A messiah, or a madman. There was a fine line between the two. Crowds flocked around him. Some stayed for moments, swayed only by curiosity. Others observed him for hours, hanging on his every word. Moscow had been Yann's home for more years than he dared to count, but the city was a stranger to him now. Nothing was holy in Russia anymore – not the memory of monarchy, or the laws of nature. No Romanov blood ran in the Olympovski pretender's veins.

Yann had a choice now. He could track down Taisiya, and join her in this goliath endeavour, or he could leave Moscow for good. As Yann watched the Tsar, he saw a whole dynasty mapped out before him. What would Moscow look like in 50 years, or 100? Would Russia be restored to Empirical greatness, or would the new country crash and burn as it had so many times before? The Russia Yann had known was a phoenix, destined to evolve and resurrect continuously. He no longer wished to stand by and watch his country burn.


Yann returned to his apartment, and gathered up his most prized possession: a stack of papers, a plan for the future. He neatly folded his clothes, and packed them into a brown leather holdall. A new life awaited him. A new name, a new future. Only one thing stood in his way.

Yann looked at the decaying flowers in a vase on the kitchen windowsill, the white lace bra hanging over a chair, pink lipstick etched on a coffee mug from the previous morning. She would be at the theatre until midnight, rehearsing for a show that would never see the final curtain close.

Yann tore off a sheet of paper towel, and grabbed an eyeliner pencil that lay beneath the mirror on the mantelpiece.

*To my Katka*, he wrote. *I'm sorry.*

Yann didn't let himself feel regret as he boarded the train to Saint Petersburg. There was no life for him in Russia now. The sky had grown dark, and his final view of Moscow was a mosaic of street lights, windows lit up in yellow and gold. And darkness. Darkness of the Russian countryside, darkness of an epoch that only he could foresee.

# Phoenix Chistikova

*October*
*2155*

"How do I look?" Drew asked. He emerged from Phoenix's bedroom in a deep-purple suit, with flowing lace cuffs that reached to the knuckles of his fingers.

"I think I'm the one who should be asking that," Phoenix laughed. "You look ridiculous, but very… you."

Drew combed his dark-blond hair back in front of the mirror, and inspected his face with a critical eye.

"You should have let me wear a dress." He turned to Phoenix, and his tone grew serious. "I know I'm not the bridesmaid you would have hoped for."

"Let's not talk about her today," she said. "Please."

Drew sat down at the table beside Phoenix, and gently lifted her veil so he could see her face.

"I know she's here in spirit," he said.

"She doesn't have a spirit, Drew. She's a— She *was* a robot. Unless someone thought to upload her memories onto a USB stick as she was dying, she's all gone." Phoenix stood up and walked to the window. She gathered up the skirt of her wedding dress in her hand, so as not to trip. The white lace felt alien against her skin. Phoenix looked out across the Rotermann quarter, to the sea beyond, searching for any trace of apprehension in her heart. She had no urge to run away. Phoenix had spent almost 23 years battling a fear of commitment, but now, on her wedding day, cold feet were far from her mind. Kai meant safety; Kai meant stability; marrying Kai meant never being abandoned again.

"I don't even know what she'd say." Phoenix opened the window, and took a deep breath of cool autumn air. "Would she cry? Would she somehow relate it to her own wedding – and that icy bastard? Would she say some classic ditsy Sphenya thing, or tease me for getting married so young?" Phoenix closed the window, and sank down into the sofa. "I'm scared of forgetting her."

"Careful of your dress." Drew gave Phoenix a hand up from the sofa, and pulled her into a gentle hug. "She'd tell you she's proud of you," he said into her hair. "So would Elizaveta."

"God, I've lost so many people. Elizaveta, Sol, Sphenya…"

"Nothing will undo that loss," Drew said as Phoenix finally wriggled out of his embrace. "But you've gained people, too. You have me, and Dr Skryabin, and you have Kai. You have a whole life ahead of you. I wish Persephone was here, I wish she could see the woman you've become. But she is gone. Don't ever let her memory hold you back, Phoenix. Persephone loved you so much. You have to live for both of you now."

"Well," Phoenix said with a sad smile, "getting married is definitely a Persephone thing to do. The perfect way to honour her memory." She snorted. "Hopefully I'll have better luck than she did."

"If you start a war against Kai in a year from now, we'll know Persephone's spirit lives on."

"Oh god," Phoenix laughed. "She would kill you for saying that."

"Come on, let's go down. You don't want to be late for your own wedding."


Dr Skryabin stood by the doors to the Institute's courtyard. He wore a purple suit, which matched Drew's in shade, but not in extravagance. The colour didn't suit his pallid complexion and pebble-grey eyes, but it warmed Phoenix's heart to see him wearing it. Her fingers stroked the purple ribbon around her bouquet as she looked from Drew to Dr Skryabin. Dressed in their complementary outfits, they looked like a small team. Her team. Two men she had learnt to call family.

The third waited outside. She could see him through the door, dressed in a lilac suit, with a purple bow tie.

"Are you ready?" Dr Skryabin asked.

Phoenix swallowed; the nerves began to hit her now. Kai's parents sat in the front row. It dawned on Phoenix that life as she knew it was over. Her solitary existence was gone; she was part of a new unit now. More than that, she was part of a family. A family built on love, instead of violence. A family that would catch her when she fell, instead of leaving her out in the cold. Phoenix Kashnikova had everything she had ever wanted, and she wasn't sure she deserved it.

"I was nervous on my wedding day," Dr Skryabin said, sensing the unease that settled over her like a heavy raincloud.

"Was he your first love?" Phoenix asked, as she tried to breathe evenly.

"Oh no," Dr Skryabin smiled to himself. "The first man, yes. But he was love number 2.5."

"You can't love half a person," Phoenix said.

"I've lived a long life—"

"You're not that old."

"Older than you'd believe. I've lived long enough that I can't list my great loves without a decimal point. I know first-hand that love is complicated. It took me decades and countless mistakes to love someone the way you love Kai. It's rare to meet the love of your life at 18, rarer still to marry them at 22. Take a deep breath, and don't give in to the nerves."

"Okay." Phoenix nodded slowly to herself. "Okay, I'm ready."

Dr Skryabin took Phoenix's arm, and Drew picked up the train of her dress.

Gold and orange leaves lay strewn across the grass of the Institute's courtyard, a vibrant autumnal backdrop to the wedding ceremony. The October air was crisp and clear; Phoenix felt instantly calmer as she stepped outside. Kai's face broke into a smile when he saw her. His eyes crinkled with joy, and Phoenix couldn't help smiling too.

"Kashnikova," Dr Skryabin said as they walked down the aisle.

"Man, that's the last time you'll ever call me that!"

"Kashnikova," he repeated. "I don't say this enough, but I'm proud of you. For everything."

"Dr Skryabin," Phoenix said. "I don't say this enough either. But I'm grateful to you. For everything."

"I didn't think I'd cry till you reached the altar," Drew said from behind them.

Kai reached for Phoenix's hand when she joined him at the altar. His touch was warm and firm, and even after all these years, her heart skipped a beat. She looked up to meet his kind, brown eyes, through the transparent lace of her veil, and the last of her nerves disappeared. This was the man she wanted to spend the rest of her life with, this was the man who felt more like home than any city or

401

apartment ever had. Her heart was his; she had known that since a drunken kiss in a student dormitory when she was 18 years old.

The words of the wedding ceremony floated like butterflies in the air above Phoenix's head. They drifted over her, and she let them cleanse her of the pain, of the futility that had marked so many years of her life.

When Phoenix finally said "I do," it was a promise to herself as much as to Kai. Phoenix Kashnikova was gone, and a new Phoenix rose from her ashes.

"You may now kiss the bride."

Kai took Phoenix's face in his hands, and kissed her softly on the lips. She could feel him smiling against her; Phoenix had never seen Kai as happy as he was in this moment.

"I love you," Kai whispered. Their faces were so close they breathed the same air.

"I love you too." She took his hand, and they turned to face their guests, the crowd of colleagues, and friends, former classmates, and Kai's family. Phoenix looked out upon the rows of connections she had made in the past four years, and her life didn't feel empty. She squeezed her eyes shut for a moment, and imagined Persephone standing beside her. The fantasy flickered out before it could take hold. Phoenix knew there was no place for Persephone in the life she had now. Persephone meant chaos; a life lived completely in flux. Persephone's death had bought Phoenix her stability.

She closed her eyes again, and counted to three. Phoenix squeezed Kai's hand, and let him tether her to reality, to the moment she lived in now, instead of the shockwaves that still hadn't dissipated almost two years after Persephone's death. It was time to look forward, instead of back. The past was of no use to her now. Phoenix looked at Kai, and broke into sudden laughter.

"Oh my god," she said. "We're *married.*"

"That is generally how weddings work," Dr Skryabin said from behind her.

"I can't believe you're my wife now!" Kai hadn't stopped smiling since the ceremony began. He looked at Phoenix like the sun and moon and stars were visible only through the vessel of her face. "I am the happiest man in this world."

Phoenix couldn't find the words she wanted to say. Instead, she

402

threw her arms around Kai's neck, and let him lift her into the air. She screamed with joy and relief as her feet left the ground. There was freedom in commitment, freedom in stability.

As Kai returned Phoenix to the ground, Dr Skryabin tapped her on the shoulder.

"Congratulations," he said. "Chistikova."

# The Tsarevna and the Book of Blood
*December*
*2158*

Madness ran in the blood of the Olympovski dynasty, and by 8 years old, Melinoë Olympovskaya was no exception.

Melinoë paced across the floor of the palace's nursery, her black, curly pigtails bobbing up and down as she marched. A blizzard raged outside the window, submerging Moscow in a swirling storm of snow. Melinoë missed the early days of autumn, days spent kicking golden leaves into the air in Zaryad'ye park, stamping on icy puddles with her fluffy red boots. Though she was a spring baby, autumn had always been her favourite season.

On the far side of the nursery, Melinoë's nanny, Anya sat in a grand, green-velvet armchair, embroidering silver stars onto the hem of a midnight-blue dress.

"Melinochka," Anya said. "Stop walking in circles, you know I can't concentrate when you do that. Come." She patted the arm of her chair. "Sit. Read a book."

"I don't want to read." Melinoë sat on the floor by the window, and watched the thick snowflakes fall. She could barely see the branches of the trees a metre in front of her, let alone the city beyond.

"Books are the best companion you can have," Anya said sagely. She discarded her sewing on the floor beside her chair, and joined Melinoë by the window. "There must be some story you like?"

"What's the use of stories?" Melinoë said glumly. "I am not a character." She turned so Anya couldn't see her face. "Every story I read is about a girl with a mother, a girl with a friend. There are no stories for a girl with a country."

"Let's go to the library," Anya said. "We can read history books. What about your great grandmother, Tsarina Gaia? She was a girl with a country."

"Or my mother. Persephone."

Anya was silent. Melinoë knew she had said something wrong.

"Tsarina Persephone didn't have a country, Melinochka," Anya said finally. "She married into one, which is a fate you don't have to worry about." She paused. "Your father wouldn't like you talking about this."

"Okay."

Melinoë continued to watch the snow. A slow anger burned inside her. She didn't know where it came from. Something deep in her bones told her that an injustice had been enacted against her, that her father and Anya knew something she didn't. Melinoë hated feeling excluded. She was too young to understand that her life would be lived on the outside, that the price she paid for security, luxury, and power was a life lived in solitude, a peripheral existence defined by her *otherness*. Melinoë wanted to be normal. If she could not be normal, she would wield her privilege like a weapon.

In her eight-year-old mind, the notion was reduced to *if I must suffer, so shall they.*

"Shall we go to the library?" Anya asked.

Melinoë nodded, and didn't say a word.


The Tsar's library was the most grown-up room in the palace, as far as Melinoë was concerned. Bookshelves stood as tall as the ceiling, and the scent of smoke from her father's cigarettes clung to the air, long after he had vacated the room. Melinoë felt ill at ease here, but she didn't have the words to vocalise her ambivalence.

Anya settled into a red armchair by the window, and returned to her embroidery. The dress was Melinoë's outfit for next week's winter solstice ball. This was the first year her father deemed her old enough to attend the event. A silver tiara would accompany the dress. Melinoë longed for the day she could wear a real crown.

With Anya once again entranced by her embroidery, the surly Tsarevna was free to roam. Melinoë didn't head for the history section. Instead, she crept to a ladder in the darkest corner of the room. After a quick glance to make sure Anya wasn't watching, Melinoë clambered up the sturdy rungs of the wooden ladder, until she stood parallel to the highest shelf. The Tsar's prized collection of scientific books stood before Melinoë, cloaked in thick, leather covers, as though to protect their anonymity. She felt the pages calling to her, singing songs in words she was too young to understand.

After much deliberation, Melinoë chose a large, red volume, and hauled it down from the shelf. Her feet wobbled precariously on the ladder, as she adjusted her positioning to account for the weight of the book.

"What do you have there?" Anya asked, as Melinoë sat on the floor at her feet, and opened the red book to the first page.

"History," Melinoë said. "See, it's red. Like Communism." She smiled sweetly, and hoisted the book up onto her lap.

"You're too young to be reading that," Anya said, though she smiled to herself a little.

"I'm not too young to know about revolution." Melinoë looked her dead in the eye. "Revolution is my enemy."

When she had sufficiently scared Anya away, Melinoë began to read. The language was as heavy as the book itself, and many words were beyond her level of literacy, but Melinoë feasted on the illustrations. Her eyes lapped up diagrams of blood and cells and DNA. The book wasn't enough. Melinoë wanted it to come alive. This book held no story, told her no tales of futures she could never aim to live and girls she could never hope to be. Melinoë had a new fantasy now, and it delighted her more than adventures in the park, or dreams of being Tsarina.

"Anyushka?" Melinoë asked. "Can you get me that book?" She pointed to a slim blue volume on a shelf nearby, a little too high for her to reach.

"Of course, my dear."

When Anya stood up, Melinoë cut the thread from the embroidery needle, and inspected the slim steel with curious eyes. It was light, small in her hand. It wouldn't cause any harm; it would merely be an experiment. Her father had always encouraged her to take an interest in science.

"Here you go, Melinochka." Anya handed her the book.

Melinoë gave her nanny a cold smile, and pretended to read. Anya searched for the needle amongst the folds of the blue dress.

"Melinochka?" she asked. "Did you take my needle?"

"Why?" Melinoë feigned confusion.

"Wait here while I fetch another one."

"Don't leave me here alone," Melinoë begged. "You don't need to finish the dress today. Read me a story instead!" She passed Anya the blue book, and climbed up onto her lap, deftly hiding the needle in her palm.

Anya put her arm around Melinoë's shoulders, and opened the book to the first page. An illustration showed a princess in a castle, with a dragon breathing fire into the moat below.

"Once upon a time," she began.

Melinoë thrust the embroidery needle into a vein in Anya's wrist. Anya screamed as bright red blood spurted onto the white pages of the book.

"Melinoë!" her father thundered as he walked towards her. She hadn't heard him enter the library. The Tsar pulled his daughter off the screaming woman, and placed her roughly on the ground.

"Are you hurt?" He picked up the half-embroidered dress from the floor, and held it against Anya's wrist to stem the flow of blood. She nodded weakly in response.

"Melinoë," the Tsar said with as much restraint as he could muster. "You will wait here until I return. Do not move, do not touch anything, and," he noticed the red book on the floor, "do not read anything."

Melinoë met her father with an ice-cold glare, and sat sulkily in front of the floor-to-ceiling windows. The blizzard continued to beat against the glass; the snow hemmed her into the confines of the palace in a cold, white, claustrophobic flurry.

When the Tsar returned, he didn't say a word to Melinoë. He grabbed her by the wrist, and led her up flight after flight of staircases, until they reached a part of the palace she had never ventured to before.

The final staircase twisted in a wide spiral, until they came to a room at the top of a tower. Wide windows dominated the walls, overlooking the city of Moscow. Melinoë had never felt more distanced from the real world than she did in that moment.

"This will be your study from now on," he said. "There will be no more nannies. You are too old for a nursery, too old to be babied. If you want to read books beyond your years, I will choose your curriculum." Her father pulled books off the shelves and dumped them on the table. Melinoë didn't understand the fire that burned in his icy eyes. "You will learn Greek, Estonian, Latvian, Lithuanian, English. You will study every day until you have curtailed your curiosity and replaced it with intellect. I will not doom you to repeat my history."

"Father," Melinoë said. "I didn't mean to make Anyushka scream. I only wanted to see her blood."

The Tsar heaved a deep sigh, and patted the top of his daughter's head.

"The first rule you will learn as Tsarina," he said, "is that your intentions mean nothing. All people see are the consequences. Do you understand me, Melinoë?"

"I don't have a choice," she said.

"I will come check on you later,"

As her father descended the stairs, a coldness settled in Melinoë's heart. She was on her own now, and this time there was no one to blame for her exclusion but herself.

Melinoë let out a blood-curdling scream, and cursed her father's name, cursed Anya, cursed the memory of Persephone, the dead mother who had abandoned her to this fate. Melinoë did not know how she would make them pay, but she had read enough stories to know what happens to those fools who lock princesses in towers.

# Acknowledgements

Thank you to Vilma Rugytė, for being the first person to read this novel, and for sending me so many enthusiastic messages while you were reading it. There's nothing I love more than talking about this book, and after so many years of clutching it close to my chest, it was so exciting to have someone to share this world with!

Thank you to Paul Robinson, for being my father and proofreader, and for instilling a hatred of misplaced apostrophes in me from a young age.

Thank you to Sanni Lindroos, for designing the cover of my dreams. I don't know if I believe in fate, but us meeting in the city where my novel is set felt like destiny. The month we spent living and working in Tallinn was the closest I've ever come to being in the world of Phoenix and Persephone; our friendship transformed my experience of that city. Thank you for being my illustrator and my friend, there is no one I would rather cry in cleaning cupboards with!

I wrote the original version of this novel when I was 14, before I'd experienced real, selfless, passionate friendship. I longed to find the Persephone to my Phoenix. In the years since then, I've had a handful of Persephones, and even the occasional Phoenix. I wouldn't be the woman I am today without the friends who have guided me, supported me, loved me, held me accountable, helped me grow. I love you all more than I can ever put into words. Seven years after I began this novel, I finally understand what it's about.

There are so many people, places, and events that have shaped this novel into its current manifestation. It's a museum of seven years' worth of hopes and dreams, of life experiences. There are lines I wrote at 15, or 17, or 21, that I still read and know exactly what inspired them. There is one person I could not have written this novel without, and she is my past self. I don't often feel gratitude towards the ghosts of Eliza past, but when I read through this novel I am so proud of the woman I've become, and she wouldn't exist without the foundation of previous Elizas I built her on.

Most of all, I am grateful to Phoenix and Persephone, for being complex and nuanced enough that I haven't gotten bored of you after seven years. I couldn't have wished for better voices in my head!

# About the author

Eliza S Robinson was born in New Zealand, grew up in the north of England, and now resides in Glasgow, Scotland. She is a writer of novels, blogs, poems, and the occasional witty tweet. Eliza studied Film & Television Studies, and Russian, East European, and Eurasian Studies at the University of Glasgow.

Eliza's literary influences are an amalgamation of the epic fantasy novels she read in childhood, and the dystopian fiction that defined her teenage years. In The Purest Form of Chaos, Eliza weaves a dystopian narrative into a fantasy style of prose, whilst putting women's experiences of power and entrapment front and centre.

When Eliza isn't writing your new favourite novel, she can be found falling down astrology rabbit holes, turning the menial details of her life into a grand, gossip-worthy narrative, and running away to the Baltic States the moment life gets boring.